MARY'S APOSTLES

VICTORIA CARO

TRAPPED IN A DREAM
ESSENCE
THE QUIXOTE PACT

---

1. http://www.victoriacaro.com

To my beautiful family

PROLOGUE

In 1948, as the world struggled through the devastating aftermath of two consecutive world wars, four Hopi messengers were elected to caution global leaders that the worst was yet to come.

Hopi, meaning 'the Peaceful Ones', is the proud name of a small nation in Arizona encircled by another native tribe, the Navajo Nation, which in turn is enclosed by yet a much larger nation, the United States of America.

Renowned for their deeply spiritual and peaceful life in harmony with nature, the Hopi hold the strong belief they are charged with a divine mission: the preservation of balance in the world to secure human salvation. In order to accomplish this formidable task, the Great Spirit provided them with prophecies that warned of great threats and the wisdom to tackle them.

Thus, horrified that the ominous prophecies were being fulfilled, the four Hopi elders set out to comply with the mission entrusted to them. Three times they tried to address the United Nations but were rejected, until 1993 when their perseverance earned them the last speech at the General Assembly Hall during the opening ceremonies of the International Year for the World's Indigenous People.

Mr. Thomas Banyacya, by then the sole remaining survivor of the initial four messengers, was not discouraged by his sparse audience, for their prophecies warned of such trials.

His speech was humble.

"Our goals are not to gain political control, monetary wealth, nor military power," he said, "but rather to pray and to promote the welfare of all living beings and to preserve the world in a natural way."

Mr. Banyacya then shared for the first time some of the knowledge the Hopi had guarded for centuries, revealing, among other things, the existence of two sacred objects.

One was the Sacred Tablet of Pahana containing an encrypted image of a long-lost White Brother who, according to tradition, had migrated to the East. His figure appears headless, meaning that his identity is unknown, only to be revealed upon his return for Judgement Day.

The other was also a sacred encrypted image, though this time preserved in the form of a petroglyph on a sandstone boulder appropriately named Prophecy Rock. Located in Old Oraibi, the founding town of the current Hopi homeland, its humble strokes are believed to contain the divine way—or Life Plan, as the Hopi call it—said to guarantee salvation on the Day of Purification.

"We still have our ancient sacred stone tablets and spiritual religious societies which are the foundations of the Hopi way of life," he explained. "Our history says our White Brother should have retained those same sacred objects and spiritual foundations."

For the Hopi to succeed, the world had to be aware and commit to doing its part, so Mr. Banyacya reminded the Assembly of its place and duty: "The United Nations stands on our native homeland. The United Nations talks about human rights, equality and justice, and yet the native people have never had a real opportunity to speak to this Assembly since its establishment until today. It should be the mission of your nations and this Assembly to use your power and rules to examine and work to cure the damage people have done to this Earth and to each other. Hopi elders know that is your mission and they wait to see whether you will act on it now."

Holding up a picture of Prophecy Rock and pointing to two of its symbolic lines, he explained that humanity had two simple choices: to follow the crooked path to destruction or the straight path to Balance and Peace.

In view of where matters stood, he concluded, "It's up to all of us, as children of Mother Earth, to clean up this mess before it's too late."

Well beyond a quarter of a century later, matters have not much improved, and we see that the crooked path is overwhelmingly the most transited path, funneling the world to its impending doom.

But not all hope is lost.

What the Hopi may not know, or perhaps do, is that the Great Spirit, as a true mother, cannot remain on the sidelines. She wishes to give her children a good, last chance, though they must learn to find their way on their own. She has strategically planted *Divine Markers* across the world containing the clues to decipher Pahana's identity and unravel the hidden wisdom encrypted in Prophecy Rock's Life Plan. Albeit there is one condition for success: Reason and Faith must be applied in equal measure. Should her latest *chosen ones* master this ultimate test, they may well secure human salvation and bring in forever global peace.

CHAPTER 1

Sofia Auru-Soto hurried into the office eager to find out what the urgency was.

Dan Hansen, owner of the magazine she periodically collaborated with, acknowledged her presence immediately and didn't waste time.

"Here, take a look at this," he said handing her a news print.

Sofia reached for it and read the title, "Disembodied Voice Saves a Baby's Life." She sighed. "You're not serious, are you? You made me cancel a session with a very disturbed young man for this?"

Dan continued calm. "In Spanish Fork, Utah, first responders working to upright an overturned car found in the river, say they heard the distinct voice of a woman crying for help from inside the vehicle. This prompted them to speed up their efforts while reassuring the woman all would be fine. To their shock, what they found inside was the woman dead, most possibly upon impact, but her baby alive. The child was unconscious."

"I know, I heard about it on the radio on my way here."

Dan craned his head forward to study her over the top of his lenses. "Of all people, *you* don't think it's interesting? Surely it must pique your curiosity a little."

"No, Dan, it doesn't. There is nothing remarkable about it. I have an endless list of patients who hear voices." Her response was defiant. She knew well where he was going with it, and it disappointed her. Sofia shook her head. "The other night I spoke to you in confidence. I hope you're not going to start calling me in every time someone hears a voice because of what I shared with you."

He avoided her gaze as he persisted. "Two police officers and two firefighters heard it. We can't dismiss them as lunatics."

"Even professionals can suffer a simple case of mass hallucination in a moment of frenzy... Stop ignoring me."

"The agents were carrying body cameras." He sneaked in an angled grin.

"Are you saying there is a recording of the voice?"

"Not exactly. A lot is going on making it difficult to discern the background noise; however, the rescue personnel can clearly be seen responding and reacting to it indicating they honestly heard it."

Sofia slowly raised a suspicious eyebrow. "Really? That's it? Stop messing with me and tell me what you really have."

"The baby's name is Lily."

Sofia paled.

Dan gave her a moment to let it sink in.

"A mere coincidence," she finally whispered true to her perpetual state of denial despite the childhood flashback that was puncturing her memory. She saw herself trapped in the darkness, terrified, and then the light...

"Maybe. Maybe not. Either way it makes for a great story." Dan considered her as he continued. "Listen, I've been thinking about what you told me and how it defined your life. Imagine how this is going to define that child's life as well, regardless of whether the rescue team really heard the voice or not. This is a unique opportunity to address the subject of miracles from a psychologist's point-of-view, but not just any psychologist; one who lived through a miracle herself. That personal perspective is priceless. I want a special edition including compelling cases occurring across the country and laced with your story."

Sofia felt the disappointment rise in her throat. "I should have never told you. I can't believe you'd do this to me. I trusted you." She turned to leave.

"Wait, you don't understand," started Hansen. "Something strange is going on."

Sofia stopped at the door.

He explained quickly. "For a society that is more secular than ever, miracles are on the rise. They are being reported everywhere."

"I haven't heard anything."

"Because most cases are dismissed when no proof is supplied. Anymore, if it's not captured on a phone, it didn't happen. Normally, I would agree, but your story got me interested. I researched a little and was shocked to learn how widespread they are and how diverse the witnesses are. But most importantly, the number of accounts is accelerating at a ridiculous pace. I want to know why, and you are the best person for the job."

Sofia turned and crossed her arms. "What about my reputation? Did you think about that?"

A sudden shadow played over Dan's eyes. He came around his desk. "Indeed, I did. It's a big part of it. Our readers have come to trust your professional insight and analysis. What if someone was to find out about your little secret?" He stared at her briefly and then softened his features. "I'm not trying to betray your trust, much less take advantage of it. However, you need to understand that I have worked hard to build this business. It was a big gamble to pull it off from a small town like this, and the digital age doesn't make it any easier. It is in the best interest of this magazine, and that of your career, that you come clean; that you tell your story in your own words upfront rather than on the defense to clear yourself. Think about it, your skepticism, even in the face of a personal experience, underscores the promise we make to our readers." He aimed his index finger at the poster on the wall behind his desk. It depicted the magazine's logo: a large, white question mark, designed purposely plain and unobscured, on a dark blue background hovering over the words, *We Question Everything.*

Sofia knew those words well; they were her life-credo and defined who she was today. Yet they were also partly an illusion, a deceptive front. Her skepticism was more emotional than logical when it came to her personal experience. She concealed a dark corner in the depth of her memory she would not question. To do so meant to confront it, and for a psychologist who spent her working hours helping patients face their fears, she completely eluded her own.

"I'll think about it," is all she'd commit to.

Dan's features drew tight. He returned to his side of the desk. Once again, he could be seen avoiding her stare. "You have until the weekend to accept the project. If not, there is someone else interested in it."

Sofia jolted and leaped several steps closer. "What? Who? You told someone?"

He lowered his voice to a conniving whisper. "No. I'm just trying to help you."

"What are you talking about?"

Dan rubbed the nape of his neck as he braved a look at her. "His name is Michael Amir. He showed up in my office a few days ago. He said he was spending some time with your people on the reservation when he heard about your miracle. He's a reporter. I checked his credentials. They're solid. He wants your story."

"Why?"

"Why wouldn't he? Two Hopi twins experiencing a Marian miracle is an intriguing story to say the least. Hell, I want it!"

His enthusiasm unsettled her. It sparked the memory of people towering over her and gawking down; all expectant to see what marvels she was suddenly supposed to be capable of.

Sofia flushed the image from her mind as quickly as it came on.

"Why did he come to you instead of me?"

"I imagine he was warned you don't like talking about it and cleverly enlisted my help." Dan intensified his gaze. "Listen, it is a win-win for everyone. He gets the story, I publish it, you save your reputation."

The clash of emotions had Sofia struggle briefly with her response. She was too angry to find her voice to yell at him and too proud to cry. The result was a stutter. "S-so you already knew? You set me up. That fatherly talk the other night was just a ploy to get me to fess up. Why the games, Dan? Why not just ask me directly?"

Initially, he focused his attention on an old scratch on his desk, but then suddenly posed it squarely on her. There was a small degree of irritation in his glare. "I don't like being at a disadvantage. Amir has a professional profile worthy of the next Pulitzer Prize. He could be stalking the President at the White House and yet has chosen to camp out here to stalk you. I demand to know why. What have you not told me?"

Sofia was appalled.

"What the hell? I have no obligation to tell you anything, let alone about my personal life. If I chose to, it was because I thought you were a friend I could trust."

Dan Hansen lingered his stare. He released some air and produced a forced grin.

"I'm sorry. You know this is a tough business. Precisely because of our long-standing friendship, it bothered me that you could be concealing a big story that someone else could snatch right from under me."

"There's no big story, okay? When I was seven, I fell into a well and suffered a minor concussion. According to my sister, she was alerted by a female voice that led her to me, saving my life. As far as I'm concerned, my life was never in danger, and she knew where to look. We often played down by it." Sofia's gaze took on a pleading quality. "Dan, you know my sister. She's imaginative, profoundly spiritual, and lives half the time with her head in the clouds. It's easy to see that when she found me unresponsive, her young mind conjured up a fantastic story. That is all there is to it." She then waved her hand dismissively. "As for this guy you talk of, why he'd be interested, I have no idea. It is very likely that my folks back home got a little carried away embellishing it. The Hopi are notorious for their storytelling mystique, and quite frankly, it's not like much else goes on in the desert."

Dan stared at her over his lenses again. "You are oversimplifying what happened. And as for this *guy*, he has a remarkable career. I doubt folklore tales would impress him easily. Sofia, you can't keep hiding from it. Take it as a sign: he showed up here days before another similar miracle takes place mere miles from your well. And if that weren't enough, coincidently, the rescued girl carries your sister's name."

"If it were a sign, that child would carry my name. Like her, I was the one rescued, not my sister."

That was the type of detail-discrimination Dan paid her for. Now he ignored it. He considered her briefly. He was aware of Sofia's tense relationship with Lily. "Have you heard from her lately?"

Sofia replied with discomfort. "No. She's been busy with her research. It has her quite absorbed." Then she shook her head to clear her mind from the brume that muddled her thinking. "This is ridiculous, Dan. You don't honestly think there is any supernatural phenomenon happening here, do you? You run a magazine named *The Skeptic Warrior*".

"Don't insult me, young lady. I've been trying to debunk the absurd for as long as you've been alive, but I'm not in the business of denying strange occurrences as a matter of course either. Our job is to suspend judgement until due research can either deny or affirm the claim. What I'm seeing *here* are two mysterious events separated by twenty-five years and the most unlikely journalist interested in one of them. And if he is, so am I." Dan rested just enough to switch back to his more characteristic fatherly demeanor. "I told him that my condition to convincing you was that you both worked as a team. Face it, the story is going to come out whether you like it or not. This is your chance to maintain control over it."

Sofia walked over to the window but didn't really look outside. She just needed a moment to gather her thoughts. "What do you know about him?"

Dan released a sigh of relief and smiled. "He's forty-five. Single. No formal residence. He spends his life surfing the globe from one war to the next stopping to report on an occasional natural catastrophe or humanitarian crises in between. The man has more visible bullet scars than a target at a shooting range."

Sofia turned to share her twisted face.

"Precisely my thoughts," he responded to her bafflement. "What does a seasoned war correspondent want with you?"

"Did you ask him?"

"Of course, I did."

"Well, what did he say?"

"Not much. He simply answered that he was tired of war and was looking forward to some peace."

"What's that supposed to mean?"

"Young lady, I suggest you go and find out."

CHAPTER 2

Sofia paced back and forth near El Molero, her favorite food stand, in Santa Fe Plaza. She had chosen to meet at the National Historic Landmark because it was a popular gathering spot downtown for locals and tourists alike, making her feel safe despite not being sure why she felt otherwise. She had several times initiated a retreat but resolved ultimately to accept that her curiosity was stronger than her discomfort.

Upon leaving Dan's office, she had called Michael Amir, and as soon as he answered the phone, she was thrown off balance. It was his voice. It was deep and strangely thunderous as if emerging from the depths of a tunnel. Though not threatening. More like that of a bass singer down to business; he thanked her for calling and instantly expressed his wish to meet as soon as possible. Sofia wasn't as eager and tried probing him a little. Michael, who asked to be called Mike, while she ignored it, masterfully dodged most of her questions in a perfectly expert and charming kind of way. Eventually, she conceded to an encounter in a public place.

She had arrived early, too restless to confine herself to the four walls of her office. The memory of her childhood trauma, its hinted link to a modern-day miracle, and her sister's name thrown in the mix had rattled her far more than was bearable for a professed cynic like herself.

With the phone ready in her hand, she thought of calling Lily but inevitably procrastinated. Sofia loved her sister. In fact, she secretly admired her. For all her bohemian flare, Lily had proven to be a strong-willed woman with a focused passion. For several years now, she had taken on the fight for women's rights both in the world at large and in her church in particular, displaying a grit Sofia lusted for herself. Yet her favorable feelings didn't help their strained relationship, which Sofia had long acknowledged was mostly her fault.

It all began the day she fell down the forsaken well. Her father, while loyal to his Ute heritage, remained neutral in spiritual matters. The problem had been the women in the family. Her mother, a Hopi elder, was deeply religious, Catholic of all things. Why the women in her family chose to be fervent Catholics was a family enigma adorned with colorful legends that went back as far as oral memory could tell. Her sister had bought wholeheartedly into it, and their combined devotion had her mother and sister embrace the miraculous event as a divine sign. For Sofia, an innate skeptic, the experience had been overwhelming. She didn't believe any of it, nor wanted to be a part of it, and fled as soon as her age allowed. Sofia converted to miles the isolation she had created for herself since the incident, a distance that only broadened with her sister's choice for a career.

It didn't seem right, she had mulled over many times. How could identical twins be so different?

Sofia looked at her phone. It had been a while since they had spoken. She took a deep breath and dialed. The first ringtone barely had a chance to ring.

"Sof!" she heard, "I was just thinking about you, so imagine my delight when I saw it was you on the screen!"

Sofia smiled. She couldn't deny her sister was also the most positive, upbeat personality she knew. Indeed, they were different.

"Hi Lily. And I'm happy to see you are as delightful as ever." She heard a giggle. "Why were you thinking about me?"

"I'm in the car and a crazy driver in a van with several stickers that read things like, '*Life is a journey, not a race*' or '*Chill Out, Be Happy*' just passed a little old lady who, I admit was moving at an exceedingly cautious pace, flipped her off, and then skipped the light ahead as it turned red. I was wondering what your Freudian take would be on that?"

Sofia laughed. "It would seem to me a severe case of Jerkitis Bladder Incontinence. The jerk is probably in a hurry to get to his bathroom after being overserved."

"God save his soul. He might not make it driving like that." Another giggle. "What do I owe this long-overdue-pleasant surprise to?"

"You could call, too, you know."

"As I recall, last we talked, you asked me to get lost."

"You were being a pain, as usual."

"I just worry about you."

Sofia rolled her eyes. "Let's not get started, okay?"

"Okay, mouth zipped!"

An instant of silence ensued long enough for Sofia to brave up and admit to the reason for calling. "Did you hear about the miracle in Spanish Fork?"

"Lord Almighty, I can't believe you just asked me that question. Are you feeling all right?"

"Ha-ha-very-funny. Now answer it. Have you?"

"Yes, of course. How could I not? Mom called me freaking out. Did she call you?"

Sofia bit her lip. "I have a couple missed calls. I haven't had a chance to get back to her yet."

"Well, she's convinced our ancestors are trying to warn me of a horrible, impending danger."

"Our ancestors? I don't understand."

"You know, our Ute side of the family? Since it happened in Spanish Fork, Utah... Ute, Utah, ring a bell?"

"I know my ancestry, thank you. What I meant is what do they have to do with a miraculous female voice?"

"Oh, not you too. There are female spirits as well you know."

Ignoring this last comment, Sofia felt a chill running up her spine. She was not immune to the beliefs of her upbringing. Somehow her family had been able to merge the native traditions from both sides together with the Christian faith and make it all work. "I'm going to guess you agree with her."

The connection went silent.

"Lily?"

"At the risk of earning your wrath, yes, I do think that someone up there, be it an ancestor or Our Blessed Mother Mary, is trying to caution me." Lily's voice had lost its playful pitch.

"You are going to have to explain yourself fast. You know I have little patience for this."

"Do I have to remind you that it was you who called me and brought it up?"

Sofia bit her lip again and quickly cleared her throat. "Fine. Why would you have to be cautioned by spirits or the *Divine* nonetheless?"

More silence.

She quickly regretted the comment. "I'm sorry, okay? I'm not trying to mock your beliefs, it's just—"

"It's not that," interrupted her sister. "I sent you a drive with information that explains it. I see you never received it."

"No, I didn't receive anything from you. Why a drive? What's the matter with email?

"I was hoping you'd keep it somewhere safe for me."

"What? Why?"

"Listen, do you remember that research I've been working on?"

"Of course, it's all you talked about last we met. You are attempting to demonstrate that a fresh interpretation of the New Testament proves that Jesus favored women's apostolic role."

"Yes, that one." Lily's voice dropped to a whisper. "Well, while at it, I inadvertently stumbled upon something."

"Are you kidding me? What in the world could you have *stumbled upon* to warrant miracles in Spanish Fork with your name and mysterious memory drives?"

"Something that big."

"Define 'something.'"

"Not on the phone. In person. I'm driving into town as we speak."

"You are?" Sofia shook her head at the rush of events. Lily lived in Phoenix. It would have taken her a minimum of seven hours to do the drive. Why didn't she let her know sooner she was visiting? "Okay, head over to my place. You know where to find the key. I'll try to finish up here as soon as possible. I have an appointment with a journalist. It's the reason I was calling. I was wondering if you had heard from him. He found out about our childhood incident back home and wants to write about it."

"I'm surprised you agreed to meet."

"Dan talked me into it. He didn't leave me much of a choice, really. But I'm not totally sold on it yet. He's a freelancer of sorts that chases global conflicts around the world. Why on earth he is interested in us is anybody's guess."

Right on cue, Sofia heard the unmistakable voice.

"Present."

She turned around and was caught off balance for the second time. Michael looked nothing like she expected.

She whispered quickly into her phone, "My appointment is here. We'll talk later," and cut the connection. Sofia didn't want her sister involved, not until she checked him out first, perhaps fearing her more than him.

Her eyes then set wide-opened on Michael.

He extended his hand. "Hi. You seem surprised."

"Oh, I'm sorry," she stumbled. "It's just that I expected you to look differently." Sofia lowered her eyes somewhat embarrassed, as they shook hands.

Michael was approximately six foot two and brawny but had a baby face crowned with neck-long, grey-free, brown curls that clashed with his purported age and risk-prone profession. To complete the discord, she feared that if he imbued his almond gaze with any more sweetness, she'd develop diabetes.

He smiled, apparently used to the reaction, which spiked the sugar in her veins.

"Thank you for meeting with me. I hope I didn't interrupt anything," he said gesturing at the phone.

"No, it's okay."

He then waved her to a bench nearby as an invitation for her to sit. She had made it clear over the phone that she wanted to meet in an open public space, so he didn't bother suggesting a drink at one of the many restaurants around the plaza.

She accepted.

They took their spots while Sofia studied his face. As Dan had mentioned, Michael had several scars, one particularly pronounced that ran across his cheek under his left eye. It didn't look like a bullet or shrapnel had caused it, rather something nastier. Upon closer examination, his features seemed more in line with his age. Still, she thought, something was off-kilter. Seeing his youthful face talk with a bass voice was like watching a dubbed-foreign film in which the voice and the image were not well synchronized. Yet, somehow, it all seemed to work nicely in the end.

Since her sister was to arrive soon, Sofia didn't waste time and went to the point. She addressed her reservations. "Please understand that the only reason I'm here is because Dan asked me to consider your offer. Personally, I'm very reluctant to do so. You are intruding in a part of my life I generally don't like to talk about. Therefore, I hope you don't mind me asking some questions before agreeing to anything. No promises."

"Fair enough." Michael crossed his legs and leaned back stretching one arm along the back of the bench. He was wearing a pair of graphite cargo shorts and a pale grey t-shirt, showing off a soft tan that suited him as if he had been born with it—which he probably had if his surname was any indication. The whole ensemble came across as that of a man very comfortable in his skin.

Her posture, however, was clearly not as relaxed, and she was now regretting having chosen to wear long, black pants. The forecast had called for a cloudy afternoon, but, of course, the sun was now shining brightly just to torment her. Luckily, there was a soft breeze, and thanks to the ample shade provided by the park's trees, her airy, white blouse expelled as much heat as her pants absorbed.

Sofia cleared her throat to get started. "Dan told me you are a war journalist."

"Most of the time, though not exclusively."

"That is a challenging career. Why did you choose that line of work? I mean, it is evidently dangerous," she clarified, gawking overtly at his scars.

"It chose me. I'm not interested in wars. What's more, I despise them. But my family is originally from the Middle East, and I speak fluent Arabic. I had no problem finding work out of college as an undercover investigative journalist in the area. Unfortunately, it was surprisingly easy for me to infiltrate extreme factions."

Sofia shared her puzzlement. "Please don't take this the wrong way, but you don't look like the type of person a terrorist would open up to... so young looking, I mean." If he looked like a kid now, she couldn't even imagine what he looked like out of college.

Michael chuckled. "No, I might not come across as an authoritative confidant, but you'd be surprised the amount of information they'll spill when intent on recruiting."

Sofia relaxed. That made sense.

"You could have moved on eventually to something else. Why didn't you?"

Michael stalled his reply as he shifted his body slightly. "The thought has crossed my mind many times." He paused. It was apparent he was struggling to come up with the right words. "Since the beginning of time, that region has been in turmoil; not that the rest of the world has been much better, but since it is the one I'm from, it was where I set out believing, somewhat naively, I could make a difference." His gaze drifted into the trees. "There is a lot of anger that feeds it all, and over the years I've come to understand that it is ingrained in human nature to foster anger as a sign of strength. History proves we don't see war as the problem but as the solution."

"It's sad."

"It's wrong." Michael's gaze was unforgiving. "We should know better by now."

"There is always hope."

He surrendered a faint grin. "Yes, and that is why I'm still at it."

Suspended silence ensued.

It was tense.

Sofia thought it would be better to change the subject. "So, tell me. What's your interest in me? I'd like to think I am as far as one can be from a warmonger."

The switch was welcomed and Michael's face lit up.

"I certainly hope so, or I'm going to be very disappointed." He suddenly stared at her with such intensity that Sofia could feel his look pry under her skin.

"Well?" she pushed.

Michael uncrossed his legs and leaned forward. "I'd like to know why an extraordinary event drove one identical twin to fully embrace it as divine and ultimately become a nun, while propelling the other to seek out a career in neurotheology to discredit such occurrences." He smiled to add, "I'm particularly interested in the roots of religious conflicts, and your sister and you present a fascinating case study."

Though initially surprised, his inquiry put Sofia at ease. She had become used to having to explain it. Sofia was now the one to sit back and relax.

"First, my sister is not technically a nun as she is not cloistered. She is a religious sister and works as a history professor in a Catholic College. Second, as for me, I prefer the term Spiritual Neuroscience if you don't mind. Neurotheology limits the discipline's scope to the realm of religion, while the spiritual experience is broader than that."

"I stand corrected."

"Also," continued Sofia, "it is not my purpose to discredit anything. While my sister thrives in the rapture of faith," she angled a grin, "I favor the joy of scientific discovery, meaning that she is content with believing, whereas I strive to know."

"And yet, most of your collaborations with *The Skeptic Warrior* have resulted in discrediting the phenomena being studied," countered Michael.

"You've read my articles?"

"Each and every one. Your essays too." He smiled. "Very interesting."

She was impressed. He had done his homework. "Michael, it is hard for human self-esteem to admit that our conception of the world relies on the information collected by our senses in coordination with the enormous number of mental processes involved in making sense of it. And both our senses and mental processes can falter at any moment. Additionally, the more we learn, the more apparent it becomes that sometimes it is necessary for our brain to play tricks on us. In fact, deception is its modus operandi in many instances. Sensory illusions are extremely common and just as often misinterpreted."

"So, for you an extraordinary spiritual phenomenon is no more than a misunderstood neuron doing its job?"

Sofia shot Michael a playful scorn. "I wouldn't simplify it that way, nor generalize, though in most cases, it has been proven to be so." She straightened up slightly. "Let me clarify: There is a great misunderstanding between the believer and the scientist. For believers there is a sense of awe when contemplating creation, but at the same time its magnificence is intimidating, calling for an immediate explanation, a creator that grounds the magic. A scientist is just as amazed, and it is precisely that wonderment that drives the thrill to unravel the mystery behind the magic wherever it may lead." Sofia drew a soft smile. "What I'm trying to say is that it has never been my intention to ruin the magic. I simply describe reality, and for me it's pretty amazing as it is, no magic needed."

"Have you ever come across a phenomenon you couldn't explain?"

"Yes, of course. I don't have an answer for everything; at least, not yet." Sofia examined Michael. "What is your position in all of this?"

"I'm in awe of the magic of creation while at the same time open to whatever science may reveal about it."

Sofia chuckled. "You know how to play it safe."

"It keeps me alive," grinned Michael. Then he sobered his gaze. "Do you mind me asking if you are an atheist?"

"No, I don't mind, and the answer is, no. I'm a skeptic. An atheist is absolutely certain that God does not exist in the same manner that a believer is absolutely certain he does. My position is simply that I don't know and won't take a position on it until I do." Sofia lowered her tone. "Unfortunately, this makes me a coward in the eyes of the first and a doomed soul in the eyes of the latter."

"Is that how you think your sister sees you?"

The question shook her a little. It took Sofia a few seconds to answer. "Yes".

"That's not true!"

Sofia bounced in her seat. Lily was standing right there, beside her, looking visibly upset.

"Why would you say that?"

"What the...?" Sofia jumped to her feet. "How did you get here so fast? Wait! How did you know where I was?"

Lily persisted. "I don't think of you as a lost soul."

"You absolutely do. Since you found me in that stupid well you have been trying to save me."

"Again, not true. What I worry about is your perpetual state of denial, as if it never happened. You regressed into your own little world that day. You've never been the same again. I don't think it's healthy, and you should know that better than anyone."

Sofia crossed her arms. "I suggest we discuss this some other time. We have company."

"Unbelievable," huffed Lily, turning to Michael, "You see what I'm talking about? She's evading the subject again."

Michael got up to greet Lily showing signs of being very amused by it all. They melted in a warm hug.

"I'm so happy to see you," said Lily as they separated. "Thank you for coming."

Michael drew his distinctive sweet smile. "As soon as I read your message, I dropped everything."

CHAPTER 3

A couple of small kids ran by chasing a dog, while a family, evidently tourists from the maps and brochures they held, stopped at El Molero to order their renowned fajita rollups. Surprisingly, the line was not as long as usual, most likely due to the bleak forecast. Since the sun was out, it was safe to presume it would soon get crowded.

Sofia was fuming. First Dan, and now her sister, both had messed with her today. She switched her pointed stare between Lily and Michael a few times until she settled it on Michael who appeared to be the common link.

"I see you know each other."

"I've known your sister for several years."

"Please don't be angry," interrupted Lily, "We had to do it this way."

Sofia turned slowly to her. "You *had* to lure me here with lies?"

"We needed to get you away from the office on a good pretext."

"Lily! I don't need excuses to get out of the office. All you had to do was ask."

"It's not that simple."

"It's not? What justifies him," asked Sofia pointing at Michael, "deceiving Dan the way he did! How do you think it will affect my job and career when Dan finds out he was played?"

"Technically, I didn't lie," clarified Michael. "There really is a great story here."

Sofia couldn't believe it. Was he for real? "After this ridiculous charade, do you really think I'm going to open up to *you* about that day?"

"No," said Lily. She pulled her sister's arm for attention, "He's not here for our story. It's much more than that. It's a story greater than us."

Sofia released herself. "I don't care what it is. You just can't do that!"

"Please, let me explain. It was my idea," started Michael.

That Sofia was sure of. Regardless of their differences, she knew one thing: Her sister was utterly incapable of employing devious means to get her way. If anything, she faltered of being too transparent, even to her own disadvantage sometimes.

"I apologize for how it was conducted," he continued. "You're right; we should have consulted with you before taking any action. Unfortunately, because of my job, I've grown to be exceedingly cautious. When Lily contacted me and told me what was going on, I became very concerned for her. We had to play it safe. I assure you some people are not going to like what she has uncovered. This is serious."

Sofia's gaze widened as it turned to Lily. "What the heck is he talking about?"

"I told you on the phone. It has to do with my research. I've stumbled upon something big." Lily looked around. It was getting busy, as the skies cleared, and lunchtime approached. She spotted another bench further removed from the fajita truck and its growing line. "Let's go over there," she suggested.

Lily pulled Sofia by the arm toward the isolated corner as Sofia turned to launch a hard look over her shoulder at Michael. What crazy ideas had this guy put into her sister's head? Lily was a religious historian, and her research had to do with women's parity in the church; hardly something anyone anywhere in the world could care less about.

She turned back to her sister, "How did you two meet?"

"In Afghanistan," replied Lily. "If you remember, several years ago I volunteered with my group of sisters to help with humanitarian efforts. As usual, women, the elderly, and children were the most in need. Still are. Mike was there doing a paper on the dire state of women's welfare under the Taliban."

Sofia looked back at him as if a lioness protecting her cub. "Really?"

Unhindered by her conspicuous misgivings, Michael explained. "I was commissioned by the United Nations to help with a global collection of data to analyze the correlation between prosperity and development, and the rights of women."

Sofia showed no signs of being satisfied, so he continued talking.

"In most societies, women come last in the concession of equal rights. Take here, the US, for instance. Too summarize it grossly, first the wealthy, white, male, property owner ruled. Despite the Declaration of Independence and the Constitution, minorities and women weren't even considered citizens initially, much less have any rights. Gradually the rest of the white males were granted the right to vote, followed by men of color, and lastly women. Global historical data shows a strong correlation between the increase in a country's national Gross Domestic Product and its awarding of rights, specifically to women. One major reason is that the wellbeing of families and communities is directly dependent upon the wellbeing of women. Therefore, women's incorporation to the workplace and more so to government offices reflects positively back into their communities. The US economy took off sharply when women jumped into the labor market in the 1940s. In short," he added to conclude, "once a society acknowledges the equal standing of every individual down to the last poor, black woman, that society's level of wellbeing on all fronts, from political and economic to technological and health, simply skyrockets. The Taliban offer a lamentable example of worst-case scenario."

"And because of my personal crusade," added Lily, "we connected and have stayed in touch since. Satisfied?"

No, she was not satisfied.

The three reached the bench, but none felt like sitting.

Sofia took a moment to probe her sister. It was like looking in a mirror. They both carried their striking features as natural as possible, one as a way of life, the other for comfort. The only alteration that distinguished them was the length of their dark, wavy hair; just below the shoulder for Sofia, neck-cropped for Lily. Otherwise, you could not tell them apart if not for the spirit that fueled their expressions. Lily was the energetic, lively one, always radiating cheer, while Sofia admitted to being the serious, stern-set, and quiet one. Even when it came to clothes, Lily wore her long, demure skirts with more pizazz than Sofia carried her perfectly-cut, office attire. Today, Sofia saw something new, an intense purpose mixed with tension, and identifying unease in Lily's eyes translated to extreme alarm for Sofia.

"Lily, what's going on?"

"I need your help."

"Why?"

"Because you're the smart twin. I've reached a dead-end in my research, and only you can help me."

Nothing was making sense. Sofia took a deep breath. "Okay," she surrendered. "Tell me what this is about."

Lily further intensified the new, grave glare that was making Sofia so uncomfortable.

"What I'm going to tell you will be very difficult for you to accept. That's why it's imperative that you listen to the end." Lily reached for her sister's hands. "Please, Sof, I beg you, no matter how absurd it may seem at first, promise me you'll listen with an open mind all the way to the end."

Sofia furrowed her eyebrows. The same person who boasted about her blind faith was asking her to be open-minded. "Just get on with it."

"No! Promise me! I'm going to be talking about miracles and divine conspiracies. You have to listen." Lily squeezed her sister's hands so hard she almost cracked a knuckle.

"Okay, Okay. I promise. No judgement or eye rolls until you're done."

"Good." Lily momentarily closed her eyes as if to perform a brief prayer. Then they popped opened with an eerie shadow. "I have reason to believe that the Second Coming is upon us, and that the Vatican is covering up all the signs."

Sofia straightened out her furrowed eyebrows and slowly raised them. "The Second Coming, you said?"

"Yes, you know, the End of Times with the coming of the Kingdom of God as prophesized by the Book of Revelations."

"As in the world is going to end soon?" Sofia's state of stupor was only surpassed by her incredulity.

Lily drew a smile not at all in line with the severity of what she was claiming. "No. It was never meant to end. That's not what it's all about. I've discovered that through the centuries there have been divine signs attempting to guide us on how to correct course, to live in peace and to put an end to suffering, but we have failed to acknowledge them."

Sofia tried talking common sense. "Lily, you don't need divine signs to figure out that the human race has badly screwed things up. And it's not rocket science that if we were all a little nicer to each other, we'd be better off."

Lily's smile angled to one side. "First, you promised," she reminded, waving a finger at her sister. "Second, I'm going to prove to you that we have indeed needed these divine signs, that we have indeed received them, and that the heads of the main churches have been blatantly ignoring them. But most important of all, I know what the signs are telling us." Lily's face glowed with hope. "Sof, we have been granted a unique opportunity to convert Hell into Heaven here on Earth. You are going to help me usher in the Day of Purification."

Sofia exasperated. There it was: the age-old Hopi conviction that they were the chosen ones to save the world. Then toss in the Christian strive to secure salvation, the family legends, and the episode at the well, and it all mixed to instilling in her sister a delusional messianic complex.

Sofia looked at Michael in search of reason.

She didn't find it.

"I read her research," he said. "She is not talking nonsense. She has solid evidence. You need to listen to this."

"You promised..." echoed Lily.

Sofia crossed her arms, more in frustration than defiance. "How exactly are we supposed to convert Hell into Heaven?"

"I don't know, but I've located a set of Divine Markers that draw a path. I believe it leads us to the answer."

"Divine Markers?"

"Real, rock-solid markers."

"And they lay out a path?"

Lily nodded.

"Where to?"

"That's where you come in. I was only able to get so far. I need your analytical genius to figure out the last stretch to destination."

CHAPTER 4

Sofia turned her bewildered look to Michael, again. She knew her sister was prone to fantasizing, but what about him? She had looked him up. It was a hasty search, to be sure, but it appeared he was a serious professional in a serious field with some serious awards to support his acumen.

Michael once more confirmed with a firm gaze and a nod. "I'm telling you, this is no joke," he insisted.

Other than her promise, the only thing stopping Sofia from stomping out was the unsettling prospect that her sister could be under the influence of this man with some kind of obscure agenda.

She'd play along for now.

"Hell, Heaven, the End Times, Divine Markers and mysterious paths, those are big words," she started. "Since it is all *divinely* inspired, why would church leaders turn a blind eye? Surely they know better than to defy the Gods."

"They're in denial," responded Lily. "They're being asked to make changes they don't like. Maybe even end the role of the papacy as we know it."

"What?" Sofia was back to being shocked. Her sister, the virtuous nun, was conspiring to bring down the Vatican? She couldn't help shooting Michael another suspicious glare.

For the first time, he showed a hint of annoyance. "I understand you find this difficult to digest. But if you give her a chance to explain, you'll see it makes sense. As for me, if my presence makes you uncomfortable, I'll leave. But know that I'm here because I am concerned for her safety."

Lily interceded. "Sof, I trust him. I would not have reached out to him if I didn't."

That did little to comfort her. Lily was excessively kindhearted. She trusted everyone.

Sofia took a moment to restrain herself. She rubbed her face and grunted to release the whirlwind of frustration amassed inside. She addressed Michael.

"I apologize. I realize I've been rude to you, but you need to understand that my distrust is out of concern for her as well." Her tone was one of cautioned conciliation.

He nonetheless approved with his irresistible smile. It helped ease the tension.

Sofia approached the bench. "Give me a moment," she requested. She sat and massaged her temples. Sofia tended to overstimulate easily and had learned to take the necessary reprieve to calm down.

Lily and Michael followed. Each sat to one side of her and waited for her to be ready.

If she was to understand what was going on here, Sofia knew she had to get a grip fast. "You know what?" she announced with renewed poise, "I actually want to hear this." She looked at Lily. "Please, start from the beginning."

"Okay..." Lily found her sister's accommodating attitude unexpected. She had come prepared for a little more resistance. She proceeded hesitantly. "I prefer to start from the end. It will help set the stage to better follow the rest."

"Whatever," ushered Sofia, waving her hand, "just get on with it."

"All right then..."

Lily gave her sister a second look. She wondered if this was the calm before the blustery winds. What she was going to reveal was trying even for the most devoted, and in the past Sofia had stormed out on her for much less.

She started slowly. "So, as you know, I was researching the New Testament to support my claim that women were more active in the early church than they are allowed today. For instance, in Paul's letters to the Romans he acknowledges the valued leadership and missionary engagements of some women. He even greets and praises two, Junia and Andronicus, as prominent 'apostles' of all things. Since then, the Church has consistently belittled the real contribution of female saints, nuns and women in general. We all know of Mary Magdalene, who rather than recognized as first among the apostles, was smeared as a prostitute for the longest time. Acknowledgement has come slow, reluctantly, and only because they had no other choice in the end."

Lily paused to check on her sister, who seemed calm. Encouraged she continued. "Anyway, the point is that I was combing through history, picking up on these flagrant oversights to justify the Church's resistance to our ordination, when I came across the Secrets of Fatima, probably their worst offense to womankind ever." Lily paused again to assess her sister. "You are familiar with Fatima, right?"

"Yes," answered Sofia, deeply curious how her sister was going to consolidate age-old sexism with the End of the World. But she was also noticing a bitter undertone in her voice that she found almost more troubling than the unease she had detected in her eyes. Lily's drive to help others was rooted in a healthy and joyous spirit. Sofia never thought it possible that something could sour it. Her protective instinct bristled. "I touched on it sometime ago. It's an interesting case in Mariology. Most apparitions can be explained by natural causes or are deemed a transitory delusion commonly witnessed by one or a handful of seers. In this case, however, the apparition came accompanied by a phenomenon predicted well in advance and, therefore, witnessed by thousands of people, including the media. To summarize, if I recall, Mary appeared to three young shepherds and told them three secrets. Two were revealed at a certain point, but the third one was kept under wraps by the Vatican until recently. When finally revealed, the secret disappointed so much it led many to suspect it wasn't the real one, leading in turn to the rise of countless conspiracies. That's as much as I know."

Lily nodded. "Then let me expand on it. The events around Fatima led me to the fundamental clue that, in turn, guided me to the Divine Markers. It's important you know the whole story."

"Right, the markers, I can't wait to hear about those." Sofia was relaxing, and it showed up in her sarcastic edge.

Lily offered her a warning stare.

Raising her palm in a sign of peace, Sofia gestured her on.

"Thank you," continued her sister. "So, on May 13th, 1917, three little shepherds were working in their family-owned fields in Fatima, Portugal, when they saw the bright image of a young girl in a short dress appear above a tree. The image asked them to return to the same spot every month on the same date, the thirteenth."

"That's it? She appeared only to ask them to return?"

"There were several, short and gentle apparitions that preceded the more famed ones, probably to make the kids comfortable with what was to come. For instance, the year before an "angel of light" appeared to warn of the future visions. The eldest of the three, Lucia Santos, was 10 years old at the time and had admonished her younger cousins, Francisco and Jacinta, to remain quiet about it. But Jacinta, who was the youngest and only seven, told her mother, who told the neighbors thinking it was children's play. When the word got out, some took it rather seriously, and over the following months, on the date instructed, the children returned to the same spot accompanied by a growing number of locals."

Lily leaning in ever so slightly. "It was on July 13when the female image revealed the Three Secrets to the kids, asking them not to share it with anyone yet. In addition, they were told that the two younger ones would die soon, while Lucia would remain longer to help communicate the Secrets at the right time. Finally, for the world to believe that they were in fact seeing what they claimed to be seeing, the vision prophesized the miracle you mentioned for October 13. Tens of thousands of faithful, together with reporters and photographers, from near and far, flocked to the spot to witness the promised wonder. It is said that most indeed saw what is now known as the 'Miracle of the Sun'. According to varying accounts, the sun changed color, rotated, and danced. The three shepherds were then informed by the 'lady dressed in light' that she was Our Lady of the Rosary and had come to ask for men to change their ways, for they were deeply insulting God. The public apparitions ended there, and as foretold, Francisco died two years later at the age of eleven, and Jacinta in 1920 at age ten."

Sofia frowned. There was something about the little ones having to die that didn't seem right.

Lily continued. "Initially the Church did not appear to pay much attention to it. But, as usual, people are hopeful, and the site became a powerful pilgrimage destination. So much so that, eventually, the Church became concerned and decided to whisk Lucia away, purportedly for her own safety, due to the enormous attention she was receiving. She was entered into a boarding school until she was transferred to a convent a year later. Lucia was 14 years old. From that day forward, up to the day of her death in 2005 at the age of 98, she remained under close surveillance. And though she continued to have visions all her life, they are scarcely known because the rules of her cloistered community limited her conversations with visitors. No one could talk to her without license from Rome."

"Poor child. Locked away like that all her life."

"I'm certain she was fine. Bear in mind that she was a humble and illiterate shepherd with a meek future who became a revered nun visited by high profiled dignities from around the world. Having read her memoirs, I believe she was very happy."

"If you say so."

Lily cleared her throat. "I could do with some water."

Michael jumped to his feet. "I'll get some."

"You don't mind?"

"Happy to. I'll also get something to eat. You continue with the story. I'll be right back."

"Thank you," replied Lily.

"It's fine with me if we go to a restaurant," suggested Sofia. "We'd be more comfortable."

"No," responded Michael sharply. "We have things under control here. It's better if we stay put for now."

Sofia gave Lily a quizzical look.

Lily patted her sister's hand. "Let me continue. There is still a lot I need to tell you. I'm not even close to the interesting part yet."

Michael took off with a trot. Sofia sat confused. And Lily resumed her account.

CHAPTER 5

Lily knew better than to abuse Sofia's patience and hurried to summarize as best she could. "Due to the growing number of pilgrims visiting Fatima, the bishop appointed a Commission of Canonical Inquiry and Lucia was sent across the border to Spain further removed from the growing devotion. In 1928, the first official Church ceremony took place at the Fatima Shrine, and in 1930, the Commission finally declared the visions 'worthy of belief', thus authorizing the official cult of Our Lady of Fatima."

"All this time the Secrets were not yet known to the public, right?" asked Sofia.

"Correct. Up to this point, they were known to exist, but not what they contained, which, as you can imagine, added to their allure. It wasn't until 1940 that Lucia writes to Pope Pius XII to express her wish to reveal them. According to Vatican records, the pope does not answer. Undeterred, Lucia claims to have the permission of Heaven and, with the support of her local bishop, goes ahead and writes her memoires anyway." Lily interjected a wink, "You see what I mean? She was fine, even feisty."

"It must be part of a nun's profile," teased Sofia.

Lily smiled, taking it as a compliment. "Anyway, while her first and second memoires are dedicated to her little cousin Jacinta and their childhood together, it's the third and fourth memoirs, published the following year, the ones that contain the first two Secrets. Then, in 1947, the Fatima phenomena received an international boost with the installation of Our Lady's statue—"

"Slow down," interrupted Sofia. "Before you go on, remind me what the Secrets were. It's been a while since I read about them."

"I was going to after ...." Lily stopped herself. Seeing her sister's interest, she happily conceded. "It doesn't matter. I can tell you now. The first one is a vision of Hell and goes like this:

> *'Our Lady showed us a large sea of fire which seemed to be under the earth. Immersed in this fire were demons and souls, like transparent and black or bronzed embers with human form, that floated in the*

conflagration carried by the flames that emerged from within them, together with clouds of smoke falling everywhere, like the sparks of a huge fire, without weight or balance, amid screams and groans of pain and despair, which horrified us and made us tremble with fear. The demons could be distinguished by their terrifying and disgusting likeness to frightful and unknown animals, but black and transparent. This vision lasted but a moment.'"

Sofia winced as she remembered. "It's hard to understand why Mary would show that to three little kids."

"Yes, well, Lucia precisely goes on to write how grateful they were that the heavenly Mother had prepared them by promising in the first apparition to take them to Heaven. Otherwise, she wrote, they would have died of fear and terror. And according to witness accounts, both Francisco and Jacinta died smiling knowing all would be fine."

Sofia doubted it. People tended to see what they wanted to see. "Still... It's disturbing. I don't recall the Second Secret as bad."

"No. It's just strange. Lucia then writes that Our Lady tells them kindly and sad:

'You saw hell where the souls of poor sinners go. To save them, God wishes to establish in the world devotion to my Immaculate Heart. If you do as I say, many souls will be saved, and you'll have peace. The war is going to end, but if you don't cease to offend God, during Pius XI's reign a worse one will begin. When you see a night illuminated by an unknown light, know that it's the great sign provided by God that he is going to punish the world for its crimes, by means of war, famine, and persecutions of the Church and the Holy Father. To prevent this, I will come to ask for the consecration of Russia to my Immaculate Heart and the Communion of Reparation on the First Saturdays. If you attend to my requests, Russia will be converted and you will have peace; if not, she will spread her errors throughout the world, causing wars and persecutions of the Church, the good will be martyred, the Holy Father will have much to suffer, various nations will be annihilated, in the end my Immaculate Heart will triumph.

The Holy Father will consecrate Russia to me, she will convert, and a period of peace will be granted to the world."

Sofia took a thoughtful moment. She then looked at her sister through the corner of her eyes with one openly skeptic and elevated eyebrow. "Am I allowed to share what I think yet, or am I still to remain silent?"

"No need. I know too well what you'd say. I'll even tell you: Typical apocalyptic gibberish."

"I would have been a little more polite than that."

"Only a little," agreed Lily with a smile.

Sofia chuckled. "So, what does it mean?"

"It appears to be predicting World War II. However, as I am sure you would wisely point out, the premonition is questionable because, though received back in 1917, it was not made public until 1941 when the war had already started."

"Not only that," added Sofia, surprised her sister would admit to that. "What about the reference to Russia? Tens of millions of people died in the war, the deadliest ever in history. And let's not forget the horrid Holocaust. But Mary traumatizes three little kids because her concern is the conversion of Russia?"

Lily narrowed her eyes as if regressing into deep thought. "That is precisely the strange part and what got me thinking. It turned out to be a clue." Lily resurfaced. "The Church's interpretation was that Mary was concerned about communism and the spreading of atheism, but I have a very different theory."

"You actually have a theory that makes sense out of all this?"

"Absolutely. But stay with me. Let me finish with the chronological account of Fatima before we get into the details. It's just now getting juicy."

"Right, the Third Secret."

"Exactly. In 1944, while still in Tuy, Spain, Lucia writes down the infamous Third Secret, puts it in an envelope, and delivers it to the Bishop of Leiria, informing him that Mary wants it made public in 1960 for '*by that time, it will be clearly understood*.'"

"That's different," observed Sofia. "This time the Secret is written down sixteen years before its revelation. And with specific instructions, no less."

Lily grinned. "For a good reason, you'll see. The envelope stays with the bishop until 1957, when, with all the expectation of the approaching date, Pope Pius XII has it sent to the Vatican for safekeeping. You can imagine the degree of speculation going on in the media over its possible content."

"I recall it vaguely. Everything from Armageddon to a UFO invasion was being debated. What happened in the end?"

"The unthinkable happened." Suddenly, Lily's bitter undertone reemerged. "In August of 1959, John XXIII proceeds to be the first pope to open the envelope. He reads the Third Secret with some close associates and allegedly says: "Let us wait. I will pray. Then I will let you know what I have decided.""

"Which means...?"

"It means that Pope John XXIII decided not to make it public."

"You're kidding!"

Lily took in a slow measured breath. "Unfortunately, not. He locked it away. This is what got to me. Here I was on a mission to change things; to prove that Jesus had always wanted women side-by-side men teaching His message. I strongly felt I could do more as a minister. It was my calling. And I genuinely believed my Church was making an honest mistake in this regard. Then I come across this and, bam, smack in the face, it hit me: What hope did I, a mere sister, have of ever getting ordained if the maximum head of my Church completely disregarded the wishes of the most sacred woman of all, the Mother of God?"

Sofia now understood her sister's bitterness. It was raw disappointment. The type that can only come from someone you look up to.

She cupped her hand on Lily's shoulder. "Maybe they simply didn't believe the apparition ever really happened. I doubt anyone in their right mind would want to defy Mary if they did."

Lily drew a soft smile. "I tried to convince myself of that, but remember, they had qualified the apparitions as worthy of belief and Her cult authorized."

"You know as well as I do that the Church considers apparitions a private revelation. The faithful can choose to believe them or not."

"I'm surprised you defend them."

"I don't. I'm with you. Their acknowledgement of women's equality inside the Church is long overdue. However, I do want to be fair. The Church may find itself in a position where they do not believe the miracle but choose to respect it in honor of the thousands of faithful who do."

Lily stared at her sister. "You always were the sensible one."

"Well, thank you."

"However, this time you are wrong. You told me once: If you really want to know someone's intentions, don't listen to their words, pay attention to their actions."

"I had no idea you ever listened to me."

"It was a weak moment."

They both chuckled helping Lily regain her spirit.

"So, what do their actions tell you?"

"A great deal." Lily seemed suddenly to spring back to life. "Something was going on backstage. The Vatican's official stance on Fatima had nothing to do with what they were doing."

"What do you mean?"

"Their behavior became stranger and stranger with time. After their press release saying that the secret was better kept sealed forever, a huge outrage followed. People inside and outside the Church criticized the move. The Vatican later smoke-screened their decision by saying that Mary had left it up to the Holy Father to make the call."

"I see. I imagine this only helped make speculations escalate even further."

"You bet. Now it was believed that the secret message had to do with the Church itself; anything from Mary warning that the Antichrist was sitting on the Holy Throne to its fall."

Sofia interrupted. "Wait. I was under the impression the Secret had been revealed in the end."

"Yes, eventually it was, making matters even worse. You see, for the next four decades successive popes read it, and like John XXIII, chose to keep it sealed. The few comments volunteered hinted to it being too tough for us to bear."

"Really? Mary showed the kids Hell in the First Secret and threatened with dire consequences in the second one. If that was okay for children, what could the Third Secret possibly contain that adults could not handle?"

"Exactly! That was the sentiment. But, wait for it, then comes John Paul II and something extraordinary happens." Lily's eyes sparkled. "On May 13, 1981, coinciding with the 64th anniversary of the first apparition, he is shot in St. Peters Square and almost dies. Because of the date, Pope John Paul II is convinced that Our Lady of Fatima saved his life, and while recovering in the hospital, calls for the sealed envelope. Thereafter, he visits Fatima on several occasions to thank Her and goes on a world tour to entrust us all to Her Immaculate Heart as She had requested. His devotion to the Virgin Mary becomes unparalleled. So, on May 13, 2000, there is much expectation because the pope returns to Fatima to beatify Jacinta and Francisco. The hope is, that if the Secret is ever to be revealed, it will be he who'll do it and what better occasion than this?"

Sofia leaned in.

"When the ceremony ended, John Paul II stepped aside and the Vatican's Secretary of State, Cardinal Angelo Sodano, took the stage. To everybody's dismay, rather than revealing the Secret itself, he instead alludes to its content by explaining that it simply foretells the assassination attempt on Pope John Paul II. He then goes on to say that the Vatican was aware it would disappoint in view of all the sensationalism created around it over the decades, and, therefore, to avoid any further exaggeration, they were going to provide the *correct* interpretation for the faithful to abide by along with the Secret.

"A typical cult maneuver," commented Sofia, "deprive followers from thinking for themselves."

"Many faithful seek and welcome the guidance," protested Lily. "In any event, the uproar in the media could be heard all the way to Mars. Everyone was shocked that the Vatican would keep it sealed for decades under the pretext that we couldn't handle the truth, only to reveal in the end it had to do with the frustrated attempt on the pope's life. Finally, in June of the same year, the actual Secret was made public together with a very long Theological Commentary by Cardinal Joseph Ratzinger, who, by the way, also orchestrated the wild presentation in Fatima a few months earlier." Lily raised an eyebrow. "Does his name sound familiar to you?"

Sofia raised another. "Isn't he who became pope after John Paul II?"

Lily nodded satisfied. "Correct. In February of 2005, Lucia Santos died, and Ratzinger rushed to seal her convent cell. Only two months later, John Paul II, the Pope of Fatima, passes away, as well. Ratzinger goes on to become Pope Benedict XVI, putting an end to the whole matter."

A brief suspended silence ensued.

"I see," conceded Sofia. "Their behavior does seem most strange. It's all over the place."

"That's my point," stressed Lily, "Why play it cool first as if Fatima was no big deal, but then keep the Secret locked away? Why justify it by saying it was too frightening only to later switch and say it wasn't all that frightening after all and blame the media for exaggerating? And why isolate Lucia in life and then lock her cell off upon her death? Something about these Secrets frightened them."

There was the bitterness, again. Sofia didn't like it. It surprised her to realize she preferred it when Lily was all faith and joy. "So, you think you have discovered what that is?"

"Yes, it is all in the details."

CHAPTER 6

Michael ran up the steps to reach the restaurant's second-floor deck. He walked over to the window and knocked. On the other side, a man that mirrored his looks, though younger with slightly shorter hair, was dinning on his own enjoying the privileged view of the plaza. Upon hearing the knock, he turned his head. Michael waved him in. The man nodded and got up to oblige.

"I don't have much time," started Michael. "How's it going?"

"I haven't seen anything suspicious. I think you're good. However, after you moved further into the center of the park, I'm having a little difficulty seeing through the dense canopy."

"I'm reluctant to suggest another move."

The young man shrugged. "I'll manage. How are things down there?"

"She's listening."

"It's a start," he said pleased.

"What about her place?" asked Michael.

"As suspected, they're watching it."

"I'm surprised they didn't show up here, then."

"They may have bugged her and don't need to get up close."

Michael nodded. "I'll take care of that. In the meantime, the plan is to eat something and then lead her to the cathedral. Keep your eyes peeled. If they're here, it will be your best chance to spot them."

"Do you want me to signal you, or should I take care of it myself?"

"If possible, give me a heads up. I'd like to take a good look at them before we act."

"Will do. Otherwise, I'll see you at Saint Francis."

Michael smiled. "Thank you, Gabriel. I appreciate your help."

"It's exciting times. I'm happy to be part of it."

The two sisters stood up to stretch their legs.

Sofia looked around. "Where's Michael?"

Lily scanned the corner of the plaza he took off to. "Maybe he doesn't like fajitas and went somewhere else."

"He's odd."

"Why do you say that?"

"I don't know, his looks, his strange voice. There's something about him that seems out of place."

Lily smiled. "What matters is that his heart is in the right place. And you have to admit he's also very charming. Some younger sisters back in Afghanistan almost reconsidered their vows after meeting him."

"He made a move on the nuns?"

Lily laughed. "No, he was a perfect gentleman. But I got the impression one or two were disappointed he didn't."

Sofia offered her a long, side look.

"No, not me. But I do like him. And I trust him."

"He's not the type of friend I'd envision you with."

"It's funny. Unlike with you, on the surface, he and I could not be more different. Yet inside we are both passionate about our common cause."

"Don't dismiss me that quick. I'm a woman. I care about our rights too."

"That's only a steppingstone. It's about the bigger picture. Have you been listening?"

"Oh, right, it's not just about women. Women's wellbeing reverts in their community and ultimately leads to the wellbeing of the world at large. Sorry, got distracted when you moved on to the Apocalypse, or was it Heaven on Earth?"

"You're impossible," said Lily.

"Well, what do you expect? You start by saying you were researching gender equality, when you stumbled on a divine conspiracy that has had the popes freaking out for decades. I'm having trouble keeping it all straight."

"You can't see it yet, Sof, but Mary is offering us the End of the World as we know it; the end of pain and suffering for so many. All we have to do is follow the path she has laid out for us."

"You sound like a true Hopi: Follow the straight path as instructed by the Great Spirit, and you shall be saved on the Day of Purification." Sofia didn't mean to mock their ancient tradition, but it came across a little like it.

It didn't faze Lily. "Only I'm referring to a real path, as on a map, not a metaphorical one."

"Well, then, tell me about the Divine Markers, already."

"Soon." A subtle plead for patience was conveyed in the single word.

Sofia considered her sister. She had not had a conversation this long with her for as long as she could remember, let alone about the type of subject that had contributed to their distance in the first place. Lily had changed. Sofia wasn't sure if her new sober aura was a good thing, but it had smoothed the fanatical edge. Either way, she had missed her and was rather enjoying having become her unlikely confidant.

"Fine. Go on then, tell me instead about the Third Secret," welcomed Sofia. "What was it in the end?"

She didn't have to ask twice.

"A vision," said Lily.

"A vision... That's it? I thought it was a message?"

"Exactly. Sr. Lucia had alluded to a message, so when a vision was revealed, some questioned its authenticity. Others wondered if the Third Secret consisted of both, a vision and a message, but the message was withheld."

"Can it get any more complicated?" Sofia was in disbelief.

"I know, right? Personally, I side with the last group. I'm not going to go into all the details but suffice to say there were witnesses that attested to the existence of a message, the Vatican archivist among them."

Sofia shook her head.

Lily pulled her phone out. "As for the vision, let me find it. I want to make sure I tell you right."

"You need to look it up? What happened to your eidetic memory?" teased Sofia. Lily had a remarkable selective memory. She never mastered the periodic table but was able to memorize every verse in the Bible if only to torment Sofia when they were kids.

"Getting old I guess," confessed Lily. When she found it, she read.

"... we saw to the left of Our Lady, slightly higher, an angel with a flaming sword in his left hand. As it flashed, it launched flames that looked as though they would set the world on fire. Yet they died out in

contact with the brilliance Our Lady radiated from Her right hand sent to their encounter. The angel, pointing to the earth with his right hand, said in a loud voice: 'Penance, Penance, Penance!'

And we saw in an immense light, which is God, something similar to how people see themselves in a mirror, when before it passed a bishop dressed in white. We had the impression it was the Holy Father. We saw other bishops, priests, religious men and women climb a steep mountain, at the top of which there was a big cross with a rough trunk, as if it were of an oak tree with its bark. Before reaching there the Holy Father passed through a big city half in ruins and half trembling with hesitant steps, grieving with pain and sorrow. He prayed for the souls of the corpses he met on his way. Upon reaching the top of the mountain, on his knees at the foot of the cross, he was killed by a group of soldiers who fired several shots and arrows at him, and in the same way there died one after another the other bishops, priests, religious men and women, and various secular people; gentlemen and ladies of different status and positions. Beneath the two arms of the cross there were two angels, each with a glass pitcher in his hands in which they gathered up the blood of the martyrs and with it irrigated the souls that made their way to God."

Sofia took a moment. Finally, she reacted. "Wow! That seems a lot for little kids to assimilate all at once. I'm sorry, but even if Lucia truly saw that, I find it hard to believe she'd be able to remember so much detail after so many years. How old did you say she was at the time? Ten? That must have made her, what, thirty-seven when she wrote it down?"

"She is renowned for her prodigious memory. Apparently, hers was eidetic for real."

"That can be said of up to 10% of children, but it is necessary to cultivate it in order to retain it," explained Sofia twisting her face in doubt. "On the other hand, I guess it was a huge event for the town. Lucia had nothing better to do than remember what she saw. Not to mention that all the attention wouldn't let her forget it even if she wanted to. Still, with the years it is easy to dress it up a little, that is... if it is the vision she saw... and if she truly saw something in the first place." Sofia arched a brow. "That is two big *ifs*".

Lily chuckled. "For a second there, as I followed your reasoning, I was starting to think you believed the apparitions happened."

"You still haven't given me any hard evidence to prove they did."

"I'm getting there. Trust me. I did my homework to give you what you need. I realized at the time that all I had was suspicious behavior. Therefore, I resorted to doing what I thought I'd never do. I decided to think like you do."

"Do you even know how?"

"In your own words, it's not rocket science. It's quite simple really. You doubt everything."

Sofia smacked her sister playfully on the arm. "I've told you a million times, I don't doubt everything, I question everything. They're two very different approaches."

"Whatever!" sassed Lily. "In any case, I'll give it to you, it worked. I set aside the Vatican's public statements and commentary, all the critics' personal opinions, the speculations and conspiracy theories, and so on, until I was left with the bare bones of verifiable facts."

"I'm surprised there was anything left."

"Was there ever. As I've explained, after John XXIII refused to make the Third Secret public, the Vatican's strange conduct became apparent. The thing is, knowing what we know now, if we go all the way back to when the apparitions happened, the behavior of every pope was strange from the start."

"I don't follow. So what? We've already established they were rattled."

Lily drew an enigmatic grin. "That was the key. The beauty of Mary's Three-Secret approach was that it rattled the Vatican in a public way for us all to see. You can question the apparitions, the Secrets, or if the message ever existed, but not how the popes reacted. So, when you go back to take a closer look at how each one dealt with the Fatima affair from the start, a pattern surfaces that leads to the why. And it was in trying to make sense of this that I stumbled on the markers."

Sofia was impressed.

CHAPTER 7

Sofia was also intrigued in addition to impressed. For her, all the talk about supernatural entities strategizing with cryptic secrets to expose behaviors, was absurd. But she knew her sister had a good head on her shoulders. There had to be something in all this that made sense at some level.

Lily rubbed her hands. "Now, pay attention. I'm going to run you quickly through the actions taken by each pope. Don't worry, I'll make it short. I just want you to see how the pattern form."

Sofia nodded.

"We start with Benedict XV. He became pope in 1914 at the outbreak of World War I. He declares neutrality of the Holy See and attempts to mediate peace fruitlessly in 1916 and 1917. He also happened to be an ardent Mariologist, so resorts to placing the world under Our Lady's protection, and on May 5th, 1917, adds the invocation '*Mary Queen of Peace, pray for us*' to the Litany of Loreto." Lily glowed. "She must have listened and thought of it as Her opportunity to finally make a statement because it was only a week later when She appears to the three little shepherds for the first time. The event goes largely unnoticed outside the Portuguese village, and the Vatican shows no public acknowledgement. However, Sister Lucia, years later in her memoires, mentions two priests sent to interrogate her on behalf of the Holy Father. It was all done very discreetly. Then," Lily stabbed the air with her index finger to stress her point, "as a consequence, or not, but suspiciously coincidental, he goes on to address the spiky issue of Our Lady being Co-Redemptrix in an Apostolic Letter; a controversial subject brought up in many apparitions but never fully embraced by the Church."

Sofia exhibited confusion.

"Just listen," said Lily, eager to continue. "It will make sense in a minute. Benedict XV dies unexpectedly in January of 1922. Pius XI follows. If you recall, this is the pope referred to by name in the Second Secret, that is, when Our Lady announces the outbreak of another war if people do not cease offending God. So, it should come as no surprise that it is he who wastes no time in appointing the Commission of Canonical Inquiry to determine the validity of the apparitions. It is also around this time that Lucia is

41

surreptitiously moved from Fatima across the border into the seclusion of a convent in Spain. This is quite telling for someone who showed very little if any interest in the phenomenon publicly."

"Wait," said Sofia. "He's not supposed to know what the secrets say, right?"

"Right, but it's hard to believe. They all play cool and aloof as if not interested in Fatima, however, as I said, Benedict XV sent investigators to interrogate Sr. Lucia, and the first thing Pius XI does as soon as he becomes pope is to set up a task force to investigate it. Yet, we are to believe they never asked her what the secrets contained?"

Sofia shook her head at her sister with some surprise. "You've become more cynical than me. It's not fair. It's all I had on you."

"You'll always be five minutes older."

Sofia was going to say something but saw Michael approach loaded with takeout bags and bottles of water. She alerted Lily.

"God bless him! There's my drink." Lily reached for one of the bottles. "Where did you go?"

"To satisfy a private affair." He winked at her and then turned to Sofia. "I hope you like hamburgers. You have one three choices: classic, turkey or tortilla."

Sofia wrinkled her nose. "Tortilla burger? No thanks, I'll take the classic."

He then let Lily choose.

"Turkey for me."

Michael smiled. "Thank you, both. You don't know what you're missing. This hamburger is wrapped in a flour tortilla, smothered in green chili and topped off with melted cheese." He sat on the bench licking his lips in anticipation. "You can't get this where I come from. Delicious!"

The sisters took their places on the bench not regretting their choices a bit.

"How's it going?" he asked Lily.

"I'm running her through the popes. Just reached Pius XI."

"That's it? Good thing I also picked up some dessert." Still, Michael did not get too comfortable. He remained tense with one eye on the restaurant across the street.

Lily recognized in his posture the need to hurry up. "So, as I was saying," she took a small bite, "eventually, in 1930, the Commission declares Fatima 'worthy of belief', just when racism, religious intolerance and social upheaval are at their worst all over the globe. Talk about offending God!"

Sofia nodded, grasping the situation. "Nazism, the spread of authoritarian regimes, communism, the great depression and segregation, women's rights, wars on all continents, development of nuclear weaponry..."

"You get the idea. The state of affairs on our planet had always been ugly, but for the first time we were on the brink of being able to destroy it altogether. Pius XI reigned between the two World Wars. The annexation of Austria by Germany that led up to the outbreak of the second one happened during his last months. *If* he knew the secret, he was certainly concerned. His pontificate was marked for his stern and relentless condemnation of all these issues and the fight for peace."

"A big step in the right direction," remarked Michael, "It's appalling how most churches have historically failed to spearhead the fight for human rights and equality, or even peace, as they should have. Rather, they have painfully lagged behind, staunch in their conservative ways, and even taking advantage of much of the abuse."

Sofia stared at Michael with curiosity. "Can I ask you what church you belong to?"

"All three Abrahamic faiths run in my family as they do in the region I'm originally from." He then chortled to himself as he returned his attention back to his burger. "It makes for interesting family reunions during religious holidays, I can tell you that."

"And to that point," added Lily, "as you know, Mary and Jesus are prominent figures in the three. So, now think about this: Fatima is a prime Muslim name, that of Mohamed's favorite daughter who is venerated equal to Mary. Mary, who we forget was a Jew, chooses to appear in a town named Fatima, of all places, to Christian shepherds." Lily paused with a heavy stare on Sofia. "I don't think Fatima's Three Secrets were intended for the popes exclusively; it was intended for the leaders of the three religions. I'm telling you, the apparitions in Fatima were unique in many ways, from the content of their messages, to how they were delivered, to whom they were addressed."

"Put that way, I see why they'd be rattled. Heck, I am."

Lily shook her head. "Unfortunately, and back to Pius XI, like benedict XV, he did not seem to glean or satisfy Mary's wishes. He died in February of 1939."

Lily took a sip of water to drown her last bite. She was the only one who, despite doing all the talking, had finished her burger.

Sofia bit into hers for the first time, while Michael seemed content enjoying his slowly.

Lily resumed. "Next up, Pius XII."

"They're not very creative when coming up with names," observed Sofia.

"Wait for the next one."

"What's with it anyway?"

"To be honest, I have no idea why they do it," answered Lily.

"Mercurius is to blame," announced Michael, to their surprise. "He was elected pope back in the 6th century. He deemed it inappropriate for a pope to be named after a pagan God, that is, Mercury, so adopted John II in honor of his predecessor John I, a martyr."

The two sisters lingered their stares on him.

"What? At one of my assignments the only entertainment we had was a Trivia board game."

"O-k-a-y," exaggerated Lily to tease him. "Where was I? Pius XII. Now is when it starts to get interesting. This pope's whole career is curiously linked to Fatima because, coincidently, and I'm going to be using this word a lot, he was elevated to archbishop in the Sistine Chapel on the day and exact time of the first apparition." Lily widened her gaze. "What are the odds? He admitted it impacted him, and when elected, placed his pontificate under the maternal care of Our Lady. Then, he goes on to become one of the most Marian popes of all time. Now pay attention, here is where the pattern starts to form. Surprisingly, according to Vatican records, when in 1940 Lucia writes to him expressing her wish to reveal Our Lady's message, he does not answer. She goes ahead anyway and publishes her memoirs. World War II is in full swing. That same year, Pius XII—as requested in the Second Secret—consecrates the human race to the Immaculate Heart of the Virgin but neglects to make a specific reference to Russia and eludes admitting that he does the consecration because of the Secrets." Lily intensified her stare on

Sofia. "First he ignores Lucia, but later complies with Our Lady's request, though only in part, all the while treading water to avoid his actions being connected to Fatima."

"Strikes me as an indecisive guy."

Lily grinned mischievously. "Our Lady took care of that. While taking a walk on Vatican grounds in 1950, he witnesses a phenomenon very much like the 'Miracle of the Sun' that occurred in Fatima back on October 13th, 1917. After that he becomes quite assertive. He goes on to proclaim the dogma of the Assumption and the Queenship of Mary feast, announces a Marian Year, and much more. It is obvious he is trying to appease her, yet again in 1952 when consecrating the *people* of Russia, rather than Russia itself, he fails to do it according to her instructions."

"There were specifics on how to do it?"

"Yes, you see, Lucia continued to have visions all her life. In one of them, Our Lady stipulates that the consecration of Russia must be done by the pope simultaneously with all the bishops."

"That *is* strange," agreed Sofia. "If they don't believe any of it, why bother to consecrate at all? But if they do, why only go halfway?"

"Exactly! That's how I noticed the pattern forming. Let's recap: The first two popes show no public interest in the phenomenon while privately sending investigators, appointing commissions, removing Lucia, and attempting to appease Our Lady by giving Her many titles. It doesn't seem Mary wants discretion or honors from them, so She anoints the third pope with very public associations to Fatima. Inevitably, Pius XII finds himself compelled to perform the consecration but does so only halfway. It became clear to me that, though on the one hand they try to please her, there was something about Russia, on the other, they refused to acknowledge or act upon, even at the expense of defying Her."

"What was it?"

"Not yet."

"Arg!" exclaimed Sofia. "You're killing me."

"All in due time." Lily was delighted with her sister's interest. She hurried up not to lose it. "Perhaps because of Pius XII's resistance or inability to fully comply, it is during his pontificate that Lucia receives instructions *from above* to write down the Third Secret. She places it in an envelope and sends it to the Bishop of Leiria who she seems to trust. Pius XII, however, orders it sent to the Vatican for safekeeping. Purportedly, he dies the following year, in 1958, without reading it. Now get this: he is buried on October 13th, the same date of the 'Miracle of the Sun', in line with his curious relationship with Fatima from the start. See what I mean? He is linked to Fatima in a very public way from beginning to end. Our Lady appears set on making them face it publicly." Lily chuckled softly. "His successor does not appear to like that at all."

Michael retrieved three sundaes from a bag. "Who wants dessert before it melts?"

Without a word, the sisters launched for theirs.

As he handed them spoons, he suddenly paused and narrowed his eyes to focus on something at the end of the park. He jumped to his feet. "I forgot the paper napkins. I'll be right back."

Lily watched him leave with discomfort.

The scene was not lost on Sofia. She was about to say something when on second thought decided it was probably wiser to stay quiet and observant.

"Next, John XXIII," continued Lily with urgency in her voice. "It is safe to say he was probably the least Marian of the popes, and openly resentful of the Fatima phenomenon. He's the one who shocked the world when refusing to divulge the Third Secret." Lily raised a finger. "But here comes the kicker: This is the year he also stuns everyone, even the cardinals, by suddenly convoking the Second Vatican Council that carried out a complete overhaul of some of the Church's most traditional, deep-rooted and inflexible stances ever. Curiously, it's done under the theme 'The Signs of the Times'."

Lily paused to let that piece of information sink. To be sure it did, she repeated it. "Do you see? He reads the secret message, decides to keep it sealed, and then calls a council to undertake a major reform of the Church, chiefly, a concerted effort to reach out to other Faiths. That caught my attention and put me on track to discover what 'Russia' really meant. And, once again, the same pattern follows: For public purposes, he tries to keep the Council separate from Fatima to the extent that in his opening speech he made it a point to reject the thoughts of the *prophets of gloom who are always forecasting disaster*."

Lily paused once again to ensure Sofia's full attention, which she no doubt had. She continued. "This is not to be taken lightly. His position is of extreme significance. Bear in mind that Mariology is a grassroots affair in opposition to the Church's authoritative command. Through the ages, simple-everyday shepherds, peasants, fishermen, women and children are the chosen ones by Mary to receive Her messages, which the Church has always reluctantly come around to acknowledging only once the phenomenon has gained widespread acceptance and devotion. So, by making the decision to lock up the Secret rather than reveal it, John XXIII sent the clear message that he, the pope, and not a child-shepherd-turned-nun, was in charge of Faith. His whole papacy was an exercise of reclaiming the supreme authority of the papacy, which has a whole lot to do with 'Russia.'" Lily leaned forward. "Talking about papal names, for instance, consider the one he chose. John XXIII had already been carried by a previous pope. In the Middle Ages there were many power struggles that resulted in two or three popes coexisting and claiming to be the rightful one. The line of Avignon prevailed eventually, and the others passed on to be labelled antipopes. The previous John XXIII was one of them. This matter had been settled for 500 years, so why select this particular name and numeral if not to make a statement of authority?"

"I'm afraid I don't quite understand," admitted Sofia. "You're saying that he was impelled to call the Vatican Council and proceed to a major reformation after reading the message, yet publicly discredits Fatima-like prophets and adopts a centuries-old name to make sure everyone knows he is the top dog?"

Lily looked into the depths of Sofia's eyes. "If you recall, Sr. Lucia said that the Third Secret was to be released in 1960 per Mary's wishes, for '*by that time, it would be more clearly understood*'. Don't you see? The Third Secret had two purposes: One, the Secret itself, and, two, how the Church dealt with it was for the rest of us *to understand*."

"But understand what?"

"That most Church leaders across all religions are more worried about their authority than doing their job. They are supposed to work together toward spreading love and peace in the world as her Son preached. Yet the past two thousand years have been a succession of ugly religious wars, when not intolerance and fanaticism. They have all failed her Son."

Sofia's rational instinct bristled. "Whoa! Lily, slow down. I think you are getting carried away. Let's put things in perspective. All you have is some papal actions that coincide with some Fatima events and a lot of speculation. Hardly the bare bones of verifiable facts you promised, and much less to reach a severe conclusion like that."

"I have more than that. I'm not done. And let me clarify, not all leaders have been the same; some have truly tried to do the right thing. I'll prove this to you. I just got a little ahead of myself. But I can assure you one thing: Mary is one mighty, pissed-off Mother!"

CHAPTER 8

Michael returned without the paper napkins and what appeared to be a dark shadow looming over his face.

"Ready for a walk? We've been here for a while."

Lily leaped to her feet.

Sofia stiffened. "I'm not moving until someone tells me what's going on."

"We'll brief you as we move," urged Michael.

Sofia did not appreciate his dismissive attitude and rose slowly. "I think you should have done that by now."

Michael glanced at Lily.

She sighed. "Fine, I'll tell you. My room was ransacked this morning. It happened while I was out running errands before heading this way. One of the sisters I'm sharing the apartment with called me about it. Luckily, no one was home when it happened. Whoever did it, took all my files and computer."

Sofia dropped her jaw. "What the... Did you call the police?"

"We don't have time for that. I didn't even bother going back for the bag I had packed. I jumped in the car and came straight here."

"Lily, are you out of your mind? Your place was assaulted. If you had been there, you could have been hurt. You need to contact the authorities."

"And tell them what? All I have is a stolen computer. Listen, I don't think I'm in physical danger. They just don't want my research made public, okay? Everything will be fine"

"Who exactly are *they*?"

"I'm not sure. A few months ago, I shared my notes with my superior seeking advice. She ran it by hers, and they did not like it. I was asked to hand over all the copies and to stop the nonsense. Instead, I reached out to a friend who works at the Leadership Conference of Women Religious. I was then threatened with being expelled or even excommunicated for disobedience."

"That's quite serious. Can they do that?"

"Of course they can."

"Still, ransacking your room is a little much, not to mention illegal. Besides, if you shared it with others, why did they bother? It's out already, isn't it?"

"I only shared a rough, unfinished draft with a handful of people. In it I hint to keeping one crucial item to myself. They were probably looking for that. Now I know I'm on the right track since it made someone, somewhere very nervous."

"What are you talking about?"

"I was fishing. Remember I said that some critics of the Vatican believe the Third Secret consisted of a message in addition to the vision? That's because, apart from the four-page description of the 'vision' that was published in 2000, Lucia also mentioned the existence of a single-sheet of paper containing the 'words' of the Virgin Mary. According to Lucia, they were written in the form of a letter that she sent to the Bishop of Leiria. Later, on another occasion, she hinted that Our Lady's words had something to do with the Apocalypse, chapters 8 to 13. The witnesses and the evidence to there being a missing letter are many, including the Vatican archivist, as I already told you. I believe that's why Ratzinger was quick to seal off her cell when Lucia passed away. She kept notes on all her visions and letters to the popes. Someone does not want those words made public."

Sofia's eyes were bulging. "You have those notes? Is that why they searched your room?"

"Not exactly, though I made them believe so."

"You lied?"

"Again, not exactly. Listen, the path I keep telling you about, I think it leads us to the message."

"How do you know that?"

"I know thanks to John Paul II. He hid a clue in a homily he gave precisely in Fatima. It reveals the location of the markers. These, in turn, delineate the path that I believe leads to the message."

Sofia needed a moment. She squeezed her eyes shut. The real-world dangers of a ransacked room were colliding in her head with the outlandish implausibility of a pope leaving secret codes about divinely placed markers in his homilies. Her logical brain was struggling to process it.

For Michael it seemed to make perfect sense. "You understand my concern, now?" he asked. "Whatever the secret is, some are determined to keep it concealed, and they must be dangerous if even a pope resorted to hidden clues. Please, let's move." He nudged Sofia gently on the shoulder as to direct her toward the corner of the park that led to *W. San Francisco Street*.

Sofia obliged, feeling disoriented. She looked up. "Where are we going?"

"To the cathedral."

"This isn't the way."

"We're taking a detour."

"Why?"

"We stalled in the park to check if you were being followed. You are. The detour is to get rid of them."

Sofia whipped her head around to see for herself. "Why would *I* be followed?"

"Most likely because of the drive I sent you," said Lily.

"No, you didn't. I never got anything."

"It's pretty apparent you didn't. Everything I'm telling you is on it. They must have intercepted your mail."

"You should have warned me of all this!" Sofia raised her voice.

"Calm down, will you? When I was asked to hand everything in, I sent you the draft hoping you could keep a copy safe for me. It was only today, after what happened at my apartment, that I realized how serious they were about it."

"Serious? You just told me that a pope had to code a call for help in one of his homilies. That didn't give you some idea?"

"Deciphering the markers was a work in progress. It took me a while to glean the path's full significance."

"What about Michael? When did he realize it was serious enough to drop everything and fly across the world to your rescue? It certainly wasn't this morning!"

Before addressing her question, Michael pointed south. "Let's go down *Don Gaspar Avenue*." He then clarified. "I've been in town for over a week. I came as soon as Lily informed me that she had been threatened with excommunication. I thought she could use my help. God knows she is going to need it." He turned to Lily. "Gabriel spotted only one man. I find that strange. While he takes care of him, I think it would be best if we headed toward San Miguel Chapel. It will help us determine if there are more."

Lily nodded her agreement.

Again, Sofia instinctively turned to see if someone was following. No one was.

"And Gabriel is...?" she asked.

"My cousin. He's a security expert in the private sector. He was watching the plaza and spotted someone suspicious."

Sofia froze in her tracks to confront her sister. "And you didn't know it was serious? He even brought a fricking expert! Is there anything else I should know?"

"We need to keep moving," said Michael.

His calm, pushy tone was irritating her to no end. Sofia remained frozen to the spot and stabbed him with her eyes. "You infiltrated my workplace. You lied to my boss. You lured me to the park neglecting to inform me you knew my sister. You had me sit there for hours knowing I was being watched. You both kept the apartment assault from me. And no one cared to mention the potential for danger was enough to warrant a professional bodyguard. I demand to know: Is there anything else I should know?"

Michael's brown eyes softened. Apologizing once more was probably worthless. He resigned to signaling her bag with a gentle gesture. "There is a good chance you have a tracking device in there. You'll have to get rid of it. I'd like to suggest we leave your bag at the chapel."

Sofia yanked the bag off her shoulder as if it had suddenly burst into flames. She held it awkwardly in her hand not knowing what to do with it.

Lily reached out to relax her arm. "Sof, I promise we didn't plan it this way. It got out of hand, I'm sorry. We obviously didn't think things through. I swear I would never put you in harm's way on purpose." She looked genuinely overwhelmed by the circumstances herself.

Slowly and reluctantly, Sofia shouldered her bag, again. "Let me assess the situation. We are being followed by anonymous men, who may or may not be dangerous, because they think you have a copy of a Divine Message that you really don't have." Lily nodded as Sofia continued. "Our plan is to shake them off and set out to look for it ourselves; a Divine Message not even a pope dared to address openly?"

Both Lily and Michael nodded this time.

The idea of just going home flashed through Sofia's mind. But, if she was being followed, that was a moot point. And, more importantly, it wasn't in her nature to abandon her sister, anyway.

She looked ahead, shaking her head almost more in disbelief than worry, and renewed their walk. "I'm going to guess you won't tell me about the markers until you run me through the rest of the popes." There was a clear irate edge to her tone.

Lily skipped to catch up with her.

"I would prefer not to."

"Then get on with it."

CHAPTER 9

Michael fell a few steps behind to keep a better eye out as Lily resumed her account.

"I left it with John XXIII. His papacy didn't last long. He died of stomach cancer in 1963 after only four years in the papacy. The Council barely had a chance to get started."

"Am I just paranoid now, or do only the Marian popes last?"

Lily released a soft breath of relief. All things considered her sister was being quite the sport. "It makes one wonder, doesn't it? It may be the reason his successor, Paul VI, chose to fine-tune the purposes of the Council to fall more in line with Mary's desires. He had been a close friend and adviser of Pius XII and shared his devotion for Her. Paul VI was the first pope to visit Fatima and made extensive contributions to Mariology, but most important of all, he specifically stressed Our Lady's new ecumenical orientation."

"What does that mean?"

"For the first time in a thousand years, The Second Vatican Council reached out to other Christian Faiths to end the Great Schism. That is what ecumenical means, the promotion of unity among the churches. And *that* is what Russia was code for in the Second Secret. Paul VI publicly acknowledged it and gave her credit for it."

"*That* makes no sense. What does Russia have to do with Christian schisms?"

"Russia has nothing to do with Russia and everything to do with the Great Schism."

Sofia's gaze conveyed clearly that her patience had depleted.

"Easy, I'll explain, okay?" Lily cleared her throat. Dealing with her sister in this instant was almost more stressful than not knowing who they were running from. "The Christian Church came to be when Constantine the Great adopted the Christian Faith as a means to unify his broad Empire in the 4th century. Overnight Christians went from being persecuted to being tolerated and even favored. Unfortunately, their rise in prominence led to internal bickering over theological issues, but chiefly, over authority. So, basically, rather than adhering to Jesus' message of unity and love as he specifically requested, Church leaders embarked into a divisive doctrine and power struggle that resulted, first in the Great East-West Schism of 1054 and later political breakoffs such as the Protestants, the Anglicans and so many others. Now, to be fair, this is true for most religions and human enterprises—"

"Yes, yes, yes, but Russia, how does it fit in?"

"The Russian Orthodox Church is the largest of the Eastern branch and the second largest Christian Church after the Roman Catholic. 'Consecrate Russia to my Heart' was code for *reunite per His wishes*; Mary's Heart being her Son, of course."

"I find that a stretch."

"Then think about this. You know what John XXIII's last words were on his death bed? *'Christ lives on and continues his work in the Church. Souls, souls, ut omnes unum sint.'* This latter means, 'Souls, souls, that they all may be one." It derives from Jesus' Farewell Prayer at the end of the Last Supper, during which he calls for unity and love among his apostles. *That they all may be one* was Jesus' final instruction to the coming church... Hardly what they did."

Lily identified fissures developing in her sister's stern front, so she felt encouraged to shock her some more.

"Another stunning coincidence: Until 1917 the Roman Catholic body of legislation included a mismatch of some 10,000 norms. It was one big confusing and conflicting mess. Pope Pius X ordered its cleansing into one comprehensive and orderly volume. Promulgated in May of 1917, it came to be known as the 1917 Code of Canon Law. Amidst the divisive directives it preserved, canon 731 forbade administering the sacraments to heretics or schismatics, and canon 1258 stated that it was illicit for the faithful to assist at or participate in any way in non-Catholic religious functions, even if Christian. That same month Our Lady appeared in Fatima requesting the consecration of Russia." Lily widened her gaze as she set it momentarily on her sister. "Paul VI, five decades later, and most probably incited by his predecessor's last words, stressed Mary's ecumenical role. You see? He was acknowledging her request and role as arbiter in the talks of peace among the greater Christian family."

"If that is the case, it would seem they were adhering to her request. How is it that Mary was still upset, and the Secret kept secret?"

"They adhered only in part, remember? According to the vision Sr. Lucia had in 1929, she clarified that the consecration was to be done by the Holy Father in union with all the bishops of the world. And this is key to understanding why the popes struggled with Fatima's Secrets. You see, prominent among the disputes between the East and West that led to the Great Schism was that the Orthodox Church does not recognize the authority of the Bishop of Rome, aka the pope, over the rest of the bishops. They consider all bishops to be of equal standing. Thus, Our Lady's condition requiring that the pope consecrate with all the bishops simultaneously is like a slap in the face. She's not recognizing their authority over them either, or at least, demanding they humble down a little for the sake of unity."

Sofia had to stop it right there. "That is a lot of reading into a vision."

"I do not come to this conclusion based on the vison alone. Regardless, I'm not the only one to interpret it that way. Why else would Pius XII choose Fatima's anniversary in 1956 to address all the bishops of the Eastern Rite and issue encyclicals addressed to the Oriental Churches calling for unity? Later, Paul VI continued in his steps by resetting the prime objective of Vatican II to restore unity among all Christians." Lily slowed her walk to face her sister. "Can it be only coincidence that he also declared Our Lady Mother of the Church during the Council and then closed it on the Feast of the Immaculate Conception?"

Sofia did not know what to think. She felt intoxicated by the overload of information.

They reached the corner of *De Vargas Street*.

"This way," ushered Michael signaling them to turn into it.

By doing so they entered the heart of the Analco Historic District, home to the oldest colonial buildings in the United States. Settled in the early 1600s by the Spaniards and their native allies the Tlaxcala Indians, the neighborhood boasted original examples of Spanish-Pueblo architecture, characterized by the adobe construction indigenous to the Southwest. Aside from its historical value, what Michael liked about it was its low structures. It made it much easier to scan.

"How many popes do we have left?" urged Sofia.

"Four. But don't fear; it'll go fast now as I'm mostly interested in John Paul II."

"If I know my history well, the next one up, John Paul I, only reigned for 33 days, right?"

"Yes, however, considering how short his papacy was, his relationship with Fatima was most intense."

"How so?"

"The year before becoming pope, Albino Luciani, at the time Patriarch of Venice, visited Fatima on a private pilgrimage and had the chance to meet with Sr. Lucia. According to his personal secretary, when he left the room, his face was 'white as a sheet of paper'. Then the following year, his brother Edoardo said that while on vacation Albino avoided company, seeming restless and worried. When asked about it, he replied that he couldn't stop thinking about what Sister Lucia had told him but wouldn't say what. Soon after came the conclave. Reacting to some insinuations that he may be elected, Luciani made it clear he would decline. Since he was elected anyway, when asked if he accepted, he said: 'May God forgive you for what you have done.'"

"I not surprised," said Sofia. "Say Sr. Lucia told him about the Third Secret. It describes a pope being shot and killed. He probably knew by then he was a potential candidate for the job and wasn't too fond of what possibly awaited him."

"How about this then? Only ten days after being elected, while John Paul I was receiving none other than the leader of the delegation from the Russian Orthodox Church in audience, the Russian Patriarch collapses right there and dies in the pope's arms."

"You're kidding!"

Lily shook her head. "Nope. Then, only twenty-three days later, it is he, the pope, who suddenly passes away."

"That is downright spooky."

"I know."

"What do you make of it?"

"I'm not sure. There are enough conspiracy theories out there doing all the guess work. Though none link it to Fatima. What struck me was a remark

John Paul I made in his Angelus of September 10th. It was addressed to a meeting being held at Camp David between the Christian US President, Carter, the Muslim President of Egypt, Sadat, and the Jewish President of Israel, Begin. This meeting ultimately led to a peace treaty between Egypt and Israel, and the Nobel Peace Prize for their Presidents. In it, John Paul I states, in reference to God, that, 'He is our Father, even more He is our Mother.'"

Sofia furrowed her brows. "Why did that capture your attention?"

"Because those words belong to Julian of Norwich, a 14th century visionary who claimed that God was both our mother and our father. Her book, *Revelations of Divine Love*, which describes her visions, is the first book in the English language known to have been written by a woman. In it she explains that in creating us, God showed his motherhood, and where there is motherhood, there can only be love. Julian saw no wrath in God, rather only in humans, which she said He forgave. She asserted that God's love flourished from combining the might and goodness of His Fatherhood and the wisdom of His Motherhood. In her visions, Jesus further emphasized this point by highlighting all the goodness and love shown by His mother, Mary. Consequently, Julian also came to learn that there was no Hell, that Hell was pain and suffering. This helped me understand that when Our Lady showed the three little shepherds the vision of Hell, She wasn't showing them the fate of our souls, She was showing them the reality of life for most humans throughout time. Life on earth has been Hell and continues to be in many parts of our world. The horrors that people still endure today, the civil wars, religious extremism, repression, and so much more ... Life, not death, has been Hell for greater part of humanity. It's not a promise we are doomed to; it's a reality we must work ourselves out of."

"You're depressing me."

"Don't be. Julian learns from God Himself that '...*All shall be well, and all manner of things shall be well...*' He forgives us all; he wants Heaven for us all."

"I'm delighted to hear that. Now back to the matter at hand, how does this fit with Fatima or schisms?"

Lily drew a broad smile. She loved it when she knew she could impress her sister. "Julian of Norwich received those visions on May 13 of 1373, the same date of the visions of Fatima. Therefore, her Catholic Feast Day is May 13 like that of Fatima. An interesting coincidence and an interesting choice for John Paul I's Angelus addressed to a peace talk involving the three Patriarch religions, don't you think?"

CHAPTER 10

They reached *Old Santa Fe Trail*. Following Michael's lead, they crossed watchful for cars and climbed the short flight of steps that led to San Miguel Chapel.

Michael stopped in front of the humble Spanish structure and proceeded to a quick scan of their surroundings. "You go in," he said to the sisters. "I'm going to stay out here a moment."

Sofia took a nervous look, as well. There were people promenading every which way. "What does someone following us have to look like in order to appear suspicious?" she asked him.

"Familiar," responded Michael curtly, and insisted, "Please go in. I'll join you both inside in a few."

Lily motioned Sofia toward the right side of the building. The visitor entrance was through the souvenir store, which was tucked around the corner in the corridor formed between the chapel and the adjacent building.

It was mid-afternoon and only a handful of tourists wandered in and out. Since the chapel was small, turnover was rapid. Inside, the space was modest with two short rows of pews and a single central aisle. Built in 1610 on the grounds of a former Puebloan Kiva by the Tlaxcala Indians for their own worship, the Spanish, colonial-mission chapel claimed to be the oldest church in the United States.

Lily and Sofia advanced down the aisle, not sure what to do.

Behind them, a boy rang the 14th century Spanish bell curious to see if its legend held true. He smiled at his mother and said in a playful accent: "We'll be back."

On the altar screen, a small statue of Saint Michael, the Archangel for whom the Chapel was named in Spanish, caught Sofia's attention. She approached the railing that separated the altar from the rest of the space. Sofia had visited the chapel a few times before for different reasons but had never paid much attention to the details. Now, she was struck by how familiar the statue's handsome, childlike features seemed, though unable to place why.

Lily tapped her on the arm and pointed to her bag. "Take your ID and banks cards out. Then, give me the bag. I'll slide it under the altar table behind the skirt."

Sofia nodded and did as instructed. She also turned her phone off hating to leave it there like that.

When no one was looking, Lily stepped over the low railing and hid the bag. She then quickly returned to Sofia's side.

"Now what?" asked Sofia.

"I guess we wait. Let's sit over here." Lily walked over to the pew in the front row.

Sofia followed. "You trust Michael alone can handle things out there?"

"I do. And don't forget his cousin." Lily seemed confident.

Sofia, not so much. A quick look around told her there were no escape routes other than the way they came in. Both the main front entrance and the small side door in the back looked like they were permanently blocked.

She crossed her arms feeling a chill. "I'm not an expert on military strategy," she started, "but I think hiding in a little building with only one way in and out is probably not the best idea when being followed." Sofia looked at Lily. "Be honest, how serious is the danger?"

"Honestly? I don't know."

Sofia held her stare as her sister's attention wandered blankly over the altar screen. If she harbored any concerns, she wasn't showing it. Rather it was serenity that Sofia identified.

Lily hinted why. "Sof, Our Lady's signs and markers are everywhere, we just never knew to see them as such." She rolled her eyes over three images of Mary present in the altar area. One was a statue of Her holding baby Jesus set upon a pillar beside the altar table. Another was a Black Madonna icon painted in the Byzantine style hanging on the wall. And the last one, also on the wall but a little closer to the pews, was a reproduction of the miraculous image of Our Lady of Guadalupe in Mexico. The three images were close together on the left side of the chapel just beyond the altar railing.

Sofia had followed her sister's eyes believing she was mesmerized by Mary's abundant presence not knowing yet of the real hidden significance of the three depictions.

Lily drew a soft enigmatic smile, ready to resume. "It's time I tell you about John Paul II. God bless him."

The way Lily said it gave Sofia more chills.

"You are going to like this," started Lily. "His papacy lasted almost 27 years."

"Meaning, he must have been a great fan of the Virgin Mary."

"Indeed, he was."

"Does he hold the record?"

"No, that would be Pius IX who reigned for over 31 years."

"What did *he* do to please Her so?" asked Sofia facetiously.

"He promulgated the dogma of the Immaculate Conception, set the stage for the promulgation of the dogma of the Assumption, and laid the foundation to promoting Her Mediatrix and Co-Redemptrix."

Sofia almost dropped her jaw. "I was only kidding when I asked the question. You don't seriously think Mary gets rid of who she doesn't like, do you?"

"Of course not. At least, not Her. In any case, it would be Him." Lily gestured at the crucifixion on the wall.

"I thought we established He was all forgiveness and love."

"Yes, but She is Mom, and nobody messes with His Mom,"

Sofia stared at Lily, hoping they were still joking.

"*Anyhow*," continued Lily with an impish wink, "back to John Paul II. While in the seminary, he came across the works of Louis de Montfort, a French priest and preacher, who was also an early writer in the field of Mariology. John Paul II admits to being deeply impacted by his teachings. When elected, he chose *Totus Tuus*, meaning 'Totally Yours', as his apostolic motto. It was borrowed from Montfort's Marian consecration prayer that says, 'I belong entirely to you, and all that I have is yours. I take you for my all. O Mary, give me your heart.'"

"He paid attention," said Sofia. "Right there already he is obliging and submitting his papacy to her authority."

Lily nodded satisfied. "He paid attention, alright. You see, he also chose the Marian Cross for his coat of arms. What's interesting about this is that, traditionally, the M for Mary overlapped with the cross. However, John Paul II designed his with the M placed under the right arm of the cross. And this is significant, because it replicates the vision Sr. Lucia had in Tuy, Spain; the same one in which Mary asked the popes to consecrate Russia in union with all the bishops of the world. In that vision, Lucia saw Our Lady under the right arm of the cross with Her Immaculate Heart in her left hand."

"Interesting..." admitted Sofia.

"Still, at first, John Paul II played it safe, not defying the old conservative ways too adamantly. But after the attempt on his life, he became brazen and went about apologizing for over 100 wrongdoings by the Church, among them injustices committed to women."

"That's nice, but he was against the ordination of women like the rest."

"I'm not so sure. In his *Letter to Women* in 1995, he commits a weird contradiction. He acknowledges women's contribution, dignity, and even leadership through his exaltation of the feminine genius but then devotes a sentence to chastising societies and cultures that fail to fully integrate woman socially, politically and economically."

"I see what you mean. If there ever was a state that excludes women socially, politically and economically, that would be the Vatican City. It was intended for his own."

Lily nodded. "I think so. As for Fatima, true to the pattern followed by his predecessors, one thing was his public stance, and another his private one. But contrary to them, John Paul II actively and repeatedly reached out to us. I've identified several concealed messages in his communications."

"It's scary to think he felt the need to proceed that way," observed Sofia. "I guess he didn't want to go the way of his predecessor."

Her sister's comment had Lily recall an interesting fact. "Did you know that his predecessor, John Paul I, was the first to take a double name and adopt the numeral I? No other pope ever did that or has since. Take Francis, for instance. He is Pope Francis, not Francis I. It is almost as if John Paul I knew he wouldn't be around long and chose his name in honor of his successor rather than a predecessor as was the custom."

Sofia shot her sister a long, skeptic look. "Maybe we are getting overly imaginative. Stick to the hidden clues. What were they?"

Lily chuckled. "If you think that's imaginative, I suggest you brace yourself. Things are going to get pretty eerie."

"Great, like I'm not scared enough already."

"Just saying, there is nothing imaginary about what I'm going to tell you. But, however intimidating, it's the type of evidence you yearn for. Are you ready?"

"No, but go ahead, please."

CHAPTER 11

Lily shifted slightly to face her sister better. "As we've seen, John Paul II displayed special sensitivity toward Fatima from the moment he was elected; then he was the target of an assassination attempt on the anniversary of Fatima, and he was later caught in the middle of that odd episode in Fatima when it was revealed that the ominous Third Secret simply prophesized the failed attack on his life. So, I paid close attention to his behavior. The first time I picked up that he was trying to tell us something was in an interview he gave to a small group of German Catholics in 1980. This was barely two years into his papacy, and, supposedly, he had not yet read the Secret. Remember, it was said he called for the envelope while in the hospital after the assassination attempt the next year. In the interview, he was asked about the Third Secret, and he responded according to the official script at the time; that is, its content was too serious to share, that communism was somehow involved as the threat, and that since nothing could be done about it, why bother to share it."

Lily paused to retrieve her cellphone. She tapped the screen to pull up her notes and read.

> *'To know implies a responsibility. It is dangerous to want to satisfy one's curiosity only, if one is convinced that we can do nothing against a catastrophe that has been predicted.'*

She looked up. "When you hear this, you can understand why the disappointment when the Secret was finally disclosed."

"I would say. *Catastrophe* is a big word."

"Right. But then he does something strange. With a rosary in his hands, he urges everyone to put their trust in Mary. He warns that soon great trials will require even giving our lives. Prayers will help, but this sacrifice is the only way possible to effectively renew the Church. He reminds everyone that it would not be the first time that renewal was driven by blood. Finally, he concludes by urging us to be 'attentive, very attentive,' to the prayer of the rosary." Lily left it there waiting for her sister to grasp its implication.

She didn't fail. "He could not have said all that without being privy to the Secret. He knows that death is involved. He probably thinks it could be him. It's no wonder he was convinced Mary spared his life."

"Not only that; he seems to know more than what the vision suggests. He is talking about trials that call for the renewal of the Church. Think about it. The Second Vatican Council that brought about the greatest changes in the Church's history had already passed. He was there. So what renewal is he talking about? And how bad can the renewal be to require the shedding of blood?"

Sofia suddenly agitated her hands. "The rosary. It must be the key to understanding this. He seems particularly interested in bringing our attention to it. He repeats 'be attentive' to it twice."

Lily bounced. "You got it!"

"Didn't you say that Mary presented herself as Our Lady of the Rosary during the 'Miracle of the Sun'?"

"Yes again!"

"So, what does it all mean?"

"A rosary is basically a mnemonic device, a string of beads that allows the user to keep track of his or her prayers without counting. Many different religions use this method. In the case of the Roman Catholic tradition, it enables the user to focus on meditating on a series of mysteries with a strong Marian emphasis. The thing is that the bible grants very little space to Mary. In fact, it doesn't even mention Her by name in the few instances she is referenced. Yet the Rosary Prayer collects them all, giving Mary a predominant role and equating her devotion to that of her Son. The idea is that through Her you reach Him." Lily paused. "For centuries, it remained unchanged, until none other than John Paul II himself added five more mysteries to it. These additional *Luminous Mysteries* elevate Mary to the heights of God himself."

Sofia widened her gaze. "Please, explain."

"John Paul II felt that in order to glean Christ's full message, it was necessary to include mysteries of His public ministry and called them the *Luminous Mysteries*, for He is '*the light of the world*'. Curiously, however, the light is not quite on Him. Two of the mysteries he added refer to Christ's Baptism and Transfiguration. In both cases God's voice can be heard saying,

'*You are my beloved Son, in whom I am well pleased*'. As I see it, the light is on God, the portrait of a loving father proud of his son. The third one is the Wedding in Cana when Mary tells Jesus there is no wine. Jesus responds '*Woman, what does that have to do with you and me? My hour has not yet come.*' Mary disagrees and tells the servants, '*Whatever he says to you, do it.*' This is not the image of a subservient woman. She is the one handing out the orders and instructing Her Son to perform His first miracle."

"So, you are saying that John Paul II chose mysteries that reflect a loving family, in which, incidentally, the mother has a strong say."

"Yes. He is elevating Mary to equal parenting status: Father and Mother."

"Which goes back to, *He is our Father, even more He is our Mother*. I'm seeing two themes forming in relation to Fatima. One is the Father-Mother duality, and the other is unity among the churches."

Lily angled a grin. "Does it sound familiar?"

"Balance and Peace: Balance through equality and Peace through unity. The Hopi Way," Sofia mirrored her sister's smirk. "You sure know how to bring things home."

Lily chuckled.

"What about the other two mysteries?" asked Sofia.

"One is Jesus' proclamation of the Kingdom of God. He claims it is near, forgives sinners and asks all to believe in the Good News, which is, the promise of Heaven, not Hell." Lily brought her hand to her chest. "Which I take as a call to create Heaven on Earth." Lily relaxed her hand. "And the last one is the institution of the Eucharist, a rite that commemorates the Last Supper. John Paul II specifically referred to John 13 when explaining why he chose this mystery. In this passage, Jesus starts by stating His love for humanity and goes on to wash the apostles' feet. His act is meant to remind them they must stay humble."

Lily read from her phone.

"*You call me 'Teacher' and 'Lord.' You say so correctly, for so I am. If I then, the Lord and the Teacher, have washed your feet, you also ought to wash one another's feet. For I have given you an example, that you also should do as I have done to you. Most certainly I tell*

you, a servant is not greater than his lord, neither one who is sent
greater than he who sent him."

"Humble," repeated Sofia deep in thought. "I'm curious now, how does the Catholic tradition justify the pope's supreme authority?"

"Believe it or not, it comes down to one word: Rock."

Sofia perked in surprise.

"Matthew 16:18 reads: '*I also tell you that you are Peter and that on this rock I will build my assembly*'. The popes of the Western-Latin Church interpret this passage as translated into Latin, in which 'Peter" and 'rock' are both 'petrus', the same thing. Therefore, when Jesus says 'You are 'rock' and on this 'rock' I'll build my church", the popes argue that the church is built upon Peter, granting them, his heirs, supreme authority. However, this is not the case for the Eastern-Greek Church. They interpret the passage in its original Greek form. In Greek, 'Peter' is 'petros' expressed in the masculine form and meaning smaller rock or stone, while 'rock' is 'petra', in the feminine form and meaning larger rock or boulder. Not the same thing. For the Orthodox, Petra represents Faith, not Peter, and thus has nothing to do with Jesus granting superior authority to anyone."

"Fascinating. Who knew?" Sofia shook her head. "Okay, where were we? Right, when asked about the Third Secret, John Paul II directed everyone to be attentive to the rosary."

"That's right." Lily slid a figure across her phone screen and showed the display to Sofia. "This is the apostolic letter where John Paul II explains why he is adding five mysteries." Lily pointed. "Look at this section. It's titled '*From* mysteries *to the* Mystery: *Mary's Way*'. In this section he states that '*the Rosary offers the secret which leads easily to a profound and inward knowledge of Christ*' in whom, he says, '*are hidden all the treasures of wisdom*'. And then he gives it a name: '*We might call it Mary's Way*.'"

"*Mary's Way* ... I presume this is the path you keep talking about, but what made you think this passage was coded and referring to a real path?"

"Initially, I didn't. It was later that I realized what it was trying to say. In fact, it's more of a reminder for the original coded message; one John Paul II inserted in a homily a couple of decades earlier. I think John Paul II feared no one had picked up on it."

"Wait, you're saying he added the five mysteries to the Rosary Prayer just so he could sneak in a reminder about an earlier clue? And what's this about decades? I thought we were in 1980 at the beginning of his papacy."

"Hold on, I explained myself incorrectly. The five mysteries are important in themselves as we've just seen. But he also inserted a coded message in their explanation." Lily showed her sister the screen. "Look for yourself. It may seem he is talking about a metaphorical path, however, once you realize he is referring to a real one, it takes on a whole new meaning." Lily pointed to the title, again. "It's no accident that he capitalizes the word 'Mystery'."

"Lily, I'm developing a headache."

"I know, I know, I'm confusing things. Please bear with me. This is not easy. I'm trying to summarize months' worth of investigations."

Someone rang the Spanish bell again. Both sisters looked back instinctively. It was a young giggling couple; most likely honeymooners guessed Sofia.

"I wonder what is keeping Michael," she said. "Should we check on him?"

Lily winced. "Let me straighten this part, first, because I forgot to mention that John Paul II added the five mysteries to the Rosary Prayer in 2002. If we were to be attentive to it, I doubt he'd keep us waiting 22 years to provide the secret message. That's how I realized there had to be an earlier one. Obviously, I looked for it in the original prayer but found nothing. I was stumped for a while. I couldn't figure out what he wanted us to be attentive to. So, I went back and raked through all his comments, speeches and writings related to Fatima, until I found his original clue."

Sofia's brain was churning. "Okay, how about I summarize to see if I got it straight. You noticed John Paul II was trying to tell us something when he responded to a question about the Third Secret of Fatima in Germany early into his papacy. His answer appeared to infer that he knew more about the Secret than what was later revealed and insisted on the importance of paying attention to the rosary. Failing to find anything in the prayer, you eventually discovered that he had provided a clue somewhere else, but since no one seemed to spot it, you think he resorted to adding five mysteries to the prayer decades later, containing the essence of the Third Secret. Then he inserted a coded message in his explanation about the mysteries, referencing the prior clue. The coded message hints to there being an actual *Mystery,* with a capital M, that Mary is the key to deciphering it, that it has to do with a real path, and the path leads to a hidden treasure of wisdom related to her Son. That treasure of wisdom is *the* lost message of Fatima, and the prior clue contains the parameters that guide us to it."

"Wow, confirmed, you are the smart twin."

"I'm not sure about that. Given how disjointed, obscure and all over the place the pope's secret messages are, I don't know how you figured out anything. Clearly, you are the genius. I mean, what was the deal with the rosary in the end if it didn't lead to a clue?"

"Actually, the rosary itself was the clue, a huge one. I figured that out later, as well. But, for now, I think you are ready." Lily, slowly, drew a broad smile. "It's time I told you about the markers."

CHAPTER 12

Sofia had her eyes glued to her sister and ears perked. She was ready all right.

"One year after the attempt on his life and believing that Our Lady of Fatima had guided the bullet away from his vital organs, John Paul II goes to Fatima to give thanks. During the relevant mass, he starts his homily commenting on the third word of Jesus on the Cross. This is when Jesus says to His mother, '*Woman, behold your son!*' And then turns to John and says, '*Behold, your mother.*' Traditionally, it is taken to mean that Jesus is entrusting the care of His mother to John, as was custom in those days, you know, putting His mother under the protection of a male. John Paul II turns it around, and explains that Jesus is instead entrusting men, symbolized by John, to His mother. But John is not just any man; he is also an apostle. And, if you remember, in the Wedding of Cana, Mary displayed authority over Jesus, Her son. Thus by extension, John Paul II is recognizing Mary's authority over all her children, and more specifically over the apostles and the Church. Now, he is not the first to recognize this, for Paul VI proclaimed Mary, on his own initiative, the 'Most Holy Mother of the Church' during the closing of the third session of the Vatican Council. John Paul II is simply reaffirming the statement with support from scripture—."

"Yes, yes, yes, the Father-Mother duality, I get it. Focus. The markers, I want to know about the Divine Markers, already."

"Fine." Lily leaned in and spoke quietly. "In this same homily he goes on to exalt the importance of Mary's shrines mentioning two specifically by name, Lourdes in France and Jasna Gora in Poland." Lily paused. "Are you familiar with them?"

"With Lourdes, yes. It is the most important Marian shrine in France and one of the largest pilgrim sites in the world. It was the location of a series of eighteen apparitions that occurred sometime around the mid-19th century to a peasant girl. I've never heard of Jasna Gora."

"I'm certain you have. It is the name of a monastery in Poland that houses the famous Black Madonna of Czestochowa. Since John Paul II was Polish, he had special devotion for her. It also happens to be the most important shrine in Poland and a major pilgrim destination there."

"It does seem vaguely familiar now. Okay, so he mentions two major shrines. And?"

"And he does it while in Fatima, the most important Marian shrine and pilgrim destination in Portugal." Lily turned to her phone and pulled up a map of Europe. "Look." She pointed at the three locations and smiled with pride, "I present you *Mary's Way*."

"Sofia took the phone in her hands to see it better. "Interesting, the three shrines can be connected by a perfectly straight line."

"It doesn't stop there. There is another marker." Lily slid her fingers across the screen to augment the map, narrowing in on a certain spot in the south of Germany. "When John Paul II was there in 1980 giving that clue-riddled interview, he made a stop to visit the oldest and most important Marian shrine in that country, Our Lady of Altötting." Lily tapped with the tip of her index finger on the screen. "See? It's on the line too."

Sofia drew the screen closer to believe her eyes. "That makes four major shrines on one straight line."

"Yes, four major shrines, all four the most important ones in their respective countries, and all four related in some way or other to popes, for guess who grew up near Our Lady of Altötting, venerates Her and is referred to as Her Pope?"

Sofia twisted her face to think. "A pope from Germany... Ratzinger!"

"Bingo! Pope Benedict XVI. Coincidentally he accompanied John Paul II on that precise trip 25 years before becoming pope himself. And, in case, you haven't made the connection yet, he chose for papal name that of the pope that was reigning when the Fatima apparitions occurred." Lily set her eyes on her sister as if looking over a pair of glasses. "Wouldn't you say John Paul II is trying to tell us something in his homily?"

Sofia handed the phone back and rubbed her face. "This is a lot to digest. Let's recap: A straight line crosses through the north of Europe from Poland to Portugal connecting the most important Marian Shrines in each country. John Paul II knew of this and revealed it to us in a homily."

Lily raised a finger. "Not just any homily. It's important to emphasize that he did it in Fatima on the first anniversary of the attempt on his life, which coincided with the date of the first apparition, May 13th."

Sofia met her sister's eyes with disbelief. "No one else has ever noticed this?"

"Not that I'm aware."

"How did you even pick up on it? I mean, yes, he mentions two shrines, but how did you think to look on a map?"

Lily bounced with excitement. "Because John Paul II tells us himself in that same homily. After mentioning the two shrines, he goes on to recite Judith 13:20, '...when our nation was brought low... you avenged our ruin, walking in the straight path before our God.' Then, just to be sure, he makes it a point to repeat the quote again at the end of the homily. That's how I knew to look for a straight path. I'm telling you; he has been inserting clues everywhere."

Sofia's jaw dropped. Literally. Before she could collect herself, Lily continued, enjoying her sister's state of shock.

"At the risk of sounding like a bad TV commercial ... but wait, there's more."

Sofia recovered fast to roll her eyes. "Cute."

Lily laughed. "The Book of Judith tells the story of a Jewish heroine, who upset with her countrymen for not standing up to the enemy, sets out to defeat them alone, and succeeds. Pretty significant wouldn't you say? Could the message be any clearer?"

"Maybe to you. Enlighten me."

"Regardless of divergent doctrines and power struggles, there is one thing all Churches agree upon: the absolute exclusion of women from authority positions. Therefore, and going back to his *Letter to Women* of 1995, it is interesting to read John Paul II's admission that the Church has diverted from God's plan with regards to women and calls for a *renewed commitment* of fidelity to the Gospel vision. He explains how the attitude of Jesus Christ himself transcended the established norms of his own culture by treating women with openness, respect, acceptance and tenderness. He then goes on to ask: '*how much of his message has been heard and acted upon?*' You see? Renewed commitment... that's the renewal of the Church he's talking about, a return to Jesus' original vision of Unity and Equality."

Sofia winced. She wondered how much of her sister's rationale was driven by *her* commitment to women's rights. "If so, for Unity to be reached, the papacy would have to renounce to its supremacy among bishops. And for Equality to come true, women would have to be given equal status, not just in the Christian Church, but across all religions, no less. Good luck with that. No wonder he expects upheaval and bloodshed."

"It's not about luck. It's about who gets the job done. Like Judith, where men failed, women will succeed. That's why John Paul II tells women to take up the mission. He believes we can do it peacefully. He ends his letter of 1995 by saying: *'May Mary, Queen of Love, watch over women and their* mission *in service of humanity, of peace, of the spread of God's Kingdom.'*"

Sofia released a nervous laugh. "World peace? The spread of God's Kingdom ...? No pressure there."

Her sister's glance was hopeful. "Do you believe me, now?"

Sofia took an instant to answer.

"Lily, I could give you a dissertation on why I question everything you've told me from the apparitions to your speculation about the popes' behaviors to the hidden clues. Granted your straight line is interesting, but at the end of the day, it's just four shrines in a row. You have to admit there are enough shrines in the world to circle the earth with straight lines many times over. And I'm certain we could easily find some commonality among them to further validate their connection. So, the answer is no, I don't believe. But I am very intrigued. I'll give you that."

"I see." Oddly, Lily displayed a triumphant smile. "She who laughs last, laughs best. You leave me no choice. I'll have to keep shocking you until you do believe."

Sofia arched an eyebrow. "There's more?"

"The straight line does not begin in Poland."

Sofia tried to visualize the map in her mind. "If it is not Poland," she thought out loud, "it must be further east... Russia?"

"Russia is a big country. That would be too easy." Lily played with her phone. "Let's narrow it down a little, shall we?" She was enjoying this moment greatly, for Lily was reliving the joy she felt when she realized it herself for the first time. She turned the screen for her sister to see. "Moscow."

"No way!" Sofia yanked the phone from her hands.

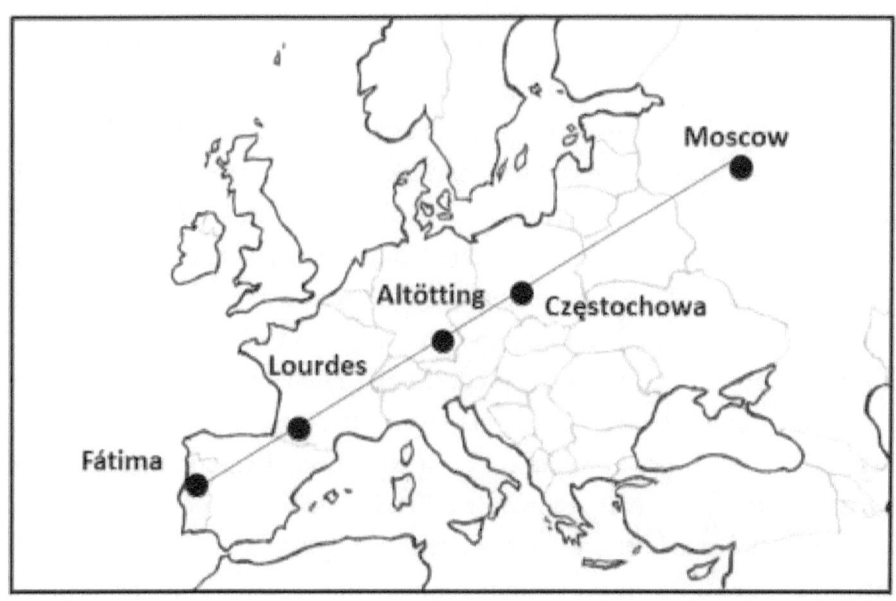

"Wait a minute. Technically, the line does not cut through the city."

"Dear Lord, Sof, it brushes the city on the north. How close does it have to get?"

"All right, close enough. Does Russia have a major Marian Shrine in Moscow, as well?"

"It used to until the Russian Revolution of 1917. Does the year sound familiar? The Kazan Cathedral, located on the Red Square, is a Russian Orthodox Church that used to house the sacred icon of Our Lady of Kazan. It was so precious it was known as the 'Protectress of Russia' for the countless times it helped the country through one war or other. Unfortunately, during the Revolution, the cathedral was burned down, and the icon disappeared... until," Lily paused for effect, "lo and behold, it appears decades later in a private collection and none other than the Blue Army of Fatima, an association devoted to promoting Fatima's message, mysteriously manages to get its hands on it. The beloved Russian icon ends up enshrined in Fatima of all places."

Sofia shook her head in awe as it rehashed in her head. "A major Marian Russian icon disappears in 1917 from Moscow, the same year that the apparitions in Fatima call for the consecration of Russia, only to reappear enshrined years later precisely there, in Fatima, while a straight line connects the two cities and all the major shrines in between." Sofia shook her head again. "Okay, you win, you can laugh now."

Lily didn't. "There is nothing to celebrate just yet. John Paul II, on one of his trips to Fatima, sees the icon and identifies the opportunity to reach out to Russia. He offers to give it back with the condition of being allowed to deliver it in person. The Orthodox Church refuses. They take it as the Vatican's attempt to proselytize and seize the heroic spotlight for delivering a Russian treasure. So, here is a pope who travelled to 129 countries during his reign, more than any of his predecessors; many of the trips important symbolic firsts like being the first to pray at the Western Wall or the first to pray in a mosque, yet he never makes it to Russia. The icon will sit in his personal study for 11 years. Finally, in 2004, ill, and seeing it was not going to happen, John Paul II resolves to return the icon through a delegate, no strings attached. It becomes the only public connection made by a pope between the phenomenon of Fatima and the Russian Orthodox Church. Not a year later, he passes away and so does Sr. Lucia. And with their passing, Ratzinger takes the name of Benedict to come full circle and put the lid on Fatima."

A brief moment of silence settled, until Sofia broke it. "So close..."

"We can't let their deaths go in vain, Sof. We have to find that message. The mission is now ours."

Something gave Sofia pause. "If we are to accept that someone—let's call them Mary— planted her shrines in a straight line to lead us to a let's-say-message, it would seem quite an elaborate effort simply to reaffirm the need for Unity and Equality. There must be something of far more value at the end of that path."

Lily's heart leaped. "There is only one way to find out."

Sofia agreed. "Where do we start?"

"We follow the path."

"Last I checked all that lies beyond Fatima is the Atlantic Ocean."

A suspicious grin formed on Lily's face. "Not that path."

"There's another one?"

"Yes. I think *Mary's Way* was a call to attention for the Patriarchs. You see, Moscow is also the See of the Russian Orthodox Church and considered the Third Rome. They've had their own internal load of bickering and schisms over doctrine and authority. While all these gentlemen continue with their ego wrestling, it is up to us, the grassroots ladies, to take the torch, and Mary has provided us with our own road map."

"I knew it! I told you we could connect a random number of shrines and come up with a conspiracy," refuted Sofia.

"There is nothing random about the new markers," clarified Lily, all smug and proud. "The clues to finding them are provided by *Mary's Way*. That's what I meant by following the path."

Sofia narrowed her stare. "I swear, if there is another straight line like that one," she said pointing at Lily's phone," I am totally going to freak out."

Lily smiled. "For your comfort, this one isn't straight, at least not at first, but it is let's-say-intriguing, nonetheless. Its markers are not shrines but one of the greatest and most overlooked Mysteries —with a capital M— of all time."

CHAPTER 13

A disturbance at the front of the chapel startled the sisters. They turned to look and saw a man in his mid-thirties and dressed in a navy suit, guide the last of the tourists out and close the doors. Sofia and Lily exchanged concerned looks. It was clear he was there for them and either locking Michael out or them in, maybe both. Instinctively, they jumped to their feet searching the chapel's whitewashed walls for an escape. To the left they spotted the side door that Sofia had seen earlier and rushed over to it, but it was locked as she had suspected.

The man, tall in stature and well-built as one would expect from a stalker on a payroll, retrieved his weapon from under his jacket and proceeded briskly in their direction.

Sofia could feel her heart pound inside her chest. She looked over to consult with her sister. Lily gestured to stay calm with her hand. She then addressed him.

"What do you want?"

"I want both of you to do as I say. You are coming with me. No one will get hurt if you do it nicely and quietly."

"We are not alone."

"Neither am I. Your friend outside is being taken care of as we speak."

Sofia's heart went from pounding to leaping up her throat.

The man reached the end of the aisle and stepped to one side. With his free hand, he waved them over, instructing them to head back toward the only exit.

Lily understood it was pointless to reason with this guy. She stole a wink at Sofia and motioned her to go first.

Sofia acknowledged her sister's cue with a barely perceptible nod. Followed by Lily, she walked up to him, veering into the aisle. Suddenly, within inches from him, she doubled over as if overcome by a cough attack. As the man looked down at her, Lily snapped his wrist and kneed him right in the groin. His fold in pain was automatic; still he managed to hold on to the weapon. Speedily, Sofia reached for his sore wrist, gripped it tightly with her two hands, and twirled under his arm to twist it behind his back, while, simultaneously, Lily wrapped her arms around his neck to lock him in place. With his body trapped in a contorted position, the unnatural bend in his arm forced his grip to open and release the gun. Not wasting a second, Lily threw her leg forward to trip his feet as Sofia pushed him forward. His whole body collapsed to the ground. The twins then immediately sat on him, but not without retaining the one arm in the impossible twist.

They noticed his breathing became heavy under their wait.

"Who sent you?" asked Lily.

The man did not answer.

Sofia forced the twist on his elbow.

He grunted. "You are wasting your time," he said with difficulty. "I know you don't have what it takes to pull all the way."

He was right. There were some inherent disadvantages to being on the good side. Sofia was getting sick just thinking about it and for Lily, in addition, it was against her vows to do so.

"Search his pockets," surrendered Sofia.

Lily did and found nothing. They were completely empty. "What did you do to Michael?" she asked.

The man stayed quiet.

"Here, hold his arm," instructed Sofia. "The others may come in any minute." She reached for her belt and removed it from her waist. She grabbed his other arm and brought it together with the first. The sisters maneuvered the best they could to secure his wrists.

Just then, as they got to their feet, the access door from the souvenir store slammed open and in came Michael running followed by the younger copy of himself. The worry on his bruised face quickly switched to surprise. He came to a stop and gawked at the man on the floor. Then he raised his inquisitive eyes. "I'm happy to see you have control of the situation."

"Years of mom dragging us kicking and crying to karate classes," said Lily with pride, "Black belt."

"I never thought I'd be happy she did," added Sofia. "It was one of the many weird obsessions she had. She was convinced we might need it someday. I hate to admit she was right." She then paused to examine Michael. "Are *you* okay?"

"I'm fine. Unfortunately for me, I never took karate. It's a good thing Gabriel showed up when he did."

For some reason Sofia was not buying his demure response. She wondered how many bruises the others sustained before his cousin appeared.

Gabriel offered his hand. "Nice to meet you, Sofia."

She accepted it. "Nice to meet you too." She appraised him. His facial features were almost more baby-like than Michael's, though his voice was not as stark in contrast. He was nonetheless just as odd, for there was nothing about him that resembled a professional bodyguard. If anything, he inspired maternal instinct. But then, she, a petite brunette, and her sister, a nun, had just overpowered a hired enforcer. Who was she to stereotype?

"He wouldn't talk," said Lily, "and, quite frankly, we weren't about to make him," she concluded unashamed.

"I'm afraid the two outside in the corridor won't be talking anytime soon, either," said Michael.

Gabriel could be seen grinning in the background.

Michael then set a severe gaze on the man on the floor. "I think you two should get going. We'll catch up with you."

Sofia was going to ask what he planned on doing, when she saw Gabriel caress his knuckles. She decided she didn't want to know and felt the sudden urge to get out of there.

"Fine with me," she agreed and dashed for the door. Her current circumstances were getting out of hand, more than she felt prepared for.

Lily gave Gabriel a quick hug. "Thank you for coming." And as she ran to catch up with her sister, she shouted over her shoulder, "please be careful."

Once outside, Sofia turned quickly toward the front of the chapel, shielding herself from looking into the corridor. She didn't care to see the two unconscious bodies. She was in full-on flee mode.

Lily caught up to her.

Sofia hesitated momentarily at the top of the stairs that led to the sidewalk, not sure which direction to take. "What if there are more?"

"I'm going to bet our good luck on them thinking that three bullies are enough to control one religious sister."

"That guy in there was a professional. I'm pretty certain his employer has the resources to know by now that you're not alone."

"Good. Let them sweat, then." Lily took the stairs and turned north on *Old Santa Fe Trail*. "This way."

For Sofia, reality had no problem sinking in. She followed her sister, claiming sanity. "Lily, this isn't a game."

"Yes, it is. It's an intimidation game. They think I have something they want and are trying to scare me into giving it to them. That's all."

"That's all?! This morning your room was ransacked and just a moment ago we were held at gun point. It might be smart to clarify that you don't have it."

"No, it wouldn't because then they would set out to look for it themselves. I provided enough clues in my report for them to know where to start." Lily pointed back toward the chapel. "You said it. They obviously have the resources. I prefer they waste their time focused on me. We can't let them get to it first."

Sofia stopped sharp in her tracks. "Lily! I don't know what you got yourself into, but by your own admission even a pope was too afraid to talk about it openly and resorted to hidden riddles. You are way in over your head."

Her sister turned with her cheeks flaring. "And what would you have me do? Hand it to them and look the other way? Go on business as usual, ignoring Mary's signs and John Paul II's cry for help? Of course this is way over my head. You don't think I know that? But I'm either the only one seeing the signs or the only one willing to do something about them!"

Lily released a forceful sigh. With a softer tone, she continued. "Sof, I'm sorry. I really am. I never meant to put you in harm's way. To be honest, despite what happened with my room this morning, until that man showed up, there was a part of me that realized I could be on a wild goose chase. All afternoon I've been trying to convince you as much as myself. No more. I believe, and even if you don't, I need your help."

Amidst the whirlpool of feelings that suffocated Sofia in this surreal turn of events in her life, one emotion rose strongly above the rest, her respect for her sister. She admired her bravery and drive to do the right thing more than ever.

"I do believe, Lily. I believe in you."

The *Closed* sign hung on the bolted door. Michael and Gabriel dragged the two unconscious men down the aisle, leaving them stretched out on the floor by the altar.

Gabriel then stepped over to the conscious one and stood tall looking down.

"Do you want some answers?" he consulted with Michael.

Michael shook his head. "They were paid for a pickup. They know nothing."

"What then?"

"Call the police."

"They'll be released; no records."

"They aren't carrying identification. The authorities will be curious about that. It will buy us time. That's all we need."

Gabriel nodded. "I'll call from the chapel's office so that it doesn't trace back to us." He started heading that way. As he walked by Michael, he stopped and asked quietly: "The shop clerk. What do we do with her? They tied her up behind the counter."

"Is she hurt?"

"No."

"Did she see you?"

"I was careful."

"Good. We need to keep a low profile. We'll let the police find her."

Again, Gabriel nodded and then ran off.

Michael approached the conscious hire. He was sitting on the floor, propped up against a pew, legs stretched out in front, and hands still secured behind his back as the twins had left them. Michael crouched slowly to whisper in the man's ear. There was no one around to hear, but he knew of the chilling effect his deep voice had up close and at low decibels; like the rumble of a tornado prowling nearby in the dark of night.

"I have a message for you to deliver. Tell Red Dragon that the twins have guardian angels. His time is up."

Michael drew a satisfied grin, rose and walked away.

The sidewalk was getting busier as the pleasant afternoon settled in. Navigating oncoming pedestrians was becoming a challenge. However, Sofia and Lily were so absorbed in their conversation, it was up to everyone else to avoid a collision.

"So, I'm studying the line that connects the shrines in search of more clues when I realize that Jasna Gora and Moscow have several interesting things in common," explained Lily. "If you recall, Jasna Gora is the name of the monastery that houses the highly venerated image of Our Lady of Czestochowa, Protectress of Poland. John Paul II, who was Polish, was particularly devoted to her for this reason. The image is a painting composed in the tradition of Byzantine art, which follows strict symbolic formulas, meaning that they all look very similar. One of the commonalties is that Mary and the child are represented in dark skin colors. That's why the Polish icon is also known as the Black Madonna of Czestochowa." Lily slowly and purposely drew a conniving grin. "Now listen to this. Due to the strict artistic guidelines, most of the Byzantine icons fall into a handful of themes. One depicts Mary holding her child in one arm, while gesturing toward him with her free hand. The Polish image belongs to this category. It's known as a Virgin Hodegetria, which in Greek means 'she who shows the way.'"

"She who shows the way... *Mary's Way*... interesting," said Sofia. "Yet, this is not the path we are to follow. You said there is another one?"

"That's right. I think Mary's Way was intended for the popes of the West and the patriarchs of the East, because it links the string of shrines in the West with a rich corridor of highly venerated Russian Marian icons, such as those of Yaroslavl and Kostroma, as it continues eastward beyond Moscow." Lily paused to assess her sister. "You see what I mean? The line doesn't end in Moscow, either. What's more, Our Lady of Kazan, you know, the Russian painting that disappeared during the revolution and appeared in Fatima, is a Black Madonna painted in the Byzantine style as well. All this can't be a coincidence. It's as if Poland's Protectress and Russia's Protectress, both Black Madonnas, serve as a bridge across the Great Schism. The message to reunite couldn't be clearer."

Sofia raised her eyebrows, impressed but remained noncommittal. "Again. Interesting. Now tell me about the second path."

"Okay, so here's the thing. There is another fundamental characteristic that pulls both sides together. For the Russian Orthodox Church, an icon is not a true holy icon unless it 'appears', that is, miraculously in a certain spot as if a gift from above. This caught my attention because in the West, the most popular images of the Virgin Mary are statues that *appeared* miraculously as well, and all of them black, as well."

Sofia inhaled a soft breath. "Lily, I'm familiar with the Black Madonna phenomenon. There are several perfectly rational theories to explain them. It's generally accepted that the early ones are based on pagan mother-goddesses like Isis. Alexandria in Egypt was one of the five major episcopal sees of the Roman Empire during the inception of Christianity. As the new tradition gained traction, Mary came to replace Isis. That's why many Black Madonna statuettes, showing Mary seated on a throne holding baby Jesus, are suspiciously identical to those of the Egyptian goddess and her son Horus. But it wasn't just Isis. Some Greek and Roman earth goddesses were depicted with black skin in many instances to represent the color of the soil. Over time, they too were reimagined as Mary. And then, the greatest boost for Black Madonna worship occurred in the twelfth century when the crusaders brought them back from the East. These statuettes were so popular they further thrived through mimicry and reproduction."

Lily listened patiently. Now it was her turn.

"I agree with most of what you just said, but you are missing two crucial points: One is the fact that the phenomenon exists in the first place. It underscores one of the greatest ironies of the Christian Church: While the male, elite priesthood commissioned extraordinary pieces of 'white' art to prestigious names the likes of Michael Angelo, da Vinci or Bernini, and built grandiose cathedrals, the lay folk in stark contrast venerated little, humble, anonymous statues of black women in humble chapels. Such has been the devotion to these images that the majority became patronesses of the towns, cities, nations and even continents where they appeared. There is no formal registry, believe it or not, but it is estimated there are approximately 500 of them. And that's only for starters," emphasized Lily raising an index finger. "Beyond this, there is a category of Black Madonnas that have no explanation. Once you take away the reimagined goddesses, the ones designed on purpose to resemble indigenous populations, the ones blackened by candle smoke or years of accumulated grime, the ones sculptured in honor of the Songs of Songs so dear to the crusaders, the reproductions, and so on, there is a residual group that remains a complete enigma. Like the Polish and Russian Protectresses, what's key about this group is that they are found miraculously and display the stubborn quality of refusing to move from a certain spot, generally the one where they were found, as if they were milestones along a divine path."

CHAPTER 14

The sisters turned east onto *Water Street* as they passed the Loretto Chapel on their right. It looked like a busy day for the once small-sized Gothic temple. Today it was a private museum, and visitors could be seen flowing in and out to admire the 'Miraculous Staircase' that led up to the choir. For Sofia, the elegance of its carpentry alone was well worth the visit, but the appeal for most of the public was very different. In 1877, an enigmatic craftsman volunteered to build the stairs. When the job was completed, the stranger disappeared without a word leaving behind a spiral staircase masterfully assembled without glue, nails or center support. Since then, legend has had it that the gifted carpenter was St. Joseph himself.

Sofia took a quick look back on their trail. No suited threats seemed to be following; nor were Michael or his cousin.

"Do you think they are all right?"

Lily pulled out her phone. "I'll text Michael."

"Wait, your phone," just noticed Sofia, "like mine, it could be bugged, right?"

"It's new. I replaced the old one as soon as I heard about my room." Lily spoke as she typed.

"I called your number earlier. You kept it. Can't they track that?"

"Michael encrypted it."

"When? How?"

"This morning when I called him to tell him about the room. It was his idea to get the new phone. As for how, I have no idea."

"Is hacking telephone numbers part of the journalist's job description now?"

"If you are stationed in terrorist territory, my guess would be yes. Besides, he had Gabriel do it."

Sofia narrowed a suspicious gaze. "What kind of private security does he dwell in?"

Lily tapped SEND and put her phone away in her skirt's oversized, front pocket. "I didn't ask."

"Don't you think it's an important question?"

86

"I trust Michael, and Michael trusts him."

Sofia frowned with disapproval.

"You don't like Michael," said Lily.

"It's not that. It's just that he seems too comfortable with all this. How do you know you can trust him?"

"I saw him interact with the refugees in Afghanistan and liked what I saw. His concern for them was genuine." Lily's gaze darkened with the hue of a painful memory. "There was this little boy—" She paused to clear her throat. "Did you know that it is an ancient custom there for warlords, businessmen or the rich and powerful to have boys as sex slaves? They are referred to as *Dancing Boys*. It's a status symbol."

Sofia's face paled as she shook her head softly.

"At one of the camps, there was a boy, eleven, who would follow Michael around. We thought it was cute, and he took it for a kid admiring his profession and wanting to become a journalist. We soon found out the boy was trying to find a kinder *guardian* than the one he had escaped from. I'm going to spare you the details of what he endured." Lily closed her eyes momentarily to rid herself of the disgust. "Poor child, he thought that was the only life he could expect and sought to make it a little easier. But the creep found him and tried to take him back. Michael stepped in to stop it; had several ribs broken and his face slashed before a group of refugees and soldiers ran to save him." Lily set her eyes on Sofia. "You see? You don't usually hear these things. You hear that women are horribly treated under the Taliban, but so is everyone else regardless of age, gender, or whatever. Where women are disdained, everyone suffers. The treatment of women is like a warning beacon on the tip of an iceberg alerting to a much broader abuse. The entitlement of dominance over one person never stops at that one person. That's why equality is so much more than gender. Equality is a state of mind where one understands that no excuse can raise you above another granting you the entitlement to disdain and abuse that other."

Sofia nodded. "What happened to the boy?"

"We were able to place him in one of our orphanages. He's in college now. Michael is taking care of that."

"Let me guess. He is studying journalism."

Lily relaxed with a chuckle. "Almost. Had his heart set on it for a while. But, no, in the end he chose Law. He's grown up to be a very brave, young man. He wants to go back to change things. It would seem the ugly practice is on the rise."

They reached the end of the small street and turned north. The Cathedral Basilica of St. Francis of Assisi appeared before them in a dramatic contrast to the smaller adobe structures in its vicinity. Archbishop Lamy, the first bishop of Santa Fe, was originally from the Clermont area in France, and had it built in the Romanesque style to simulate the architecture he was familiar with.

The sisters crossed the road and climbed the short flight of steps that led up to the right side of the building. A merry choir of chanting birds received them.

Lily smiled. "Have you noticed how birds never cease to sing in this corner?"

Sofia looked up at the branches of the tree that loomed nearby. Then she assessed the sky. A gray cloud had drifted in front of the sun. The little feathered creatures did seem unusually cheerful despite the momentary lack of warm sunrays. "No, I wonder why?"

Lily had a hunch. The secluded corner was dedicated to St. Francis' love of animals. Beside the tree, laid a small garden with a bird fountain and a plaque displaying his *Preaching to the Birds,* a sweet ode to their blessed freedom to sore the skies. In Lily's mind it was no coincidence birds perpetually sang their praise to his sensitive soul.

"Why are we here?" asked Sofia.

"There is something inside I want to show you."

As they approached the front door, Lily stepped over to curtsy in front of the statue of Kateri Tekakwitha, the first North American Indian to be canonized, explaining her prominent spot in front of the cathedral. For Lily, she was much more. Like her, Kateri was a Native American woman and Catholic, a mixture that occasionally acted up inside. The jury was still out on how much of their faith had been enforced or not on their ancestors, so it was difficult to reconcile at times. In Kateri's case, conversion and the vow of virginity had been her free choice, motivated in part by the ugly alternative, enforced marriage. Hers had been arranged when she was eight. Orphaned, half blind and scarred because of smallpox, she wasn't the most desirable prize for a man and could not expect the best treatment. So, she refused to marry and chose instead to serve others. And that she did very honorably. Lily admired Kateri's resolve, and beyond faith and career choices, shared with her an additional personal bond. Katari was also known as Lily of the Mohawk and had been the inspiration for her name.

Lily led her sister through the two front bronze doors into the cathedral. She looked down the aisle, crossed herself and immediately turned toward the north side.

She motioned toward the back corner as she explained. "In order to understand the paving of the Black Madonna path, we need to go back to the beginning of Christendom. But don't panic, I'll try to summarize 2,000 years of historical nuances into as few minutes as possible."

"Well, thank you. I truly appreciate that," welcomed Sofia with a touch of teasing.

Lily smiled. Her sister was being a true sport, and she was about to try her patience to the limit.

"Just so you know, some of the historical nuances will be legendary apparitions and miracles. I need you to listen until the end no matter what you think of what I'm saying. It will eventually all come into focus, I promise."

Sofia, who was now imbued with loyalty to her sister and much curiosity, agreed with a tamed sigh of surrender.

They came to a stop before a small, gated chapel, the only remnants of an adobe church built in 1626 that once stood on the site.

With her hand, Lily signaled she was ready to begin. "So, Jesus ascends leaving his disciples with the Great Commission of spreading the Good News, meaning the promise of Heaven—"

"Geez," interrupted Sofia. "When you said the beginning, you really meant it."

"Shush and listen. As the apostles head out on their respective missions, Mary moves to Ephesus, in Turkey, with John. Not seven years pass when she performs her first recorded apparition, surprisingly, on the farthest possible side of the Mediterranean in Spain. It's the year 40, and the Apostle James, John's brother, is preaching in what is now known as the city of Zaragoza.

He is heartbroken because he's not being very successful. Mary, who is alive and well in Turkey, appears to him in Spain, in the flesh, upon a pillar, to encourage him by assuring James that people will eventually have faith as strong as the pillar of jasper she is standing on. She then asks him to build a chapel, leaving behind the pilar to mark the spot, and upon it a little, dark, wooden image of herself holding baby Jesus. A Black Madonna. Tradition has it that after he established the church, James returned to Jerusalem where he was martyred a few years later. His disciples return his body to Spain by boat where it is buried in *Santiago de Compostela*. Over time, the site became the destination of one of the most important Christian pilgrimages in the world, *The Camino* or *Way of St. James*; only rivaled by Rome and Jerusalem. As for the pillar and its statuette, they remain, to this day, unmoved in Zaragoza. You can even touch the pillar if you want."

Sofia couldn't help herself. "She appeared in Spain while still alive in Turkey. Seriously?"

"It shouldn't surprise you. You have heard of bilocation before."

"Indeed, I just wasn't aware it was such a common means of transportation for the saintly."

Lily crossed her arms over her chest.

"Fine," said Sofia. "Is this where our road trip starts? Not that I'm complaining, mind you. I've always wanted to visit Spain. Will we be bilocating there or taking a plane?"

"You're impossible."

"Hey, if I have to sit through 2,000 years of miracles, you're going to have to tolerate a joke or two, girl."

Her sister had a point. Lily conceded by rolling her eyes with a smile. "No, we are not bilocating, flying or otherwise to Spain. Leaving aside all the powerful elements in this tradition, which you will come to understand in due time, Spain is where the path leads us to... and where I get stuck. I only mention it first to follow Mary's work chronologically. This was her first apparition, during which, she establishes herself as the overseer of the apostles through guidance and support. What I want you to take away from it is that Spain was chosen for a specific fate, and Mary marked it from the beginning with a solid, tangible milestone."

"Why a pillar?"

"I'm not sure. To be honest, I always found it odd. It's the only such case in Marian apparitions."

"Maybe it's meant to symbolize the 'rock' of faith, as in 'on this rock I will build my church' per the Eastern Orthodox tradition."

Lily shrugged. "Could be, after all Christianity saw its birth and consolidation in the East. During the first century, the Roman Empire was almost at its zenith, reaching the Atlantic Ocean to the west, Syria to the East, the British Isles and Germany to the north, and Africa to the south. There are no canon laws or Gospels, just faith and the faithful, Jewish men and women preaching among themselves and to the gentiles, while converting at the risk of sporadic prosecution. As Christianity swiftly spreads, the second century brings the Gospels and other biblical writings. Despite their very little mention of Mary, her oldest known image is of this time. It can be found in the Catacombs of Priscilla, a noble woman and benefactor of the Christian community in Rome, who lent the space to the Church in a time of heavy prosecution. In spite of the hardships, Christianity continues to grow and, naturally, leadership stratification develops to oversee urban Christian populations. Five centers gradually become pivotal to early Christianity, each with a ruling patriarch: Jerusalem, as its birthplace, Rome as capital of the Empire, Antioch and Alexandria as major political and commercial ports, and finally Constantinople when made imperial residence in the 4th century. As I mentioned before, it is the Emperor Constantine the Great, the founder of Constantinople, who issues the Edict of Milan, officially legalizing Christian worship, thus ending its prosecution and initiating its emergence as a state religion."

"Yes, but technically, he does it to unify his Empire, not out of any personal conviction. He didn't even convert until his later years," clarified Sofia. "I know that much."

"True. And I'm happy you bring it up, because it raises an important point I like to highlight often to my students. Though he is known for the 'Triumph of the Church', the credit should really go to his mother Helena. Of humble origins and abandoned by her husband, who sought marriage into nobility with another, younger woman to boost his career, Helena never remarried and dedicated herself to her son as a single mother. In turn,

Constantine always showed deep regard and affection for her. When he was promoted to Augustus, he honored her with the title of August Imperatrix and gave her access to the imperial treasury to pursue her devotion, for she was the true Christian. It was she, Helena, who traveled to Jerusalem, who identified all the sacred enclaves, and secured them for posterity. Good examples are the Nativity in Bethlehem, the Mount of Olives and the Holy Sepulcher. It was she, too, who found the relics of the cross, some nails of the crucifixion, and the Holy Tunic. No other apostle, pope or patriarch did for Christianity what this woman did to solidify its rise. So much so she is considered equal-to-the-apostles by the Eastern Orthodoxy. Yet for the West, she is but a Saint who helped the poor and found the True Cross, no more. Women were instrumental in the early years of the Church as we see with Mary, Priscilla, and Helena, but their invaluable contribution has been systematically obscured. They were the *true* apostles."

Sofia grinned in response to her sister's passionate protest. It helped Lily realize she was getting carried away and refocused.

"Anyway, eventually, the Christian Church became the state church for an Empire of far reach. Inevitably, power struggles disguised as theological bickering followed. The nature of Jesus and His relation to God were so hotly debated that Constantine had to call the First Council of Nicaea to create a unified system of beliefs and practices for all Christendom. It settled little. Further contentious aspects of doctrine arose with the years, pitting theologians against one another and leading to the first schisms. One major source of friction was the debate over if Jesus' divine and human natures were distinct or not. Eventually, of course, another woman stepped in to settle the matter."

"Of course," said Sofia amused.

"You don't seem to be taking me seriously," said Lily.

"Trust me, I am entirely on your side."

Lily scoffed but continued. "For your information a woman stepped in because the problem was yet another woman. Jesus' nature was being debated indirectly, for the real problem was His Mother. Mary had gained much primacy from early on, especially in the East, and was being venerated as the Theotokos, meaning the *Bearer of God* in Greek. This was a problem because if Christ's human nature was distinct from God, and God could not me born for having always existed, Mary could not be referred to as His bearer. Instead, *Bearer of Christ* or Christotokos was being suggested as a more appropriate title."

"Are you kidding me? They really fought over that?"

Lily raised her eyes to heaven and exclaimed, "The wars that have been fought over so much less!"

Sofia studied her sister with open interest. "How did you become a nun? Your discord almost exceeds mine."

"My discord is with human corruption, not Faith."

"Quite frankly, I don't know why Mary didn't quit right there and leave us to our own devices."

"Luckily for us, above all, She is a mother regardless of the *nature* of Her Son, and She wasn't about to allow His death go in vain."

"Amen," celebrated Sofia.

Lily raised an eyebrow at her sister.

"I said it with utmost respect. Please, continue."

Lily shook her head. "As I was saying, in the year 431 the Council of Ephesus was called by the Emperor Theodosius II to determine what title to give Mary and hopefully prevent any more schisms."

"In Ephesus, you said?"

"Yes."

"Wasn't that where Mary moved to after Jesus' crucifixion?"

"Indeed, which gives you an idea where matters were tilting toward. What's more; the Church of Mary in Ephesus was built specifically for the occasion."

"Right, no pressure for those who wanted to downgrade her," said Sofia.

"They never stood a chance. You see, though historical records refer to Emperor Theodosius as calling the council, what they don't readily tell you is that, again, a woman's hand was behind it. Theodosius rose to emperor at the tender age of seven upon his father's death, so his older sister Pulcheria at the age of fifteen became his regent. She was diligent in ensuring her brother received proper education to become a successful ruler and a virtuous Christian leader. He proved incapable of either, so she did what she could to retain enormous influence over him throughout his life. Her faith has never been in dispute, but it is also acknowledged that her vow of virginity helped her retain power by avoiding marriage. It only worked until her brother, following a riding accident, died. The senate would not allow her, a woman, to rule alone. She conceded to marrying but on condition that her husband accepted her vow, which he did. So basically, and returning to the matter at hand, since Pulcheria favored the title of Theotokos for Mary, and since she pulled the strings, it's no coincidence her position prevailed. Such was her influence that Western popes would skip over her brother and sought her aid directly, and during another council, the Council of Chalcedon, bishops acclaimed her a 'New Helena'. Pulcheria spent the last years of her life devoted to the Theotokos and helping the poor in life and death, because in her will she instructed that her wealth be distributed among the poor."

"I get it. She contributes significantly to Christianity, especially to Mary's worthy place, while keeping with the message of her son; the signature of the true apostle."

"The signature of Mary's apostles," clarified Lily as her eyes sparkled. "You know what else Pulcheria did? She built two major churches in Constantinople dedicated to Mary. One was the Monastery of the Panaghia Hodegetria to house a precious Virgin Hodegetria. Pulcheria made her vow of virginity upon receiving it as a gift from her sister-in-law who had obtained it in Jerusalem."

"Hodegetria, *she who shows the way*. Isn't that what the Black Madonna of Poland is?"

"I'm impressed. Yes, and depending on the sources you consult, it may even be *the* one. Legend has it that Pulcheria's icon made its way to Poland and once it reached its current location in Jasna Gora, it has refused to move. There are several legends and miracles that attest to it."

"Interesting."

"It gets more interesting. The other church Pulcheria built was St. Mary of Blachernae that housed the icon of Blachernitissa, venerated as the Protectress of Constantinople and the entire Eastern Roman Empire. Also a Virgin Hodegetria. Guess where this one ended up?"

"Please, shock me."

"I shall... Moscow!"

CHAPTER 15

Lily's phone beeped. She hurried to check the screen.

"It's Michael. He says they are on their way. They notified the authorities and waited to see them show up. That's why it's taken them a while. The three men have been taken into custody, but he asks that we stay vigilant nonetheless."

Sofia's nagging fears were confirmed. "He's concerned there could be more."

"I guess."

The serene illumination inside the cathedral and perhaps more so its solid walls had given Sofia a degree of comfort. Michael's caution put the reality of their situation back into perspective: There was a lurking threat, and it was potentially big enough to require more than three enforcers.

What the hell? thought Sofia. Who were *they*? Why was Michael personally involved? And what in the world had her sister gotten herself into?

She rubbed her arms as if a chilly breeze had suddenly filtered her airy sleeves. What about her? What was she doing? She had committed to an eerie mission that she felt utterly unsuited for and wasn't sure why other than supporting her sister seemed the right thing to do. This was the closest they had been in a long time.

"I need to step it up," said Lily. "Where were we? Yes, the 5th Century. So, rifts are forming, the heirs to the apostles are drifting apart from each other and away from the original Message. And the more they do so, the more Black Madonnas *showing the way* back to it start appearing and gaining prominence."

"As if thorns in their backsides..."

"That's right," smiled Lily.

Sofia's gaze turned reflexive. "Not to be a pain in yours, but you said our path was marked by Black Madonnas who shared the affinity of appearing miraculously. These first two icons you just mentioned didn't. Bad start."

"Technically, they both have miraculous origin stories. Beyond that, they are fundamental to setting the stage. Look, the icon that was housed in the

Monastery of the Panaghia Hodegetria, which ended up in Poland, was the first Hodegetria of its kind, the original one. Apparently, the monastery was located in the proximity of a spring with healing properties. According to tradition, Mary would appear to blind pilgrims and guide them to the spring so they could have their sight restored. Thus, the name of the icon: *she who shows the way*. What this tradition exemplifies on a spiritual level is Mary's role in guiding the 'blind' toward her Son, because he *is* 'the way'. It goes back to John 14:6 when Jesus says *I am the way, the truth, and the life.*" Lily paused. "Can it be coincidence that this painting would then end up in Jasna Gora to do just that, show the way? *Mary's Way*?" Lily intensified her stare. "Then there is the other icon. It too a Hodegetria. And none other than the Protectress of the whole Christian Eastern Roman Empire. The fact that this one ended up in Moscow to mark *Mary's Way* as well, goes to strengthen the core role of 'Russia' in Mary's call for unity, don't you think?" Lily asked the question raising her eyebrows as if the logic could not be more obvious.

But she was not finished. "And let's not forget they belonged to the woman who singlehandedly secured Mary's prominent role as the Mother of God. Pulcheria then placed her icons in churches at the reach of everyone rather than confining them to a palace or chapel for private worship, as was the custom. By proceeding in this way, she made Mary accessible to all. Mary rapidly rose to represent a source of comfort for the disadvantaged because it was Her, a humble woman, who God kindly asked to share a son with. And She, of free will, consented. It is often forgotten that Mary is the only chosen one in the Bible to consent to God's request."

Sofia warmed up to the thought. It was heartening that someone so humble would garner such respect from an almighty. Mary's widespread popularity among the underprivileged was easy to understand. In addition to being a loving mother figure, she was one of them. And if she was worthy of respect, they were too. "You make a good case. From a symbolic perspective it is very powerful," she acknowledged.

"It transcends symbolism, Sof. That's the point Mary is trying to make. She built a path that is very real so we can *see* that so is *The Way*. That's why it is so important that we complete the final segment of the line. She is guiding us to an all-to-real Message."

Once thing was to sympathize with a kind tradition, another to give up on exercising healthy skepticism. For Sofia, the fact that Byzantine art limited the number of themes meant that Hodegetria icons, or some variation, had a high statistical possibility of being found in most Marian shrines and Christian churches in general. You'd be hard-pressed to draw a random straight line across a Christian continent and not connect several in a row. Therefore, that the line could be extended was not in question in Sofia's mind, but that it pointed to a specific destination with a specific purpose was yet to be seen.

Oblivious to her sister's rationalizing, Lily took an instant to recalibrate and then expressed urgency with her hand. "Moving on, we are still in the 5th century and the Roman Empire is about to collapse, particularly in the West. The Eastern Byzantine half held on another millennium, allowing for Mary's shrines and icons to spread, which She rewarded with an emerging body of miracles. Meanwhile, the West crumbled under the pressure of the Northern Germanic tribes. In the upheaval, new kingdoms were formed more focused in recruiting soldiers than worshiping maternal figures, so Mary did not channel, initially, as much attention as She had in the East. Still, it was during this tumultuous time that the earliest Marian shrine in Rome was built, the Basilica of Saint Mary Major. It was done in honor of Her proclamation as Mother of God during the Council of Ephesus. With time, it would become one of only four Major Basilicas in the world, one of five Papal Basilicas, and home to the most venerated Marian icon in the capital, the *Salus Populi Romani* or Protectress of the Roman People. It too a Hodegetria and Black Madonna."

"Rome is not on Mary's Way," said Sofia succinctly.

"No. It's not." Lily drew a mischievous grin.

"So, this icon is important because ..."

"Because, aside from being the Protectress of the capital of the first Christian Empire and the city where the Vatican is located, do you remember Pope Pius XII?"

Sofia had to think. "Wasn't he the one with the public relationship with Fatima, like witnessing the 'Miracle of the Sun' in the Vatican Gardens?"

"Yes. Following that experience precisely, it was this icon that he carried through Rome to initiate the first Marian year in Church history and then crowned it the next year to introduce the Queenship of Mary. Thereafter, every pope has honored Her with personal visits. Paul VI declared Mary the Mother of the Church before this image, and the first thing Pope Francis did on his first day as pope was to pray before Her."

"Are you insinuating that this hyped-up deference toward Rome's Hodegetria following Fatima's events, infers they knew what the Message was, that is, a call to get back on track?"

"No. Well, yes, I believe that's the Message, but not where I was going with it."

"Hold on," said Sofia raising her hand, "I think I know. The Third Secret describes a city in ruins at the foot of a steep mountain, which a bishop in white climbs amidst corpses. At its top, the bishop is killed. I imagine the popes understood the city to be Rome and, since this icon is the Protectress of Rome and its people, they resorted to a whole lot of honoring in hopes of saving the city and themselves."

"Good guess, but still not where I'm going with it."

"All right, let me try again," insisted Sofia. "The scene was interpreted as the assassination attempt on John Paul II, so if the danger is over, why would his successors Benedict XVI and Francis continue to show such reverence for Her? Do they fear the danger has not yet passed?"

"That's where I was going with it."

"I admit it is bizarre," noted Sofia. "It would appear they believe. But if they believe, I can't imagine what would stop them from acting upon a divine request, even if it were to surrender their supremacy. What on earth could be more powerful? Or maybe it is something else entirely." Sofia briefly paused to give it some thought. She looked at Lily. "You covered Benedict XVI somewhat, but what can you tell me about Francis?"

"Pope Francis' behavior was divergent from his predecessor's. While Benedict sought to put a lid on the Fatima affair, the first thing Pope Francis did was pray in front of Rome's prime Hodegetria, as I already said, but also immediately asked the Bishop of Lisbon to consecrate his pontificate to the Lady of Fatima, bringing her right back to the forefront."

"Well, it makes sense to a certain degree. I did the numbers. When elected, he was the pope poised to preside over Fatima's 100th anniversary. He was probably feeling the pressure."

"He had many reasons to feel pressure. He was also the last pope according to St. Malachy's Prophecy of the Popes. Of the 112 popes listed, Pope Francis matches up to the one foreseen ruling during the Apocalypse."

"I was wondering when you'd bring that up."

Lily grinned. "Personally, I doubt it keeps him up at night. It is generally accepted that the list is an elaborate forgery. Regardless, there are many who take the prophecy very seriously and are feeling the jitters."

Sofia whistled softly. "In his world, it can't be a good thing to have two major doomsday prophesies converge on you. I wouldn't like to be in his shoes."

CHAPTER 16

Lily eyed the time on her phone and sighed. "This is taking longer than expected."

"How much more left?" asked Sofia.

"Not all that much. But I fear that every minute I spend briefing you is an hour we fall behind whoever we are racing."

"Can't we just skip to where you got stuck? I think I got the general idea."

Lily shook her head adamantly. "You have no idea. Let's keep going. You'll soon see what I mean."

"Okay, if you're going to be that categorical about it ..." Sofia felt her legs tire. She leaned against the tall back of one of the pews and listened.

Lily jumped right back in. "Eventually, in the West, Marian devotion is adopted by the monasteries and spread through missionary efforts. Meanwhile, popes are barely holding on via precarious alliances and submitting to new rulers. Then comes Charlemagne, King of the Franks, who in the 8th century manages to reunite most of Western Europe under his influence. He is a friendly figure to Rome, and the pope sees it as an opportunity to bring the Christian center of power back to Rome by crowning Charlemagne the legitimate Holy Roman Emperor. This was not well received by Empress Irene, who—ironically—was ruling in Constantinople over what was left of the original Roman Empire. It was the beginning of the end for the Byzantines. Not only were they delegitimized by the West, but they were also confronted with the rise of Islam. The convulsion had Patriarchs and Emperors of the East questioning everything. For instance, in the case of the icons, since Islam believed in the impropriety of iconic representation, it drove some Orthodox Emperors to wonder if their battle losses were due to God being discontent with the Christian abuse of relic and iconic worship. It led to a couple of iconoclastic periods. Barely any survived, thus the extraordinary value of the ones that did," emphasized Lily. "Regardless, the Western Church, which had long begun its drift away from the Eastern one, did not care for such matters, adding to the many factors driving the wedge further in between them. The Great Schism of 1054 came about, and Pope Gregory VII, encouraged by his moment of strength in the West, officially implement papal supremacy over the Church and over secular rulers."

"Wasn't it Lord Acton, the English Catholic historian, who said: *Power tends to corrupt, and absolute power corrupts absolutely?*"

Lily added, "And corruption fosters formidable foes. The greatest and most widespread explosion of miraculous Black Madonnas followed. You see, barely forty years after the Great Schism, and overwhelmed by the advances of Islam, Byzantine Emperor Alexius I sought help in the West. Pope Urban II answered by calling the First Crusade. His goal was to recover the Holy sites, reunite East and West, and all under the freshly declared papal supreme authority. What followed instead were two hundred years of religious wars spiraling out of control. It wasn't just Christians fighting Muslims, which is bad enough, it was the slaughter of unfortunate Jews caught in the middle and the persecution of incipient Christian groups labeled enemies of Rome. Such was the madness that the Fourth Crusade resulted in the brutal sacking of Constantinople rather than its rescue. This was the deathblow to what was left of the Eastern Roman Empire. The Christian Orthodox Branches were eventually engulfed and isolated within Muslims boarders, except for the Russian rite."

Sofia shook her head. "So much senseless suffering."

"Indeed," said Lily grimly. "Religious conflict was at its worse, and all sides were guilty. Consequently, Black Madonnas spread like wildfire East and West, appearing under miraculous circumstances in caves, rivers, trees, buried, you name it. But nothing Mary did, caught the attention of those at the helm."

"Someday you'll have to explain to me why Mary couldn't just slap them straight. It would have spared the innocent a lot of suffering."

Lily's gaze was thoughtful. "Do you remember when we used to watch Star Trek?"

Sofia arched an eyebrow at the odd question. "Yes ...?"

"When the Enterprise encountered a new planet with primitive life, they'd espouse the Prime Directive and not interfere with their natural evolution."

Sofia could not believe her sister was quoting Star Trek to justify divine behavior, and worse yet, that she was about to debate it. "They didn't interfere at all," she protested. "Mary, on the other hand, according to you, is doing a lot of appearing to hint the way."

Lily shrugged "She is a mother. She can't just stand on the sidelines doing nothing while her children suffer." Lily suddenly lowered her tone to a conniving whisper. "So, brace yourself, it is going to get very interesting again."

"Okay ... I'm listening..."

"As we've seen, Black Madonnas were spreading East and West to denounce the barbarism of religious conflict. But in the West, they particularly concentrated in the Languedoc region in the south of France, where the persecution of the Cathars brought about the establishment of one of the most infamous institutions ever, the Inquisition. It was brutal."

"Right," interrupted Sofia, "but so was the mass hysteria that led to horrid witch hunts across Europe and North America, as another round of religious wars took place with the Reformation Schism. I wrote a research article about it. The deaths at the hand of Protestants superseded those at the hands of Catholics. Why didn't Mary torment them? I mean, you know it's bad when even the Spanish inquisition was so disturbed by it that they prohibited the burning of witches in Spain."

"Because she is drawing a path, remember? A path, which, I'll remind you, is headed to Spain precisely."

Sofia wasn't convinced but let her sister continue. After all, apparently, she knew nothing.

"So, as I was saying," continued Lily, "there seemed to be no end in sight to the death of innocents in the name of God."

"I'm not getting the interesting part. It's pretty horrifying to me and a good reason to become an atheist."

Lily gave her sister a scorning look. "Can you stop interrupting and let me finish? Obviously, it is horrifying, and hardly what Jesus had come to predicate. What I meant was that the spread of Mary's veil of Black Madonnas across the East in the form of painted icons and the West in the form of statuettes calling for the return to *Jesus' Way*, went largely ignored by the Patriarchs. Nothing she did moved them. She resorted to appearing to monks, friars and nuns, renowned mystics and saints that tried to alert

again and again of God's anger in view of what was happening. All failed."
Lily angled a grin. "What's interesting is what she did next."

Sofia widened her eyes.

"Mary laid out another straight path."

CHAPTER 17

Sofia felt a grip of apprehension girth her chest. Discussing wonder-working statuettes was child's play, she was confident she could reasonably debunk them all. But another straight line with a discernible pattern built through space and time beyond the frame of a reasonable coincidence, was intimidating.

She took a quick look around. The walls of the cathedral, which just moments ago comforted her, now appeared to be closing in. Why had Lily brought her here?

"You said you wanted to show me something," she urged.

"I'm getting there."

The unsatisfying response moved Sofia to scan the space again. What could the promise of a new divine line in Europe have to do with the cathedral they were standing in on the other side of the Atlantic? She knew the building had endured many mishaps having been built with little resources but great aspirations. The cathedral had gone through several renovations, and it was a miracle it stood at all. Funds were so short at the time that Archbishop Lamy resorted to local Jewish merchants in search of financial contributions. He acknowledged their aid by including a keystone above the main entrance with the four Hebrew letters that represented Yahweh. Other than that refreshing act of collaboration, there was little else she could see at plain sight that would warrant their presence. There was the expected nave divided into three spaces by two rows of columns. In its center there was a relatively new baptismal font, and along the walls she could see the traditional Stations of the Cross, which were also relatively new. Sofia ran her eyes toward the east space reaching the sanctuary under which Lamy and other Archbishops laid buried in the crypt. Nothing jumped out at her there either. She then raised her eyes and came to rest them with interest upon the San Damiano Cross that presided over the altar.

Lily had followed her sister's eye-wandering. "It's just a replica. The original cross hangs in the Basilica of Saint Clare in Assisi, Italy."

"It's Byzantine style," noted Sofia, "an icon."

"Yes," smiled Lily. "But not what I wanted to show you. You're not too far off, though. That cross is very symbolic of what both Mary and Jesus had to resort to with hopes of veering the Church back on track." Lily said this with much reverence as she appraised the cross. She turned her attention back to her sister. "Black Madonnas, apparitions, and miracles had not had the intended effect on Church Fathers. Either the popes were ignoring Her on purpose or were blind to Her efforts, which is quite ironic considering that the Hodegetria's first body of miracles was restoring sight to the blind."

Sofia tensed up. She noticed her sister's eyes starting to glitter as when she was about to reveal something wondrous.

Lily continued speaking softly. "Now get this, something very difficult to explain happened: In the same year, 1206, three prime mendicant orders with no relation or link to each other and separated by thousands of miles, suddenly sprung up." Lily intensified her brown stare to make her point. "All three had one crucial miraculous occurrence in common: Either Jesus or Mary appeared to the founding saint with a severe request to correct the ways of the Church."

Lily abruptly paused with hesitation. She eyed the screen on her phone. She was getting distracted. It was not her plan to talk about the medicants orders, at least not yet.

"Don't dare leave me hanging," said Sofia. She definitely wanted to hear this. "Are you're saying the humble and harmless mendicant orders took the vow of poverty as a way to *rebel* against the Church?"

"Something like that, but I really need to tell you about the new line." Then Lily seemed to reconsider. "On second thought, I guess it takes me to the same place. All right, I'll explain quickly." Lily took an instant to rearrange the order of her narrative. "Let's see, until then monks isolated themselves from the world in monasteries. But in view of what was going on with the Crusades, some were inspired to call for a return to the kind ways of Jesus. Like Him, they set about to preach the true way by example since the heirs to the apostles were not doing so. Now, here is what is so amazing: On the extreme east of the Mediterranean, Berthold, a French crusader and son of a Count, while in Antioch, had a vision of Christ denouncing the evil ways of the soldiers. Naturally, it impressed him, so Berthold retired and became a hermit in Mount Carmel in Haifa, Israel. He adopted Mary as his model and grew a community of followers, which in 1206 became the Order of the Brothers of the Blessed Virgin Mary of Mount Carmel with a spiritual focus on prayer, community and service. The Carmelites were born."

"Wasn't that the order Sr. Lucia joined?"

"Good catch," said Lily, "but pay attention. At the same time, another soldier by the name of Giovanni, son of a wealthy Italian merchant, was also headed to battle with the Crusades when he too had a vision that stopped him from going. It impacted him enough to go from being a spirited, young man to completely withdrawing from the earthly comforts he was accustomed to." Lily directed her finger up to the cross. "He was St. Francis, and while stopping at the Chapel of San Damiano to pray before the original of this cross, Jesus spoke to him and literally asked him to repair His Church because it had fallen into ruins."

"Literally?"

"Yep, '*Francis, repair My house for it is falling into ruin*'. Those were Jesus' exact words, and He spoke them from that cross," reiterated Lily pointing up. "It can't get any clearer than that."

Sofia raised her keen eyes to it. "This cathedral is named after St. Francis, but you say it isn't the reason for us being here ... Any connection to Pope Francis and Fatima?"

Lily grinned. "You tell me. When Pope Francis was asked why he took St. Francis' name, he explained: '*He brought to Christianity an idea of poverty against the luxury, pride, vanity of the civil and ecclesiastical powers of the time. He changed history.*'"

"He changed history? A little overstated if seven hundred years later Mary has to make the sun dance in front of the cameras in Fatima tired of waiting for the changes to happen."

Lily chuckled. "Exactly what I thought; but you get the idea. The instructions could not be more specific: Return to Jesus' kind message and ways."

Sofia was amused. "So basically, what you are saying is that elaborate heavenly miracles did nothing for the popes; what they needed was a mundane instructions manual."

"Not just any manual," said Lily with an impish smile knowing she would have the last laugh again, "the Rosary."

"What do you mean?"

"What I mean is that exactly at the same time as the Carmelites took form in the East, and the Franciscans started their preaching journey in the belly of Europe, thousands of miles to the West another saint, this time Spanish, will receive a divine visit as well. Only this time it was none other than Our Lady of the Rosary; the first time she appeared as such."

Sofia widened her gaze in recognition. "St. Dominic, founder of the Dominican Order."

"You got it."

"Why Mary in his case?"

"Because St. Dominic had realized on his own that a change in the ways of the Church was necessary. Mary appeared to supply him with the tool that would help him carry it out, the Rosary. It was he, St. Dominic, who introduced the Rosary as we know it today."

Sofia's frown of confusion turned skeptical.

"Fine," sighed Lily, "let me explain. Dominic was on a diplomatic mission with his bishop for the King of Castille when they came across the Cathars in Languedoc at the time of their horrid persecution. Dominic was concerned with the pomp and ceremony displayed by the Church while trying to convert people, such as the Cathars, who lived in a state of self-sacrifice. So, he volunteered to preach to the Cathars in a manner they would better relate to, that is, in the humble way Jesus had proceeded. He also favored learning and virtue. It is the reason the Dominican Order became strong in universities. So, in 1206, he established his first order in Prouille, France, for women. Ironically, the convent, which was run by converted Cathar women, became a refuge for Catholic girls whose families could not maintain them."

"I see, the heretics were the ones doing the charity work."

"Exactly. Dominic saw the good in them and the bad in his own. It would be there, in that convent, where he received Our Lady's visit. Like St. James, he was angst by the low conversion rates, especially because the pope's legate was murdered, purportedly by the Count of Toulouse, but the Cathars were conveniently blamed for it. Pope Innocent III called the Albigensian Crusade to gain power over the region. You can imagine Dominic's desperation. I mean, this was a man, who while studying in Plasencia, Spain, sold his textbooks, which was all he had, to feed the poor during a period of hunger that swept the city. He did not think that the slaughter of woman and children by the thousands was *the way*. So, Mary appeared to encourage him and gave him a rosary to confirm that Her love, that of a mother, was the guide to Her Son, not the sword."

Sofia shook her head feeling a healthy dose of aggravation. "With due respect, Lily, the Rosary Prayer sounds nice, but it did little for the Cathars. What's the point?"

"The point was to condemn what was happening. This apparition is a vital milestone. It marks the beginning of a new straight line. The Black Madonnas guided us here and concentrated in big numbers for this reason. And Mary appearing for the first time as Our Lady of the Rosary signals this new line's connection to Fatima. As for the Cathars," Lily sighed, "it gets worse. The few who survived the Crusade were then taken care of by the Inquisition, which was established for that purpose. And even worse yet, with time the inquisitorial duties were assigned to the Dominicans and Franciscan friars. Though this happened after St. Dominic's death, the unfortunate association resulted in him being labelled *The Inquisitor*."

"That is awful," said Sofia. "All their work for naught. What does it take to get a message across?"

"An angry Mother, apparently," said Lily. "It would seem Her Three Secret strategy in Fatima finally worked, at least in part. It certainly captured their attention. Major changes have taken place since and most of their grandiose and ceremonial expressions have been dropped. And let's not forget Pope Francis' choice of name, it's signaling 'message received.'"

"Maybe too little, too late," said Sofia.

Lily seemed shaken by the comment. She set an eerie glance on her sister. "Explaining why the mission has been entrusted to—" She paused, hesitant. "*you*."

"What?"

"It's true. Those of us inside the Church, we are no longer trusted. We have failed."

"What are you talking about?"

"Look, I told you about John Paul II's *Letter to Women* where he tells us that we, the women, have a mission, but there was another one he wrote a month before, *Ordinatio Sacerdotalis,* in which he addresses the subject of female ordination. You know how he repeats himself in case we aren't paying attention. Well, in this first letter, he starts by laying out the usual excuse held on to by both the Western and Eastern rites, that is, that Jesus chose apostles only from among men, and thus the Church follows dutifully by imitation."

"I don't recall any of the apostles being Polish, Argentinian, or Russian either," interrupted Sofia. "The nerve of these guys. They completely forgo imitating Jesus' humble ways but boast pride in being sticklers when it's to their convenience."

Lily waved it off. "It's questionable on several levels because clearly Mary Magdalene was one. But stay with me, because he then refers to several points of Pope Paul VI's *Declaration Inter Insigniores*. Among them, he asserts that the exclusion of women from ordination is part of God's plan; that Christian women need to become fully aware of the greatness of our mission, and that today our role is of capital importance for the renewal and humanization of society and for the rediscovery of the true face of the Church." Lily paused. "I'm not sure what he means by 'rediscovering the new face of the Church' exactly, but you see he mentions women's special mission again as related to some kind of renewal. Then, and this is the key, he clarifies that the greatest in the Kingdom of Heaven are not the ministers but the saints."

Sofia furrowed her brow. "I'm not sure I follow. Yes, he acknowledges that the ministers are losing points in Heavan, but how does that exclude you from our mission? You're not a minister and you are the closest thing to a saint I've ever seen."

The compliment did not have the intended effect. Lily's tone came glum. "The 'saints' he is referring to are outsiders, Sof. Mary and Jesus have had more success with them. Neither St. Francis nor St. Berthold were of the cloth but soldiers when Jesus appeared to them asking for help. And not one of Mary's apostles belonged to the Church either. What's more, in the following centuries it will be an outsider again, a woman again, who will do more for Christianity than all the ministers of the West and the East combined."

CHAPTER 18

Gabriel walked up to the two sisters.

Sofia saw him approaching. "Hi, is everything okay?" she asked with alarm.

"Yes, please don't worry. Michael wanted me to check on you and let you know we are here. He's waiting outside."

"We are almost done," said Lily. "I'm about to construct the new line." She paused unsure if he was privy to the whole story. "How much did Michael tell you?"

His smile was mischievous. "Enough. I know we are on the hunt for a secret message that hopefully might bring in world peace."

"You seem amused by it?" questioned Lily.

His young face lit up. "My understanding is that the Divine Message might compromise the Church or at least question the role of its highest representative, perhaps even topple him. I think it is funny we are helping a nun to do it."

"Whoa, slow down! I'm not out to topple anyone," cautioned Lily. "Please do not misunderstand my intentions. There are wonderful people in my Church, the grand majority, in fact. And I have a strong gut feeling Pope Francis is truly trying to do the right thing. In no way do I want to jeopardize his efforts. All I'm doing is answering a call. There are enough signs to indicate that Mary is not happy with how things have been handled. I believe she wants us to usher in equality and unity in our institutions as the stepping-stone to securing balance and peace in the world, and that we all could pitch in a little."

Gabriel gained an uncharacteristic maturity in his gaze. "Tribulation is inevitable. Large religious institutions have grown into mammoth organizations with far too many personal interests that get in the way of what is right. Your mission demands an extraordinary shift in their internal dynamics. Opening the doors to equality and unity requires them to let go of their centralized power. Heads will have to topple for change to take root."

Sofia felt a shiver. *Tribulation*? Who talks like that? Gabriel's odd word choice made the alarms go off in her head. It was clear he was far more acquainted with the prophecies than he was letting on.

Lily seemed unfazed. "I disagree. If there is one thing Our Lady has been trying to tell us all along is that peace is the way, not the end. You are right in that the leaders of these organizations might find their maneuverability limited. It might be the reason why in many instances She has had to resort to outsiders. Our mission is to sow peace with a gentle hand, and to this end I'm convinced Her line leads us to the instrument that will help us accomplish just that."

"You do justice to your people," smiled Gabriel. "Let's hope you are right. As a Jew, I grant you it is time we all found peace."

Understanding fell upon Lily's face. "Indeed, *your* people have suffered greatly. I'm sorry; I see where your reservations come from." The catholic in her felt the pinch of guilt.

"We are not entirely innocent, either," he gracefully acknowledged. "No one is. When it comes to mindsets, a quick look at the Old Testament shows ours has been quite stern in seeking wrath and punishment where love and peace would have been preferable. And when it comes to excluding women, we've done our fair share. Some orthodox groups still do today. If we all started by recognizing our historical responsibility in the damage done, maybe we'd stop pointing fingers at each other and rather walk together along the straight path," he broadened his smile to ensure the compliment was received, "as the Hopi would say."

"Thank you," said Lily moved by the praise.

Sofia stood baffled. *Who is this guy?* "Gabriel, do you mind me asking what your background is? You seem unusually insightful in religious matters for a man your age."

He grinned. "My father is a rabbi and, to top it off, my ancestry is Sephardi."

Sofia wrinkled her nose. "I get the rabbi part, but I don't quite understand what you mean by Sephardi."

Gabriel was happy to explain. It was the whole point of being Sephardi, a strong pride and a long, rooted attachment to their identity. "Under the Roman rule of Palestine, a large group of Jews from Jerusalem was exiled to Sepharad, the Hebrew name in biblical tradition for Spain. It became our home for the next 1,500 years, and during some extended periods of peace that we enjoyed with Christians and Muslims alike, we thrived to offer Judaism some of its richest contributions. The religious harmony would not last. Eventually, we'd be expelled again, spreading through North Africa, the East and even the New World colonies, but we never forgot the homeland left behind and the identity forged there."

"You guys have paid a hefty price for trying to keep your identity," admired Sofia. "Resisting assimilation into the surrounding majority has made you the perpetual 'others'. Not a good thing when the concept of tolerance is lacking."

"You should know," conceded Gabriel. "Native Americans did not fare well for the longest time under the succession of dominant invaders either."

"It wasn't meant to be that way," interrupted Lily. "The horrors of the Old World were never meant to reach the shores of the Americas."

"Now wait a minute," protested Gabriel. "Let's *all* be fair. Those horrors were well established here long before the 'Old World' ever arrived. Wars, slaughter, slavery, human sacrifices, domination, were all part of the way of life among natives of the Americas as much as anywhere else."

Lily raised her hand in sign of peace. "You're right. All people on all continents, including the Americas, sought conquering their neighbors as a means to expand, dominate and collect slaves. No religion, race or gender is free of that crime." She offered him a soft smile. "What I meant to say was that I believe America was part of God's greater plan to spread his Kingdom if all else failed in the Old World. Unfortunately, the project ended up corrupted here as well."

"Like a Plan B of sorts?" asked Sofia, wondering where this was going.

"Yes. I told you. Mary marked Spain from the beginning. Since matters were messed up so badly in the East and the West and everywhere in between, it was time to set sail."

"Oh, I have to listen to this," said Sofia raising an eyebrow. "Please continue."

Gabriel too showed interest.

Lily displayed a playful, smug face. "You should know by now that I am very capable of impressing you."

"I admit you certainly have captured my attention. However, I reserve my right to examine the evidence and play the Devil's advocate as soon as I'm allowed to. I'm sure there is a perfectly reasonable explanation for all this."

"Like what?"

"I don't know, Earth's magnetic lines to explain the shrine placements, a masonic conspiracy... aliens," she teased. "Until I study it thoroughly from different angles and with access to all the data, anything goes, and the possibilities are endless."

Lily sighed at her sister but rapidly recovered to offer Gabriel a wink.

"It has to do with an amazing woman," she announced, animated.

"Naturally," he smiled.

Lily realized that she could be overwhelming when it came to her cause, but it didn't deter her. She not only admired this woman profoundly, but Lily also had proof that this queen had been placed in the right place at the right time to carry out an extraordinary mission.

"Let me tell you her story," she started with a little drama. "She was born a princess, daughter of the King of Castile, the land of castles, but with no fanfare for no one cared about the second born, especially a female."

"Oh brother," exhaled Sofia at the theatrics. "Here we go."

"Shut up and listen," exhorted Lily, happy to torment her sister. She focused on her new fresh and willing victim, Gabriel. "Her whole worth was reduced to that of a bargaining chip when the time to negotiate her marriage came. She'd be sold to the highest and most convenient bidder in the best interest of the realm or, most likely, the king. It was the year 1451. The Iberian Peninsula was divided into four Christian Kingdoms and one Muslim Emirate named, Granada. The Muslim stronghold was all that remained after eight centuries of Christian *Reconquista*. It had all begun back in 711. As Europe crumbled under belligerent rulers, Spain was left exposed and vulnerable for the taking. Islam walked right in encroaching into the south of Europe with little resistance." Lily widened her eyes as they went wild sparkling. "Until, that is, Our Lady's miraculous intervention in 722 to aid Pelagius of Asturias, a Christian Visigoth, during a crucial battle against Moorish forces; the win kick-started the *Reconquista*. This is important because our forlorn princess was heir to the Pelagius lineage and their Christian pride, defining her sense of destiny. Her name was Isabella, and while still a toddler, her father died and her mother fell mentally ill, leaving her and her little brother, Alfonso, pretty much orphaned. Her much older brother, Henry, the only son of her father's previous marriage, became king and their guardian. He cared little for his younger siblings, so shamelessly ignored his father's will and steered Isabella's titles and inheritance to his lovers and allies. Isabella, third in line to the throne, grew impoverished, away from the court, and isolated from the world. Her only company was the stories of martyrs and heroines such as Joan of Arc who had recently been burned at the stake with the excuse she wore male clothing."

"Lily, is the extended biography really necessary?" asked Sofia. "I think we all know who Queen Isabella is." She looked at Gabriel for support.

He displayed an impeccable poker face.

"It's very important. This woman defined the world as we know it and was handpicked by Mary. She is central to our mission, and its success depends on knowing the details that made her the most powerful woman on the planet ever!"

"Okay, if you're going to put it that way... I just wished I had known I was going to spend the night in this cathedral. I would have brought coffee to keep me awake."

Lily ignored her sister with a wave of her hand and continued talking to Gabriel as if she weren't there.

"When Isabella turned six, her brother Henry, the king, started negotiating her marriage contracts, which he repeatedly broke in accordance to his capricious needs. Then, as it became apparent that he was impotent, and thus unlikely to provide a male heir to the kingdom, Isabella, and more so, her younger brother, Alfonso, became a threat to him. At the time, royal relatives had no problem killing one another for the throne. So, at age ten, Isabella and her little brother were brought to the court to keep a tighter noose on them. It would be a frightening period because, additionally, Isabella found the libertine atmosphere of the court dangerous, having to resort to seclusion to protect herself. Later, after being offered in marriage to two different brothers in the neighboring Kingdom of Aragon, to the heir of England, and to a royal in France, things turned to the worst. Her brother, in the midst of court conspiracies for his poor management, offered her to the despicable Master of the Calatrava Order. Isabella was horrified, as were the few who cared for her." Lily spared a teasing look at her sister. "Isabella spent two days praying to Mary on her knees, requesting that either the Master or she died to avoid the marriage. Isabella must have been favored because, curiously, on his way to take her as a bride, he suddenly dropped dead."

"Are you serious?" asked Sofia.

Lily shrugged her shoulders. "Just repeating what the history books say. Isabella was profoundly Marian as were most in her realm. You can imagine how this episode marked her sense of divine protection and destiny thereafter."

"I would say."

"Anyway, her older brother's wife finally has a baby, a girl, who obviously no one believes is legitimate. And with crime rampant, finances in dire straits, and the Moors in the south sensing weakness due to the king's poor governance, the Spanish nobility carry out a coup to remove Henry and install Alfonso as king at the age of thirteen. The poor kid dies of plague shortly afterwards, leaving Isabella distraught. They had always been very close, and the wrenching suspicion that it wasn't a natural death will harden her badly."

Lily raised her pay-attention finger, "Here is when she starts to shine. You see, Alfonso had named Isabella his heir. However, sensing a lack of support from Alfonso's supporters and fearing for her life, she wisely agrees to negotiate with her older brother to restore him to power. In exchange, she secures herself as the official heir and claims the right to choose her own husband. Her genius had publicly surfaced for the first time: She had achieved a legitimate path to the throne in the eyes of the kingdom, while immediately saving her neck. True to her brother's weak and deceiving nature, he fails to keep his promises. He rushes to offer her in marriage to the King of Portugal to get rid of her, but just as swiftly, Isabella, who is no dummy, arranges her own marriage in secret to the heir of the neighboring Kingdom of Aragon, a young prince her same age. Prince Ferdinand sneaks into Castile disguised as a pauper risking his life to marry Isabella in 1469. They were but teenagers, yet with their marriage had become heirs to more than half of the peninsular, and soon to the world."

"And they lived happily ever after," interrupted Sofia. "Lily, really? Are we going anywhere fast with all this?"

Lily cupped her hands on her waist. "You used to love fairytales. What's happened to you?"

"I grew up. Come on. We've been standing in this cathedral forever. I'm tired, hungry and, oh yes, overwhelmed by the unsettling turn of events in my life this afternoon. Can you get to the point?"

"All right," said Lily waving her hands in the air. "For your information, this woman was extraordinary, and, unlike poor St. Francis, she changed history in her time for real. She deserves a little respect."

Sofia exhaled her last breath of patience while Gabriel simply smiled.

Lily went on.

"Unfortunately, her life was anything but a fairytale. Her husband Ferdinand, like herself, was born to the second wife of the king and had an older brother and sister in line for his kingdom's throne. But unlike Isabella, he was favored by his father, so his two older siblings conveniently die." Lily waved her hands in the air again, "To think this was her best choice. It gives you an idea of the kind of thing this woman had to deal with. Her brother, the king, despised her, the same brother who she suspected had done away with her younger brother. And she had married into a family whose members were just as kind to each other. In addition, she was well aware Ferdinand's family had agreed to the nuptials only because they had their eyes set on her kingdom. Her neck was being stalked from every angle. And if things were not already bad enough at home, in the world at large the second wave of Muslim invasions were hitting hard in the East with the incursions of the Turk Ottomans. Constantinople and Athens had fallen, and no doubt, as with the first wave, the Iberian Peninsula was again ripe for the taking thanks to petty internal squabbles within and among the kingdoms. Isabella's monumental challenge would be to prevail in such a man's world without becoming one of them." Lily glowed with pride. "As would be expected, her genius rose to the occasion. When the time came and her brother was agonizing on his death bed, she came forward to dutifully claim the throne of Castile, while conveniently sending a very, very slow messenger to alert her husband, who wanted it for himself. By the time he found out, it was too late. She alone had been crowned Queen of Castile."

CHAPTER 19

Lily felt her legs tire as well. She looked at the pews and suggested sitting down with a gesture of her hand. "I guess this is taking a little longer than I thought. I promise to get to the juicy part fast. I thought it was important to establish that, despite everything against her, Providence would want her to take the throne. Next, I'd like you to see that she embodies all the qualities of a true apostle, and how it helps establish the new line."

Sofia welcomed the suggestion to sit. She chose the pew right next to her and slid over to allow space for the others. Lily sat beside her. Gabriel took a moment to text Michael. Then he sat on the pew in front of the sisters and turned to look back at them. He seemed genuinely interested.

Lily resumed the story without delay.

"So, Isabella, the brand-new Queen of Castile, was now confronted with placating her husband, the soon-to-be King of Aragon. She agreed to a public power-sharing agreement: His name would come first on documents while in truth she retained all governing power. The agreement only applied to Castile. In Aragon, his kingdom, women were not allowed to rule, so when he took the throne there, no reciprocal concessions were made for her. The historical consequence was that he got the credit for all her extraordinary achievements. While he was off fighting his wars, she reorganized her government system, assigned real professionals —rather than allies or relatives— to prime jobs, she brought the crime rate to its lowest in history, and unburdened the kingdom of the enormous debt her brother had left behind. But perhaps most famously, she went on to win all her wars. For instance, The King of Portugal, the one she had left at the altar to marry Ferdinand, ran to marry her 'illegitimate' niece as an alternate route to claiming the crown of Castile. A war ensued for which she was the strategist and Ferdinand the operative. They won. Then, as the Ottoman threat grew, she set out to secure her southern border by finally completing the *Reconquista* her late ancestor had started eight hundred years earlier."

"Lily," interrupted Sofia, "technically, going to war makes her very much like the men of her time. I'm not saying she had a choice, but we all know wars are ruthless. You don't win them playing the harp."

"And," added Gabriel, "let's not forget that after winning, she exiled Jews and Muslims from her dominions, as had other European countries before; an extremely tragic episode for those people."

Lily chose her words carefully. "History for the most part has been written by men," she started, "and from the biased perspective of the winner or the loser." She focused on Gabriel, "Please don't take me wrong. I understand that for your ancestors to be kicked out of their homeland the way they were must have been a horrifying experience. I don't blame you if you consider her a monster."

Gabriel affirmed with a gentle nod.

"There are several factors we must keep in mind, though. One, when she went to war to reconquer Granada for the Christian side, as history puts it, what was really going on was that the Muslim ruler of Granada, knowing of the Ottoman successes in the Mediterranean, and that a woman now ruled in Castile, believed her vulnerable and felt encouraged to test her. He endeavored to carry out skirmishes on the border. Neighboring towns were being sacked and slaves taken. Meanwhile, further east, the Ottomans had clearly stated that Rome was their first target, and the rest of Europe would follow. By her time, they had already managed to reach Venice, and the ruler of Granada had reached out to them for help. Isabella had no option but to protect her southern border. Her land had once been taken, and she was not about to let that happen again. It was self-defense, not an arbitrary religious invasion.

"Second. Wars are brutal no matter which side you're on. We all know that. From her perspective, the stories that reached her of what happened when Ottomans conquered were dreadful. People were slaughtered by the thousands when not miserably tortured. Women, girls and boys were massively raped and enslaved for perpetuity, the royals being the most prized. She had four daughters. The prospect was unsettling, but most importantly, it was not her way. Harm and casualties were reduced to the minimum, and she certainly never welcomed her soldiers to do their will with women and children. This said, yes, there are instances of brutality, but in her writings, she expressed repeatedly how the deaths of her enemies and her own weighed on her, never boasting of such brutality to portray strength and instill fear as did other rulers, specifically the Ottoman."

Lily took a moment to ensure their attention. This part was particularly important to her, because it exemplified Isabella's extraordinary character.

"Third," she continued. "Isabella inspired utmost respect among her own soldiers, which was by no means the norm either, least for a woman. The reason was they knew well of her own bravery. You see, at the beginning of her reign there was an uprising in Segovia where her eldest daughter, only seven, was held captive. Defying her advisers, she rode into the town all alone to calm her subjects and save her daughter. Think about it, she grew up in an atmosphere where the men around her killed their immediate family members for power. She, however, risked being ripped apart by an enraged crowd for her daughter. Actions like these set the stage for the respect and loyalty her subjects developed for her, but it also won her the trust of her enemies. Many towns under Muslim rule in the south willingly surrendered to her on the condition that she was present. She'd personally ride into the city accompanied by one of her children as a guarantee that the people of the town would suffer no harm. By no means the norm in those savage days, either. Episodes such as these left such a lasting mark that in the game of chess, as we know it today, the Queen became the single most powerful piece on the chessboard in her honor." Lily was beaming. "A woman, this woman, had memorialized herself as the most powerful player in the ultimate game of war ahead of men!"

Lily toned her excitement down and set her gaze on Gabriel.

"As for the expulsion of your ancestors, that had not been her intent or wish. What she had asked them, as she had done with the Muslims, was for them to convert with the hope of protecting them precisely from exile. You see, the Inquisition had been in full force in Europe for several centuries by her time. Castile, her kingdom, was one of the few that had never implemented it. That is not to say there were no fanatic outbursts against Jews, but they were not state sponsored. Unfortunately, in the Christian psyche, the Jews had killed Jesus and that was reason enough to blame them for any disaster like plagues or periods of hunger. To make things worse, in Spain, there was also the historical memory of the Jewish contribution to the first Muslim invasion. The Moor conquest of the Iberian Peninsula had been swift because, among other things, they'd go in, subdue the Christians and leave the Jewish population in charge of the town. This freed the Muslim forces up to continue north with the conquest. The Jewish population had no loyalty to the Christians because of their strained relations, but for the Christians it was perceived as betrayal. With the second wave of Muslim threat heading their way, for most, Jews represented the key to their success again. Isabella had many Jewish friends, and more importantly, she had entrusted some of her chief governmental positions to them. She did all she could to protect them from the true instigators of the measure, her husband and the Inquisition."

"Yes, the Spanish Inquisition. What about that? Wasn't it she who established it?" asked Sofia.

"Isabella was a woman trying to keep her head afloat in the water while balancing the weight of two elephants on it. One was her husband, and the other was the powerful Church. Bear in mind that at that time the Vatican was heavily powered by a Spaniard, Rodrigo Borgia, future Pope Alexander VI, who also happened to be a subject of her husband. They teamed up. Ferdinand, like other European rulers, saw the institution of the Inquisition, chiefly, as an instrument for control and power. Additionally, it could also serve as a source of income since they were entitled to the possessions of the person charged with heresy. This was the reason the Templars were eliminated in France, for instance. It was Ferdinand who bought it to Castile. Isabella delayed its implementation for as long as she could and tried suggesting measures aimed at sparing the convicted, when possible. Unfortunately, just as Ferdinand got credit for her good, she got credit for his bad, and she went on in history as the Queen of the hideous Spanish Inquisition. Which, for the record, wasn't even close to being as bad as the others, but again, that too, was corrupted by history to defame her and her soon-to-be empire."

Lily paused for a breath.

Sofia and Gabriel both shook their heads back to reality. They had finally been sucked into Lily's story.

"Wow," said Sofia, "I had no idea. You're right; this woman deserves more respect than she has received. I'm very curious now, how does she fit into the whole Fatima-Secret-Message-Marian-Line thingy? I mean, you mentioned a new line. I imagine she forms part of it. How so?"

Lily, momentarily, closed her eyes. She was getting ready for a major revelation.

"When I showed you Mary's Line, you saw it connected the leading Marian Shrine in every country it crossed between Russia and Portugal."

"Right."

"All except for one country: Spain."

"Really? I missed that." Sofia stretched her hand out. "Give me your phone. I'd like to see the map again."

Lily reached into her pocket for it and tapped the screen until the map was up. Then she handed it to her sister.

Sofia scrutinized it.

"Wait, what about Switzerland? The line crosses it, too."

"Yes, it brushes south of Einsieldeln, home to the country's most important Black Madonna."

"Okay, but it is not directly touching it," mumbled Sofia. She searched some more. "The Czech Republic?"

"There, the line brushes north of Brno, home to another venerated Hodegetria."

Sofia looked up. "Not touching it either, but close enough. I won't bother asking about Belarus. The line cuts its capital Minsk in half. Surely there is a major shrine there. So not in Spain, not even close. Why?"

Lily delayed her reply to ponder how to best approach it and then started slowly.

"It is safe to say that Spain is the most Marian country in the world. The number of festivities celebrated in Mary's honor, and the intensity of the devotion is unequaled. Most of its towns, cities, regions, and the country as a whole have Mary as their patron saint and Protectress. For the longest time, every woman carried *Maria* as part of their first name. Spain leads in the worship of miraculous Black Madonnas, and, yet, despite its amazing number of shrines, *Mary's Way* doesn't hit one even by accident as if trying to avoid them altogether. What it does do, however, is run right through a little out-of-the way town called *Madrigal de las Altas Torres* that has no other claim to fame than being the birthplace of Queen Isabella."

Sofia whistled her awe. "What are the odds?" she said as she checked the mystery on the map for herself. She then turned the screen to share it with Gabriel. "Why was she born in that little town?"

"I'm not sure. It wasn't the location of the court or anything at the time. Her mother lived there long enough for Isabella to be born and then moved to another larger town."

"It's almost as if her birth had been orchestrated to happen there just to fall on the line," said Gabriel.

Sofia surrendered giving Lily her phone back. "Okay, you made your case. She was chosen. What I don't fully understand is what point is Mary trying to make? Chosen or not, why have Isabella's birthplace coincide with her shrine line? What I'm trying to say is that Mary's other apostles were not born on her line to be validated, at least no line we are aware of. Why Isabella?"

"*Mary's Way* is our source for clues. Isabella's birth on the line not only confirms that she was central to a divine mission, but it also helps us define the new line. *Mary's Way* avoids shrines in Spain because Spain has its own shrine line and Isabella points us to it."

CHAPTER 20

Gabriel's phone buzzed. He took a look at the screen. "It's Michael. He's asking why it's taking us so long."

"Two thousand years of history, that's why," retorted Lily somewhat peeved or just tired.

Gabriel chuckled. "I'll go out to keep him company."

"Now? Just when it's getting interesting," said Sofia. "You don't want to know about the second line?"

"Michael can tell me." And he walked away with an enigmatic grin.

Sofia trailed him through the corner of her eye until he disappeared, wondering if to be grateful they were there protecting them or concerned they might be the reason they were in harm's way in the first place.

"All right let's keep going," suggested Lily, rubbing her face. "To make sense out of this, let me recap: We are looking for Fatima's hidden message, and I believe Pope John Paul II gave us the clue to find it. This is so because on the first anniversary of the attempt on his life, he traveled to Fatima to thank Our Lady for saving him. In his homily, he named the shrines that, when connected, delineate a straight line, and followed up the hint by quoting Judith's straight walk before God, twice. Then, I discovered that these three shrines are the most important ones in their respective countries and that, in fact, the line connects the most important Marian shrine in every country it crosses between Russia and Portugal ... except for one, the one in Spain."

Lily stared forcefully into her sister's eyes. "Can you guess what shrine that might be?"

"Since you ask me as if I should know, and knowing it is in Spain, the answer can only be one," figured Sofia. "It's the shrine that houses the pillar."

Lily nodded, "The Cathedral-Basilica of Our Lady of the Pillar in Zaragoza." But it was important to her to emphasize the extreme importance of this detail. "If you recall, it was Mary's first apparition, and she left behind the pillar, a rock-solid milestone, together with her first Black Madonna. Today, the cathedral built on the spot is the most visited Marian shrine in the country, and yet, for some mysterious reason, Mary excluded it from Her shrine line. The only one. Why?"

Sofia could not be more amazed. Leaving aside her deep doubts about whose hand was behind the shrine line, the fact was that the shrines were lined up. And regardless of how she felt about the pillar legend, the fact was that it existed and had existed for centuries. Therefore, the combination of both inevitably contributed to a fascinating enigma, because why, indeed, would Spain's major shrine be excluded from a major-shrine-alignment, especially if, as legend had it, it was the first and only one with an actual milestone?

Sofia conceded. "It marks another path, a fundamental one."

Lily smiled, satisfied. There was a flicker of hope in her glance. "Plan B. I've been able to identify three locations along this new path and they are intimately related to Spain and the discovery of America. That's why I think Spain was chosen from the beginning. But now I'm stuck. I don't know where to go from here."

Sofia shook her head. "If Spain was chosen from the beginning, that would make her part of Plan A, not B. And I thought you said Prouille, where St. Dominic received the rosary, was the head of this new line? How does that tie into America?"

Lily was struck by the new perspective. "You're right. Maybe there is no A and B." She gave it some more thought. "Maybe both lines were meant to work together from the start."

"What do you mean?"

"Well, of the three markers on this new line, I concluded that Prouille's role was to link the new line to Fatima so that we knew we were on the right track. But, if this line was planned from the beginning, it's more likely the two lines are working in sync with each other."

Sofia did not disguise her growing confusion. "Does that mean the third spot gives away the America connection then? Because I'm still not seeing it."

"Sorry, I'm doing it again. It's confusing because this second line was not as straightforward to construct as the first one. I only figured out that Prouille was on it after I discovered the third spot. I kind of when backwards." Lily raised a finger to request a moment. She briefly closed her eyes. "Okay," she said when ready. "I'll explain, but if you don't mind, I'll skip the more boring details and go straight to the highlights."

"I appreciate that very much, thank you."

Her sister's little jab elicited a grin from Lily. She was about to stun her again and that offset the fatigue of summarizing months of work. "So ... Our Lady of the Pillar's feast day, due to her longstanding popularity, is celebrated with honors on the 12th of October, which is Spain's National Day. And it is Spain's National Day because it is the day that Columbus discovered America, spreading Hispanic culture. For this reason," she paused for emphasis, "John Paul II declared Our Lady of the Pillar the Patron Saint of the Hispanic Peoples. You got that?"

"Got it."

"Good. Now let's go back to Queen Isabella's time. Back then, the shrine of Our Lady of the Pillar was located in the Kingdom of Aragon, making it the most important shrine in her husband's kingdom, not hers. In Isabella's kingdom, the most important Marian shrine was in a small town she referred to as her *little paradise;* its name: Guadalupe. Ring a bell?"

"Of course ... Our Lady of Guadalupe ... she is huge in the Hispanic world, especially in Mexico."

"That's right, and there's a good reason for it." Lily quivered with excitement. "You see, having won the war to take Granada for her kingdom in 1492, Isabella traveled to *her* major shrine to give thanks to *her* Lady of Guadalupe. While there, and with her finances freed up from the war, she summoned Columbus and agreed to sponsor his adventure across the ocean. The Kings of Portugal and England had scoffed him off. Even her husband Ferdinand had shown little interest in the enterprise. Only Isabella bet on Columbus' crazy idea, taking full ownership of it for her kingdom. Subsequently, it was men and women from the Guadalupe region, Extremadura, who initially travelled to America, taking their worship of Our Lady of Guadalupe with them. It spread fast and wide, so her intimate relationship with the discovery led Our Lady of Guadalupe to be designated the Queen of the Hispanic Peoples, the Patroness of the Americas, and for Her feast day to be celebrated on the 12th of October, as well."

Lily paused for a breath.

"Okay. Interesting. Two major invocations of Mary in neighboring kingdoms, both celebrated the same day, and in connection with both Spain and the Americas."

"And ..." Lily widened her grin, "did I mention that her statuette is also a Black Madonna that miraculously appeared to mark a spot?"

"Really?" Sofia was genuinely impressed. Again, not because she gave any credence to miracles or their associated legends, but because the legends existed, tying into the overall pattern.

"Long story short," said Lily, "in the 14th century, according to written records from the time, a humble cowboy by the name of Gil Cordero was looking for a stray cow near the Guadalupe River when he saw a vision of Mary. She asked him to dig up her statuette and build a chapel on that precise spot. That chapel became a monastery and with time the most important Marian shrine in Castile."

Lily shifted to look straight at Sofia as her hands came together to emphasis the point she wanted to make. "Think about it, Sof. We have these two shrines, with their two Black Madonna markers, rising over centuries

to become the major shrines in their respective kingdoms. Then in the 15th century, the heirs to the two kingdoms marry, bringing their territories together and setting the foundation for Spain as we know it today. And those two same royals go on then to discover America, setting the foundation of the Spanish Empire, as well."

"I get it. As a result, Our Lady of the Pillar and Our Lady of Guadalupe become patronesses and queens of both Spain and America, thus the connection."

"And what happens when you connect their milestones on a map?"

The question was rhetorical. Lily reached for her phone. She cancelled the current map on the screen and retrieved a different one. She then turned the screen to Sofia as their shoulders came together.

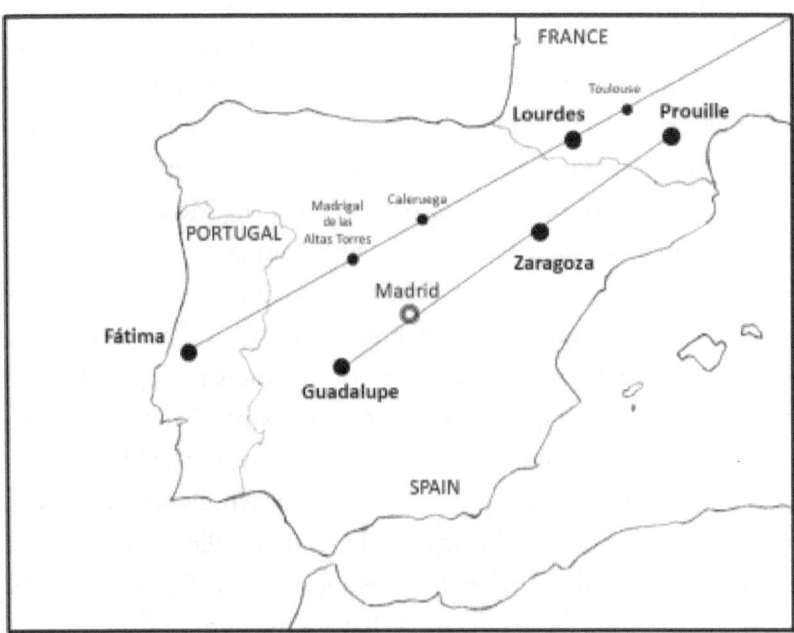

"Look. If you draw a line from Guadalupe to Zaragoza and continue north, check out where it ends ... or starts, whichever."

Sofia narrowed her gaze on the spot. "Prouille ..."

"That's right."

Sofia took the phone in her hands to better assess the line. Indeed, it was straight. If she had been standing up, her knees would have buckled. This was beyond freaking her out at this point. Nonetheless, she put her brain into high gear to find a reasonable explanation and shared her thoughts out loud.

"A straight line is the shortest distance between two points. Connecting the two most important shrines in neighboring realms with a straight line is not remarkable. It becomes remarkable when the third connecting point follows a consistent pattern with the first two. In this case it doesn't. I'm sorry, Lily, I admit that Mary appearing to Dominic in Prouille is tempting, but the line can just as easily pass through many other little towns with a Marian tradition. Prouille is not the location of a major Marian Shrine, nor has anything to do with Spain or America. It's located in France."

Her sister's analytical nitpicking did not dim Lily's grin. If anything, it drew wider. "I forgot to mention a little detail."

"Oh boy," said Sofia looking apprehensive. "What?"

"In St. Dominic's day, Prouille was under Spanish influence. But leaving this aside, Prouille is not just where the Rosary as we know it today was born, or where Mary appeared as Our Lady of the Rosary for the first time, or the place where a major mendicant order was founded miraculously at the exact same time as two other major orders across the Mediterranean. Either one of these facts and their relationship with Fatima would warrant its spot on any line. But you're right, in staying with a consistent pattern, it just so happens that St. Dominic was born a Spaniard in Castile like Isabella, and like Isabella, his birthplace, the adorable out-of-the-way town of *Caleruega* is on Mary's Line." Lily tapped the screen to show her. "That's what I meant by Isabella's birthplace pointing to the Spanish Line, it provides the pattern. And, in case there remains any doubt he is a chosen marker, while his first community was founded on the Spanish Line in Prouille for women, his first male community was founded in Toulouse, just north of Lourdes, on Mary's Line." Again, she tapped the screen. "What are the odds of that?"

CHAPTER 21

Sofia was feeling dizzy. The way her brain worked, she couldn't just take information and dump it in a pile until she could get around to it, she had to meticulously store it in sorted heaps for easy retrieval later. Right now, her sister was throwing so much information at her that her brain was at a choke point, struggling to keep up and about to burst.

Lily continued excitedly. "I realize that in terms of Mary's apostles, St. Dominic doesn't exactly fit the bill, he was not a woman. But the first house he founded was for women in Prouille, an oddity in the usual order of things at the time. And the purpose of his order was to spread Jesus' teachings in a humble and humane way, as St. James had tried in Zaragoza, and as Isabella would later try to do in Guadalupe."

Sofia just stared at her sister, stunned with what was turning out to be a formidable case.

"Don't you see?" said Lily, trying to elicit a reaction from her. "Isabella was the ultimate apostle chosen to spread Jesus' message to all nations as He had requested. And it all happened in Guadalupe, Extremadura, at the shrine of yet another major Black Madonna, who, incidentally, I'll remind you, went on to become the prime Marian invocation in the Americas."

Sofia winced and raised her hand. "Don't take me wrong. I'm impressed with this new line. I really am. But I'm not so sure about Isabella as one of Mary's apostles. Yes, I realize she was an extraordinary woman for her time, maybe even ours, but there was nothing peaceful about the discovery and subsequent conquest of America."

"I agree. A conquest is a conquest. But it was the way of the world, and I've already explained how Isabella's way was different. That's why she was the chosen one. She gave explicit written instructions to Columbus on how he and his men were to interact with our ancestors:

'Treat the said Indians very well and lovingly and abstain from doing them any injury, arranging that both peoples should hold much conversation and intimacy, each serving the other to the best of their ability.'

"She instructed him to severely punish anyone who mistreated a native in any way. Columbus failed to deliver on this front as on many others, so

129

she bypassed him and sent other expeditions, all with the same instructions. Did you know that when Columbus captured several hundred natives and brought them back to Spain for sale, she had them freed and returned? The same expedition that took them back home brought Columbus in chains for disobeying. Spain would become the wealthiest and most powerful nation in the world, the first truly global superpower; Christianity would spread to the Americas and beyond, but, inevitably, harm was still inflicted so far from Isabella's reach, and it would weigh on her all the way to her deathbed. In her will, signed on the 12th anniversary of the discovery of America, she added a special addendum to specifically clarify that the principal intention of taking custody of the new lands across the Atlantic had been their evangelization; and asked her heirs to ensure that the residents of the New World were not injured but their person and goods treated justly. Sof, this would lead Spain, in 1542, to be the only European country to officially prohibit our slavery or segregation, while centuries later Anglo colonists, for instance, still promulgated bounty laws rewarding our headhunting, including children."

She concluded. "Thanks to Isabella, Christianity is the largest and most widespread religion in the world. She, an outsider, did it."

"So what? She was just one person, and you literally just walked me through the history of Christianity to highlight how most of its leaders failed to implement its spirit: Love. Peace. Tolerance. It's not about the numbers. Face it. None of that truly came about until modern democracy offered separation of state and religion; and with it freedom of and from religion."

The rueful nun lowered her gaze. "Yet again another reason why Mary may resort to outsiders."

Sofia studied her sister with sympathy. "The problem with insiders is that their loyalty can be blind. We all know the horrors committed in the name of blind faith in every religion, no exceptions." She then reached for her sister's hand and squeezed it. "But we also know of extraordinary insiders devoting their lives to doing the right thing as well. Maybe Mary wants one huge, global effort of teamwork inspired by faith and moderated by reason."

"Amen to that," said Lily squeezing her sister's hand back.

They smiled at each other.

"Well then," started Sofia with renewed energy, "we have a new path. Is this the one we follow to Fatima's Secret, or whatever it is Mary wants us to find?"

Lily hesitated. "I'm not sure. As I said, this is as far as I got in my research."

"Seriously? How do you expect me to help? I don't know anything about Spanish history."

"I do have an idea where it *might* lead, but I need your help to verify it."

"Okay, so where do you think it leads?"

"Right here, to Santa Fe."

Lily got up and gestured her sister to follow. She walked over to the gated chapel.

Sofia was puzzled. The gate guarded the only remaining vestige of the original St. Francis Church that had been torn down and replaced by the cathedral. The reason for its survival was the treasure it held: a three-foot statuette of a beautiful blue-eyed, dark-haired Virgin Mary. Her gaze wandered off into the distance as if lost in mournful meditation, for to Her left hung Her son crucified on the wall.

"Our Lady of the Rosary," announced Lily, pointing at the revered image. "She is what I wanted to show you."

Sofia studied her with deference. She was well acquainted with *La Conquistadora*, the oldest Madonna in the United States. Her annual procession through the city was followed with days of festivities, arts & crafts, parades and music. The Queen of Santa Fe, as she was also titled, was so sewn into the fabric of the city's identity that Sofia had not thought to single her out in the cathedral. The statuette had been carved in Spain long before the 17th century, though the exact date was unknown, and her garment painted in crimson with overlays of gold leaf in the arabesque style as if to dress a Moorish princess. However, few people ever saw this original gown, for she had a rich wardrobe counting well into the hundreds of garments. In Sofia's opinion, her most striking feature was the serene yet authoritative character of her poise.

La Conquistadora inspired respect, the type you didn't mess with.

"Apart from her link to the rosary, what else makes you think she is connected to Fatima?" asked Sofia, feeling oddly enchanted.

Lily cleared her throat. "A strong hunch based on a few coincidences. Not exactly what you like to hear, I'm afraid."

Suddenly, one of the coincidences struck Sofia. She shared it. "Santa Fe was known by our Puebloan ancestors as the *Dancing Grounds of the Sun*."

"Yes, I was hoping you'd pick up on that one." Lily started to look a little anxious. "Another is that, while it is not known how She made Her way across the Atlantic, we do know how She ended up here in Santa Fe."

Lily paused. She had been dreading this moment. She knew the *how* could rub her sister the wrong way.

"Well, are you going to tell me? How did she end up here?"

Lily took a deep breath. "It was Friar Alonso de Benavides; he brought Her in 1626. He had this chapel built just for Her. Later the cathedral was built around it."

Sofia froze. *So that was it*, she realized. The past several hours had been hazy for many reasons. To an extent, it made sense that Lily would be pursuing a Marian prophecy; her sister always carried herself as a chosen one for something. What did not make sense was Lily's persistence in dragging her into it. But the mention of Friar Benavides clarified it. It went back to another one of their mother's obsessions: The Lady in Blue. This was the legend of a Spanish nun who was said to have bilocated to the Americas to evangelize Native Americans. In the 17th century, Friar Benavides, while stationed in the Santa Fe area, encountered natives who talked about her miraculous visits, and he reported the oddity, making the legend over time become an integral part of Southwestern folklore. Their mother took the legend far too disturbingly serious because the rumor was that the Lady in Blue had appeared to one of their ancestors, which in turn justified the family's devotion to Christianity and their sense of fate.

Lily was trying to find the evidence that drove the Marian Lines home.

Sofia confronted her sister. "You're convinced you've been chosen like all those lady apostles, aren't you? You didn't stumble on John Paul II's hidden message; you think you were guided to it as you were guided to me in the well."

"Sof, you can't deny the signs. Yes, I do think I was guided, but I didn't come to you sooner because I feared that if I told you what I had found without more information you wouldn't help. Those lines are real. I didn't make them up. And I don't think our involvement in deciphering them is accidental."

"You mean *your* involvement. Just because you found me in the well doesn't mean I have to be involved. Why does it have to be a family affair?"

Lily bit her lip. Clearly, she was restraining herself. "I've already told you. I can't do it without you."

Sofia took a deep breath and closed her eyes momentarily. Her sister was right. She would not have collaborated. She would have gotten angry as she always did when the subject came up, and she would have accused her sister of pathetic superstition or something worse.

She opened her eyes again and turned them to the lovely statuette that waited patiently for her son's pain to have a meaning. Could it really be that she was destined alongside her sister to find a divine secret? Sofia chuckled to herself as a harder question came to mind: was she really entertaining such a possibility? Surprisingly, she was, and more surprisingly, it didn't bother her anymore. Her sister's strategy had worked. Chosen or not, the two lines were incredibly intriguing, and her skeptic curiosity wanted to see the puzzle put together.

Sofia slowly turned her head to scan her surroundings, avoiding her sister's gaze a little longer. She wasn't quite ready yet to admit surrender. Could the secret be hidden in the cathedral, right there at their reach? She saw the signs to the crypt. "If we have to go down there to find your message, you're on your own," she finally said, only half-jokingly, to overcome her pride.

Lily released a soft sigh of relief, but, wisely cautious, picked her words carefully, "I don't know if it's here. All I know is that there is yet another coincidence pointing to Santa Fe."

"What?"

Lily motioned toward the statuette. "She, *La Conquistadora*, is connected to the Lady in Blue through Friar Benavides, and the Lady in Blue is, in turn, connected to Queen Isabella in a very fundamental way."

Sofia narrowed her stare. That series of connections was flimsy at best. A simple four-degree separation in the Six Degrees of Separation principle. But she listened.

"There is another enterprise that Queen Isabella undertook which is very little known: It was she who personally got involved in helping St. Beatrice to establish the Order of the Immaculate Conception."

Though it was vaguely familiar, Sofia made it abundantly clear she needed further explanation to connect the dots. "Who? What?"

Lily's hands started to gesture as they usually did when she got excited. "Isabella's mother was Portuguese. When her mother moved to Spain to marry her father the King of Castile, she was accompanied by Beatrice da Silva, her lady-in-waiting. Beatrice was said to be of extraordinary beauty, thus the king, as everyone else in the court, was bewitched by it. Isabella's mother, who is reported to have been unstable emotionally or mentally, maybe both, became dreadfully jealous. Legend has it that she lured Beatrice to the dungeons and locked her up in a chest. During this scary episode, St. Beatrice received the visit of Our Lady who consoled her and assured her she'd be freed to pursue a special mission. Three days later, and thanks partly to the intervention of Beatrice's father, she escaped her imprisonment and fled to a Dominican monastery in Toledo where she led a life of holiness for the next thirty-seven years, though never became a member. She stubbornly chose to remain another outsider." Lily sighed in resignation. "Anyway, maybe to make up for what her mother had done, or because Isabella was on a divine mission of her own, when she grew up, Isabella befriended Beatrice and agreed to support her promise of founding a new order in gratitude to Our Lady. Isabella donated the Palaces of Galiana in Toledo to the cause." Lily's eyes began to sparkle. "Guess what the new monastery was named?"

"Santa Fe," whispered Sofia recognizing the legend.

Lily was now beaming. "Then you should also know that aside from donating palaces and mediating with the pope so that St. Beatrice could found the Conceptionist Order, Isabella went as far as to personally design their conspicuous blue cape. Can you believe it? It was Queen Isabella who designed the blue cape that gives the Lady in Blue her name."

Sofia's jaw dropped to the floor.

CHAPTER 22

Sofia needed some fresh air. She signaled it to her sister and pivoted on her heels to head toward the exit when the flicker of the votive candles burning for Mary broke her flight. She stood frozen. They were calling to her. Candles always did. She teetered. Generally, she'd ignore them. Today, for the first time in twenty-five years, she resolved not to fight the spell.

Sofia turned and approached the candle table. Slowly, she reached for a stick, dipped its end in one of the burning flames and proceeded to light a solitary one in the corner of the candle tray. The gentle ritual submerged her in a long-time evaded memory. It placed her back in the well. It was deep, humid, and dark. She was terrified ... until *She* appeared, the most beautiful woman Sofia had ever seen dressed in a magnificent glow. In one hand, the woman held a candle. Its defused light helped smooth the rough walls that imprisoned Sofia while highlighting the vision's comforting smile.

Then the woman spoke ...

"Sof," interrupted Lily, "are you all right. You look pale."

"I'm fine," she lied, and forced a grin.

"Let's see about that fresh air and get something to eat while at it," suggested Lily.

"No, I've changed my mind. I'd rather not waste any more time. Please go on." Sofia finished lighting the small flame and replaced the stick in its holder.

Lily observed, hopeful. She had spent the same twenty-five years waiting for her sister to open up about that day. It would appear the time was near. She'd be patient a little longer.

Sofia turned, urging her sister with a set gaze to continue.

Lily complied. "So, um, as you see, Queen Isabella designing the famous blue cape can't be coincidental. This was a woman who discovered the Americas leading her little realm to rule the globe, all the while raising five children, strategically uniting the surrounding realms to create Spain as we know it today, and keeping her husband, the Church and potential invading forces in check. Finding the time or care to design a cape that defines none other than the Lady in Blue has to be a sign of something. It just has too! The

Lady in Blue must tie into this somehow, and you know more about her than anyone, even mom.

Sofia didn't know about that. What crossed her mind was that comparing her life accomplishments to those of that queen made her feel utterly unsuited to be chosen for anything.

She rubbed her temples. "Let's refocus. We have two lines. One is Mary's Line which crosses Europe from Moscow to Fatima. It, in turn, gives us the clues to construct a second line specific to Spain. Then based on some interesting coincidences, you have concluded that the Spanish Line points to Santa Fe where, either *La Conquistadora* or the Lady in Blue, perhaps both, hold more clues." Sofia was doing this mental exercise for her own benefit. She looked at the statuette. "The lines are straight and meaningful. If they are going to point to Santa Fe, or more specifically to Her, it has to be with something more substantial than a few interesting coincidences." She turned to her sister. "Do you have any idea how *La Conquistadora* made it to America from Spain?"

"There are no records, but I have a theory."

"You keep using that word. What you may have, in any case, is a hypothesis, and it's only good if it is linked to the lines."

"Absolutely," smiled Lily, amused by her sister's pickiness. "So, here's the thing: Everywhere the Black Madonnas are referred to as just that, black. Everywhere, that is, except for in Spain. There, they've always been labelled the *Morenitas*, an endearing nickname meaning something like the 'little tanned ones'. This is significant considering Spain's role in the evangelization of America." Lily raised her hand and placed its back against the skin of her face. "We are not black but rather tanned, and that subtle difference was crucial to Our Lady of Guadalupe's success among indigenous people in Mexico and contributed to her rapid spread throughout the rest of the Americas."

"Right, Our Lady of Guadalupe in Mexico derives from of Our Lady of Guadalupe in Spain, whose tanned features made her easily relatable." Again, Sofia repeated this for her own benefit. It helped structure the information and ease the choke point in her head, which was imperative if she was expected to start figuring things out from this point.

"Exactly. And that's how we get from Spain to America. Because think about this: most of the initial explorers were originally from Extremadura, a Spanish province with no access to the sea but home to Isabella's *paradise*, the Shrine of Our Lady of Guadalupe. So not only was this shrine where the queen signed off the discovery of America, it was its image who accompanied most early explorers. They venerated her and thus took her with them. Further, when Hernan Cortes, who was born in Medellin, a town not far from Guadalupe, conquered Tenochtitlan, capital of the Aztec Empire, he carried a banner emblazoned with her imagen. It is well recorded how much he worshiped her."

Sofia twisted her face as if struck by pain. "Lily, I don't know where you are going with this but considering the casualties on both sides, I'd hate to think that that was what Mary wanted."

"Our Lady wanted slaughter in her name as much as God wanted witches burned on the stake in his. Humans have the vicious and innate ability to corrupt everything. For this reason, I also believe she was as horrified with the Aztecs as she was with the Old World's doings. Like we said before, brutality, slavery and human sacrifice were widespread here as everywhere else. Some of our native brothers were more blood-thirsty than others for sure, but it was a common theme throughout all America. Let's not forget our own Puebloan sacrificial and cannibalistic deeds recently uncovered in Mesa Verde. In the particular case of the Aztecs, at the time of the European arrival, it is calculated that tens of thousands of men, women and children were sacrificed annually. Warriors were trained to wound —not kill— in order to collect as many live victims as possible for the blood fest."

Lily paused.

"Sof, it would be there, at the capital of the Aztecs, where the brutality of two worlds clashed, where Our Lady of Guadalupe from the Old World appeared to a native of the New World, leading to the establishment of the most popular and visited Marian Shrine—not only in Mexico—but in the whole world today. If that's not a divine extension of the Spanish line to America, we might as well give up right now."

For Sofia it wasn't as clear cut. Lily was relying on personal impressions and unverifiable miracles to make her case. Worse yet, she had bent a straight line, which was the only verifiable fact they had. Sofia pictured it in her head.

The extension of the Spanish Line beyond Guadalupe, without bending it, had it crossing the Atlantic to Brazil. Far from Mexico, and further yet from Santa Fe. Meaning that, the only thing keeping her hooked to this mission was being brushed away.

Sofia sighed. It was becoming hard to simply stick to facts. Because, on the other hand, the overarching symbolism of the universal Mother Goddess pleading for all her children to stop the madness was powerful. Maybe, if only out of respect for that, she'd humor her sister ... reluctantly.

"So, you have extended the Spanish Line across the Atlantic by breaking it and leaving us with an extraordinary leap of faith as only recourse to link the Shrine of Guadalupe in Spain with her notable shrine in Mexico."

Her sister's blunt skepticism did not faze Lily. She nodded.

"Okay, then. Where does she come in?" asked Sofia, pointing at *La Conquistadora*.

"I'm getting there." Lily was unable to disguise the thrill she experienced sharing her *hypothesis*. "As I was saying, Our Lady of Guadalupe appeared to the native Juan Diego in 1531 on the Hill of Tepeyac just north of Mexico City. The reason he was able to recognize Her as Our Lady of Guadalupe was because there was a chapel there dedicated to Her with Her statuette. But that image would soon be replaced with a far more valuable relic. You see, when Juan Diego went to report the apparition to the archbishop of Mexico City, he was instructed to supply proof. Juan Diego asked Our Lady for one during a following apparition, and She happily provided it. Apparently, She appeared to him several times," clarified Lily. "So, despite it being winter, Our Lady of Guadalupe asked Juan Diego to collect flowers from the barren hilltop. Miraculously, of course, he found rose blossoms, but the type only native to Castile; a clear link back to Her shrine in Spain."

Lily's eyes began to sparkle as she continued. "Juan Diego placed the roses in his apron and ran to present them as proof to the archbishop. Upon opening the apron, the flowers fell to the floor revealing the miraculous image of Our Lady of Guadalupe emblazoned on the fabric." She felt the need for an incision. "Sof, that image, to this day, is a mystery. It has been thoroughly tested, but its enigmatic pigmentation, inexplicable craftsmanship, and strange resistance to decay remains unexplained." She continued. "In any case, and back to the story, the apron, or *tilma* as they call it, went on to replace the statuette in the chapel. With time, Our Lady of Guadalupe, whose image once led Hernan Cortes' men into the city of Tenochtitlan, three hundred years later led the country's independence movement, becoming the ultimate symbol of Mexico's Identity. The first President of the independent state even changed his own name to Guadalupe Victoria, meaning *Guadalupe Victory*. Understandably, it spread quickly throughout Central and Southern America."

Lily paused. "It's not clear what happened to the statuette when Juan Diego's *tilma* replaced it in the chapel. There are no records as far as I was able to find. However, records do say that when Friar Alonso de Benavides was promoted to custodian of New Mexico, he was searching in a warehouse in Mexico City for items to take with him, when he stumbled upon a box. Inside he found her, *La Conquistadora*."

"Wait," started Sofia, impressed. "So, you are implying that this statuette here, *La Conquistadora,* could be the same statuette of Our Lady of Guadalupe that ultimately gave rise to the most important Marian shrine in the world ..." Sofia assessed the image with renewed curiosity. "That would award her the medal to the most important divine marker of all."

"That's right. You see what I mean? The line leads here, it has to. Remember, we are to be attentive to the rosary, and She is Our Lady of the Rosary. So, the Spanish Line starts with St. Dominic's reception of the rosary in Prouille; then runs down through Zaragoza to the Shrine of Guadalupe in Spain. From there it makes its way to the Shrine of Guadalupe in Mexico, where Benavides finds her, extending the line north to Santa Fe. The evidence is overwhelming."

Sofia raised an eyebrow at Lily's loose understanding of the word "evidence". It was every researcher's temptation to force the outcome to expectation, and her sister had forced it enough to turn a straight line into an arch. She was having a hard time taking it seriously.

She looked up at the statuette. "I wonder if she hides the secret inside. Should we break her open?"

Lily's gaze turned to shock. "You'd better not, unless you want to be lynched by the locals, and me."

Sofia chuckled. "Relax, I was kidding."

"Luckily for you, it won't be necessary. In 1997 she was x-rayed. She's pretty solid. I wasn't relying on finding something inside, as much as outside. It was not all that uncommon for artists to carve messages on their statuettes as a way to leave their personal mark on their work. That's why we are here."

The two sisters appraised the statuette for a moment.

What a great story if it were true, thought Sofia. But she feared her sister would be disappointed. There was too much discord between straight lines designed according to tangible markers in Europe and the disorderly jump to Santa Fe based on an intangible miracle and a couple of hunches. They were missing something.

CHAPTER 23

Suddenly Sofia felt a cold breeze again. It brushed her arms as it headed toward the candles to play with their flames.

"Ladies," came a male voice from behind, "I couldn't help noticing you have been admiring our lovely Madonna for a while."

The sisters jolted and tuned to see who it was.

"I apologize," said a man with a dignified appearance. "I did not mean to startle you."

Tall and impeccably attired in a grey suit, his generous amount of neatly cut hair and trimmed moustache rejuvenated his otherwise conspicuous senior age.

"My name is Simon Gomez. I am a member of the *Caballeros de Vargas*. I'd be pleased to provide information on *La Conquistadora* if you seek it."

"I'm sorry," started Sofia, "you said you were a member of what exactly?"

"The *Caballeros de Vargas*. It is a brotherhood, if you may; the official Honor Guard of Our Lady *La Conquistadora*."

"Ah, yes, I've heard of you," said Lily as she offered her hand. "An old boy's club, if you may, that prides itself in perpetuating the fine virtues of Don Diego de Vargas, the peaceful conqueror of Santa Fe. Nice to meet you. My name is Lily Auru-Soto, and she is my sister Sofia."

Sofia remembered now. The brotherhood was central to the parades and fiestas celebrated in the Madonna's honor. She had always been curious about them.

"Why does she need guards?" she asked.

Mr. Gomez released Lily's hand and offered his to Sofia. "You'd be surprised, young lady. She was kidnapped in 1973 by two teenagers attempting to commit extortion. Our city mourned for three weeks. Fortunately, she was found unharmed. Be that as it may, our service is honorary in nature, one of old tradition. In truth, we are a colorful club dedicated to preserving the rich Spanish History, Culture and Faith of our Holy City. We work closely with the ancient confraternity that attends to her personal upkeep."

"That's a lot of people watching over her."

"Indeed, and we are all profoundly honored to do it," he smiled.

Lily could not believe their luck. "Perhaps you *can* help," she said. "You wouldn't know by any chance if the artist left a message on her?"

The *caballero* tilted his head slightly. "A very interesting question. Not really. The job of dressing her falls on the confraternity. They would be in a better position to know, though I've never heard anything to that respect. Why do you ask?"

"Just curious. I read somewhere that artists did that sometimes," replied Lily. "One other question if you don't mind: *La Conquistadora* and the Lady in Blue have Friar Alonso de Benavides as a common denominator. I was wondering if there were other associations you may be familiar with."

The senior gentlemen showed his surprise. "Well," he thought for a moment, "I would say we don't usually think of the Lady in Blue as a local legend. True she did appear in New Mexico and as far as Arizona; however, she belongs more to the Texan folklore."

Sofia was struggling to follow the conversation. She was distracted by the persistent chill. Where was the breeze coming from? Even the candle flames seemed to complain by showing unusual agitation ...

Then it hit her.

She stared at them. *Candles ... The candle ...* she recalled. *That was it. The woman in the well held a candle in her hand.* Sofia just realized the mistake her sister was making. It was as if a flash of lightning had her visualize the correct path in her mind. She'd have to confirm it on a map, but if she was right, Santa Fe was still in play. Her sister had got the destination right but had taken the wrong path to get there.

As usual, Lily was oblivious to her environment. "Folklore?" she asked, surprised. "You don't believe the story?"

Mr. Gomez offered an assured smile. "I am a man of unwavering faith, yet a nun claiming to bilocate across the Atlantic to preach to the Indians can hardly be taken seriously."

Lily was stunned. This seemed most uncharacteristic for a devoted Knight of Vargas. Traditional Catholic Faith was at the core of their loyalty to *La Conquistadora*. They took their faith and mission very seriously. "I do not see why not. Bilocation is a gift attributed to many great saints and mystics."

"With due respect, I must insist. Hundreds of men endured dear hardships in person to bring the Word to these lands. A simple, uneducated woman from her cloistered cell in Spain can't take the credit for their work and sacrifice."

Paying attention to the conversation again, Sofia was stunned; though it wasn't the debate over bilocation that had her baffled. It was the weird vocabulary. What was up with it lately? This man spoke and carried himself as if he had just walked out of the 19th century.

Meanwhile, Lily waved her hand at *La Conquistadora*. "You serve a simple, uneducated woman. How can you question the contributions of another?"

"My young lady, I beg you not to compare the Vessel of our Lord with a mere nun."

Sofia embraced herself. He should not have said that.

"A mere nun! That nun served as personal advisor to a king, wrote a bestseller based on the life of Our Lady, and converted my ancestor's by more peaceful means than some of those men you speak of. How can you discredit her merits like that?"

At the front of the cathedral, the doors opened. Sofia could see it was Michael visibly on alert. He turned his head in several directions, presumably looking for them.

"We reach an impasse," concluded Gomez with an unsettling sneer. "I consider it opportune to leave now." With a tilt of his head, he took off with haste.

"Unbelievable!" exclaimed Lily, fuming.

Sofia, a little more aware of what was going on around them, found the whole episode rather unnerving.

Michael approached them running followed closely by Gabriel.

"Is everything all right here?"

"Yes," said Lily shaking her head. "He was just another typical male chauvinist."

"Who?"

"What do you mean who? Simon Gomez, the man we were just talking to. He's a member of the *Caballeros de Vargas*, the group that helps promote devotion to *La Conquistadora*."

Michael's composure stiffened. "Which way did he go?"

Lily looked at him with surprise and pointed toward the altar.

"You stay here." Michael's order was addressed to Gabriel. He then ran off after Gomez.

The sisters exchanged concerned stares before settling their eyes inquisitively on Gabriel.

"If he didn't know we were talking to someone, what alerted him to come in?" asked Sofia.

The young man shrugged it off. "He has a sixth sense for these things."

Michael was quick to return. He was holding his phone to his ear. "Yes, good afternoon. I am trying to locate one of your members... His name is Simon Gomez... Are you sure? Could I have mistaken the name or surname?... No Simon or Gomez listed as member... Please, could you hold on a second?" Michael looked straight at Lily. "What did he look like?"

"Tall, maybe in his late 70s, still had plenty of brown hair, wore a trimmed moustache... distinguished looking..."

Michael returned his attention to the phone. "Sir, did you hear that?" The reply did not seem to please him. "I see. Well, thank you, anyway." He disconnected. "You described Captain Diego de Vargas, and half their membership takes pride in looking like him." Michael set his severe gaze on Lily. "I think it is safe to conclude he was an imposter. What did he want?"

"He offered to provide information about *La Conquistadora*."

"Did you tell him anything?"

Lily's chest swelled in proportion to the paling of her features. She brought her hand to her mouth in horror. "Oh no! I asked him if he knew of any association between *La Conquistadora* and the Lady in Blue. I'm so stupid. I blurted it all out with his first question."

"Lily, don't worry," comforted Sofia, "that hardly reveals anything."

"You don't understand. I make no mention of either one in my report. I just supplied that man with extra information."

"And with their resources, they'll jump ahead of us easily," added Michael.

Sofia examined him. "How did you know he was talking to us and that he could be of concern?"

"Call it a hunch," he grinned.

Sofia wasn't amused, and she showed it. "Don't dismiss me like that. Who are *they*, and what do you know about them?"

Lily interrupted: "Look!"

A group of five people, three men and two women, approached their corner with a purposeful gait.

They didn't appear to be menacing or even mindful of their presence, but Michael and Gabriel, nonetheless, positioned themselves in front of the sisters.

The group solemnly passed them by and stopped at the gate. The man at the front retrieved a key from his pocket to open its doors. The group followed him in. It was then they saw one of the women carrying an exact replica of the Madonna, though dressed slightly different. A second man carried a ladder. He opened it and placed it before the retablo. The man who had opened the gate climbed it, reached for the original Madonna and gently brought her down delivering her to the second lady. The woman with the replica then handed it to him, and he placed her on the spot. All the while the third man appeared to keep watch. When the switch was completed, the first man climbed back down. The group collected their things and began their retreat.

Lily stepped in front of Michael to address the first man who appeared to be the leader of the group. "I'm sorry, what are you doing? Where are you taking Her?"

The man, whose eyes reflected joviality, smiled making the rest of his face match them appropriately. "Oh, please don't fear. I am her *Mayordomo*. Our beloved *Conquistadora* has been claimed for a very special mission."

Lily knew that the *Mayordomo* was the president of the confraternity that took care of Her. But she also knew that *La Conquistadora* rarely left the chapel. That's what the replica was for. "What sort of mission?"

"She will preside over a mass at the Children's hospital."

"Is that usual?"

"Not quite. It was a special request from a very generous donor. His child has turned for the worse; it just happened this afternoon. It's very tragic. *La Peregrina* will take Her place until Her return."

Sofia stepped forward. "Shouldn't it be the other way around? It's *La Peregrina* who is taken out in her place in order to protect the original."

"That is correct. However, exceptions are sometimes granted, especially if children are involved. This is a severe and very urgent case. If you excuse me, we must be going."

Lily turned to Michael with despair. "What do we do? We need to stop them. It's clear the generous donor is Gomez."

Sofia reached rapidly for her sister's arm and pulled her back. When Lily looked at her, Sofia shook her head and signaled with her lips a stern order to stay put.

The group hurriedly left.

Lily then wasted no time to question her sister. "Why did you stop me? They have Her. What if there is a clue carved on Her?" She turned to Michael. "We must do something!"

"Gabriel and I will follow them. We'll see what we can find out."

"What about us?" Lily felt desperately helpless.

"You are going to have to figure out the Lady in Blue's role in all this and fast. If you come up with something, let me know."

"He's right," said Sofia. "We'll go to the library. It's not far from here. Maybe we can resolve it before they do."

Michael and Gabriel took off after the confraternity group.

Lily nodded, feeling the weight of failure on her shoulders. "I need a minute," she said. She stepped over to one of the pews and sat down. Her look of desolation was heartbreaking. "I've failed Her. I've failed Our Lady like everyone else over two thousand years before me. I failed. I failed. I failed—"

"Lily—"

"No, don't say anything. You don't understand. From that day you fell in the well, and She led me to you, I knew we were chosen. You might not believe it, but I always have. I've spent my life trying to figure out why; yearning to know what She wanted from us and hoping to live up to Her expectations."

"Lily, listen—"

"You know how I really figured out there were clues in John Paul II's homilies?"

Sofia wanted to say something but accepted it was better to let her sister vent first.

"In a dream, that's how. No, it wasn't through investigative work. It was handed to me in a dream. In it, I stood in the middle of a barren landscape. Only the horizon lay before me. Then John Paul II appeared beside me. He read me the two passages from his homily and then pointed to the ground. A path formed making its way to the horizon. As I followed it, you know who stood at the end?" Lily set her wrenched stare on Sofia. "You! The path led to you! I'm always led to you! They don't want me, Sof. They want you!" Lily lowered her gaze. "They want the outsider, and it is obvious why. We the insiders perpetually fail them." Lily hid her face in her hands.

Sofia sat with care next to her and wrapped an arm around her shoulders. She spoke softly. "You have it all wrong, Lily. You misinterpreted the signs."

Lily raised her watering eyes with a furrowed brow. "What do you mean?"

"Mary fed you a single clue in a dream. From it you've unraveled the greatest quest of all time; a two-thousand-year plan to have a simple message delivered to all humankind. Most have been blind to it. Only you saw it. Lily, you *are* the path."

Her eyes dithered confused. "What about you? Why am I always led to you?"

Sofia smiled. "Like the rosary was given to St. Dominic as his tool, I'm given to you as yours. A certain someone central to this mission expressed it most eloquently:

'Faith and Reason are like two wings on which the human spirit rises to the contemplation of truth; and God has placed in the human heart a desire to know the truth.'

Illumination lit Lily's face. "John Paul II. I guess it makes sense. I am Faith and you are Reason ... teamwork." She nonetheless sighed. "Still, I have failed as did St. Dominic."

Sofia jumped to her feet. "Nonsense! You simply made a very convenient mistake that will keep them distracted for a while."

"What do you mean?" Lily rose to her feet as well.

"They won't find anything on *La Conquistadora*. As with all the other statuettes, she is but a marker. No doubt important to sketch a divine line, but meaningless if you don't know where the other ones are."

"Are you saying there are more?"

A broad triumphant smile crossed Sofia's face. "And I know exactly where."

CHAPTER 24

Sofia led out the front doors of St. Francis as Lily followed behind excitedly.

"Where are we going?"

"To the library."

"Still? I thought you said you knew where the other markers were?"

"I have a strong suspicion but need to confirm it."

They reached *E. Palace Ave.* and turned left.

Sofia took a deep breath. "Lily, there is one thing I never told you about my experience in the well."

Lily felt her heart perform a somersault.

"I didn't simply hit my head and go unconscious. I was well awake and terrified after falling. You know how I feel about tight spaces, and it was dark." Sofia looked at her sister askance. "Mary appeared to me. At least, I think it was her." She quickly removed her gaze and looked forward. "At the time, it felt real. Afterwards, I concluded it was a dream or an illusion. Now I wonder if there is something else at play. What I'm trying to say is that I'm not ready to settle for a miracle and leave it at that. Nature is rich with miracles that we've been able to explain through science. But if I'm confessing this to you it's because that experience helped me moments ago fill in an important gap in your research. And I want to understand why."

Lily didn't dare say a word. She had waited too long for this confession. She simply nodded.

"As I remember it," continued Sofia, "when she appeared, in her left hand she held a lit candle and in the right one a rosary. She then smiled and asked me not to fear, which was needless since her bright presence had comforted me already. Then she said: 'If you ever find yourself lost, follow the light'. As she did so, she brought the candle across to illuminate the rosary. Finally, she smiled again and said, 'now you may sleep my dear child', or something like that. I'm not sure. I heard the last words as I passed out."

The sisters kept quiet as they reached *Washington Ave* and turned right.

Lily's eyes had welled again. "I always knew there was more to your story. Thank you for sharing it with me. Can I ask you a question?"

"Sure."

"Even if you thought it was just a dream, why did you keep it to yourself? Why deny it?"

"You know I never shared the intensity of your spirituality. Since mom has an altar at home with candles and a rosary, I concluded I had merely incorporated elements of my environment into the dream. Especially since it was dark; the candle made sense as wishful thinking. Then your side of the story alone was enough to have everyone harass us. We became a freak show. I dreaded all those people following us everywhere and trying to touch us, calling us *little angels* and all that. I still get goosebumps just thinking about it."

Upon reaching the library front, Sofia stopped to face Lily.

"I was scared, all right? I was scared of what it could mean. I guess you are braver than I am. For you to be chosen was inspiring, for me it was unnerving. It's the reason I set out to study the Lady in Blue and so much more, to ground it in reasonable facts that I could handle."

"I wasn't all that brave," confessed Lily. "I was probably as scared as you, but my way of dealing with it was finding refuge in Faith. It could be said that while you worked hard to make sense of it, I chose not to think about it at all. It was easier to let others tell me what to think. I obediently accommodated to the traditional Truth of how these things were to be understood."

Sofia laughed. "Not for long. You're possibly the most rebellious nun I've ever known."

"It took me a while, but I finally came around," giggled Lily.

They stood quietly for a moment looking at each other.

Lily then hugged her sister gently. "I'm happy you finally confided in me," she whispered into her ear.

"I should have a long time ago."

Bells tolled on the hour in the distance.

"Shoot!" exclaimed Sofia, stepping back. "We better hurry. The library will close soon."

She sprinted toward the library's front door cutting through the courtyard.

Lily sped to catch up. "So, what are we looking for?"

"Maps."

Inside, Sofia walked up to the reception desk.

"Excuse me. Where can I find maps?"

The lady she addressed took a moment to look at her and her sister, performing the usual double take they were accustomed to. "It depends. Are you looking for a city map or a country map?"

"I'll need a world map and a map of the Southwest. One of Spain, too, if possible."

The woman gestured to a far end of the building. "Over there to the left of the table."

"May I also borrow a ruler, please?"

"Yes, certainly."

The librarian took a quick look around her station and seeing there were none signaled she'd be right back.

Lily leaned into Sofia's ear.

"I'm guessing you don't want to use the maps on my phone. You think we are being tracked with it?"

"Correct."

"Shall I get rid of it?"

"Yes, leave it on, but mute it," she whispered.

Lily reached for it and did as instructed.

"Here, now give it to me," said Sofia. She took the phone, reached over the reception counter and dropped it in an open box on the floor. The shadows hid it from plain view.

"What if Michael tries to get hold of us?"

"He knows where to find us."

"What if we want to contact him?"

"Old-fashioned, library phone. I still have the note that Dan gave me with his number in my pocket."

Lily looked at her sister. "It's Michael, isn't it? Why don't you trust him?"

"I told you. Something about him does not add up. I can't put my finger on it. He seems too comfortable with his bodyguard role."

"And I explained it comes natural to him. He risked his life to help a boy."

"I don't deny it. By he is hiding something. How do you think he knew we were talking to the old man?"

Lily shrugged her shoulders.

Sofia told her. "I bet he asked Gabriel to hack your phone to listen into our conversations. That's how."

Lily pouted. "If it turns out that he is one of them, I'll never be able to trust anybody again."

Seeing her sister's disappointment, she threw her a rope.

"Don't think the worse. He could just be an overly zealous journalist not wanting to miss out on any detail of his big story. I'm simply saying we should be cautious, that's all." She changed the subject. "As for *them*... I'd love to know who the heck we're up against."

Lily gave her sister a somber look. "Maybe it's just *He*."

Sofia rolled her eyes. "Please spare me the Devil allusion. There is enough evil in humans to have to worry about a mythical dragon with horns, or goat, or whatever it is."

The librarian returned with the ruler.

Sofia took it with a thank you, grabbed a pencil from a cup on the counter, put there for the library's patrons, and proceeded to the area indicated. They retrieved the maps they needed from the shelf and brought them to the table nearby. Sofia rolled the world map open first. Lily placed books on the corners as holders.

The two sisters leaned over it.

With pencil in hand, Sofia then went on to mark the sites of the shrines. She located Lourdes, in France, and Fatima, in Portugal, quickly.

"What was the name of the Polish shrine again?"

"It's here in Czestochowa." Lily pointed to the spot.

Sofia marked it.

"And this is Altötting in Germany."

Sofia marked it as well.

"I don't think you should be writing on the map," said Lily.

"I promise to make a generous donation," responded Sofia, while concentrating on connecting the shrines with the pencil along the ruler's edge. She then stood back to admire the miracle. She couldn't get over it. It was wild, wild enough to have the better of her seriously considering an unearthly intervention.

"Don't forget Moscow," reminded Lily.

Sofia completed the line to the East, though her real interest for now was in the West.

"Did you ever continue the line across the Atlantic to see where it took you?"

"Yes. It crosses through Venezuela and Colombia."

"And?"

"Nothing." Lily shrugged. "There are Marian shrines in those countries, no doubt. They are all very Catholic. But I couldn't find any reasonable connection to Mary's Line."

Sofia extended the line across the ocean. "So, you disregarded potential evidence because it didn't fit your preconceived expectations." Sofia clicked her tongue as she shook her head with an angled grin. "Not very scientific. It's no wonder Mary needs me."

"You're going to rub it in my face every chance you get, aren't you?"

"Absolutely!" chuckled Sofia. "That's what big sisters are for."

"Then report big sis: What does your scientific approach say?"

"Hold it, I'm not done. You'll see."

Having completed Mary's Line, Sofia reached for Spain's map. It was a little smaller, so she was able to place it on the right side overlapping the bottom corner of the world map for an easy viewing of both. She then drew the Spanish Line starting in Prouille, running it through Zaragoza, but rather than stopping in Guadalupe, her pencil continued to one more location. She then circled the name of the two cities where each line had been extended to.

Lily shook her head in disbelief. "How in the world did I miss that?"

CHAPTER 25

Lily was more in shock than disappointed with herself. "Both lines end in cities named Medellin."

Sofia nodded as her grin grew broader to boast she had known from the offset they would. Her hunch was confirmed.

"Medellin in Spain is the town where Hernan Cortes was born," recalled Lily.

"I know. It caught my attention when you mentioned it earlier. Things started to add up a little then."

"How does he come into play? He's hardly someone I'd think Our Lady would choose for anything, let alone to be one of Her apostles."

"She probably had no choice. It's not like they were sending pious women over here to do the exploring and evangelizing."

"Well, technically, one did come."

"Yes, right, the Lady in Blue. In any event, I don't think Cortez's role was that of an apostle, but rather a clue. Hernan Cortes was a devoted believer. On one hand he worshiped Our Lady of Guadalupe, but, on the other, he also venerated another depiction of Mary; one he carried on a medallion around his neck. Most Spanish adventurers and sailors of the time did."

"Who?"

"Our Lady of Candelaria, otherwise known as Our Lady of the Candle or Candlemas in English."

Lily recognized her immediately. "Yes, she is yet another miraculous Black Madonna."

"Then, you should also know of her association with your precious Queen Isabella."

"Of course ..." whispered Lily, retrieving the information from her memory. "Devotion to *La Candelaria* started in the Canary Islands, more specifically in Tenerife, where two local natives found Her statuette back in the 14th century. It must have fallen off a Christian boat and washed up on the beach. The natives associated Her with their Mother Goddess and venerated Her in a cave nearby, until quite some time later a converted native recognized Her as the Christian Mary. Her first official Catholic mass was held two centuries later when Queen Isabella took over the islands around the time of the discovery of America."

Sofia picked up from there. "And due to their strategic location in the Atlantic, the port of Tenerife was designated the last stop in Castilian territory before heading across the ocean. That's the reason many explorers and sailors carried Our Lady of Candelaria close, because their last prayers were offered to Her before departing to the unknown. As the port of departure and entry, the islands developed strong ties with the Americas, so later in the 17th century, when an economic crisis hit them hard, a massive flow of emigrants headed to South America. For political reasons of the day, Venezuela was particularly favored, and a large group settled in Caracas, bringing their Patroness with them. There is a major Candelaria Shrine there."

Sofia stabbed the map where Mary's Line cut right down the middle of the Venezuelan capital, as she continued. "It's estimated that up to 70% of the white population in the region is descendent from the Canary Islands alone." Then she dragged the tip of her finger along the line, across to Colombia and stopped at the end of it. "Consequently, her devotion spread fast. Our Lady of Candelaria is also the Patroness of Medellin in Colombia."

Lily narrowed her stare as she realized something. "Our Lady of the Candle receives that name because the Black Madonna found on the beach in Tenerife holds a candle in her left hand. In the vision you had, Mary held one in her left hand as well. Is that why you know so much about the Candelaria and her worship?"

"Yes," confessed Sofia.

"How does She help us move forward, though? I get it that She is worshiped along Mary's line in South America, but Her Black Madonna is in the Canary Islands, and neither line cuts through them."

Sofia locked her smiling eyes with her sisters'.

"She fills an important gap in your hypothesis. You were wrong about the Spanish Line leading to Santa Fe. But you were right about *La Conquistadora* being a marker as a result of connecting to another marker, or better said two, in San Antonio, Texas."

"Come again."

"Look, around the same time that immigrants from the Canaries settled in Venezuela and Colombia, Spain was having trouble fending off French incursions here in the Southwest. Large groups from the Canaries were therefore encouraged to also settle in New Spain to secure the area. Fifteen families landed in Texas and founded the city of San Antonio. They, too, immediately proceeded to build a shrine, which inevitably was dedicated to their beloved Patroness, Our Lady of Candelaria."

"Excuse me. If my leap from Guadalupe, Spain, to Guadalupe, Mexico, was questionable because it bent the Spanish Line, how do you justify a random leap from Medellin in Colombia to San Antonio in Texas?"

"First, you didn't bend the Spanish Line, you curled it. Second, all you had was a miracle and an unverifiable guess that *La Conquistadora* is the same statuette replaced by the miraculous tilma."

"Yeah? Well, all you have is a vision of a candle."

Sofia was now the one enjoying her ability to stun her sister. "What I have is a process that stays true to the lines. By keeping them straight, they led us to two cities with the same name. Then, you, yourself, pointed out that Mary's Line provides clues on how to construct the Spanish Line. Consequently, if both lines lead to cities named Medellin, it follows that the Medellin on Mary's Line is trying to tell us something about the Medellin on the Spanish Line. Which it does."

Lily was blown away. "How would you even know? When did you learn about these cities to know?"

"I don't need to know about these cities. I only need to know about the history of Our Lady of Candelaria and, as you would say, *it just so happens* that the full original name of the Columbian Medellin was 'The Town of Our Lady of Candelaria of Medellin.'"

Lily blinked at the unusual long name. "That's a mouthful ..."

"Which makes it difficult to forget, especially since I also know that Medellin in Spain—after which it was being named—did not worship Our Lady of Candelaria. I always thought it was strange. Now I realize it was a clue, because what 'Lady of Candelaria of Medellin' do you think it is referring to if she wasn't worshiped there?" With a wave of her eyebrows, Sofia welcomed her sister to answer.

"The one its most famous resident, Hernan Cortes, wore around his neck."

Sofia nodded. "That has to be it, right? I mean, there was no other Candelaria related to that town. But he also worshiped Our Lady of Guadalupe. Therefore, just like both Ladies converge on him, I think the lines are trying to tell us to look for a shrine where they also come together."

Lily crossed her arms and glanced at her sister, shaking her head. "And you still don't believe in miracles? Do you realize Mary had a city named with a whole sentence just to guide you the right way?"

"I realize someone went to a lot of trouble to draw lines across the world. The who, how, and why is up for debate."

"Someone? Mary appeared to you with a candle in her hand so you could follow Her clues. You literally saw her with your own eyes."

"I also see colors everyday and yet they don't exist; it's my brain interpreting the wavelengths of light. Lily, I'm with you. You stumbled on something powerful here, and I'm willing to call it Mary for now. But until I don't get a chance to thoroughly study it, I'm not settling for any explanation."

Lily raised her eyes to the ceiling and said, "Please forgive her. Somewhere deep, deep, deep inside, she is good at heart."

"Real cute."

"Just looking out for you."

"Can we get back to this," said Sofia, tapping the map.

"Sure, you believe the shrine where both Ladies converge is in San Antonio."

"I don't believe. I know. Before the Canary settlers founded San Antonio, soldiers and natives from Mexico had set up a presidio there. Their loyalties were to Our Lady of Guadalupe. They demanded that she have a prime presence in the new church as well. So, the soldiers, the natives and the new settlers all reached a compromise. They agreed to consecrate the Cathedral of San Antonio, the oldest cathedral in the United States, to both, Our Lady of Guadalupe and Our Lady of Candelaria."

Lily did not need any more convincing, but for the sole purpose of teasing her sister she questioned the logic. "Very impressive, but when it comes down to it, your leap of faith is almost worse than mine. You left

Mary's Way hanging in Medellin, Colombia, and jumped to San Antonio, Texas, where you fashioned a third line by connecting San Antonio to Santa Fe. That is only two points, which is unremarkable for a straight line, and more so since there is no pattern. Because what links San Antonio to Santa Fe?"

"The oldest cathedral to the oldest church and the oldest Madonna in the United States, plus a little something else."

Sofia gave her sister a triumphant look and doubled over the world map reaching for the ruler. She ran the pencil from Santa Fe to San Antonio and then continued south through the Gulf of Mexico and the Yucatan Peninsula all the way to Medellin.

"There, better?" she said as she straightened back up. "Dear little sister, faith-leaping is your thing, not mine. Santa Fe and San Antonio are connected on a perfectly straight line with Medellin, Colombia, where they link to *Mary's Way*."

Lily fanned her face with her hand. She could feel her cheeks flare up with the excitement. "WOW! Just, WOW!"

Sofia's smile turned smug. She wasn't done stunning her sister. She reached for the third map. This one framed Central America, the Gulf of Mexico, and the Caribbean. But it also covered a large section of the Southwest of the United States, allowing for better appreciation of finer details than the broader world map. She laid it over the previous two, having the books now hold down all three. She then redrew Mary's Line, only this time she added an extra mark to the line between Santa Fe and San Antonio.

She stepped away. "*Voila*," she exclaimed.

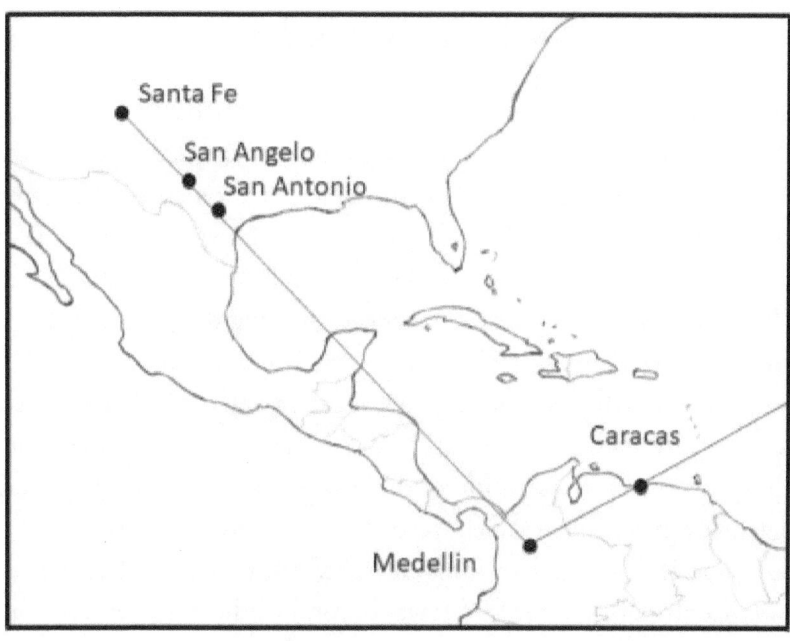

Lily looked at the map and back at her sister. "What?"

"Don't you see?"

Lily squinted as she looked closer at the location. "I don't understand. Why did you mark San Angelo in Texas?" Then it dawned on her. Her eyes shot wide open. "Holy Mother of God!"

CHAPTER 26

Lily marveled at the wonder her sister had performed. Not only had she confirmed with a tangible line a wishful leap, but she had also located the Lady in Blue's connection to the Divine Line. San Angelo was the camping grounds of the Jumano Indians who claimed to be visited by the Lady in Blue. They weren't the only ones. But they were the ones interviewed by Friar Benavides, whose report then reached the king of Spain and the pope, contributing to cementing the legend.

For this reason, today, San Angelo was the capital of the Lady in Blue.

And, to Lily's delight, it was on Mary's Line. "I knew it! I knew she was somehow involved in this. With all the stunts she pulled off, she fitted the ultimate pattern; she qualified as one of Mary's apostles. I knew it!"

Sofia nodded. "Looks like you were right." She then considered her sister. This was deeply personal for Lily. It was beyond vindicating the contribution of yet another extraordinary woman to her faith. For Lily, it was about validating her family's sense of destiny. And she, Sofia, the black sheep, had helped her do it.

Lily shook her hands with excitement. "Tell me everything you know about her. She is the key to finding what we are looking for. She has to be!"

Sofia cupped one hand on her waist while leaning with the other on the table. "Why is it that you don't know more about her? Apart from mom's stories, you are a Catholic sister in the Southwest. That alone should make *you* the expert."

Lily shrugged dismissively. "I took her for granted. For me, her miracles were part of a tradition where miracle-workers abound. I never thought to inquire any further beyond her religious persona. Until now, that is. I had plans to do it. Never got the chance."

"She's not just any miracle-worker. She is one closely related to our family. Didn't that pique your curiosity?"

"Sof, I'm not like you. I'm not captivated by the fine details. It's the big picture I care about."

Sofia drew a wry grin. "Leave it to a skeptic to be the source of information for a bilocating nun." She stood straight again. "Fine, here's what

I know: She was born Maria Coronel y Arana in 1602, in a small town called Ágreda, in Spain, very close to Zaragoza. Her family was extremely religious, if not outright fanatical. Since the Inquisition was still alive and strong, it is suspected that her parents' intense devotion was to make up for their Jewish ancestry. They couldn't hide it since theirs was from a renowned lineage—" An unexpected connection gave Sofia pause. "I just realized it isn't only the blue cape that connects her to Queen Isabella. One of Maria's ancestors was a high-ranking administrator at her service. You might know him ... something Coronel, I can't remember his first name."

"Coronel...?" deliberated Lily, "Yes, I think you are referring to Abraham Senior. He was one of the queen's most trusted allies from an early age. He even intervened in her secret marriage to Fernando. When the Jewish exile was enforced, Isabella convinced him to convert under her protection to save him and his family from having to leave. He took the Christian name Fernando in honor of the king, probably to ingratiate himself with him." Lily grinned. "The baptismal ceremony happened precisely at the Shrine of Guadalupe, and Isabella presided as Godmother." Lily shook her head. "Amazing ... that queen's reach never ends. By protecting him, later one of his descendants would become none other than the Angel-Winged, Blue Nun of the Southwest."

Sofia chuckled at the extravagant description. "Yes, well, going on, Maria's mother converted their home into a Conceptionist Monastery, having her daughters join it. Maria was a teenager. She took the name Sister Maria de Jesus and soon displayed mystical giftedness such as performing levitations and experiencing raptures. They were widely witnessed, so word got out quickly, reaching the ears of the Inquisition, who decided to leave her be for the time being. Shortly thereafter, she starts saying that during her trances she is transported by saints and angels, namely St. Francis and St. Michael, to a strange land with strange peoples who she teaches the Gospel to. Her confessor is impressed by this and decides to send a letter to the Archbishop of Mexico to inquire if the friars have heard of a mysterious nun preaching in the area. Meanwhile, in New Spain, missionaries are, in fact, coming across unrelated tribes who seem oddly familiar with the Christian liturgy."

"Yes, such as the Jumanos from San Angelo." Lily was in rapture herself, thrilled that the family's legend was linked to the line. She looked down at the map. "Growing up and hearing these stories, I always wondered why Our Lord would go to all the trouble of flying a nun across the ocean to preach when the Franciscan friars were already in the area. There must have been a special reason. Now I'm convinced it's related to Fatima. It must be."

Sofia winced. "Lily, this might disappoint you. What most people don't know is that the Jumanos encountered Spaniards as early as 1535. They had been exposed to Catholic ways long before theses impressionable missionaries arrived."

"It was more than just being exposed. The Jumanos showed up at the Isleta Mission asking for a friar to go live with them because a divine woman had instructed them to. It's recorded."

"They were suffering Apache raids. It is very likely that they told the friars what they wanted to hear as a way to lure them into their settlements. They were in search of protection, not spiritual guidance."

Lily insisted. "Her visits are quoted at over 500, expanding as far as Kansas and Arizona. For decades the Spaniards continued to encounter Native Americans across the Southwest who remembered her. There are many testimonies of natives requesting blue cloth for burials and shrines. They genuinely believed in her."

"True. But by then the word had gotten around and the Franciscans were all too happy to feed the legend. The Jumanos, as other pacific tribes, were forced to find refuge closer to Spanish settlements due to the aggressive advance of the Apaches, the Comanche, the Navajos and the Utes. To this day, the Lady in Blue represents a symbol of protection."

Lily pouted haughtily. "Congratulations on ruining our beautiful legend."

"To Maria de Jesus' credit, there is much about her that remains fascinating. She doesn't require miracles to justify her worth."

"She might not, but we do if we are to find a Divine Message. Please, keep going. You'll see, I'll be the last to laugh as usual."

If there was one thing Sofia had learned in the past several hours, it was that that could very well be.

She continued. "As we were saying, the Jumanos showed up in Isleta Mission one summer asking for a friar to go back with them to San Angelo. Friar Juan de Salas, who was in charge, could not spare one because he was shorthanded, but recorded the oddity, because, as you can imagine, he wasn't used to natives walking in voluntarily asking to be converted. Then in 1629, a new custodian arrived in Santa Fe to replace Friar Benavides, carrying a letter from the archbishop of Mexico inquiring about the mysterious nun. That's when Friar Juan de Salas, who was in Santa Fe to welcome the new custodian, remembered the oddity and informed the new custodian and Benavides about it. Since it is summer, the Jumanos were scheduled to show up for trading purposes. The three men set out to the mission to investigate the enigma. When they asked the Jumanos why they wanted a friar, these revealed the existence of the Lady in Blue. They explained that a beautiful, young woman had been descending from the sky dressed in blue and spending time with them teaching them many things. One day, she told them about the Spaniards that would come and instructed them to go ask for a friar because she no longer could continue to visit." Sofia leaned in to share an anecdote she knew her sister would like. "Maria de Jesus later told Benavides, when they met, that, indeed, that had happened. She thought better to end her travels when the Inquisition knocked on her door."

Lily smiled.

Sofia continued. "Having been replaced, Benavides heads back to Mexico with the stunning story, and the archbishop dispatches him to Spain to inform the king about it. It's 1630, and Benavides writes his invaluable *Memorial* for the king, a comprehensive report on the state of the missions and settlements of New Mexico. It's considered of great historical value for its detailed descriptions of the American Southwest and our people. In it he reports on the Lady in Blue and connects her to Sr. Maria de Jesus. Then he wastes no time heading to the town of Ágreda to meet her in person. She turns out to be just like the Jumanos had described her: young, beautiful, and a Conceptionist nun wearing a blue cape. In turn, she confirms much of what he knows to be true about them and the geography of the area. He adds these new findings to his revised *Memorial* of 1634, which he delivers to the pope in Rome. This time the Inquisition decides to pay a visit to check her out. But so does the king. Having read his copy of the *Memorial*, King Felipe IV is captivated by her story and schedules a stop to meet her on his way to battle. They hit it off, and she becomes his spiritual and political advisor for the next two decades until their deaths, mere months apart, in 1665."

Lily widened her smile. "Not bad for an uneducated woman restricted to the four walls of a convent."

Sofia winced again. "Let's not lose sight of the fact that she was a celebrity. Benavides needed her claims to be true to procure financial support from the king and the pope to subsidize the efforts of his Franciscan peers in the New World. I'm not saying he lied about it, but he could have very well overenthusiastically chosen to believe it and accordingly sell it. And it worked."

Lily waved her sister's rational perspective away. "I suggest we focus on the book she wrote. Mary dictated it to her. Logic says that if the Lady in Blue holds a clue to the whereabouts of a hidden message, that's where we'll find it."

"*The Mystical City of God*," whispered Sofia. The title was a metaphor for the Virgin Mary. The book was supposed to be Mary's autobiography since Sr. Maria de Jesus claimed she had written it as dictated to her in private revelation by Mary herself. Sr. Maria de Jesus had resisted for years to pen it fearing the Inquisition. Eventually, her superiors, and purportedly God, had ordered her to do so. The result was four massive volumes that took the nun over eight years to complete, only to burn all the copies when a substitute confessor chastised her for writing it. He did not believe it was a woman's place to draw attention to herself. Later, subsequent confessors and clergymen encouraged her to rewrite it. When she did, the pope proclaimed it a miracle, in itself, because she had managed to do it word-for-word. Sofia was not all that sure she had. The possibility that the humble nun had self-censored some of it to appease the Inquisition was not lost on many.

"I read it," said Sofia. "Or better said, I read the second copy. It was a while back. I found it a difficult read, and all I can remember about it is how painfully self-deprecating Sr. Maria de Jesus is throughout it."

"She had no choice. She had to stay in line with the low esteem a woman was to display in theological matters." Lily grinned. "Yet, and despite that, her activism for women's equality emerges within its lines. She not only dares to portray Our Lady as an active, all-knowing woman equated to her son in glory and power but goes even further. She writes that God, himself, instructs the angels '*to admit as a superior conjointly with Him, a Woman.*' Picture it, Sof: In a profoundly misogynist time driven by religious zealots, when women were forbidden from learning and burned at the stake for petty absurdities, Sr. Maria de Jesus got away with teaching herself to read and write and penning a bestseller centered on a *Woman* raised to the heights of God. Say what you want, but that woman was one miracle after another. Even her body remains incorrupt to this day. It's on display to the public in her hometown."

"What she was, was a genius," concluded Sofia. "Did you know that after ten days of interrogations, the inquisitors were so impressed with her that they asked her for souvenirs before leaving?"

Lily sighed. "What I'd give to read the original version of her book. I wonder how much of it she felt necessary to delete or modify."

"Wait." Sofia paused in thought. "Not all copies were burned. She had given one to the king and warned him in a letter not to tell anyone about it."

"Really? What if the message we seek is contained in the king's copy? Why else would she entrust its safekeeping to him rather than have it burned with the others? Do you have any idea what came of it?"

"Not the slightest," mused Sofia. "With a little time, I could find out. It could be in Spain's National Library."

Lily's gaze turned timid. "There might be yet another."

Her sister responded with surprise. "Another copy of the original manuscript? Where?"

Lily braved her stare. "I know you don't believe she bilocated but please humor me. Why would Sr. Maria de Jesus be transported across the ocean to do a job the friars could do? Why go to all that trouble?"

It took Sofia a moment to glean that she had been set up. "Are you suggesting she was brought here to deliver a copy of the original manuscript to our ancestors?"

"A copy, a summary, a secret message ... Sr. Maria de Jesus said she handed out crosses and rosaries to the different tribes during her visits. What if she also delivered the secret message we are looking for?"

"Even if that were the case, where do we start looking? She's said to have appeared over 500 times across four states."

"We start with the Jumanos. San Angelo is on the line. It's clearly a sign."

"No one knows what came of them. They disappeared from history."

"Not entirely. They dispersed and mixed with other tribes, like ours. You know many peaceful tribes were welcomed on our mesas in those tumultuous days." Lily fortified her stare. "I think we should ask mom."

Sofia knew that's where her sister was going with it, still, it felt like a punch in the stomach. She stood tight-lipped refusing to admit that there could be any credence to her mother's obsessions after so many years disavowing her.

Lily reached out to squeeze her sister's arm softly. "Sof, we are chosen, and mom obviously knows something. Our time has come. This weekend's miracle back home in Spanish Fork is telling us so. We must meet with mom."

Sofia looked up at the ceiling as she exhaled her frustration. Why was it so hard for her to admit that maybe, just maybe, her mother's claims were not all that crazy after all? She then took a last look of denial at the map, pleading it to display a hint of a marker somewhere as far from Spanish Fork and her mother as possible.

Her body tensed.

Mary's words floated back to her: *If you ever find yourself lost, follow the light...* Sofia remembered Mary taking the candle in her left hand toward the rosary in her right one. She realized that Medellin in Colombia at the beginning of the new line was the candle as symbolized by Our Lady of Candelaria, while Santa Fe, at the end, was the rosary as symbolized by Our Lady of the Rosary. The direction she was to follow was north. She ran her eyes along the line northward beyond Santa Fe, judging from there where it would lead.

When she saw it, she burst into a hysterical laugh. There was no way around it. The stars had aligned to support Lily. "I can't believe it," she surrendered. Sofia reached for the ruler to confirm with a penciled line what her eyes had surmised.

She stepped back briefly to register ... well, yes, the miracle.

The line reached Spanish Fork in Utah, their home.

Sofia marked it with a big, fat, black X, the sign of a buried treasure.

A fireball of satisfaction swelled in Lily's chest when she saw it. "Mom it is!"

CHAPTER 27

The black SUV came to a stop alongside the curb where the sisters waited. Sofia appraised the vehicle as the passenger door opened. Out stepped Michael.

"Nice," remarked Lily, approving their ride.

Sofia did not think that was the correct adjective. The truck belonged to Gabriel, and it seemed awfully *official* for a young man. She continued to study it, feeling unsettled. Against her wishes, and after an awkward scene to recover the phone, Lily had insisted on calling Michael to inform him of their travel plans. The fact that the Lady in Blue had been confirmed as an integral part of Mary's Line and on top of that the line led home—of all places—reaffirmed Lily's trust in her intuition and by extension in Michael.

Deep down, Sofia knew they needed the cousins. The trip would be long, on dark, lonely roads, and they didn't trust their own vehicles. In the end, she agreed reluctantly; the dark-lonely-road part being decisive to persuade her.

Gabriel offered his vehicle, supposedly a rental.

Security must pay well, thought Sofia, as she also wondered why *official* was the word that came to mind upon seeing it. She acknowledged she had no arguments to justify her persistent distrust toward the two men. Rather the contrary, they seemed to genuinely care for their safety. But she too enjoyed a healthy dose of sixth sense—or, as she would put it, observational skills— and the nagging feeling that something was off with the cousins gnawed at her mercilessly.

Michael kindly signaled Lily to take the front seat. "Gabriel will need directions when we get there."

As soon as Lily settled in, he closed the door and moved to open the back one for Sofia.

Just great, thought Sofia, feeling the bite of guilt. *He is indeed a gentleman*. She couldn't remember the last time someone showed her such courtesy.

"Thank you," she said and took her place.

Michael closed the door and ran around the back to the other side. Once in, Gabriel hit the accelerator.

"You can input your parent's address into my phone's navigator," suggested Gabriel. His phone was standing in a dashboard holder. "It's the latest in GPS apps."

"We can try," she said as she typed it in, "but I doubt it will work. Satellites can't seem to pin down their ranch. It's a little out of the way, all back roads up a mountain."

She then turned slightly to talk to Michael. "You said you were blocked at the hospital?"

Michael had told her over the phone that they were denied entry into the children's intensive care unit for security and privacy reasons. They were waiting around to see if the statuette came back out when Lily called.

"Yes. As we waited, I asked some questions. The hospital personnel knew little or nothing about the sick child, but most didn't think the Madonna's presence was all that strange. She had been brought in before."

"It doesn't matter now. We think *La Conquistadora* was just a marker," said Lily.

"What did you find out?" he asked. "Why the sudden visit to your mother?"

Lily went on to explain as Sofia stared out the window, overwhelmed by the heavy sense of inevitability that pushed down on her. Could it be a simple coincidence that the line cut right through her parent's property in Spanish Fork? Little coincidences... big coincidences... so many coincidences. What kind of logic could explain divine lines halfway around the world pointing to her childhood home?

Why them?

Why *her*?

As Lily wrapped up the account, Michael repeated Sofia's thoughts precisely.

"Any idea what you or your family have to do with the Secret of Fatima or the Lady in Blue?"

"I wouldn't be surprised if it comes down to our Hopi heritage," leveled Lily.

"Why do you say that?" asked Gabriel.

Sofia remained silent in the back as she tallied the reasons in her mind. Her mother's obsessions and quirky behavior started to make sense.

Meanwhile, Lily explained. "Our people believe we've been entrusted with the divine mission to safeguard universal balance and harmony for the benefit of the entire world.

Sofia scoffed.

Michael threw her a glance. "You don't share that sentiment?"

"We can't even get running water up on the mesa in Oraibi but, apparently, we have the power to control the forces of the universe."

"Obviously, what I just said was meant to be symbolic narrative. It helps us preserve through oral tradition the memory of the ancient wisdom handed to us," clarified Lily.

"And their lays the problem, oral tradition," rebutted Sofia. "Ask two different elders and they'll tell you the story with a different twist. Who knows what the ancient knowledge was, if anything."

"You're exaggerating."

"Hardly. Heck, ask the same elder twenty minutes later and you'll find there is a new nuance to the story."

Lily waved her off. "Don't mind her. She's grumpy because she has issues to work out before we see mom."

Sofia treated her to a mean look but left it at that because Lily was right and, to Sofia's credit, right trumped pride. She sunk into her corner and got to work.

"The knowledge we are to protect," continued Lily, "is coded in an image carved onto a boulder we call Prophesy Rock. Its central tenet is that balance and harmony should rule among all peoples and nature, which is to say, in essence, peace should be our guiding star. Thus, our name, The Peaceful Ones, or Keepers of Peace. Now, to be clear, peace should not be understood as passive inaction. It requires an active, mental focus rooted in reverence and respect for all things, which implies fortitude of spirit to tame the arrogance that justifies the disparagement and abuse of our environment and others." Lily offered a subtle sigh of newfound assurance. "Our mother is convinced that our family was chosen to play a central role in the Hopi divine mission."

"How do you reconcile your Hopi heritage with your Christian faith?"

"Easy, we believe all faiths are weaved together. In the case of our family, the mesh is particularly strong with the Catholic faith and goes back several generations. How it happened is shrouded in a family mystery linked to the Lady in Blue. We're hoping our mother can shed some light on it."

The trip was uneventful. After calling their mother to announce their visit, they had stopped to get something to eat and then took turns driving and napping. They were on the last stretch of the trip, and Lily was at the wheel.

Sofia sat by her side wide awake holding her breath. She had not seen her mother in several years. It was quite ridiculous really. There had never been a fight to justify it, just excuses to never find the time to come home. It disturbed her to realize how deeply her unresolved issues affected her.

The house came into sight, and other than the trees looking taller in the front yard, the rest appeared as she remembered it. It was a contemporary ranch that from the road seemed deceptively modest in size. In truth, it hid another generous floor on the other side, clinging to the hillside with gorgeous bird-eye views of Spanish Fork sprawling at its feet.

Lily parked in the driveway, turned the ignition off, and leaned back to rest without rushing for Sofia's sake. "Whenever you're ready."

Michael and Gabriel preferred to wait outside the vehicle and had half their bodies already out the doors.

Sofia waved her hand in surrender. "Let's just do it!" She didn't want to extend the torment of anticipation any longer than necessary.

Once out, Lily led the way to the front door while Michael and Gabriel fell behind to gauge their surroundings. The house was not as secluded as Lily had led them to believe. While it wasn't in a populated suburban neighborhood, the mountain side was sprinkled with private lanes and hidden homes within easy reach. The good news was that at least the access to this part of the elevation was limited and easy to keep in check.

One of the front double entry doors to the house opened before Lily had a chance to knock. An attractive woman stood smiling in its frame. Her long, white, cotton shirt fell over a pair of comfortable black leggings that hinted to a petite built. And if it weren't for the natural gray highlights that adorned her chest-long braids, she could have easily been confused for yet another sister. Overall, excluding her shrewd stare, nothing about Ms. Soto fulfilled the expectation one usually had of a tribal 'elder'.

"You're here early. I hope you didn't drive too fast."

"Of course we did," said Lily, hugging her mother.

Sofia stood waiting her turn and feeling miserably anxious.

Her mother made it easy on her. No drama, no reproaches, just a step forward to hug her daughter with genuine joy. "I'm so happy to see you." She then stood back, took one good look at Sofia and quickly turning her attention to the two men so Sofia could escape inside.

Ms. Soto examined them thoroughly.

When both realized they were being scrutinized, they approached the door.

Michael took the initiative. "Ms. Soto, I am Michael Amir and this is my cousin Gabriel Avishalom.

"Amir. Avishalom. Cousins. Interesting." She gave them an enigmatic smile, "Gentlemen, welcome to my house," and showed them in.

Ms. Soto led them through the great room toward the back deck where a table was set with a generous breakfast.

Sofia, meanwhile, wandered in the great room taking in the familiarity of the space. It looked, smelled, and felt like home in a very good way. She had forgotten how much she missed it. This was her favorite room. Its highlight was the wall of uninterrupted windows designed purposely to draw the eye to the breathtaking views hidden behind the house. During the day, it gave the space the impression of being suspended over a void as if to mimic a Pueblo cliff-dwelling, while on a clear night, it displayed the majesty of the starred sky as if nothing stood between the observer and the universe.

Sofia slid her gaze toward the right wall. Gracefully put together, it exhibited a colorful hodgepodge of artifacts her mother had collected over the years. It was a little more crowded than she remembered. Her mother had been busy.

Michael joined her to admire the eclectic assortment.

"Is your mother an art collector?"

"Not exactly, more of a memento collector. She's an archeologist. These artifacts are from her diggings in nearby Ancient Puebloan sites." Sofia studied each item with renewed interest. As she ran her eyes over a couple of baskets, a shell necklace, and some geometric designed ceramics, she raised her hand to point at a mug. "That is from the 13th century. Most people mistake it for a modern-day tourist souvenir."

"What about these dolls?" He was referring to a selection of figurines decorated with colorful attire wearing animal masks and elaborate feathered headdresses.

"Those are kachinas. They represent spirits. There are hundreds of them. We believe that everything in nature has its own guardian spirit. They are carved out of cottonwood root and given to girls to learn about the traditional dances." She drew a nostalgic smile as she caressed the feathers on a cute green and red dancing doll with googly eyes. "This one was mine. They aren't made with feathers anymore to protect migratory birds."

Next up were a series of framed photographs lined vertically in pairs. They were pictures of rock art.

"Are these all Anasazi? What do they represent?" asked Michael.

Sofia gave him a playful look of disapproval. "Just so you know, we don't like the term Anasazi. It is a Navajo word that describes us as 'enemy ancestors'. We prefer the more neutral term 'Ancient Puebloans'."

He accepted the correction with his irresistible smile.

Unarmed, Sofia continued. "As for our rock art, the themes usually repeat themselves to represent hunting scenes, animals, spirits, and so on. I recognize the ones on the left. They are typical of the Four Corners region." She narrowed her stare with curiosity. "However, despite the similarities, I'm not familiar with the petroglyphs on the right."

Ms. Soto was heard calling from the deck. "The coffee is getting cold."

Michael saw how Sofia's eyes lingered on a small Christian altar. It contained a little wooden statue of the Virgin Mary holding baby Jesus flanked by a rosary and a candle. He noticed that within the altar piece was another kachina, this one decorated mostly in blue. And crowning it all on the wall was a paper parchment showing some strange drawings. He was interested in asking about the ensemble but also noticed how Sofia's gaze reeled away to an alternate plane.

He stepped away silently.

"Where is dad?" he heard Lily ask as he joined the party outside on the deck. The fresh morning breeze felt heavenly.

"Working as usual," answered Ms. Soto. "He left at dawn hoping to finish up early and get back quick to see you." She offered coffee to the men and both accepted. "He is a reservation ranger," she clarified for their benefit. "There have been many reports of trespassing lately. He went out to do his round."

"You need a permit to access a reservation here in Utah?" asked Gabriel.

"It depends. Generally, out of respect, you should ask permission for certain areas, but you can usually get away without it. However, my husband's specific area of responsibility falls within sections considered off-limits because they are sacred to the local Utes."

"Why do people trespass?"

"Gold. This region is infamous for its legendary 'Lost Mines'. The good weather brings out the gold-diggers and treasure hunters every year."

Sofia finally joined the group. Her face had lost some color. No one seemed to notice. She reached for a toast and then stopped to smile. Her mother had made her favorite bitter orange marmalade, which no one in the world liked but her. The color returned to her cheeks. This her mother did notice pleased.

"Ms. Soto, thank you," appraised Michael, "everything is delicious." He was hungry and honestly appreciative.

Gabriel nodded in agreement with his mouth full. He was serving himself a second round.

"Please call me Sakwa."

"May I ask what it means?"

"Indeed you may. It means 'blue'. I was born on a clear-skied day much like today."

Gabriel swallowed. "Nice," he said glancing at the uninterrupted blue skies that extended before him. "What about Soto? Is it Ute?"

"No, Auru, my husband's surname is Ute. Mine, Soto, is Hopi. My grandmother chose it." Sakwa chuckled at the memory. "Traditionally, the Hopi did not have surnames. That is the white man's custom. My family resisted the imposition for as long as possible until my very wise grandmother concluded that embracing the new for one's own benefit was as important as loyalty to the old. In other words, the elders in my family had decided to send me off to college." She angled a grin, "You'd be surprised how stubborn college secretaries are about having to fill out the family name box if you want to be accepted." A strange shadow settled over her gaze. She paused to run it across her audience slowly and deliberately. Then she spoke. "Since the women in my family are the guardians to the secret of the '*Blue Star*', Soto, meaning 'Star' seemed most fitting."

Sofia and Lily exchanged stunned looks.

Lily then voiced their surprise.

"Guardians? Secret? Blue Star? What in the world are you talking about? You never told us any of this!"

Their mother leaned back comfortably in her chair claiming her rightful aura of a tribal elder; her gaze now pungent. "No, I never did, but the time has come. It's the reason you are here, isn't it?"

CHAPTER 28

The Auru-Soto sisters stared at their mother with intense expectation.

Sakwa started by directing her attention to Lily.

"Let me ask you first: I read your report and studied your map; most fascinating. However, nothing in the report hinted to our family's involvement. How did you conclude you had to come here?"

"Wait!" said Sofia. "You sent mom a copy too?"

"Of course. I sent her one when I sent one to you and Michael. You're the only one who never receive it." Lily then gestured with her hand toward her sister as she responded to her mother. "Sofia figured it out yesterday. Mary's Line does not end in Fatima. It continues across the Atlantic all the way to Medellin in Colombia, while the Spanish Line runs into Medellin, Spain."

"Medellin..." repeated her mother. "How interesting."

"It doesn't end there. Come," said Lily jumping to her feet. "I'll show you."

Lily grabbed the bag at her feet, which carried the maps together with the snacks they acquired at a stop and led her mother inside to the dining room. The rest followed and took their places around the table as Lily retrieved the maps. She first unfolded the largest one, the world map, and then placed Spain's on top as they had done at the library. Sofia and Michael helped her keep them flat by holding down the edges though their need to roll back up again had considerably diminished with the folds inflicted on them.

Sakwa stood by Lily.

"Look," explained her daughter, "the Spanish Line crosses the town of Guadalupe, home to the original Lady of Guadalupe, a Black Madonna. This you knew. But then it heads to Medellin where Hernan Cortes was born. He had devotion for Our Lady of Guadalupe, but also for Our Lady of the Candle, who is yet another Black Madonna. Now, in my report I explain how I suspected that *La Conquistadora* was the forgotten statue of Our Lady of Guadalupe in Mexico, originally brought from Spain, and how Friar Benavides found her tucked away in a box in Mexico, choosing to bring her to Santa Fe for his new mission. That is how I traced a route from Guadalupe,

Spain, to Santa Fe. At this point I was at a loss but felt strongly that the Lady in Blue had a role to play since the same Friar was intimately connected to her legend as well."

Sakwa nodded. "I see. It makes sense."

"Only in part," said Sofia. "She was right about Santa Fe but wrong about how to get there. The lines were proving to be too precise and elaborate to suddenly hang in Guadalupe and perform an awkward leap across the Atlantic. A more solid clue, consistent with the lines, had to be found to confirm Santa Fe as a marker, and that clue was provided by the city of Medellin in Colombia. The city's full original name pointed back to Hernan Cortes and his worship of Our Lady of the Candle. So, since the two lines seemed determined to bring our attention to the two Madonnas through Cortes, it occurred to me they—combined—were the anchorage we were looking for, and I knew the cathedral of San Antonio in Texas is consecrated to both."

Lily stabbed the map with her index finger. "And was it ever. Here is Medellin, Colombia. As you can see, Mary's Line turns northwest toward Santa Fe running through San Antonio precisely. But not only that," announced Lily, sliding her finger up along the line, "San Angelo in Texas falls on the line, as well. It is the irrefutable sign that the Lady in Blue holds the key!"

Her mother stunned her with an unexpected question. "Why would she?"

Lily froze her puzzled look on her. "W-well," she stammered, "she seems to fit the pattern that warrants her being an apostle ... San Angelo, the capital of her legend in the States, is on *Mary's Way* ... And *Mary's Way* leads straight here to Spanish Fork where you, her greatest fan, happens to live ... We were hoping you might have the answer."

Sakwa shook her head in awe as she drew a broad smile. Then she appraised her daughters proudly. "I always knew this moment would come, that both of you would find your way to the secret. But I must admit I never thought it would be spelled out on a world map."

The twins stared at their mother with renewed expressions of deep anticipation.

Sakwa turned silently toward the great room. She approached her exhibit wall and stopped before the altar. As if performing a ceremony, she reached for the old rosary and returned with it to the dining room. She stretched her two hands out with the rosary laid across her open palms and offered it to her daughters.

Sofia nudged Lily, inviting her to take it first.

"I've always told you that you were destined for something big. I knew it the day you were born," said Sakwa

"Yes, but how did you know?" asked Lily enthralled with the rosary though not sure why. "You never did tell."

"You're twins. In our tradition that's an omen."

"Twins are born every day in the world," said Sofia. "We can't all be omens."

"True, but not all are born Hopi and heirs to a prophecy."

Lily handed the rosary to Sofia, who for now was more interested in what her mother had to say. The two sisters ushered her on with their unblinking eyes.

Sakwa started slowly. "For many generations a secret has been passed down in our family from mother to daughter. It started with a distant ancestor we simply call Grandmother, and it tells the story of her encounter with the Lady in Blue. This much has been hinted to you already. It is time you knew the full story."

Sakwa paused to seize the moment in honor of her own mother and grandmother lamenting neither one was present to enjoy it. Both were alive to see the twins born, so both died knowing the time to solve their long-guarded family prophesy had arrived.

"Maybe you'd like to sit down," she suggested once ready to proceed.

Lily shook her head. "We've been sitting for hours. Please, just tell us."

"As you wish." Sakwa took a deep breath. "One night a long time ago, as everyone slept, Grandmother, while still a girl, heard a strange noise. No one else appeared to be stirred by it, and since it did not seem menacing like that of a wild creature but more like a soft whisper, she decided to check it out on her own. The memory of where she lived is lost, yet we know it must have been a Pueblo because the story says she climbed out of the house rather than walked out of a hut. In any case, once outside, she saw a blue star twinkling brightly in the sky to one side of the Pueblo. She walked in its direction to get a better look, when the star swiftly descended toward her. She soon discerned the profile of a woman carried by two angels who gently deposited her on the ground at arm's reach. The woman's glow had relaxed with her proximity, revealing that its blue hue was the reflection of the blue in the woman's cape.

"Grandmother was understandably startled at first, but the Lady's gentle voice soothed her, and though she spoke a different language, Grandmother had no difficulty comprehending her." Sakwa paused to claim close attention. "I was made to memorize their conversation and will repeat it word for word." She lowered her eyes briefly and then spoke.

'Who are you' asked Grandmother.

'I am a friend. I come from far to seek your help.'

'How can I, a simple girl, help a spirit?'

'I am not a spirit but a mortal like you, and like you, I was chosen to guard a secret. This secret I must now pass on to you.'

'Why me?'

'Tumultuous times await the world and your people. This will lead many to forget the wisdom of their ancestors. The Great Mother sees much courage and promise in you as in the daughters that will come from you. For this you have been chosen to ensure that the ancient wisdom is not lost. I will provide you with a prophecy. You are to guard it and pass it on to your daughter, and she to hers, and so forth. When the world is ready, the prophecy will reveal the secrets that will help heal it.'

'May I ask what those secrets are?'

'It suffices for you to know they hold the Great Spirit's true face and true name.' The Lady in Blue then asked, 'Do you believe you can

honor the Great Mother and the trust she has put in you by taking
on this responsibility?'

Grandmother did not blink and responded resolute, "I believe and
know that I can and will!'

Sakwa smiled at this part. She loved the strength of character her
ancestor had displayed. Then she gestured at Sofia, as she continued.
"Pleased, the Lady in Blue handed her that rosary you now hold and
prophesized the following words:

'For the True Pahana to reveal itself, a pure heart must find the
straight path that leads to it, and a wise soul must see its true nature.
Only then will balance to the world be restored, and the people of all
nations live in peace.'

Sofia dropped her eyes to study the rosary in her hands. A thin film of
sweat formed as she realized she could be holding one of the rosaries the
Spanish nun was said to have handed out during her bilocations. Curiously,
it was unremarkable for a relic of such nature, just a normal wood-beaded
rosary you could find anywhere. One detail did stand out though. She
examined the small medallion that connected the cross to the ring of beads.
It contained a peculiar image on the front and markings on the back she did
not recognize.

"Wow," exclaimed Lily, having quickly derived the implication of the
prophecy. "It is talking about us. That time is now. It means the Day of
Purification is near. I knew it!"

Sofia reacted with a chuckle. "Great job selecting our names, mom: Lily,
the flower of purity, and Sofia, 'wisdom' in Greek. It's called self-fulfilling the
prophecy."

Her mother displayed her best version of an innocent face. "Honey, how
was I to know you'd grow up to be the wise skeptic and Lily the pure-hearted
believer?"

Sofia bit her lip.

Sakwa then laughed. "I'm kidding! Of course I knew. From the day you were born, your hands were closed in a tight fist, while Lily's were always open. It was a no brainer."

"I'm sorry," interrupted Gabriel, "I'm not following. Who is Pahana?"

Sakwa looked at him as if seeing him for the first time. She studied him with piercing intensity, it was almost uncomfortable. She then did the same to Michael.

"Would you prefer that Gabriel and I left?" asked Michael.

Sakwa shook her head. "I have the distinct feeling that you are meant to be here, and that your help will be much needed in what lays ahead for my daughters. I ask that you stay."

"Thank you," he said. "It will be our honor to help."

Gabriel confirmed with a courteous nod as if agreeing to an unspoken covenant.

Sofia observed the scene trying to decide what concerned her more, the comment on what lay ahead, or her mother's strange complicity with two men she had just met.

Sakwa, meanwhile, attended to Gabriel's question.

"Allow me to explain," she started. "According to Hopi tradition, we used to live underground until the Great Spirit and Creator of all things, led us to the surface. Two brothers then took very different paths. The younger one became the leader during an extensive period of migration, which eventually brought us to our current home in Arizona. The older brother, who we refer to as the White Brother, or Pahana, went to the East with the promise of returning in the future coinciding with the prophesized Day of Purification, at which time he'd present proof of his identity. In short, Pahana's return will usher in peace to the world as long as we can recognize his true face."

Sakwa waved at the two men. "Please follow me; I want to show you something." She led them to the parchment that Michael had noticed earlier on the exhibit wall. "What you see here are the two sides of a sacred Hopi tablet. The Great Spirit gave us four tablets. Three of them represent land titles and instructions on how to take care of them. They are in custody of the Bear Clan. The one you see here is the fourth tablet and it is held in custody by the Fire Clan. If you look closely, one side of the tablet has a headless human figure etched into it."

Sakwa aimed the point of her finger at the lower left-hand side and proceeded clockwise to explain the other markings. "Surrounding the headless figure are various Hopi symbols, representing water, brotherhood, land and maybe corn."

Michael pointed at the symbol that looked like a V. "Is that the corn?"

"Yes, we think so, it is not quite clear. Whatever it is meant to represent must be important since it is repeated twice on one side and then again on the other."

Michael nodded and Sakwa moved on to the depiction of the back side of the tablet.

"The other side has what looks like a swastika, which for the Hopi represents the four cardinal directions of wandering. This is in relation to the migrations our people undertook until we settled in Oraibi. There is also a snake or river, the face of the Great Spirit, a moon enclosed on two sides signifying the end of a path, and again a V, which may or may not be corn. You'll also notice down here," Sakwa pointed to a bottom corner, "that a piece of the tablet is missing. It is said that Pahana took it with him so that upon his return he could prove his true identity with it."

Ms. Soto then began walking across the great room back to the dining room.

Gabriel caught up to her. "Yet, if I understood correctly, according to the prophecy handed down to you, it will be Lily, the pure heart, and Sofia, the wise soul, who are destined to identify Pahana."

"As *I* understood it," clarified Lily, "my job is to find the straight path that leads to him, as in the lines that brought us here. Now it is up to Sofia to figure out his true face."

Her mother appraised her, once again, with deep admiration. "I'm so impressed you deciphered an actual path. We always thought it was meant to be a spiritual one."

"My work here is done," smiled Lily, playfully smug.

"Well, apparently, mine has just begun," said Sofia focused on the rosary. "I must use wisdom to identify Pahana and usher in peace to the world. No pressure." She looked up as her shoulders dropped. "I'm sorry, mom. I realize I have always rejected your claims. I never gave you a chance. But please understand it's in my nature to question everything. It's who I am. And I'm going to need more than a family legend or a common rosary to usher in peace anywhere."

Sakwa approached her daughter. Gently, her hands cupped her face.

"Don't *ever* apologize for using your gifted brain, you hear me? The herd mentality never helped anybody. Far more questions should have been asked throughout history to prevent the suffering of so many. We've been tasked to protect the wisdom of our ancestors. What that wisdom holds is that peace is about balance. An inquisitive mind and a noble heart must go hand in hand if the world is ever to find peace."

Sakwa released her daughter who praised her mother. "I'd bet my two pennies *you* are Pahana."

"I'd wish. All I have are nice words that aren't even original. Our elders tried convincing the United Nations with them once. They fell on deaf ears. History tells us that nice words alone don't do the trick. Ask Jesus, his got him crucified and went largely ignored thereafter." She set her intense stare on her daughter. "Where there are deaf ears, we must make eyes see. These lines might just do that trick and, according to our family prophecy, they lead to Pahana. Now, it is up to you to reveal his face."

Sofia exhaled overwhelmed by the challenge. "Where to start..."

She began by pacing the length of the dining room as she organized her thoughts out loud.

"It all began because Lily discovered a concealed message in the speech that John Paul II gave in Fatima. That message led her to discover *Mary's Way*, which in turn took her to the Black Madonna markers, which in turn took her to the Spanish Line, and all eventually brought us here."

Sofia stopped sharp and dropped her eyes once more to study the rosary. She then pointed her shrewd quizzical stare at her mother. "Why here? Why are we in Spanish Fork? If the ancient wisdom of the Hopi is central to the enigma, why are we in Utah and not Arizona? Shouldn't the line have led us to Oraibi?" Sofia then stretched her hand out holding the rosary to show her mother the reverse of the medallion. "And what are these markings?"

Her mother's pride could not glow any brighter. "You did not disappoint. Those are two excellent questions. Those markings are the reason I became an archeologist and explain why we are all here."

CHAPTER 29

Sakwa directed a quick look through the dining door into the kitchen to check the clock on the wall. What she had to reveal would take time.

"How are we doing? Is anyone hungry? Do you need a break before I get started?"

All four guests adamantly shook their heads. Apart from still digesting breakfast, they would allow nothing to distract them from hearing about the mysterious markings.

Sakwa chuckled to herself. Who was she kidding? She had waited too long for this moment to stop now. "In that case, we need to go back to my exhibition wall."

They followed her to the composition of six framed pictures. The images were organized vertically in three pairs, each with a common theme.

Sakwa stood in front of them as if a tour guide. "The secret was revealed to me by my mother when I was fifteen. It was the standing custom until I broke it with you," she said addressing her daughters. "I knew you were the chosen ones, and that you'd have to find your way to it on your own."

Sakwa then widened her attention to include the men. "When I was handed the rosary, those markings intrigued me immediately; I wondered if they were a secret code of sorts that led to the location of Pahana or offered clues to his identity. My young mind saw exciting possibilities and I read everything I could get my hands on about ancient scripts. In my senior year of high school, I came across the work of Barry Fell, a professor at Harvard, who was making headlines for his controversial claims about ancient American inscriptions. In short, he was of the opinion they were in reality the legacy of Old-World civilizations who had visited America long before Columbus."

"I've heard of him," said Sofia. "My understanding is that his conclusions have been generally rejected."

"The situation with Mr. Fell is not so much of rejection as of lack of support. No one has been able to refute his claims but neither has anyone set out to confirm them. We must bear in mind that he was not a historian or an archeologist, but a marine biologist with a specialty in starfish and sea

184

urchins. It was hard for the established academia to accept the intrusion of an unqualified outsider, more so when he was questioning their life's work to rewrite history. Additionally, stacked against him was that the inscriptions he was basing his claims on were considered forgeries by the same academia he was defying."

"Why forgeries?" asked Lily.

"From the beginning of colonization, ancient stone buildings and artifacts with strange inscriptions have been turning up everywhere. Some of the more renowned were found in the early 19th century such as the tablets of Grave Creek in West Virginia, the Davenport Calendar Stele in Iowa, or the inscription of Monhegan Island in Maine. Their symbols looked very much like Old Irish Celtic but weren't exact. This led many to conclude that the finders were trying to pull off clumsy hoaxes. And to be fair, there were indeed many trying to pull off hoaxes. That said, Fell argued that not all were, and the artifacts that weren't had been compared against the wrong scripts. You see, it was around his time when older Southern European scripts were being discovered and deciphered. The recent findings revealed that the Old Irish Celtic language was a younger variant of the Iberian Celt. What's more, scholars were starting to wonder if the Celtic language was Celtic at all, but rather an ancient Iberian language adopted by the Celts and spread back across Europe. So going back to the inscriptions found on American soil, Fell realized they were more like the older Iberian script, which was unknown in the 19th Century."

"So, what exactly was his claim again?" urged Lily.

"He was convinced that Celts, Phoenicians, Libyans, Egyptians, and other peoples of the Mediterranean had visited America and established trading posts as far back as two millennia before Christ. And he thought this based on inscriptions found on a variety of tablets, artifacts, and gravestones unearthed across the US."

"If he was a marine biologist, how would he know about ancient inscriptions?" asked Sofia.

"Fell was born in New Zealand in 1917 and—"

"Wait! 1917?" interrupted Lily.

"Yes. Why?"

"The year of Fatima's apparitions..." Lily looked inquisitively at her sister. Sofia shrugged it off as if saying 'add it to the pile'.

Sakwa continued. "As I was saying, he was born in New Zealand and knew of the Polynesian petroglyphs that bore mysterious resemblance to Libyan inscriptions, which is a variant of Egyptian. Because he was a marine biologist, he studied this oddity with the hope of understanding human dispersal across the planet, perhaps at the mercy of winds and ocean currents. It sparked his interest in epigraphy, that is, the study of ancient scripts. It became a sort of hobby for him."

"In other words, he was an amateur," remarked Sofia. "I can see the reluctance to accept that the Atlantic was a busy highway four thousand years ago based solely on his personal interpretations of some strange symbols."

"He wasn't the only amateur. Archeology, as we know it today, has come a long way with regards to professionalism, technical resources and, more importantly, new discoveries. One thing you need to understand is that when the artifacts were being unearthed, American academia belonged to a New World set on severing ties with the Old. The last thing on their minds was finding evidence of ancient ties unless it was to justify their providential right to the land. Finding America's new identity as a nation for the white colonist was more important than understanding the ancient identity of the 'savages' whose land they wanted. The mindset, circumstances, and archaeological know-how of the time didn't favor an open mind toward genuinely caring about ancient native artifacts."

"You think Fell was on the right track, then?" asked Michael.

"I do. I enjoy the benefit of time, new technologies, and recent archaeological discoveries that start to back him up. The scripts Fell based his claims on are today much better understood and appreciated."

Sofia raised the rosary medallion. "I am going to guess that you identified these markings as belonging to the Iberian script and that's why his work caught your attention."

"That's right. My career path was set. I went into archeology to find out for myself what they meant."

"And did you?" Lily could hardly contain her curiosity.

"Unfortunately, not. We have been unable to decipher this Iberian script yet." Sakwa drew a smile. "However, I did discover something in relation to it that may shock you."

Sofia was certain nothing could shock her anymore, and Lily just wanted to know if any of this led to Fatima's secret. Michael and Gabriel both leaned in displaying eager interest and readiness to be shocked.

"We're listening," ushered Lily.

Sakwa turned to the panels displayed behind her. "I want you to look closely at this rock art. I'm sure you'll recognize the three examples on the left, they are all Native American."

The twins nodded, whereas the men conformed to accepting it as fact.

"Well, their equivalent ones on your right are not."

Sofia and Lily approached the panels to look closer.

Sakwa explained to Michael and Gabriel. "I took the top left picture southeast from here, near the Colorado boarder, on the Golf Course trail in Moab. It is Puebloan. Our ancestors lived in the Four Corners regions, an area that reached well into Utah, Colorado, New Mexico and Arizona. The rock art in that picture has traditionally been thought to depict a hunting scene because of the men with spears and the bighorn sheep. Now compare it to the scene in the right picture."

"It is very similar," remarked Sofia already on it. "You're saying it's not native?"

"Not native, not even American. It's a carving found on a stele unearthed in the province of Cordoba, in the south of Spain. Steles like this one have been popping up all over the Iberian Peninsula within the last 50 years. They are considered warrior steles dating back to the first millennia before Christ and as such portray a dead warrior or leader with his weapons and some luxury items to highlight his elevated status. On this particular stele, you see the deceased wearing a horned helmet surrounded by his spear, shield, an ivory comb, a mirror, and a harp. These burial accessories were common in the Mediterranean, specifically in the early Greek Minoan and Mycenaean cultures. Many graves have been unearthed with actual ivory combs and mirrors or harps in them. However, the horned helmet denotes the warrior's Iberian Celtic ethnicity. Just for the record, it wasn't the Vikings who wore horns on their helmets, it was the Celts. Some Mycenaeans and peoples of the Near East did as well."

Sofia was in awe. "The resemblance is remarkable. I would have sworn it was Hopi. The postures of the Puebloan hunter and the Iberian warrior are identical. Both are depicted looking forward with their elbows drawn high to the sides and hands hanging down open, showing four fingers ... They are wearing the same horns—"

"And what about the shields?" interrupted Lily. "They are represented with the exact same three concentric circles." She rapidly rolled her eyes back and forth over the two compositions. "Even the spear and the little people around them are the same. This is crazy!"

Sakwa nodded. "This is only one example. I could show you hundreds. Scenes like these are repeated throughout the Southwest of the United States as they are now being discovered throughout the southwest of the Iberian Peninsula. So, as you see, the similarities go beyond just a script, the rock art is identical too."

Sakwa kneeled to reach for one of the doors of a cabinet sitting under her exhibition wall. From it she extracted a large photo album.

"I prepared this for this moment." She opened it to show them two more comparable renderings. Her audience of four gathered around her to look over her shoulders as she held open the album.

Moab   Cordoba

She explained. "This one on the left is another example from Moab. It too is a petroglyph you can see at their Golf Course rock art site. It depicts their city's icon 'Moab Man', a cute friendly figure who looks like he is waving. He wears horns on his head and two sphere-like pendant earrings." She ran her finger across to the opposite page. "Well, this figure is found on another Spanish stele from a town also in Cordoba, like that first one on the wall, which in their case depicts a warrior wearing horns and ball earrings. You can see his sword hanging from his waist. Two different Moab renditions much like two different steles from Cordoba, Spain."

Sakwa then turned to another page. "As for the accessories, I've found mirrors and comb-like objects on many Native American pictographs and petroglyphs, which obviously are not being understood as such here. Like in this picture of Dawa Park back home on our reservation: You see the mirror? Or this one in Crow Canyon: You see the combs?"

"Incredible..." whispered Gabriel.

Michael directed his eyes to the next pair of pictures on the wall. "What about those two in the middle? They show equivalent hunting scenes on horseback. How is that possible for the Native Americans? There were no horses until the arrival of the Spaniards."

"Rock art is extremely difficult to date," explained Sakwa. "Though there are some scientific methods available, it is generally done in relation to artifacts found nearby or via association with other sites. One general rule of thumb is that if there is a horse in the scene, it must have been done after the Spanish arrived. This American picture on the left is a close up of a large panel found also here in Utah known as Newspaper Rock. It is one of the largest collections of petroglyphs and has been carved over time by different groups. The horse is simply assumed a rendition added after colonization."

"And yet it contains many of the elements seen in that sculptured hunting scene on the right, wheels, dog, and all."

"Eerie, isn't it? That sculpture is a votive chariot found in Merida, Spain, and dates back to around the 6th century B.C. It was common in the Mediterranean to bury warriors with symbolic chariots as well. It symbolized their bravery and victories. So, the choice of elements should not be taken lightly. Many of the Spanish warrior steles depict chariots alongside their shields, weapons, and the rest of their status symbols." Sakwa turned a few pages until she found the one she wanted. "Here," she said pointing at another stele. "This one is displayed in a museum in Seville, Spain. As you see, in this example, the warrior is shown with a sword, a bow and arrow, and the usual shield, but also, in the upper, right-hand corner, you can see the sketch of a chariot as if looking at it from above rather than from the side." She then drew Michael's attention to the picture on the left. "This is an American comparative I came across a few years ago. It is a close up of a different section of Newspaper Rock." Sakwa's finger pointed to a strange looking thing that on its own would have been difficult to interpret but placed side-by-side the Spanish warrior stele made sense. It was clearly the rudimentary sketch of a chariot as seen from a bird's-eye view."

Sofia leaned in to see it better. Her eyes went back and forth between the two schematic chariots. It was bizarre. "How is that possible? This would mean that those people from prehistoric Spain carved a chariot on a rock here in Utah hundreds of years before Christ."

"Or even thousands," affirmed her mother solemnly with her head. "As I said, I could show you comparatives all day. I've found chariots at other Native American sites. One in Albuquerque, New Mexico, is drawn from the side pulled by a horse that leaves no doubt. But to make my point, please allow me to share two more. It's important I prove that these commonalities are not limited to stick characters and odd sketches of purported chariots. That could ultimately be argued as a reasonable coincidence." Sakwa launched a side look at Sofia and winked.

"Most wise of you," smiled her daughter.

With a gesture of her hand, Sakwa drew their attention to the third and last pair of pictures on the wall. Sofia recognized the Hopi Mother Earth symbol immediately. Of two types, the one her mother had chosen to display was the square labyrinth.

Gabriel approached the picture seeming particularly interested, so Sakwa addressed the explanation to him.

"It's called a *Tapu'at*, meaning mother and child. It symbolizes our people's spiritual rebirth during our emergence to the surface. It is also suspiciously identical to the Cretan Maze, a labyrinth typical of the Minoan culture and seen replicated throughout the Mediterranean in art, buildings and coins. This is important because, in the case of buildings, this labyrinth became the foundational design for most Phoenicians temples. The Phoenicians were the master builders of the Near East around the 10th century B.C. In fact, King Solomon entrusted the building of his temple to them."

And that was why these pictures had caught Gabriel's attention. He turned to the picture of the floor plan on the right. "I see what you mean. The direction of entry into the Hopi labyrinth and this building appear to highlight the importance of that common square area in the center. Is it, too, a temple?"

"You are very perceptive," admired Sakwa. "Yes, it was an inhabited sanctuary. The entrance indeed directs the visitor into that square room, because it is the altar. What sets this temple apart from the other Mediterranean ones, is the interesting altar symbol found carved on the floor, a circle with a triangular crossbar on its tangent. It is believed to symbolize Tanit, a Great Mother Goddess of the Mediterranean."

"Both relate to a Mother Goddesses," mused Lily.

"This sanctuary is a good example of how recent discoveries can help support Mr. Fell's claims. It is located near Merida, Spain, the same city where the votive chariot was found, and is known as Cancho Roano. Though the site was discovered in the 1950's, archeologists did not get their hands on it until 1978."

"Mom, why haven't you come out with it?" wondered Lily in awe.

"I can't. We were handed the medallion for a reason. We have a responsibility. This knowledge may very well lead us to Pahana. Remember that Pahana is said to have gone to the East. It could be a reference to these people."

"Yes, of course ... So, who are these people?"

Sakwa drew an enigmatic grin. "They are the legendary Tartessos, and until a few decades ago, they were believed to be but a myth."

No one seemed to recognize the name.

"First references to them can be found in Assyria and Greece, and then later in Rome. They are also repeatedly mentioned in the Old Testament in relation to King Solomon who had close commercial ties with them.

There are up to two dozen mentions of their fabulous riches throughout the Bible. However, it is the Greeks who truly idealized them in their writings. Some allusions are imbued with mythological flare, like the stories related to Hercules. However, Herodotus, considered the Father of History, mentions them on a more factual basis. The point is that they were a prosperous civilization of infamous wealth thanks to their precious metals, domain of metal work, and trade. Furthermore, they were purported to own a powerful fleet for trading purposes, while their capital was located on the southern coast of Spain beyond Gibraltar, that is, on the Atlantic side. As you can see, they were well poised to have been able to reach American shores."

"Mom," started Sofia, "Barry Fell found traces of many Mediterranean people on American soil. What make you think it was only the Tartessos?"

"I don't know for a fact that it was only the Tartessos. But you said it a moment ago. It is hard to envision the Atlantic being a busy highway three to four millennia ago only for such widespread knowledge to fall into oblivion until Columbus. One advanced civilization, with good ships, displaying influences of many other people, and situated on the Atlantic seems more likely."

"Right, but anymore, it is accepted that the existence of land beyond the Atlantic was well known by many before Columbus," insisted Sofia.

"True, it's widely accepted the Vikings, for instance, established some settlements prior to him. But they did it much later and not to the wide extent that Iberian traces show. Bear in mind that examples of Tartessian inscriptions and rock art are found across the whole country. But there is something else to support their early crossings: a circular current system in the Atlantic Ocean named the North Atlantic Gyre. What is interesting about this system is that the current flows from the Iberian Peninsula down to the Canary Islands, then across the Atlantic to the Caribbean, north along the East coast of North America, and then back across the ocean straight to the Iberian Peninsula. Therefore, while crossing the ocean for the Vikings would have been a challenging undertaking against the current, the Iberians pretty much just had to let themselves be dragged across and back. It was a very doable crossing for these ancient peoples, and since they were merchants, I doubt they would have been inclined to spread the word. They would have sought to protect their business."

"How do you explain the wide range of Mediterranean traces found then?"

"The Iberian Peninsula was rich in gold, silver, copper and tin; metals that the rest of the rapidly developing Mediterranean craved. The Tartessians were skilled traders open to outside influence that contributed to strengthening their commercial ties. That was the secret of their success. In sum, they wrote in an ancient pre-Punic form; their burials were Greek, their iconography was markedly Egyptian, their gods a blend of the Mediterranean pantheons, and their temples Phoenician. Talk about diversity."

Sofia's eyebrows remained furrowed deep in thought. "All the Mediterranean civilizations at the time were equally influenced by each other to a great extent. What specifically made you think it was the Tartessians who left their mark here?"

Sakwa smiled broadly. "You shine again. You are right. There is a cultural trait that singles the Tartessians out. I saved the more impressive comparative for last."

Her audience regrouped around her ready to look over her shoulders. She turned the pages until she settled on the last two pictures. The one on the left was a photograph of a young Hopi woman. The one on the right a finely sculptured bust, it too of a beautiful woman."

Sofia lost her breath in astonishment.

"No way!" exclaimed Lily.

CHAPTER 30

Sakwa waited. She knew her daughters needed a moment to digest the significance of what they were looking at.

Gabriel wasn't all that sure he knew what he was looking at. He turned his puzzled gaze to Sakwa.

She explained. "It has been a long-standing tradition for Hopi women to wear our hair rolled up in a whorl, one on each side. It's meant to indicate our fertility upon reaching the age of marriageability. You might recognize it as a similar hairstyle made famous by Princess Leia in Star Wars. We refer to it as Squash Blossom and have always thought of it as unique to our people."

"Not so unique anymore, I would say," remarked Lily.

"Right, it turns out there were other women who wore it as well; those in Spain 2,500 years ago. At least, that is the estimated age of that bust."

"Who is she? She is stunning."

"The Lady of Elche; a Spanish treasure. Her perfect features were carved into a delicate limestone that was once colored in red, blue and yellow. If you look close enough, you can still see traces of them. There remains much mystery as to her identity, but since a few other similar statues have been unearthed in several necropolises across the region with Phoenician influences, it is likely she represents the Great Mother Goddess Tanit, who true to her gender, was believed to guard over fertility. In any case, for all the external influence they received, her elaborate hair dress was unique to the southern Iberians."

Sofia finally came around. "I have to hand it to you, mom, you managed to shock me. The evidence is overwhelming: inscriptions, rock art, buildings, symbols; even unique female hairstyles." She stared at her mother. "There appears to be an odd affinity between the Tartessians and us, the Hopi. Their impact must have been great on us. Why? I mean, the zeal with which we have conserved their memory for thousands of years seems unreal. Not even the Spaniards care for that hairstyle anymore. You'd think that after so long we too would let it go. Why did we stick to their influence so passionately...?" Sofia trailed off as the realization formed in her mind.

Silently, Sakwa watched her daughter reach the answer on her own.

"... We *are* them," murmured Sofia. Her jaw dropped.

Now the mother spoke.

"The Iberian Tartessians found their identity and ways morph due to the successive invasions and cultural exchanges endured throughout the next three thousand years. They did not live in isolation as we did. Carthaginians, Romans, Visigoths, Muslims, Jews, and Christians; all occupied the Iberian Peninsula for extensive periods of time," explained her mother. "The Spaniards are who they are today as a result of their rich, layered history, whereas our identity and ways remained largely unaffected and, therefore, unchanged."

Sofia readjusted her jaw to share the connections rapidly forming in her head. "Our legends, they make so much sense now. Pahana, for instance: one brother stayed behind leading the migrations, while the other went east. That could mean that one group of Tartessians was left behind to settle and scout for, let's say gold mines, while another went back and forth to Spain to fulfill their trade commitments." She jerked at another realization. "Our sacred tablets... Of course they represent titles to the land; they were probably mining claims."

Sofia set her wide-open, sparkling gaze on her mother searching for confirmation.

Sakwa nodded. "What's more, are you aware that the word *symbol* derives from the Greek *symbolon,* which means *token,* as in a part that completes a whole? For the Greeks, a token was one of two parts that when brought together formed a meaningful unity. For example, when a transaction was agreed, a clay seal was broken in half. One piece was given to the client to serve as a voucher, while the other remained with the provider. Bear in mind that in those days, if you ordered goods from faraway lands, it could take months, if not years, to get your goods delivered. So, when the time to collect came, if the client's piece completed that of the provider, the product was handed over. Obviously, the Tartessians were privy to the practice and most assuredly used it. Does it sound familiar?"

"The fourth sacred tablet and its missing piece," answered Sofia. "The group that left took the piece as their identification token. Those that stayed behind had instructions to only supply or reveal the location of the mines to whoever came back with the piece. It was their way of protecting their prosperous business."

"What if the piece was lost?" asked Michael. "It would seem an enormous risk to tie a transoceanic trade route to one single piece, or even a single bearer."

Sofia looked at him. He made a good point. Her face suddenly paled as the answer exploded behind it. She looked up at the rendition of the fourth tablet hanging on the wall; her eyes fixed on the decapitated figure. It wasn't headless because of the broken piece, the body had been carved headless on purpose, and now she knew why. She slowly turned to the album her mother still held open in her hands. The answer was right there before them.

Everyone observed her with expectation.

Sofia inhaled a deep breath. Could it be? Had she figured out the true identity of Pahana? Had she unraveled the prophecy that was so central to her people, and more so to her family? She spoke almost in a whisper.

"I think I know who Pahana is." She first looked at Michael. "You're right. The Tartessians could not have bet their livelihood on one small piece of clay. The piece itself is irrelevant though extremely symbolic." Sofia gestured with her hand toward the copy of the fourth tablet on the wall. "The human figure is headless for a reason. In Hopi art, there is only one single difference between the representation of a man and that of a woman: the woman is depicted with whorls."

Her mother exhaled a loud breath of recognition. "Dear Lord, of course! The Tartessians venerated Tanit as we saw in their sanctuary, and it's believed that the Lady of Elche is likely her, as well. Further, she wasn't only a Goddess of fertility, Tanit was also the Protectress of seafarers. The missing piece, which may have depicted her female head, must have been a sacred code of sorts. She, Tanit, their Protectress, was the identification code."

"Pahana is a woman?" celebrated Lily. "I love it!"

The three women squealed with excitement as they hugged each other.

"We did it!" shouted Sofia.

"I'm so proud of you," cried Sakwa at her daughters. "You fulfilled the family prophecy! I knew you would!"

They hugged and jumped around. Sakwa reached out to include Michael and Gabriel who were happy to partake in the festivity. Finally, they paused to stare at each other until Sofia asked a fundamental question: "Now what?"

Everyone looked at Sakwa.

"I don't know," she mumbled as if caught off guard. "I never thought beyond this point."

"Should we tell the other elders?" suggested Lily.

Her mother appeared suddenly somewhat forlorn. "To be honest, I don't think they'll take it very well. It's another reason I have been reluctant to come out with this information. Think about it. Our people's zeal to conserve our ancient traditions, our legends and our prophecies has been exceptional. They are core to our identity, our reason for being. It is our belief that we are the chosen ones to keep the balance of the world, to teach the sacred value of the Great Spirit's Life Plan. Pahana is meant to bring in peace to the world. How do you go from that to explaining we are in reality but descendants of mineworkers whose traditions were designed to protect a prosperous metal trade business?"

Shoulders slouched; all's but Lily's.

She shook her head. "We're missing something. Let's be reasonable, even our traditional Life Plan talks of a straight path. It can't be a mere coincidence that two straight paths in Europe lead to a third straight path in the Americas and to our Hopi Straight Path. And they certainly don't do it just to tell us we were once Spanish gold miners. I doubt that's what Our Lady had in mind when She appeared in Fatima."

Michael and Gabriel exchanged looks. Then Gabriel asked the question. "The Hopi have a straight line as well?"

Lily sighed. "Not exactly, at least not like the Marian and Spanish ones. Remember when I told you about the ancient wisdom we received from the Great Spirit? I said it was coded in an image etched into a boulder in Oraibi we call Prophecy Rock. We name that image Life Plan, and it represents a schematic summary of our belief system. In brief, it depicts the Great Spirit instructing us to follow the 'straight path' meaning, in essence, a balanced way of life in harmony with nature. The petroglyph also shows a group of people on another line above the straight one, which trails off crooked, symbolic of its evil ways." Lily raised her hand to show her palm in sign of caution. "Please understand this is a gross simplification of a very ancient prophecy. There is more to it, but you get the picture."

Sakwa shook her head sadly as she flipped back some pages in her album. She then turned it for everyone to see.

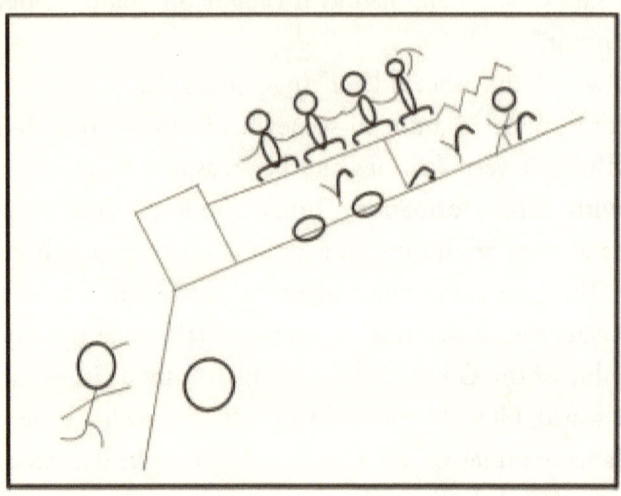

"This picture on the left is the image of our Life Plan on Prophecy Rock." She held it open, facing Michael and Gabriel. "You can see here the straight and crooked lines Lily was talking about." She pointed to them. "The bottom one is straight, the top one ends crooked. Now look at the comparative on the right. It is another votive chariot from the time of Tartessos."

The side-by-side comparison offered a completely new perspective of what the Life Plan resembled.

"Are you kidding me?" exclaimed Lily. "Our precious Life Plan is in reality a chariot?"

Even Sofia, who had never paid much credence to the prophecy, felt disappointed. Unfortunately, as she switched between the two pictures, that is exactly what it looked like, a schematic chariot with wheels and all. How could she have never noticed that before? How had no one else?

Sofia strained to understand the scene displayed on the votive chariot. "It's difficult to tell what I'm looking at. What do the figures on it represent?"

"I'm sorry, the picture is not very good, and the piece did not hold up well," admitted her mother. "It was found in Monte da Costa Figueira, north of present-day Portugal, and has been dated to the 4th century B.C. It's believed to be the scene of a sacrificial ritual, that of an animal. The human figures are priests, men and women lined up in pairs as if in a procession. I realize the compositions are not identical. The point I'm trying to make is that our Life Plan depicts a chariot displaying a scene in the same manner that the votive chariots did. But also, it's important to note that the composition of this particular votive chariot, though Celtic in nature, is uniquely Iberian. It is yet one more example of our distinct connection to ancient Iberians.

"Mom," started Sofia, "I see what you mean, but, technically, scenes generally require some sort of stage. The fact that our Hopi Life Plan scene is displayed on what could be construed as a chariot may simply be coincidental."

Sakwa's facial response was grim. She didn't like dethroning their sacred prophecy any more than anybody else. "It's difficult to see, but if you look closer, you'll notice that some of the people on the votive chariot are wearing backpacks and playing a flute."

As the twins dropped their jaws again, their mother explained to Michael and Gabriel. "One of our most charismatic and iconic kachinas is Kokopelli, a humpback flute player." She then turned the page. "Since we're at it, you might as well see this picture, as well." She showed it to them. "This is a warrior stele found in Ategua, a town located in the province of Cordoba in Spain. "The reason I bring it to your attention is because at the bottom there is the usual schematic chariot common to Tartessians steles. To its right there is a larger figure believed to be the driver, who is equivalent to the character we interpret as the Great Spirit standing to the left of our Life Plan. And see under the chariot on the stele? There is a group of little people holding hands identical to the one standing on our Life Plan's crooked path. In each rendition, one of the little people is even holding up the same cane."

"Lily was appalled. "Great Spirit is a chariot driver? That's just wrong!"

"Well, look at the chariot's wheels," said Sofia.

"Oh, no." Lily brought her hand to her mouth in shock.

"What about it?" asked Gabriel.

Sofia explained. "As you see, the wheel is a ring with four spokes. That is also the Hopi symbol for earth and our people. It's the center piece in our flag and it can be found in a lot of our rock art."

Sakwa was frozen in thought. Something had clicked in her mind. She put the album down on the cabinet's surface and crouched to look for something in it. She retrieved a folder with loose pictures that had not made it into the album.

"What is it mom?" asked Sofia curious.

"I just realized something." Sakwa stood up and flipped through the pictures. She quickly found the one she was looking for. Everyone crowded around and sneaked a peek over her shoulders.

Sakwa explained as she underlined a series of images with her finger.

"These are the four decorated sides of a cubed administrative seal found in the Tartessian Sanctuary Cancho Roano. The cube is irregular; two sides are larger than the other two. On one of the larger sides, you can see a chariot and its driver." Sakwa paused to look at it closely as if seeing it for the first time. "I kept this picture as another example of our Life Plan's resemblance to a Tartessian chariot scene. In this case, the schematic lines of the chariot and the position of the driver, who stands behind the chariot rather than riding on it, are even more comparable."

"I guess," accepted Sofia exercising some imagination. "The inclination and angles of the strokes that outline the chariot are very similar. So?"

Sakwa then pointed to the other large face of the cubed seal. "Look here. There is a man accompanied by a number of animals that I think look like a bird, an ox, and two lionesses portrayed as serpopards. The serpopard was an Ancient Egyptian mythological lioness with a long, snake-like neck. They were usually depicted in pairs with their necks intertwined. Here, due to the small size of the stamp, the necks are simply fused together.

"What about the two smaller sides?" asked Lily. "Both have a pair of animals facing each other."

Sakwa started by waving them off. They were irrelevant to the focus of her interest. "One shows two griffins and the other two goats..." She then trailed off again in thought.

"Okay, so what are you realizing?" asked Sofia.

"This seal is quite unique. Aside from being cubed instead of cylindrical as was the norm, experts are having trouble interpreting its overall meaning because it contains a hodgepodge of unrelated symbolic scenes from the Near East."

"So?" asked Sofia again.

"Look at the two male figures."

Sofia studied each one. She smiled. "Yes, I see. The one with the animals is no doubt a man; his private parts are displayed to make this clear. However, the chariot driver is missing his."

Michael and Gabriel leaned in to see better with a subtle wince.

"The chariot driver is a woman," said Lily picking up quickly on the implications.

Sakwa nodded but soon turned to shaking her head with a frown. "I can't believe I fell for the traditional male-centered interpretation. Me, of all people! I even noticed that oddity when I first saw it but thought nothing of it."

"If she is a woman," continued Lily, "that means she is a goddess. In the ancient Mediterranean, while male drivers could be warriors, leaders or gods, the female chariot driver was most certainly a goddess." She looked at her mother. "Does that mean the Great Spirit in our Life Plan depicts a woman? She is not wearing whorls."

Sakwa took a moment to think. "Not necessarily but could be. This seal is from the 7th century B.C. and its iconography is Phoenician. The rampant goats were closely associated with their Great Mother Goddess Asherah. Asherah later evolved into Tanit when Tyre, the Phoenician capital, fell to the Babylonians, and Carthage became their capital in the 5th Century. The Mediterranean goddesses Asherah, Astarte, Tanit, Nit, and others, were in essence all the same goddess. It's a long story. The point is that Asherah was considered God's female manifestation as it related to humans, since in creating us He was our Mother. Later, Tanit preserved this understanding. She became the Protectress of Carthage and her epithet remained 'The Face of Baal', meaning the *Face of the Lord*."

"*He is our Father, even more He is our Mother*," whispered Lily.

Despite the feeble connection back to Fatima, Sofia felt a wave of discomfort. They had gone from Marian apparitions and mysterious Black Madonnas to unravelling a mythical ancestry whose art butchered their most sacred beliefs. Her perfectionist brain struggled with the disjointed and chaotic amount of cross-continental cultural, historical and mythological data that piled up without a discernable end.

"How does any of this help us?" she asked frustrated. "Where are we going with it?"

Her mother was blunt. "I have no idea."

They resorted to taking a lunch break.

CHAPTER 31

Sofia stood before the scenic windows in the living room. They had just finished lunch, and she sought a moment alone to gather her thoughts. Spanish Fork spread at her feet on a persistently clear-skied day, and the sun was on the descent toward the western horizon. In the background, chatter from the kitchen could be heard, and an odd mixture of thrill and defeat still filled the air. It was apparent to everyone that discovering the true identity of Pahana, as the family prophecy called for, was by no means the end of their quest. And call it tribal pride or denial, none of the three Hopi ladies in the house were about to accept that their people had been conserving an ill-understood tradition for thousands of years. There had to be more to the Hopi Way than met the eye. Sofia was proud of her firm skeptic stance in life, and just as she had questioned superstitions, religious beliefs, rituals and what not, she was now determined to question what little rational evidence they had in the interest of her people.

Gabriel appeared through the kitchen door carrying a tray with coffee and cookies. He stopped in the hallway between the living room and the dining room, uncertain where to place it.

"Please leave it on the coffee table in the living room," said Sakwa from behind. "We'll be more comfortable there."

He obliged.

Lily and Michael followed.

Sakwa gestured them to sit on the sofa.

Before anyone had a chance to get comfortable, Sofia spoke as if trying to dislodge a painful splinter.

With her back to the room, she started solemnly. "Our people have been performing ceremonies around the calendar for centuries upon centuries because we genuinely believed it was important to the wellbeing of the world. Rarely do believers of other religions perform rituals for the sake of others as we do. Most do it to save themselves, and those who do not adhere to their beliefs are dismissed as pagans, heretics or infidels rightfully doomed to some horrific punishment for daring to dissent." She eased around, displaying hope in her features; not the spiritual type, but the kind fueled by loyalty. "We are the Peaceful Ones, the Guardians of Balance and Harmony. We care for all people no matter if they think like us, pray like us, or look like us; as we do for all creatures and nature."

Sofia paused, for that had been the Hopi in her speaking; now her rational mind took over again. She addressed her sister. "You said it. The European lines point to our ancestor's land and whosever hand is behind it—let's say Mary—seems keen on highlighting the importance of that potential ancestry as it connects us back to Europe. That cannot be a coincidence or meaningless. However," she continued as she retrieved the rosary from the side pocket of her jeans and turned to her mother, "I have a problem with this. I struggle with the concept of a bilocating nun no matter how extraordinary she was as a woman of her time. For skeptics like me, Mary has been providing tangible evidence supported by a discernable pattern to don the lines with credible weight." She displayed the reverse of the medallion. "These markings sparked your interest in archeology, which ultimately led you to the Tartessos-Hopi link. If we are to give that link any credence and continue down this track, we must first find its validation on the lines."

Lily's shoulders slouched, fearing there might not be any. "We've been working on the premise that Mary wants us to follow the path back to her son. Why then would She care to bring our attention to a possible European ancestry rooted in people that disappeared long before her son was even born?"

Sakwa answered. "I don't know about that, but I can tell you that Tartessos and our Puebloan ancestors are definitely linked through the lines, both lines."

The twins looked at her with surprise.

"Both?" said Sofia. "That would be definite. The lines feed each other; they're intertwined."

Her mother nodded, "I know, you mentioned that earlier." She got back up from the sofa. "Come, I'll show you."

They eagerly hustled to the maps in the dining room. Michael trailed behind in his characteristic silent-but-all-ears demeanor, while Gabriel lingered just enough to take a few quick sips of his coffee. He doubted he'd get back to it while still warm.

Flanked by her two daughters, Sakwa explained. "Earlier, when you walked me through your new findings on the maps, you explained how both lines led to cities named Medellin. It caught my attention because Medellin in Spain is the location of the most important Tartessos necropolis unearthed to date. Among a variety of valuable artifacts, an amulet with an image like the one on the front of the medallion you are holding was found there."

Sofia looked at the rosary in her hand with a mixture of bewilderment and relief. The fact that she, the skeptic, was indeed being supplied with the evidence she needed was almost more formidable than their mythical ancestry being validated by divine lines.

Lily burst with satisfaction. "That not only puts the Tartessians on the line, but it also connects our family legend to it."

"I would agree, but it is more than that," announced their mother. "If you extend the Spanish Line further southwest beyond Medellin, it continues to Merida." She showed them on the map. "That's the city where the votive chariot was found. This is important because Merida, inland, became the center of the Tartessians region after their coastal center was damaged by a tsunami. Their necropolis in Medellin is close by, as is their sanctuary, Cancho Roano. Aside from these two major sites, within a short radius around Merida, other important Tartessian settlements have been discovered, including more rock art like ours." Sakwa turned to Sofia. "I can show you pictures if you want."

Sofia waved her offer off. "I believe you."

Sakwa then drew an imaginary oval with her finger that framed an area encompassing the south of Portugal and the Southwest of Spain. "This was the general area they controlled during their formation period as demarcated by their warrior steles," she explained. "It's crossed down the middle by the Spanish Line."

Sofia deposited the rosary on the table and reached for the bag to retrieve the pencil and ruler she had taken from the library, which she promised her sister she'd compensate for generously as well. She then completed the line on the Spanish map by extending it to Merida.

She stood back. "Good, we have Tartessos well established along the Spanish Line." Sofia then studied the US segment of Mary's Line on the world map. They had considered naming the section between Medellin in Colombia and Spanish Fork in the US the Americas' Line. However, for Sofia, the fact that they touched in Medellin had her feel it was meant to continue as one. Her eyes zeroed in on an area short of Spanish Fork. "And Mary's Line cuts through our ancestor's Four Corners region."

"Yes," confirmed Sakwa, "but if you want to be really picky," she pointed to a spot in Utah, "it runs right through Moab where I have found the highest concentration of Tartessos and Hopi equivalencies." She gestured toward the pictures on the wall where two examples hung.

It was difficult to appreciate on the world map. Sofia fetched the Central America-Southwest map from the bag, and laid it open on top.

And there it was. Everyone could see it. Moab was on the line.

The general sentiment was of awe. The Spanish Line cut through the middle of the Tartessos region, touching specifically its main center, while Mary's Line cut through the middle of the Hopi's ancestral region, touching specifically its main center of art equivalencies with the Tartessos. Not the freakiest coincidence in the world could accomplish such a feat. It was clear that the Tartessians and the Hopi were connected, and Mary wanted it to be known.

Yet the critical question still floated in the air.

Lily voiced it. "My question again: Why would Our Lady bring our attention to an ancestry that predates Jesus' birth? How can this possibly relate to Fatima?"

"That's a very good question," said Sofia thoughtfully. Her eyes slid over to the rosary. It was the only lead they had. She picked it up again and turned to her mother addressing the medallion once more. "You said an image like this was found on an amulet in Medellin's necropolis. It may hold the clue. I imagine you researched it. What did you find out about it?"

"It was a necklace pendant. The theme was relatively common and widespread among Egyptians, Phoenicians and Greeks alike."

"You've mentioned the Phoenicians several times. I have a vague idea who they were, but do you mind expanding on them?"

"Sure. They were the Biblical Canaanites. They originally lived on the coastal strip of land we know today as Lebanon. Curiously, though they invented the alphabet we all use today, most of their writings were limited to commercial transactions. What we know of them is largely thanks to the Greeks who were the ones to call them Phoenicians, meaning purple, for the monopoly they had on the purple dye used in royal and priestly clothing. They were prosperous merchants with trade posts and colonies across the Mediterranean. When their Canaanite city of Tyre was invaded by the Babylonians first and the Persians soon after, one of their colonies, the city of Carthage in current Tunisia became their powerhouse. Later, the Romans came along and referred to them as the Punic. During their three grueling Punic Wars, Carthage fell, so yet another colony, New Carthage on the southeast coast of Spain became their stronghold until it too eventually fell to the Romans. In short, the Canaanites, the Phoenicians, the Carthaginians and the Punic were all—more or less—the same people, whose commercial enterprise dominated most of the Mediterranean for over 1,000 years."

"Understood." Sofia now centered her attention on the finer details of the rosary's medallion. "I see what looks like a mountain at the bottom, a vertical snake on each side, a circle in the center crowned with a crescent moon, and a pair of opened wings at the top. What is it supposed to represent?"

"That depends on who you ask," started her mother with a touch of mystery in her tone. "For the Egyptians it represents Creation. For the Phoenicians/Carthaginians it symbolizes Tanit. For the Greeks it's interpreted as the oracle of the center of the word. And for the Tartessians, I imagine a little of everything."

Sofia raised a mocking eyebrow. "Well, that clears it up."

Her mother chuckled. "It's not really all that confusing since they are different versions of the same thing. I'll explain. It starts with the Egyptians. The mountain is the primordial mound that emerged from the ocean of chaos and, as such, is considered the center of the world. Upon its peak, the sun god—either Ra or Amon, depending on the source—came to be. The two cobras represent his sovereignty, like the Uraeus you see on the forehead of a pharaoh in paintings or statues. And his divinity is confirmed by the winged disc seen at the top." Sakwa paused briefly, signaling a slight adjustment in narrative. "That original mountain-island, called Benben, was represented in temples by a sacred stone in the form of a cone or pyramid believed to have the power to connect heaven and earth, anointing the temple with the aura of a cosmic center. You may be more familiar with the Greek version of this: the notorious oracles. For the Greeks, the sacred stone was called Omphalos, and since it connected heaven and earth, their sanctuaries became pilgrim centers where people went to consult the gods. The more famous one is the Oracle of Delphi in Greece."

Sofia nodded. "How does that relate to the Goddess Tanit?" she asked.

"Well, here is where it gets interesting. Egypt juggled several creation stories at the same time, each with its own creator. The oldest one, from before Egypt was even Egypt, had the Goddess Neith as Creator." Sakwa paused with a twinkle in her eye. "She was said to weave the world into existence."

Lily leaned into Gabriel to explain, while Michael appeared distracted with the maps. "We also have a female spirit said to weave the world into existence. We call her Spider Woman."

"Neith was worshiped across the northern coast of Africa," continued her mother. "When the Phoenicians founded Carthage in current Tunisia, they adopted her and called her Tanit, because Tanit means just that, Land of Neith. Now, look at the outline of the composition. The mountain in the form of a triangle is her body, the sun in the form of a circle is her head, and the snakes are her arms. This profile looks like the modern icon of a woman and was known as the Sign of Tanit. Basically, it portrays Tanit as the personification of Creation. And since God is not visible, but his Creation is, she was also known as the Face of the Lord."

Sofia understood. "The true face of Pahana."

But her mother wasn't done. "And now look at the crescent moon. It functions as a sort of diadem. This matters to us because in Tartessian territory, long before Carthage was founded, instead of the Sign of Tanit or profile of a woman, it was her diadem that took on a life of its own as a symbol of protection. You see, there were two categories of stone slabs in Tartessos. One was the warrior stele we've already seen, and the other was the diadem stele for the diadems its figures wear. It's not quite clear if the figures are warriors protected by Tanit's diadem or Tanit herself. Maybe both. Either way, I have found diadem-themed rock art here too."

"Indicating once more that it was the Iberian peoples who visited," concluded Sofia.

Lily shook her head in utter confusion. "Creation, goddesses, sacred rocks and oracles... What is Mary trying to tell us?"

The twins looked at each other feeling awkwardly lost, like when you're in one of those hedge mazes thinking you are near the exit only to find yourself closer to its claustrophobic center.

"Ladies," they heard Michael call, "I think you need to take a look at this." He pointed to three spots on Mary's Line.

Sofia was first to glean what he meant.

"What the...?!"

CHAPTER 32

Just when she thought nothing could shock her anymore. Sofia rubbed her eyes in disbelief. "Exactly how many cities named Merida are there?"

"I don't know, but whatever the number, three of them are bisected by the lines," said Michael. "There is this one we already know on the Spanish Line, and then there are these two in Venezuela and Mexico on Mary's Line."

Sakwa looked on in awe. "Spain, Venezuela and Mexico... That's one per segment ... Remarkable ..."

Gabriel was curious about the statistical probability of what they were looking at and pulled out his phone to find out. Meanwhile, the women ran their eyes along the lines several times counting Meridas.

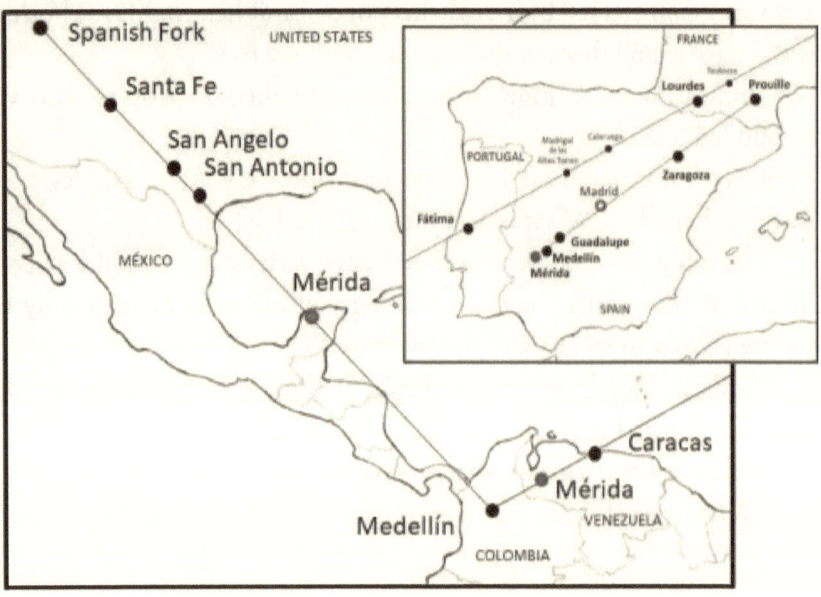

"That's all there are, three," said Gabriel. "There are a couple of smaller locations in Mexico and a municipality in the Philippines named Merida, but as a city, there are only three in the world, these three, and the three are the capitals of their respective provinces."

"That's crazy!" Lily's eyes were bulging. "So, if two cities named Medellin brought us here and gave us the Lady in Blue-Tartessos-Hopi link, what is three Meridas trying to tell us?"

Many blank gazes were exchanged.

"Let's think," started Sofia, and then she did what she always did, summarize the situation to register it better. "There are only three cities in the world named Merida, and the three are located on the lines, but not just anywhere on the lines, one per straight segment." She shared her look of shock with her sister. "There is no way that is an accident. There must be something of such importance about Merida that the city's presence on the lines was tripled so we wouldn't miss it." Sofia then turned to her mother. "You said Merida was the center of Tartessos when they moved inland. Is there anything else about that city you can think of that can justify something like this?"

"Not really. What little I know has to do with its prehistorical archaeological sites. Other than that, I only have a rough idea of the city's historical outline. Bear in mind it is worth 2,000 years."

"It's not just Merida in Spain," said Lily. "What if one of the American Meridas holds the key like the American Medellin did? Or what if it's a combination of the three?"

"Agreed," said Sofia. She took a moment to assess their monumental challenge. Three cities in three countries whose prehistory was just as rich as their history, if not more. Where to even start looking for a clue? After some thought, she concluded there was only one way to go about it: systematically. "We have a lot to tackle, but there is five of us, so let's divide the load. And let's be practical. We must stay true to the lines. Focus on any piece of information related to Tartessos, Marian Shrines and so forth." She addressed her mother. "I'd like you to take another look at your notes regarding Tartessos and their sites around Merida. But before you do so, give me the run down on the city's historical outline to get an idea on how to divide it up. Since it is the original one, we should start there and then move on to the other two."

Sakwa played with a strand of loose hair as she combed through her memory. In getting ready to speak, she tucked it behind her ear. "Okay, let's see. Merida was founded by the Romans as an up-scaled retirement destination for its veterans of war. For the longest time, scholars believed that the site was void of prior settlements, which is an oddity since, typically, invaders set up camp in preexisting towns and cities. I remember this because we now know that Tartessos artifacts are being unearthed in the vicinity, not to mention that a 6,000-year-old dolmen, one of the largest megalithic structures on the peninsula, can be found there too. So, the site was occupied and of great importance long before the Romans chose it. Whatever its appeal, Augustus envisioned a second Rome for the spot. He spared no money building the city. It was provisioned with all the infrastructure of a prosperous urban enclave, from two aqueducts, bridges, and roads to a circus, two theatres, a celebratory arch, temples, a forum, and all sort of grandiose buildings, both public and private. The place was impressive even by today's standards, let alone back in 25 B.C. My understanding is that it ranked within the ten most important cities in the whole empire. After the Romans, I think Merida continued to be an important center with the Christian Visigoths, though it lost ground to the city of Cordoba during the Muslim occupation in the 8th century. Eventually it was later taken back by the Christian side in the 13th century ..." Sakwa suddenly froze. She then smacked her forehead. "I just remembered something. There is this medieval legend ... It connects the Spanish Merida with the American Southwest and even us."

Eyebrows arched high and eyes opened wide as if what they were looking for had magically materialized before them.

"Are you serious?" said Sofia in disbelief. "There's actually a medieval legend that connects Merida with us beyond the Tartessos? How is that even possible?"

"It's possible because it likely digs its roots in Tartessos, and from there, it ties into the legend of Cibola or the Seven Cities of Gold," said Sakwa. "Look, it goes back to the Moorish invasion of the Iberian Peninsula in the 8th century. According to the medieval legend, seven bishops from Merida fled with precious golden relics and took off across the Atlantic to save them. Which is to say that the locals seemed to think crossing the Atlantic was feasible long before Columbus. I suspect they conserved a vague memory of the Tartessian travels." She shrugged. "As for where the bishops went is unknown, but since most of the early Spanish explorers were from the area, the legend fueled their ventures in search of the Seven Cities of Gold that led the Coronado expedition to our Hopi mesa, and to the subsequent exploration of most of the Southwest."

Sofia was familia with the legend of the Seven Cities of Gold that led Spanish explorers to their mesa in Arizona, but never in a million years would she have thought it had any basis in reality. "Okay," she said shaking her head, "I guess one of us should look into that legend's historical background."

"Dibs!" called Gabriel. His youthful face lit up with the prospect of tracking down lost treasures.

"All yours," chuckled Sofia. She then rubbed her face. "Just what we needed, lost relics. Like we don't have enough going on already: Marian Secrets, enigmatic Black Madonnas, lost mythical civilizations, and all laced with Divine Lines. I'm surprised the Order of the Knights Templar isn't involved as well."

Lily gave her a sympathetic squeeze on the arm. "Hang on in there, sis. If Christian relics are involved, you can bet the Knights Templar and maybe even the Holy Grail will find their way into this."

"I say we go big or go home," started Sofia in jest, short of going delirious. Her skeptic mind was on the verge of imploding. "How about we top it off with the Ark of the Covenant."

Everyone laughed. It truly was becoming a bewildering, all-inclusive quest.

With all the joking, Gabriel was no longer sure if Sofia was serious about looking into the legend. "So, drop the legend of Cibola then?" he asked.

"No," responded Sofia a little more sober, "It is too much of a coincidence that the legend links Merida with our people. Please, go ahead, look into it."

Relieved, Gabriel nodded.

Lily quickly moved to pick her research topic. "While Gabriel searches for lost relics, I'll settle for something a little more prosaic like the 15th century. I bet Queen Isabella is connected in some way to Merida. The city was in her realm after all."

"And I bet you're right," scoffed Sofia. "That woman's hand was behind everything. In fact, she may be behind the American Meridas. From their locations, they were probably found shortly after the discovery. Do you mind looking into it?"

Lily nodded and turned to her mother. "Do you have a spare computer I can use?"

"Use the one in my office. My notes are securely saved to several external drives. I can access them with my tablet. And for you Sofia, if you need one, your dad's laptop is in the kitchen." Sakwa then addressed Michael. "I have a spare tablet somewhere. I can look for it."

"No, please don't trouble yourself. I have my phone."

"Good, I'll get to work, then."

As her mother and sister left the room, Sofia consulted with Michael. "That leaves you and me with the Visigoth and Muslim periods. Any preference?"

"Definitely the Muslim period," he answered, pulling his phone out of his back pocket. "Our time in Spain was our Golden Age. I love that part of our history. Besides, I'm familiar with it; it'll be easier for me to sort through the hay."

It was settled; the Visigoths was for Sofia. Not her area of strength to be certain, but in light of Merida's overwhelming presence on the lines, she couldn't wait to see what she dug up.

She headed to the kitchen and sat at the desk in front of her dad's laptop. As a professional researcher, she was adept at finding the sources of information she needed. She began with a cursory skim over Merida's chronology and found that her period began around the 5th century, which made sense since it followed the fall of the Roman Empire. The collapse had started as a slow crumble at the edges around the 2nd century. Hispania, located on the far western limits, was among the first to suffer the onslaught of several Germanic invasions. However, the Empire's worst hit came from its northeastern European border. It took these Barbarians a couple of centuries to make their way southwest across Europe, where they arrived as the Visigoths. Through the chaotic transition, Merida suffered greatly but retained its prime place as a major capital, and with the conversion of the

Arian Visigoths to Catholicism in the 5th century, the city rebounded to splendorous heights.

Sofia searched for a Marian Shrine and of course there was one, the cathedral. When she read about it, she winced. It did not quite fit the pattern ... except maybe for one thing that made her roll her eyes and exhale in desperation.

CHAPTER 33

A couple of hours passed, and everyone reconvened in the living room around a fresh pot of hot coffee served with an assortment of cookies, the same ones untouched earlier.

Spirits drooped low.

No one had found the silver bullet that warranted Merida's predominance on the lines. Not even Gabriel, who had the best shot at it.

Lily was perhaps the most discouraged of all, for, though Merida was in Queen Isabella's realm, nothing she read stood out remotely promising.

Despite or in view of the generalized dwindling mood, Sofia took the lead. "I realize no one found anything, but, nonetheless, I'd like to hear a summary. I'm sure we all agree there is something to be found."

Everyone nodded halfheartedly.

"I suggest we follow a chronological order. Mom, can you start please?"

Sakwa hurried to swallow her last piece of chocolate chip cookie. She helped it down with a sip of coffee.

"All I found is yet another potential ancient link between Merida and America. It's much older than the comparatives I showed you earlier. I'm not sure how it helps us, though."

"Tell us anyway," encouraged Sofia.

"In that case, let me explain ... The oldest hominid remains of Europe have been found on the Iberian Peninsula, so it's not surprising that some of the oldest rock art in the world is also there. And it's pretty impressive, too. The 15,000-year-old paintings in the Cave of Altamira, for instance, are true masterpieces; they even humbled Picasso who expressed he had nothing on them when he saw the bulls and used them as inspiration. Anyway, recent finds have also unearthed a 7,000-year-old, blue-eyed individual. It came as a surprise since it was believed that the blue-eyed gene had been imported to Europe from the Black Sea around 5,000 B.C. Yet this Iberian already had it at the farthest possible point from the Black Sea. All this is important because it starts to question the traditional East-West flow theory. Or, at least, its exclusiveness. There's enough evidence to suggest the occasional

West-East flow as well." She raised a finger. "The fun facts don't end there." She paused to sip more coffee.

Sofia cursed silently at herself. Her mother, like her sister, tended to ramble on topics they enjoyed. She wondered if she should have bypassed her when she had the chance. She'd give her a couple more minutes.

Her mother continued. "An interesting phenomenon occurred during the Neolithic period on the European Atlantic front that has scholars confounded. Starting in the 5th millennia B.C, huge megalithic structures began to pop up in distinct pocket-areas with no known connection between them. This happened from Spain and Portugal all the way to Scandinavia, passing through France and the British Isles. The largest concentrations have been uncovered in Brittany, France, but some of the oldest can be found on the Iberian Peninsula, largely within the Tartessos area of influence. An idea being kicked around is that these people were accomplished high-sea fishermen who left their mark navigating along the northern Atlantic Coast. That's why there is no land trail. And a recent DNA analysis supports it. It indicates that the ancient settlers of the British Isles came from Spain, meaning in sum that there was an ancient flow of emigration and influence fanning out from the Iberian Peninsula."

Sofia cleared her throat.

Sakwa looked at her askance while patting the air with her hand asking for patience. "This is very important because in Merida, as I said before, there is a 6,000-year-old stone grave, the largest in Spain, built in the passage-grave style." She raised a sheet of paper. "Here's its schematic. It looks a lot like one of the controversial root cellars of New England, a stone chamber found in Upton, Massachusetts." She raised another schematic. Side-by-side they could be mistaken for the same place. She looked at her audience. "Are you familiar with the latter?"

She saw a lot of heads shaking, so she explained. "The northeast of the United States in general, but especially the New England area, is dotted by hundreds of stone chambers once believed colonial root cellars. Current archeological studies are questioning this assumption. Barry Fell mentions them extensively in his book and even ventured to link them to Iberian Celts because of the inscriptions found in them. I knew of this, but I didn't expect to find one in Merida predating the Celts by more than 3,000 years. It suggests the Tartessos, or better said their ancestors were visiting America much earlier." Sakwa could be seen wandering off in her mind, probably in awe of the implications.

Sofia embraced the opportunity to move on.

"Well, I'm not sure if what I have will help either. Regardless," she paused to focus on her sister, "you are going to love this: The cathedral in Merida is dedicated to Saint Mary Major, and its main entrance houses a statue of Our Lady of the Good Guide or Way."

"Really? Like the Byzantine Hodegetria?"

"Not exactly. This one is much more current, a local version, and white. There are no Black Madonnas in the city that I could find. Interestingly though, the cathedral does have a strong link with the Byzantine East. During the cities prime period in the 6th century, two bishops, an uncle and a nephew from Greece, ran the place. The uncle built the cathedral in the 6th century on the site of an earlier temple. It was originally named Basilica of Saint Jerusalem, which his nephew remodeled and dedicated to Mary. A novelty at the time since, as you know, Marian devotion did not gain traction in the West until later. Other than that ..." Sofia paused hesitantly. The cathedral was associated with yet another legend and the better part of her resisted sharing it because, of course, how could it be otherwise, it concerned relics from Solomon's Temple.

She exhaled a sigh of defeat. *What the hell. Why not!* She addressed Gabriel with a rueful smile. "Talking about relics, there is another legend that might tie in with yours."

Everyone leaned in to listen. It never failed; despite all the fascinating historical data they were dealing with, it was the legends of lost treasures that caught everyone's interest.

"I read an article based on the account of a Muslim historian, I think his name was Al-Razi. He claimed that Merida's cathedral housed items that once belonged to Solomon's Temple."

"No way," exclaimed Lily, "don't tell me we truly are searching for the Ark?"

"Not necessarily. Apparently, Solomon had no shortage of fantastical relics gone astray. The ones that made it to Merida were pillaged during Nebuchadnezzar's invasion. One was a rock that emitted light, enough to illuminate the cathedral. There was also a pot of pearls, and a table made of gold or emerald or something like that. According to Al-Razi, these items were found by the Muslim forces upon taking the city. Normally, I would have discarded the account as nonsense because, apart from the shinny-rock-thingy, there is no proof King Solomon ever existed. That said, there was a temple in Jerusalem regardless of who built it, so fine, let's call it Solomon's Temple. But even then, the dates don't add up, either. The Babylonians destroyed it in 586 B.C. while Merida wasn't founded until 25 B.C. There was no city or Christians to build cathedrals to house anything." She turned to her mother to continue. "However, you told us there was a major Tartessos sanctuary in the vicinity, and we know from the Bible that Tartessos had strong business ties with King Solomon. Is it conceivable that relics from Jerusalem made their way to the Merida area, and later moved to the cathedral when it was built? I mean it was originally named Basilica of Saint Jerusalem after all."

Sakwa pondered the question a moment and then nodded her head. "Indeed," she answered, "and for several good reasons: The Tartessians were Solomon's providers of gold, gems and other precious metals. *They* were his fabled goldmines. Also, Solomon commissioned the building of his Temple to the Phoenicians, who we know set up a major trading post next door to the Tartessians for their supply needs. Therefore, one way or other, maritime traffic was highly active between these opposed ends of the Mediterranean during King Solomon's time. As for the Temple relics, I don't know about them," she admitted, "but there are several references to Tartessos in the Bible as a safe haven of sorts. For example, the Hebrew prophet Jonah tries to flee Israel by boarding a ship with destination to Tartessos."

A sudden idea gave Sakwa pause. She was stunned by its possible implication. She turned to study the framed picture of the Tartessos sanctuary on the wall. It took her a few seconds to react and explain. "Cancho Roano was built around the time of the destruction of Solomon's Temple ... In fact, its floor plan is suspiciously similar to the vision Ezekiel had of the New Temple that was to replace it."

She checked with Gabriel, who agreed with a nod. "I would say their floor plans are identical. But to be fair, it was a relatively common layout."

"Common in the Levant," clarified Sakwa. She looked at her daughter displaying amazement for her own conclusion. "The sanctuary could have been built to house the relics."

Sofia was probably more stunned than her mother. She really had not expected her casual question to have a valid answer. With this new information, she too addressed Gabriel. "Okay, so if a magic rock, pearls and a precious table is what the Muslims found left behind, did you find any specifics on what the bishops would have thought more valuable to run off with? And please don't tell me it was the Ark."

Grabiel smiled. "Relics are mentioned. But no specifics. It's the gold that spurs the chroniclers' imagination."

She sighed with relief. "That doesn't surprise me. I read the Visigoths had the custom of donating gold items to their local churches. Sources rave over the riches the temples held, and those in Merida were up there among the richest of the richest. The cathedral had a whole room dedicated to them." She shook her head feeling their attention was drifting away from more serious matters lured by age-old fantasies of lost treasures. "Look, I understand the alure of King Solomon, but let's be serious, what's the likelihood relics from the First Temple made it to Spain. Besides, even if they had, they'd be common temple artifacts. No real magic. Why would they matter to us? We need to refocus. I say we call it a dead end and move on."

Michael raised his hand to gesture his wish to intervene. "Before we do, there is something you should know about the table spotted in the cathedral. It could well be the table from the First Temple." He grinned. "Let's call it Solomon's Table. Al-Razi is not the only Muslim source to place it in Spain."

Sofia wrinkled her eyebrows. "I never even heard of Solomon's Table until now."

"It's very popular among treasure hunters for its fabled material wealth. According to Alexandrian sources of the 2nd century B.C., Ptolemy II, King of Egypt, donated the table to the Second Temple of Israel. It was meant to replace the one lost from the First Temple. Ptolemy II wanted to ingratiate himself with the Israelis by crafting one worthy of Solomon's luster. Later,

Roman sources tell how in the year 70 A.D., Titus, who would become Emperor, sacked Jerusalem and took the table to Rome. You can see it depicted among other spoils-of-war on his triumphal arch. The table remained there until the Goths took over the city in 401 and removed it to Carcassonne in the south of France. This area, too, ended up falling in battle, so one way or other the Visigoths managed to bring it to Toledo, Spain, where Muslim sources pick up. In brief, Musa bin Nusayr, commander of the invading forces, sent his second, Tariq bin Ziyad, in 711, to lay the ground for his arrival. Tariq, knowing of the table, sought it and found it in Toledo. Accounts then differ on what came of it. Some say it is still there hidden. Others that it got lost on its way to Damascus. And others yet that it made it to the Calipha's hands." Michael shrugged, "Who knows."

"I'm confused" said Sofia, "Sources place it anywhere but Merida."

"Not all sources. And you're right to be confused, that's the point I'm trying to make. Treasure hunters insist on confusing the table that King Ptolemy II donated to the Second Temple with the original Solomon's Table. The original one, thoroughly described in the Book of Kings, is the one we should care about. And that's the one most likely spotted in Merida's cathedral."

Sofia shook her head. "Aside from belonging once to King Solomon, which I'm sure would make it extremely valuable—if he had existed, that is—why should we care about it? Even the bishops left it behind."

Michael exchanged glances with Gabriel. "Why don't you explain it?"

Gabriel suddenly seemed to add ten years of maturity to his facial expression. His eyes rolled ceremoniously over the three ladies. "Jewish tradition holds that God commanded Moses to build the Tabernacle for His Divine Presence. Among the vessels built for the Tabernacle, there was the Ark of the Covenant, in which the tablets of the Ten Commandments were kept, the menorah, and a table to hold the bread offerings. This table is therefore known as the Table of the Divine Presence. Later King David wished to provide God's Divine Presence with a more worthy dwelling and entrusted the building of the First Temple to his son Solomon, who furnished it with vessels crafted of gold and gems. The new Temple and its rich vessels were therefore meant to replace the ones built by Moses." Gabriel's face rejuvenated again as it lit up. "However, legend has it that the true value of Solomon's Table is not in its precious materials, but in what Solomon engraved on it. In Jewish tradition, God's name cannot be pronounced other than by the High Priest on Yom Kippur. No practicing Jew ever does. We rather refer to Him as Our Lord. Then the esoteric branch of Judaism, Kabbalah, takes it a little further by asserting that His real name is not even known because it's kept secret. Kabbalah asserts that God shared His name only with Moses, who entrusted it to his brother Aaron, the first High Priest, and thereafter it has been handed down from High Priest to successor. Solomon was privy to it because he was not only king but also the High Priest." Gabriel paused. "It is said that Solomon etched God's forbidden name, or *Shem ha-Meforash*, on the table's top in the form of a geometric or hieroglyphic code. And this table was kept in the Temple for the Highest Priest's eyes only."

Sofia checked on everyone to see how seriously they were taking this. It would seem very much. She started to feel overwhelmed in addition to being restless for having to depend on so many legends, myths and fables to progress in their mission. It was getting absurd: First the Christian legend of lost relics, then a Muslim legend about a fabled table, and now a Jewish legend that spoke of secret divine names.

Lily, on the other hand, was having the time of her life. She leaned in. "May I ask why God's name must be kept secret?"

Gabriel appeared delighted to explain it. "Because of its power. It has to do with God creating the world through the Word. When He said, 'let there be light', for instance, light was created because the word 'light' carries the essence of light itself. Thus, it follows that all words carry the essence of the concept they represent. Based on this understanding, Kabbalah, the mystical branch of Judaism, and its fundamental text 'Zohar' hold that true wisdom can be obtained by studying the 'words' of the Torah and reaching the ultimate comprehension of their intrinsic essence."

"How?"

"By progressing along four levels of interpretation. The first level is the literal understanding whereby if you read the word 'light' it means simply that *light*. The second level interprets 'light' metaphorically as in *enlightenment*. The third level finds associations between similar words or sentences to weave deeper complex meanings, and finally at the last and highest level, skilled interpretation leads to the word's inner secret or vital energy. If you apply this to God's name, the fourth level gives access to His wisdom and maybe even power."

"I see," admired Lily, "that's why it's kept concealed. And you say His 'secret name' was written on the table?"

"Not written but coded in a geometric or hieroglyphic form, in the sense of esoteric. Only the High Priest and his successor knew how to interpret it."

"So, whoever gets their hands on the table, if they figure out how to decipher it, would have access to God's wisdom and power."

Gabriel smiled. "That is the rumor."

Lily reacted with a glimpse of horror. "Oh, no! The Spanish bishops left it behind. They probably didn't know this."

Michael stepped in. "I would suspect the contrary. The table was laminated in gold. It is said that the coded design was engraved on the top plate. Merida did not fall under Moorish control until two years into the invasion. That gave the bishops ample warning to remove the engraved plate and escape, leaving the rest of the more cumbersome material-rich table behind."

CHAPTER 34

Lily walked up to her sister. Per Sofia's request, the group had taken a break and even a nap. Later, while Michael and Gabriel sought a private corner to attend to some telephone calls and other personal matters, Sofia had chosen to take a stroll down the back hill. Over time her parents had built small, walkable terraces that led down to a modest landing. At its far end, the well laid in forgotten silence. That's where Lily found her.

"You okay?"

Sofia turned looking surprisingly relaxed with a broad smile. "I am. It's funny you know. I'm shocked by how small and harmless it looks. I can't believe I've spent my life thinking of it as the mouth of a vile volcano ready to suck me in."

Lily assessed it for herself. There really wasn't much to it. The well was but a round brick construction secured with a locked iron lid. Following Sofia's incident, their father had sealed it. Somehow in her mind it appeared more imposing too.

She chuckled. "I think it shrunk. There is no way your butt fit through that little opening even back then."

Sofia smacked her sister playfully on the shoulder. "What ever happened to sweet, pious nuns?"

Lily's gaze saddened as she lowered it to the well. "I wonder myself sometimes."

"What?" Sofia was struck by the sudden downturn.

"Lately I've found myself doubting about too many things too often."

"Really? Like what?"

She shrugged her shoulders. "You know; everything." Lily raised her eyes and settled them on her sister. "Why do I bother fighting an institution riddled with age-old ways? It is run by men wearing extravagant garb designed thousands of years ago. Why expect their mentality to update with any agility. I feel sometimes like I joined the wrong club."

"Has your faith wavered?"

"No ... Yes ... I'm not sure. I mean, I believe there is something more. I truly believe Jesus came to save us, and that Our Lady is trying to tell us something. But I find myself questioning many, fully defined precepts that are no longer that clear to me. Like the crucifixion. It is central to Christianity that God sacrificed his only son for our sins, yet I find it increasingly difficult to accept that any loving father would destine his own son to such a horrid fate. This idea whereby human sacrifice, animal sacrifice, blood and suffering fix anything just seems wrong. God is all powerful; surely he can find other ways of dealing with human sin."

"I'm with you. If he exists, I hope for everyone's sake he is better than that."

"Sof, I'm a religious sister. I should not doubt any of this for a second."

"Why not? Who says faith can't be reached through doubt, questions and reason? What's it worth if blind and dictated? Isn't there more value in taking ownership of what one believes?"

"What if I reach the wrong understanding? The Church's role is to guide us."

"Technically, most churches coerce. You either believe what they say, or you're doomed to hell. Listen, guidance should be welcomed and respected if you feel you need it, but at the end of the day, it should be your responsibility to make decisions on what you believe, and that too should be respected." Sofia could see her sister was still struggling. "Remember the five mysteries John Paul II introduced in the prayer of the rosary? Two had God saying loud and clear that he was proud of His son and how He loved him, right?"

"You are my beloved Son, in whom I am well pleased," quoted Lily.

"Exactly, so what's the risk in concluding that God would never send His son to be tortured to death? He's probably up there pissed off everyone thinks He did."

Lily shook her head. "You're impossible." She then sighed. "But I'm inclined to agree, which furthers the argument that I'm a misfit in their club."

"It's not their club, Lily. It's God's Club, and if they are mismanaging or misrepresenting it, someone has to step up and do something about it. That's the problem with insiders, they don't. The line between being loyal and becoming an accomplice is a difficult one to discern sometimes." Sofia then poked her finger into her sister's shoulder. "And if you think you can drag me this far into this only to drop out now, you've got another thing coming, girl!"

Lily awarded her sister a gaze of gratitude. "I know this is not easy for you. I don't think I would have got this far without you."

Sofia furrowed her eyebrows in discord. "I'm not sure I should get all the credit."

"Since when are you so humble?"

"Haven't you noticed that whenever we are a little confused or unsure about how to proceed Michael steps in to guide us the right way?"

"Sof, you got us here and figured out Pahana all on your own."

"Correction, you got us here. But to the point; what about the three Meridas?"

"Any one of us would have come across them sooner or later. They were right there, in front of our eyes. In fact, the Meridas' clue revealed itself only because you insisted on staying true to the lines. With my faith-leaping between the two Ladies of Guadalupe we would have cut the corner that goes through Venezuela and Colombia and never known of them."

"Well, there is no way I would have ever stumbled on that Solomon Table lead. And then there is Gabriel. How is it that he knows all the Kabbalah trivia facts that are so convenient to our quest?"

"He's Jewish."

"So what? Half the Christians I know wouldn't win a Christian trivia game if their salvation depended on it."

"Now you are just exaggerating."

"I don't think so. What about their angel names? I bet they have another cousin called Raphael."

"You are reading too much into it. They are good guys with their heart in the right place simply trying to help. Mom's help has been priceless as well."

Sofia folded her arms over her chest staring intensely at her sister. "Why are *you* being so reasonable?"

"Perhaps because we're spending too much time together. You are dangerously rubbing off on me."

Sofia smiled and turned to head back up. "Unfortunately, I can say the same."

"Really? In that case, what do you think about God's secret name?" asked Lily, falling in step with her. "Could that be what we are looking for?"

Sofia scoffed. "God's secret name with access to His wisdom and power of all things? Are you kidding me? We might as well be looking for Thor's hammer. Besides, why would the lines lead to it? Hardly the best way to keep it safe and hidden."

"Listen, I doubt it gives access to His wisdom and power. I'd like to think that would require more than just knowing His name. But still, it may provide access to some important knowledge or message. You know, like identifying Pahana did. It wasn't so much about *who* Pahana was as *what* Pahana represented."

"Great, Pahana all over again. A secret name... A secret identity... Only this time we don't have a tablet to help us."

"The gold laminate with the engraved geometric code equates to our tablet. Maybe that's what we're supposed to find."

Sofia shook her head; a gesture she had come to automate. "I feel like we are chasing fairies. We need to ground this with something more sensible."

"Our Lady, Mother of God, has laid a path for us to follow. If we are to believe that I don't see why we can't consider that it may lead to a Divine Message or Knowledge contained within God's Name. It's not that farfetched to me."

Sofia glanced warmly at her sister. For her, every single word Lily had just pronounced qualified as farfetched, yet hearing her tone imbued again with her characteristic trust and hope, somehow comforted Sofia immensely.

Up on the deck, as the sisters approached, they heard a deep, familiar voice.

"Dad's home!" exclaimed Lily, picking up her pace.

They found him engrossed in a conversation with their mother, Michael, and Gabriel. From his stunned gaze, it was apparent they were bringing him up to date. It morphed immediately to reflect joy when he saw his daughters. His arms opened wide. "There you are!"

The three hugged at the same time.

"What took you so long?" asked Lily as she stepped back. "I thought you'd be home sooner."

"I wish I had. From what I'm hearing, I almost missed out on all the fun. Quite an exciting mission you have going here." He then fixed his look on Sofia.

Sofia said in words what his eyes spoke silently. "It's good to see you." She was pleased he had not changed and looked good. And she especially liked he had not cut his long, grey ponytail as he had considered doing once. Growing up, she thought he was cooler than other dads for it. Not just because it was long, but because she found he carried it with more elegance than most men carried their hair trimmed. She knew she was biased about it, unapologetically so. Her dad was a loving gentle man, and she looked up to him for it.

A cool breeze reminded all that the evening was about to turn uncomfortable with falling temperatures.

Rubbing her arms, Sakwa led everyone inside. She turned to her husband. "Kyv, would you mind lighting the fireplace?"

As he did, she studied her young guests.

"Despite the break, I'm certain you are still tired. You've had an intense 24 hours. Would you prefer we suspended our quest for the evening and picked it up again tomorrow?"

The four looked at each other like that was crazy talk.

"Mom, we are on the brink of finding none other than God's secret name," said Lily. "I'm not sleeping until we do." And she looked serious about it.

Her mother laughed. "Thank goodness. I was hoping so. But had to be polite and ask."

Kyv was definitely not about to wait, either. He had just joined the group and was eager to know more. "Let me see if I understood," he said talking over his shoulder. He was crouched down with half his body inside their large fireplace sorting the logs. "King Solomon engraved a coded name on a table that may or may not be related to Fatima's Third Secret, which you are looking for out here in the Southwest because a divine line points this way?"

Upon hearing it said like that, Sofia felt the imperative need to claim caution. "We are not totally settled on the table. For now, we are trying to figure out why each of the three straight segments cut through a city named Merida. We've started by focusing on the oldest one. All we have so far are tales of ancient relics hurdled across the Atlantic that *may or may not*," she emphasized, "have anything to do with anything."

"With so little, why are you following that lead at all?" asked her father.

"We want to exhaust it before moving on. We thought it was an interesting coincidence that the legend of Merida would drive the Spanish explorers to look for gold this way, while one of the lines crosses through three Meridas on its way here as well."

Kyv stood up and let out a subtle groan as he rubbed his knees. "Which beckons the question: Why this way? Did the bishops leave a map behind indicating where they were going?"

Sofia widened her eyes. "Good question." She turned to Gabriel. "Any idea why this way? Could they have had a map?"

Though Gabriel started his response with a negative, his head was nodding. "Nothing I came across seems to indicate there was a map. That's not to say there wasn't one. Take the Antilles, for instance. I read that the archipelago was named after a phantom island called *Antillia* shown on many charts before 1492 and believed to be associated with the Seven Cities of the Cibola legend precisely. It may explain why Columbus knew to head straight there." His eyes shined again with the promise of treasures. This had every alarm in Sofia's leery mind wailing. "As for the explorers," he continued, "records allege it was a chain of events that led them to your mesa. However, I find it extremely interesting that the Spanish explorers would risk so much of their own money, time and prestige in the search of the Seven Cities of Gold if all they had was a skimpy 800-year-old legend and the dubious word of a friar who said he had seen one of the cities."

There it was again, thought Sofia. *So well-articulated for a security guy ...* And he had just supplied enough bait to keep them down this trail.

Her sister swallowed it whole. "Can you develop on that friar?" asked Lily.

"A little; the Cibola legend is sketchy. Some chroniclers talk of seven Portuguese bishops, whereas others say they were Spanish. In truth, this is irrelevant because back in 713 Merida was the capital of a region named Lusitania that included most of current Portugal and the Spanish region of Extremadura. Therefore, there is no contradiction. What all accounts agree on is that they took off across the ocean and built seven cities of gold. How people back in Europe knew about the cities is anybody's guess, unless we accept that traffic back and forth was more common than we thought. In any case, the legend was all but forgotten until Hernan Cortes conquered

Teotihuacan with its enormous riches followed a few years later by a fanciful report from a friar. This friar was Marcos de Niza who swore he had spotted a city greater than the Aztec capital while on a scouting mission in the Southwest. Since many of the explorers were from Extremadura and knew of the legend, the connection was made and the search for the Seven Cities of Gold launched. Viceroy Antonio de Mendoza organized the well-known Coronado expedition. It departed from northern Mexico in 1540 making its way to Arizona. When they ran into the Zunis, who were supposed to be one of the seven cities, Vazquez de Coronado realized they had been sent on a wild-goose chase. Nonetheless, he sent Pedro de Tovar to probe your people, who told him of a great river and its rich spiritual value to them. Coronado then commissioned Garcia Lopez de Cardenas to survey the river, which turned out to be the Colorado River, making Cardenas the first European to see the Grand Canyon."

"Wait," called Lily. "Did you say Cardenas?"

"Yes. Why?"

"Do you know if he was related to Alonso de Cardenas?"

Gabriel shrugged his shoulders. "I can check."

The name caught Sofia's ear as well. "Why does that name seem familiar?" she asked.

Lily drew a broad, mischievous smile. "I'm happy you ask because here is where the Knights Templar come in."

"Thank goodness," grinned Sofia, with a conspicuous roll of her eyes. "I was starting to worry."

"Well worry no more. Did you know that the Kingdom of Castile was the only one in Europe that never embraced them? Castile happened to have a major Christian pilgrimage cross through its territory, *El Camino*, but never warmed up to the idea of letting a powerful, foreign knighthood protect it like the Templars were doing with Jerusalem. Instead, they created their own local order, the Knights of St. James."

"I'm confused. If that is so, where do the Templars come in?"

"They don't. That is what's so remarkable, their absence. They were the ruling bankers of Europe for a couple of centuries; they literally raised a king in the neighboring Kingdom of Aragon and were wholeheartedly embraced and protected from massacre in Portugal. Yet Castile, sandwiched in the middle and home to a major holy site, did without them. In fact, what little presence they had was cloaked, making it a mystery itself. Isn't that amazing?"

Sofia looked at her sister like maybe she should consider some sleep.

"They are related," announced Gabriel with his eyes still on his smartphone screen. "Alonso de Cardenas was the explorer's great grandfather."

"Hmm," mused Lily, "how interesting ..."

Sofia exchanged looks with everyone before posing the question. "What?"

"Alonso de Cardenas was the last Grand Master of the Knights of St. James. I know because Queen Isabella took charge of the order after his death."

"Of course she did"—Sofia shook her head—"and aside from being the first woman to lead a knight's order, it'll turn out that she also invented freemasonry. Want to bet on it?"

"No, because I'd be sure to lose," chuckled Lily.

"Okay, so back to the Grand Master, what's your interest in him?"

"A coincidence. What else? During the Christian *Reconquista* of the peninsula, it was this order who took back Merida from the Moors, so the Christian king at the time placed it under their jurisdiction as their reward. In exchange for its rents, the order was responsible for maintaining the city and its adjacent lands. And, *coincidently*, it was Alonso de Cardenas who carried out a major renovation of Merida's cathedral."

"I remember now ..." said Sofia. "I read he enlarged it."

"Exactly, the same cathedral that is central to the legend of the Seven Cities of Gold," said Lily. "What are the odds that his descendent would be a prime member of the expedition sent to find those cities precisely?"

"Actually," started Gabriel, looking down at his phone, "I'm seeing here that most explorers in the first wave were members of that order."

"So, what are we saying here? That the Grand Master found something like a treasure map in the renovation and its members set out to find it?" asked Sofia. "

Lily agitated her hands excitedly. "It would explain a lot. When I looked up the other two Meridas, I read that the one in Venezuela was founded by an explorer looking for El Dorado. The cities official name still to this day is *Merida of the Knights of St. James*. And get this, it was founded by the same guy who founded Caracas; quite astonishing, since it's the only two cities he founded yet both are on Mary's Line. That can't be a mere coincidence."

"What about the other Merida, the one in Mexico?"

"This one, I'm not sure how it ties in. Its founder was not from Merida nor associated with the order as far as I know. From what I read he founded the Mexican Merida on the ruins of an abandoned Mayan city that reminded him of the Roman ruins of the Spanish Merida. Thus, the name. Knowing what to look for now, with a little more time, I could probably find a link to the order."

"The Mayan city could be connected to Merida in Spain through the Tartessian, not the order," said Sakwa. "If these explorers had access to a map with the route followed by the bishops, it's because it was the same route travelled by the Tartessians. I've found rock art equivalencies in Central and South America as well, specifically in Venezuela along the line between Caracas and Merida. I can show you pictures. It's likely that their Atlantic crossings were remembered by the locals and at some point documented and kept in the cathedral's archives."

Sofia groaned with intellectual pain. "Let's straighten it out. On the one hand, we have a legend that talks of seven bishops from Merida who fled across the Atlantic with relics and built seven cities of gold. On the other hand, we have Spanish explorers also from the Merida region who eight hundred years later set out to look for those same seven cities. Since the Tartessos were from the area, and there is evidence of their presence along the same trail followed by the explorers, we are concluding there must have been a map of their ancient voyages stored in the cathedral."

"Agreed," said Kyv. He had been trying to keep up with the conversation by checking the claims on the maps in the dining room. "Has anyone noticed that the Old Spanish Trail that runs between Santa Fe and Spanish Fork coincides with Mary's Line down to the inch for over 550 miles? There definitely was a map and it was darn precise, too."

Sofia walked over to see for herself. She had missed that, and it was disappointing. Spanish Fork got its name from the Spanish friars who explored and mapped the Old Trail. Fatigue was dimming her mental acuity.

She rubbed her face. "Okay, so let's say there was a map of ancient voyages stored in the cathedral. It is possible that it referenced the Tartessian gold mines, leading the legend over time to talk of cities of gold rather than mines of gold."

Sakwa lifted her finger to insert a thought. "Those bishops fled in the year 713, right?" Her question was obviously metaphorical, so when she followed it by falling into a momentary trance, everyone waited silently, knowing she was making one of her connections. She rapidly explained. "Our ancestor's sudden transition from living in pit houses to building masonry villages is dated precisely to the early 700s. Maybe the bishops did spur the building of cities, not of gold, but where the gold was."

"That's it," settled Lily. She focused her pointed stare on her sister. "Sof, we need to take this line of thought seriously. It can't be happenstance that Mary's Divine Markers draw the same path those bishops followed. They must have fled with something as extraordinary as God's secret name and She wants us to find it."

Sofia let out a heavy sigh. "Fine, I know better than to doubt your intuition anymore." She turned to Gabriel and let her stare linger for a few seconds. With a historian, an archaeologist, and a journalist in the room, it was he, the security guy, she more often turned to for information. Clearly, something was off with this picture. She proceeded. "We have God's secret name linked to the Spanish Line via a table reportedly seen in Merida. Are you aware of anything in Jewish tradition, however small, that may connect God's secret name to Mary's Line? You know the routine; it could help us validate it and maybe even locate it."

Gabriel slowly drew an enigmatic grin. "There's a link all right. But it's not on Mary's Line. It's on the Spanish Line again, and I assure you there is nothing small about it."

CHAPTER 35

Gabriel led the way back to the dining room, and though his explanation was addressed to everyone, he knew this piece of information was most important to Sofia.

"The answer to your question is Kabbalah. Kabbalah is a school of thought believed to be as old as the Torah itself. It was practiced by sages with the goal of acquiring transcendent insight into the secrets of the Torah and, ultimately, prophecy. As I briefly explained earlier, this was accomplished by successively mastering the four levels of interpretation of its words. Consequently, the lore of God's secret name and how you get to its inner esoteric truth is rooted in Kabbalah."

Gabriel paused to check in with Sofia.

"Got it," she said. "The whole idea of God's secret name comes from Kabbalah, which claims that God's name is more than just a name."

He continued. "One of the most esteemed sages of Kabbalah is Simeon Bar Yochai who lived during the 2nd century in Jerusalem at the time of Roman persecution. Jewish tradition has it that he hid in a cave with his son for thirteen years, during which time he wrote the *Zohar*, the foundational work for Kabbalah. The work was lost until it reappeared around 1270 in Spain, said to be taken there by a group of exiled Jews. A Spanish rabbi by the name of Moses de Leon claimed to find it and spent several years copying and editing it. However," Gabriel paused, "there is some controversy over this. Contemporary scholars believe Moses de Leon wrote the *Zohar* himself. Be that as it may, the Zohar, meaning 'radiance', is revered as the third most important text in Judaism and considered quasi canonical." He intensified his look on Sofia. "It was found, or *written* if you prefer, here in Guadalajara." Gabriel placed his finger on the Spanish Line northeast of Madrid.

Sofia's pupils dilated as she looked at the map. "You're saying that the magnum opus of Jewism mysticism and cradle of God's secret name hails from a Spanish city that falls squarely on the line?"

Gabriel nodded matter-of-factly.

Her look sharpened as it turned to him. "How do you know all this, Gabriel?"

"I told you. I'm Sephardi, descendent of Spanish Jews. Believe it or not, Judaism flourished with the Muslim and Christian faiths in Spain. There were extended periods during which the three religions coexisted peacefully. It was a Golden Age for us all. You wouldn't think that possible now," he lamented.

How convenient is what she thought.

"Well, I guess that validates it," celebrated Lily. "We have God's secret name anchored to one line in a pretty impressive way. The question now is why twice on the Spanish one? The pattern tells us it should be cross-referenced with Mary's Line."

Sofia started to feel nausea. The table containing God's secret name and the book with the instructions on how to decipher it were both on the Spanish Line. How in the world was that possible? No human hand could orchestrate such an extraordinary coincidence. But it also raised new questions, because the most outstanding quality of Sofia's genius was the picky alarm in her head that alerted her to incongruences, however minute. At that moment it was on high alert, and its source was the table. Compared to a holy text that defined a powerful tradition like Kabbalah, a simple table seemed wholly unsuited to be the vessel of something so precious as the Creator's Secret Name."

"Something doesn't add up," she started. "I get the Zohar, but not the table. Why a table? We are talking of God's secret name—of all things—which gives access to His wisdom and power—of all things—. Yet Solomon's great idea was to engrave it on a piece of rudimentary furniture meant to hold bread. Why not store it safely in the Ark with the Ten Commandments?"

A moment of silence ensued. No one had thought to pay attention to that detail, and it certainly raised an interesting conundrum.

Finally, her mother spoke. "Come to think of it, it does have a perfectly reasonable explanation," she said, surprising everyone. "From time immemorial in that part of the Mediterranean, bread was the offering of choice to the Gods. The oldest evidence has been found in Egypt where it was placed on a mat at the feet of the relevant god. This caught my attention when I was in college because the Egyptians, like us, believed in the need to keep balance and harmony in the universe, and it was the pharaoh's duty to maintain them by making offerings to the gods. Now, offerings were not limited to bread, but it was the staple, so the image of a loaf of bread on a mat became the symbol and hieroglyph for offering. Over time, as the Egyptians gained sophistication, the mat evolved into an elaborate table of stone, retaining its symbolic mat form, and instead of actual offerings, symbolic images of offerings were engraved on it." Sakwa nodded as she continued. "Therefore, yes, it was normal to engrave images on the temple's offering table. They were by no means a piece of rudimentary furniture but a sacred element of the temple."

She paused briefly, reflecting great concentration. Slowly, Sakwa spoke again. "Moses was Egyptian born and raised as a prince in the pharaoh's palace. All the items of the Tabernacle that God instructed him to build, including the Ark, the Menorah, and the Offering table, equate to those of an Egyptian temple, only they had to be portable. Much like the portable temple of a Pharoah when travelling for war. According to the Old Testament, the Table like the Ark was made of acacia wood overlayed with gold."

"I see," said Sofia. "The legend does make sense then."

Her mother seemed to drain color the more she thought about it. "The thing is ancient Egyptians also believed in the power of the Word. In fact, Pharaohs kept their birth names secret because they feared that an enemy could curse them by writing their name on a ceramic or clay figure and then breaking it. They referred to these writings as 'Execration Texts'. And, curiously, the oldest written mention of Jerusalem found to date is on one of these broken pieces of ceramic."

Sofia understood her mother's train of thought. "Jewish mysticism may well be rooted in Egyptian mysticism."

"It would be reasonable," concluded her mother. "The region of Judea was under direct control of Egypt for several centuries and indirectly for thousands of years."

"If that's the case, where the legend says that Solomon engraved the secret name in a hieroglyphic form, it could mean he literally used Egyptian hieroglyphs or symbols in the Egyptian tradition as handed down through Moses."

Upon hearing her daughter's suggestion, Sakwa jolted. "Holy Mother of God..." She then turned her head hastily in several directions looking for something. Her eyes stopped on the living room table where she had left her tablet. Sakwa ran for it, and as she returned, she stared at everyone in shock. "I think I know what God's secret name is!"

The silence in the room was electrifying.

Sakwa focused on her tablet briefly, and when she found what she was looking for, she turned it for everyone to see:

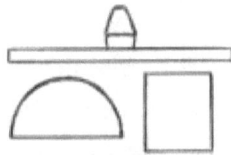

They all looked in closely and saw what appeared to be a hieroglyph containing three images, two of them geometric, just like the legend held.

Sakwa confirmed with Gabriel. "What do you think? You said the code had a geometric or hieroglyphic form."

"It could be. It does meet both conditions. What does it mean?"

"This is the Egyptian hieroglyph for offerings that I just mentioned and for that simple reason was often engraved on the offering table. At least, that was the thinking ... Now, I suspect there was an alternate reason".

This did not clarify anything; in any case it contributed to confusing everyone more, and they did not disguise it.

"I'll explain," said Sakwa. Her eyes opened wide reflecting the awe she felt for what she was going to share. "Egyptian hieroglyphs can be made up of ideograms, that is, images of what they represent; logograms or symbols that designate full words or syllables, and phonograms, which are symbols that represent sounds or phonemes like our alphabet. And it is important to note that they only wrote down the consonants of words, no vowels." Sakwa pointed to the image on screen. "In this hieroglyph, on top we see an ideogram. It is the image of a loaf of bread on a mat. By itself it can mean 'table of offerings' or simply 'offerings', which in Egyptian reads *hotep*. However, for stylistic reasons it was often accompanied by its phonemes *t* and *p* because, coincidentally, the symbol for *t* was a loaf of bread in the form of a semicircle, and the one for *p* was the mat, a rectangle. The result was a redundant hieroglyph."

"Right," accepted Sofia, "but what does that have to do with God's secret name? And since when do you know about Egyptian hieroglyphs?"

"I know nothing about Egyptian hieroglyphs," responded her mother. "What I'm sharing I know because I'm Hopi and Christian. As I said, the pharaoh held the position of High Priest; it was his duty to keep the balance and harmony of the universe by 'appeasing' the gods with offerings. Consequently, this hieroglyph for offering table also came to mean 'peace'. Since Hopi means 'Peaceful' and we believe our purpose is also to maintain the balance and harmony of the universe, the word *hotep* and its hieroglyph stuck with me." She paused to underscore her point and swiftly continued. "Then, as a Christian, another hieroglyph caught my attention." Sakwa searched for its image on her tablet and shared it. It was similar to *hotep* with one difference, instead of the image of a loaf of bread on a mat there was something that looked like a twisted string next to the semicircle and rectangle.

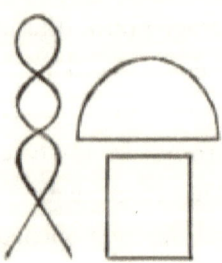

"This hieroglyph is another way of writing *hotep*," she explained. "The ideogram or image of the loaf of bread on the mat has been replaced by the letter *h*, because the word is written using phonograms exclusively, that is, the letters *h*, *t* and *p*. Again, only consonants, no vowels." Sakwa ran her eyes over her audience. "Here comes the magic," she announced. "Hieroglyphs can be read left to right or right to left. The direction is indicated by the hieroglyphs themselves. For instance, if a duck is looking to the right, then you must read from right to left. Who can tell me the reading direction for this hieroglyph?"

No one knew what to say.

"The three are symmetrical," observed Sofia. "It's impossible to know."

"Exactly!" celebrated Sakwa. "It can be read in either direction: htp or pth. And it just so happens that pth, or Ptah, is the name of a god." She allowed the revelation to linger as she drew a grin. "But Ptah is not just any god," she continued. "For the ancient Egyptians, Ptah was the main God Creator, the one who created balance and harmony where there was only chaos, and he did it with the Power of the Word. Does it sound familiar?"

Indeed it did. Everyone was speechless, except for Sofia who instinctively summarized the bewildering picture that was coming into focus. "Depending on how you read the same hieroglyph, you get offering table or the name of the god creator for whom the offerings are meant for." She reproduced her mother's wide gaze of awe. "And that was all we had in Merida, the hint of a table. And that simple table turned out to be the clue and the answer to the extraordinary puzzle of God's secret name. It's no wonder Merida's presence was tripled on Mary's Line."

Suddenly, the usually discreet Michael broke out laughing. "I can only imagine the shock when treasure hunters and esoteric believers alike find out. They have not left a rock unturned in Spain looking for the table hoping to get their hands on God's secret name when the table itself was the clue."

Lily, however, was scandalized. "How can you all be so cavalier about this? Do you realize what you are implying here? You're suggesting that God derives from a mythical Egyptian divinity. Moses fled Egypt guided by Yahweh. There is no way a Jewish king would engrave 'Ptah' on a table, coded or otherwise."

Her mother reached out to share her sympathy. They had always enjoyed a special bond thanks to their faith. "Honey, I felt the same initial distress, but it's really a question of perspective. When I read that Ptah created using the Power of the Word like Yahweh did, I researched Ptah a little further and discovered another coincidence. According to Egyptian tradition, since there was nothing but a sea of chaos in the beginning, Ptah had to create himself first before he could go on to create everything else. He did it by pronouncing the words 'I am'. And, as you know, according to our Judeo-Christian tradition, when Moses asked God what his name was, God's response was 'I am'. These words in Hebrew are said to be the root of Yahweh. Think about the beauty of it. The Muslim religion is rooted in the Christian Religion. The Christian Religion is rooted in the Jewish Religion. And the Jewish Religion is rooted in the Egyptian Religion. As a Hopi, you understand that all religions are intertwined. In the end we all believe in the same God."

Lily was coming around, still she turned to Gabriel wondering how he was taking it.

The young man responded with his odd wisdom. "God is more than just a name. What matters is his essence."

Lily stared at him, taken aback a little by having to be reminded of something so fundamental and powerful. She closed her eyes momentarily to collect herself, and after some thought, suddenly sprung back to life. "God is more than just a name, and his name is more than just a name ... If Mary has brought our attention to God's secret name, Ptah, there must be a good reason for it."

Sofia nodded with a smile. The alarm in her head had paid off big time and she knew exactly what Mary wanted.

CHAPTER 36

Sofia explained. "God's secret name appears linked twice to the Spanish Line. Thanks to the table in Merida, we have deduced it is Ptah. That leaves us with the Zohar in Guadalajara." She addressed her sister. "Lily, I think Mary wants us to interpret Ptah esoterically and handed us the instruction book to do it."

The general response was to freeze. What did they know about esoteric interpretations? Ancient sages, whether Jewish, Egyptian or otherwise, spent their lives studying to know how to do it.

Kyv gave them the nudge they needed. "Come on, you didn't make it all this way only to give up at the most interesting part."

For Sofia unraveling divine lines or exercising as a Kabbalistic sage was the same thing. She had felt utterly unqualified to do the first and yet here she was. She started pacing as she strategized. "All we have to do is ascend through four levels of understanding." She consulted with Gabriel. "The first one is the literal interpretation, right?"

He nodded somewhat restrained.

"Okay, then," she continued. "Ptah is *literally* a name, that of an ancient Egyptian God Creator ... That's it?"

"I guess," he answered. "I've never done this."

Great, she thought, *now* he's shy. She retained the question in her eyes and turned them to her mother. "Do you know anything else *literal* about this god that might help?"

"Well, I know he is one of the oldest gods of the Egyptian pantheon and hardly changed over the three thousand years of Egyptian history, which is quite remarkable in and of itself. And there is little mythology around him because he is the only one without a personal life. He was the patron of Memphis, the first capital of the unified kingdom of Egypt, so always enjoyed a prime position among the rest of the gods. In fact, the country's name 'Egypt' derives from the corrupted Greek name for Ptah's temple, which I'm not even going to try to pronounce. Let's see, what else?" She paused to reflect. "Yes, he was considered the 'Master of Magic' because of the power of his Word, and, anecdotally," she added, looking askance at her daughter Lily, "as creator he was also the 'Master Builder', that is, patron of the builders. Moses and the Israelites of Exodus would have known him well."

Lily dropped her shoulders in surrender. "Yes, I get it... The Israelites who Moses liberated were builders. Ptah would have been their patron. And it was Moses who transmitted God's secret name down to Solomon ..." Lily turned to her sister. "If your head hurts, mine is about to burst. Nothing of what I knew about my identity or faith remains standing."

Comforted by their shared sentiment of existential upheaval, the two sisters suffered a laugh attack. They were soon joined by the rest of the group.

Following the welcomed therapeutic pause, Sofia suggested they continued swiftly. It was either that or she was going to bed, because she was on the verge of collapsing out of exhaustion. "Let's move on to the next level. If I recall, it was the metaphoric one ... What could Ptah mean metaphorically?"

Her mother was already looking it up. "His name was also used as the verb 'to create' since he was the Creator, and 'to engrave' in the sense of writing the Sacred Word. It's the reason hieroglyph means *sacred writing*."

"All right, then", continued Sofia. "This is what we have so far: Ptah is the name of a God creator who created by employing the Power of the Word, and since the Word has Power, its engraving produces sacred writing ... I guess it sounds promising. We are looking for a Divine Message, after all." She nonetheless sighed. This impromptu exercise of esoteric analysis came anything but natural to her and doubted it would be productive, but she had learned to expect the unexpected. "Moving on, the third level ..."

"The association and combination of letters and words," volunteered Lily. "How are we supposed to tackle this level if we know nothing about hieroglyphs?" She turned to her mother. "Anything?"

Sakwa shrugged of her shoulders slightly. "We may know nothing about hieroglyphs, but we know what we know about Ptah's hieroglyph: Reading it in one direction, it gives us Ptah. Reading it in the opposite direction, it provides us with offerings and peace. Then, while the hieroglyph uses phonograms, two of them happen to be the image of a loaf of bread and a mat, meaning that, regardless of which direction you read it, it contains the image of a table of offerings ... And, while at it, incidentally, mat, *p*, followed by the loaf of bread, *t*, spells *pet*, which means 'sky' or 'heaven'. Just throwing it in there."

Sofia widened her look. "I must admit it is pretty nifty what you can do with a single word. What those ancient sages would not have done with an entire text."

"Wait," interrupted Lily. Her look was wider than Sofia's for what she had just realized. "There is one more combination of letters to consider. Think about it: Just like pth spells *Ptah*, the Creator of Balance and Harmony, and htp spells *Hotep*, the offerings that maintain Balance and Harmony, well ... hpt could spell *Hopitu*, the Guardians of Balance and Harmony."

She paused briefly to marvel with her parents and sister. Then she explained it to Michael and Gabriel. "The term Hopi is the anglicized short version for our native name *Hopitu*."

There was a new instance of generalized marveling as they all exchanged silent looks wondering if it could be a mere coincidence. Because if it was, it was a heck of a coincidence. Eventually they all silently agreed: *Hell no, it was no coincidence.*

Lily turned to her sister. "Sof, I think this confirms the golden plate ended up here in our ancestor's hands. It's the reason for our name."

Sofia squirmed because she realized she had no option but to agree. What was more, the ancient legends of her people were now confirmed true because the esoteric exercise was working, and if it had worked this far ... what to expect from the most intimidating level: grasping the supreme wisdom.

She took a deep breath and turned for support to Gabriel, who reading her mind shrunk as if to say "don't even look at me". And that's how the skeptic in the group resigned herself to being the chosen one destined to take on God's Power and Wisdom.

"We are the Peaceful Ones," she started solemnly, "the Guardians of Balance and Harmony. The fourth and last level holds a supreme truth. We were once assigned its protection and are now asked to extract its essence." Sofia drew a soft smile addressed at her mother. "I believe and know that we can and will do it."

Her mother's gaze filled with pride.

Sofia then took another deep breath. Everyone one did.

"Here it goes. Ptah... the God Creator... created through the Divine Word... that's why his name also means *to create* and *to engrave*... and regardless of how we place the letters or in which direction we read them, one thing remains constant, the image of a loaf of bread and a mat, the offering table, which also means *peace*—" Abruptly, Sofia paused. Slowly, she looked at her sister, the other chosen one. "Lily, His literal name maybe Ptah, but God is more than just a name; His name is more than just a name. What is the one thing that is constant in his name and, consequently, reflected in our name?"

"Peace," understood Lily. "God's true secret name is Peace because His essence is Peace. His Power was to create Balance and Harmony, that is, Peace. God is Peace."

For the first time in her life, Sofia felt a soothing connection with the universe as if the tension of gravity had been lifted and what remained was ... well ... tranquility ... Peace.

But she wasn't done.

With an intensified stare, she claimed her sister's attention once more and summarized the esoteric escalation by repeating a number of select words deliberately. "God... peace... create... balance and harmony... engrave the Sacred Word... table."

Lily immediately grasped the great honor her sister was bestowing on her. Those words combined, as if by magic, to compose a powerful message:

"God's secret name is 'Peace'
For his wisdom was to create Balance and Harmony where there was chaos.
Such power is now ours
As attested by the sacred writing engraved on the table."

The sisters rejoiced, sharing deep emotion in their eyes. That had to be Mary's message. If not, it was very close, which meant, there was no existential upheaval after all, but rather the contrary, affirmation of the most ancestral message common to all religions and people of good faith.

Lily voiced it. "Sof, the message is clear: God's essence is Peace; God created Peace; God's power is Peace... Heaven on Earth is Peace. We must find the golden plate. Mary doesn't know what else to do to *engrave* in our brains the way to her son. The plate is the physical proof that the Three Secrets of Fatima, the Divine Lines, the Black Madonnas, the secret name of God, all of it, is an elaborate plan orchestrated through centuries and millennia, through nations and continents, so there is no doubt that Balance and Harmony is the way to bring Peace to the World. God wants Peace and we have the Power to Create it!"

The solemn moment was grossly interrupted by the sound of a phone. Kyv hurried to retrieve it from his pocket. He checked the screen. "I'm sorry, I must take it. Please do not continue without me. I don't want to miss anything." And he hastily stepped outside onto the deck.

"Good time for a bite," celebrated Sakwa.

CHAPTER 37

Sofia paced restlessly alongside the dining room table. Deciphering the Divine Message had felt exhilarating. Now, all they had to do was find the legendary tabletop that could prove it. She glanced at the world map at each pass. *Where was the golden laminate?* She had removed the maps of the Southwest and Spain to have a good full view of *Mary's Way*. The line had provided extraordinary clues, and itself was a wonder, but there was something more. Sofia had the aching feeling she was missing something vital, and whatever it was, it was right there before her eyes.

The rest of the group had dispersed in part due to lack of appetite. Kyv remained tied up with calls on the deck; Gabriel had disappeared on the excuse he needed to stretch his legs; Sakwa was in the kitchen determined to feed her young guests knowing they'd eat if she put the food in front of them, and Lily was helping her.

That left Michael. He wandered in the great room, always vigilant, with one eye on the ladies inside and the other on Kyv who he observed through the window. Aware of Sofia's restless pacing, he approached her.

"I'm very impressed with how you are handling things. Legends, miracles, divine lines and secret names, it's a lot for a skeptic to take in all at once." His tone carried a playful tease.

She smiled. "It's not all that bad. I'm just being opened-minded as any self-respecting and exceptional skeptic would."

"Humble, are we?" he smiled. Then he sharpened his stare. "Seriously, you deserve a lot of credit. It is human nature to reject what does not fit with one's preconceived reality. Your accommodating attitude is laudable."

"I confess to being guilty of the contrary." Her eyes drifted in search of her mother and sister. "I think that for the first time I am truly open to all possibilities." She returned her attention to Michael with an added smirk. "And they are pretty crazy possibilities." Sofia then tilted her head slightly to show curiosity. "Gabriel and you have taken this to heart. What's your stake in it?"

"The same as everybody else's, I guess; a simple choice: World Peace vs World Havoc."

"There is nothing simple about that."

"It should be. Well over half of the world's population adheres to one of the three Abrahamic religions. The three worship the same God, whose name, as it turns out, is Peace. The three converge in Jerusalem, 'the city of peace', where we all greet each other either in Hebrew or Arabic by literally saying 'may peace be with you'. Still, all that region can show for it is a lot of pain and suffering." Michael's gaze took the intensity of a warrior, "It has to end."

"It will."

Sofia's firm response took him by surprise.

She explained. "A cursory walk through history tells us that for all the pain and suffering the French crusades and Inquisition caused, France rose to give the world The Enlightenment and the Declaration of Human Rights. For all the pain and suffering that Spanish greed for riches caused, they rose to become the most generous country in the world, ranking the highest in donations, adoptions, equality and tolerance. For all the pain and suffering that British racism and supremacy caused, they planted the seed for some of the strongest democracies in the world. For all the pain and suffering that American slavery caused, United States rose to become a beacon of freedom. And let's not forget Germany. Guilty of starting two world wars in Europe, today they spearhead a European project of unity that has resulted in the longest and most stable peace period in the history of that continent. Everyone is guilty of pain and suffering, but history has proven that we can overcome our worst and rise to offer much good. Michael, your region has long endured wars and disarray, but with a little help from the rest of us, it can, and it *will* rise to give the world peace. It's your fate."

Her words struck something in the heart of his long-time, dimming confidence. "Thank you." he whispered.

"You are tearing me up," said Lily, sneaking up behind her sister.

"Oh, shut up and let's get back to work." Sofia looked away to hide her blush. "Is dad back yet?"

Right on cue the door to the deck opened. Kyv did not look happy.

"Was that work?" asked his wife, placing a tray of snacks on the living room table. "Is something wrong?"

"It's nothing." He relaxed the expression that betrayed him and fixed his eyes on Sofia. "I apologize for the interruption. We can continue." Then he scanned the room. "Where is Gabriel?"

"He went for a walk," volunteered Michael. "I'll text him."

Sofia studied her dad for a moment.

He urged her to continue.

She obliged and renewed her pacing along the dining table. "We are looking for a gold laminate. The question is where could it be?" Once more she stopped to look at the map. She could tell *Mary's Way* was screaming it out to her, but all she received was a muffled impression. It bugged her tremendously, and because it did, she knew it was best to give it a rest and not think about it. The human mind had the stubborn habit of defying imposition and established its own agenda when it came to eureka moments. She continued pacing and moved on to the next thought. It has been demonstrated that looking for indirect associations aided inspiration, and that's why the skilled psychologist had developed the habit of reviewing, summarizing and ordering the information she had. She reflected out loud: "We think the line is telling us it is somewhere here in Spanish Fork ... which necessarily implies it is susceptible to being found because, otherwise, what are we doing here? Once this is established, the question then is how does one go about hiding something like God's secret name on a golden plate for so long in such a way that it can be found? Surely it can't be completely hidden. It has to be somehow in plain sight. Maybe disguised ... or, maybe, its location is marked in some way."

Sofia paused. She knew in her heart she was onto something.

She then turned to her mother. "Mom, I'd like you to try and visualize our rock art from the perspective of an offering table. You said that bread was not the only offering, so I imagine that usually a stone table in the temple would display more images than merely its hieroglyph. Consequently, what if the golden plate also contained other relevant imagery. Can you think of equivalent symbolism in our art?"

While Sakwa furrowed her brow in thought, Gabriel walked in silently, exchanged a swift look with Michael, and then headed straight for the food tray.

"You raise an important point," said Sakwa. "Yes, Egyptian offering tables displayed a variety of images, different offerings, pharaohs offering them, and gods receiving them. I'm going to need some time to think of comparable symbolism."

"Sure, but don't limit yourself to Egyptian iconography, after all, the table belonged to a Jewish temple ..." her words trailed off as a silly question hit her. She addressed Gabriel. "What does Jewish tradition say happened to the Divine Presence when the Temple was destroyed? I mean, if it was built specifically for it, what happened to it once its 'place of dwelling' was no longer there?"

For most of the group, that was a strange question. What did the Divine Presence have to do with the table's plate location in Utah? For Sofia, as she had exceedingly demonstrated, no end could remain loose for it could be the knot that tied everything together.

"It flew away," settled Gabriel.

"Really? That's it?"

He chuckled. "There is a lot of transcendent symbolism packed in those three words."

"Of course there is, especially if Kabbala is involved."

"Precisely because Kabbalah is involved," clarified Gabriel. "What we know about Shekinah leaving the Temple and her prophesied return is thanks to Ezekiel, the prophet, and the visions he had during exile—"

"Wait. Shekinah?"

"Yes, well, Shekinah is the name for God's Divine Presence. It derives from "to dwell" in the temple."

"Exactly how many names does God have?"

"72," smiled Gabriel. "And it might interest you to know that in the case of Shekinah, she is central to keeping balance and harmony. Jewish mysticism holds that God has two aspects: one that is male, which we cannot grasp because it is transcendent, unknowable, infinite, while the other is revealed to us through His Creation. This aspect of Creation, its manifestation, is feminine and we call it Shekinah. For Kabballah, the balance and harmony between the two is essential to avoiding chaos."

"Are you saying that according to Kabballah God is a woman?" asked Lily incredulous.

"No. In essence he is both, male and female. However, as God relates to human beings, that perceptible Presence, yes, it's feminine."

"The same Divine Presence for whom Solomon built the Temple and the table?" she insisted.

"That's right," reaffirmed Gabriel with a hint of subdued amusement.

"And it's female?" she rehashed overjoyed. "I knew it!" she squealed, looking at her sister. "It's like Pahana all over again!"

"Not like," intervened Sakwa. "It is Pahana. Shekinah is Tanit, 'The Face of the Lord'. Solomon worshipped the Canaanite Mother Goddess Asherah alongside Yahweh in the Temple. The Bible says so. She was also considered the 'Queen of Heaven', but the patriarch movement eliminated her to favor Yahweh exclusively. And as I already explained, Asherah later became Tanit." Sakwa sought Gabriel for confirmation.

He nodded. "Scholars believe that Kabballah reintroduced Asherah as Shekinah because there was a yearning for the maternal element. Kabballah teaches that returning her to the Temple would bring in the Messianic age of Peace, since balance would be restored."

"In other words," started Sofia. "More of the same: God is our Father and Mother, Balance through Equality. In Judaism the maternal aspect was reintroduced through Shekinah, the 'Face of God', while in Christianity it was done via Mary, the 'Queen of Heaven'." She suddenly addressed Michael. "Just curiosity: Is there something similar in Islam?"

He nodded. "Shekinah, precisely. However, the word is understood more as a quality than in terms of gender. It is God's tranquility, the 'Peace of God'." He angled a grin. "It is a very popular female name, though."

Everyone shared celebratory smiles. No doubt they were on the right track. Sofia did not want to waste their good traction. "So, as you were saying, where did Shekinah go?" she asked Gabriel.

"It's not really known. Ezekiel only says that he saw her leave waiting to return upon the construction of her New Temple."

This gave Lily, who was familiar with the prophet's visions, an idea. "And it is also Ezekiel who describes that New Temple, the same one that happens to be identical to the Tartessian sanctuary in Spain." She said this, pointing to the Cancho Roano floorplan on the wall. "He describes it in minute detail. Therefore, if he *saw* the Divine Presence leave, it would be interesting to analyze exactly what he *saw*." She now turned to her sister. "Because just like Solomon engraved God's name, he could have also engraved God's face, and what Ezequiel *saw* was the Name and Face of the Lord leave as engraved on the table."

Sofia was impressed. "Lil'sis, you are a genius. *The Table of the Divine Presence* ... We should be thinking of the table in terms of the Presence, not the offerings. What Ezequiel saw was the Presence engraved on the table leaving to her New Temple in Spain and offers all the details. His description could indicate what iconographic elements to look for here."

Lily could be seen concentrating. "In his first vision, the prophet said he saw the glory of God upon a strange flying chariot." Without elaborating more, she set her inquisitive gaze on Gabriel. "If God's secret name was important in esoteric study, I can only imagine the interest his image would have spurred, especially coming from a prophet. The Zohar might contain the clue."

He agreed. "Indeed. Ezekiel's vision promoted a mystical school all on its own: *Merkavah*, meaning 'Chariot Mysticism.'"

Suddenly, upon hearing this, Sofia felt the force of a lightning strike shake her to the core. Her face lit up as the 'eureka' moment detonated behind it. She knew! She knew what *Mary's Way* was trying to tell her. The visualization was so powerful she almost choked on it. She knew what they were looking for. She knew where it was. She knew everything!

But just as Sofia was about to share it, Michael shushed her. "What was that?" he asked, looking toward the front door.

Kyv whistled with such energy, it almost provoked hearing loss in all those present. The front door slammed open as did the back one. Two men entered through each one, all holding rifles. They surrounded Michael and Gabriel making it brutally clear they were not to move.

Lily jolted and clutched her mother's arm. They remained frozen, momentarily terrified not daring to breathe, until quickly realizing the men were all Native Americans. An older man followed through the main entrance. He displayed much authority, and *he* they recognized.

Kyv addressed him. "Thank you, Bode. I appreciate you responding so quickly."

"Anytime, old friend."

Sakwa was in shock. "What on Earth is going on here?"

Kyv launched a quick side look at Sofia before responding. "Earlier this afternoon, Sofia called me. She explained roughly what was going on and asked that I check into Michael and Gabriel's background. She was concerned they were hiding something. I had Bode look into it."

Lily shot a look at her sister reflecting a mixture of confusion and disappointment.

Sofia stood her ground. "I simply asked dad to make a few phone calls just to be safe." Her gaze turned apologetic when she set it on Michael. "Please understand, what happened yesterday was very serious. And something about you and Gabriel does not add up."

"You did the right thing," settled Bode; his eyes pointed at his two captives. "I am Bode Muwac, Chief of Police for the Uintah and Ouray Reservation. My demand is simple: You collaborate. Period."

Michael seemed unreasonably calm. "I believe you are out of your jurisdiction Mr. Muwac. We are not on reservation land."

"Consider me a good friend on private property who considers you dangerous."

"On what grounds?"

"On the grounds that neither you nor your cousin exist."

Kyv explained it to his wife. "Bode texted me earlier. He could not find anything on them other than what he thought were well-planted, work-related articles. It alarmed me. I asked him to come over. The call a moment ago was to let me know they were taking their positions around the house. Unfortunately, I couldn't find the opportunity to alert you."

"Why all the concern? I still don't understand. What happened yesterday?" Her eyes were opened-wide with bafflement.

"Mom," began Sofia, "Yesterday morning, Lily's room was ransacked, and later, an armed man tried to abduct us. We didn't tell you so as to not alarm you."

"What?" shrieked her mother.

Lily protested. "Nothing happened. In fact, Michael and Gabriel took care of them. They've been watching over us."

Sofia turned to Bode with a hopeful gaze. "Were you able to find out if they turned those men in as they said they did?"

Bode shook his head. "I called a colleague in Santa Fe. He found no such report. He said there was no notice of anything out of the ordinary happening at San Miguel's chapel."

Lily spun her perplexed eyes to Michael.

He responded with a contained sigh of resignation. "They are powerful. They must have made the report disappear."

"Who are 'they' and why?" asked Bode.

"I don't know who, and I'm not going to tell you the why."

"Listen buddy, you don't understand, you have no option."

"Mr. Muwac, indeed, I do. I suggest you check my back pocket." Michael's solid look was unbreakable.

Bode gestured at the man standing beside him, who reached into the pocket and retrieved an identification badge. He rapidly handed it over to Muwac with a concerned gesture.

"National Security," read Bode. He studied Michael. "What kind of National Security exactly?"

"The type that is none of your concern." Michael refortified his composure. "Chief of Police Muwac, you have grossly overstepped your authority here. However, since you were doing what any well-meaning Samaritan would do for a friend believed in jeopardy, how about this: I did not see you, you didn't see me?"

What Bode did not do was waver. He handed the badge over to Kyv. "It's your call."

"I don't want you in any trouble. This looks legit," replied Kyv, troubled.

"How would you know? Not even I have ever seen a real one. A secret agent... within a secret branch... within National Security? That's the stuff of movies. I don't buy it."

Kyv addressed Michael with caution, but sternly. "I don't care who you are. My concern is the safety of my family. You came into our house employing lies. You're going to have to convince me you are not a threat."

Lily made an attempt to approach Michael, which made the armed men jolt very nervously. She strayed them with a stay-calm look and pursued. "Michael, please, tell us what is going on."

"I will, but they must leave." He directed his eyes to her parents. "I am not armed, nor is Gabriel." He waved at the men who clearly were. "They can confirm it. Would you agree to Muwac and his men stepping outside while I explain? They may remain a few steps away from the door."

"Yes!" responded Sakwa immediately.

Kyv stared at his wife with a disapproving glare.

She insisted. "My intuition says he is to be trusted."

Bode obliged without waiting for his friend's command. Sakwa had spoken, and her intuition —and authority— were legendary. Grudgingly, he had Michael and Gabriel searched. They were clean. Bode then consulted once more with Sakwa and Kyv.

"Are you sure you want us to leave?"

Sakwa's gaze was firm. Kyv's not so much. He assented with a nod, nonetheless.

The four men retreated through the doors they came in. Bode resisted, his stare fixed on Michael. Following a tense moment of standoff, he finally turned to leave. "Whistle if you need anything."

CHAPTER 38

The tension lingered in the atmosphere. Kyv stood at a close distance as if forming a protective barrier for his family while heaving his distrust. Sakwa and Lily looked disconcerted a little further back, and Sofia stood a step behind her father biting her lip not knowing what to think.

Michael saw no reason to delay. He spoke firm and straight to the point.

"Within National Security there is a directorate that focuses on organized groups. Within it, there is a specific division that identifies and monitors suspicious cult associations"—his eyes darkened—"and I'm not merely referring to fanatical terrorists, neighborhood gangs or the KKK to name a few. Those are dealt with openly in front of the public eye by the Department of Defense or local law enforcement. I'm referring to well-funded and organized secret sects, cults or societies that lurk in our cities with a pervasive agenda, and of which no news broadcast knows or talks about. Their threat is great because their members are powerful, their tentacles reach deep into every major world organization, and they are too smart to make the evening news. Gabriel and I work for a unit within the division that surveys major world religions."

"Why?" asked Lily. "What threat do they pose?"

"A formidable one. Religion holds extraordinary sway over its believers, far more than any government. Yet, unlike governments, religious institutions go unquestioned by their faithful."

Lily revolted. "Their faithful are moved by love and trust and come together to form communities of volunteers that do far more for others than most governments."

"Lily, in no way am I implying that religion or its organized institutions, let alone their honest followers, are inherently corrupt or a threat. What I'm saying is that powerful forces within these institutions are the threat, and they are there as they are in any other respectable institution or industry. Where there is money there is power. And it follows that the larger the institution, the more money, the more power. Unfortunately, let me emphasis this, religion, due to its divine nature, has the crucial advantage of going largely unquestioned. You know that an organization, say like the

Red Cross, would have long disappeared with a single case of pedophilia, especially if they had covered it up. And no donor would tolerate their finances kept undisclosed. However, with the billions that pour into religious organizations, financial transparency is abysmally lacking. Think about this Lily, you are American. American Christians demand more transparency from their own president than they do from the pope, a foreign ruler, for instance. You, yourself, are frustrated with such complacency. Free women would never tolerate in their workplace the inequality they tolerate in their church. Religious institutions get away with what no one else can, and this kind of power, when in the wrong hands, is an enormous danger."

Michael took a breath to assess his audience. No doubt they were hanging on to every word. He continued.

"The NSA's inception can be tracked back to 1917 when Congress declared war on Germany." He paused to allow time for the connection with the year to be made. "A code and cipher decryption unit was established to monitor World War I cable and telegraph communications. Within months, amidst the turmoil, the brand-new military branch picked up on an unexpected frantic flow of signals between the Catholic Holy See and that of the Russian Orthodox. It raised eyebrows, for both Sees dwelled in no man's land, literally, while in the middle of it all. In the case of the Roman Holy See, the annexation of the Papal States by the Kingdom of Italy back in the 19th century had left the pope without a territory. This situation was resolved later with the Lateran Treaty of 1929 that gave him rule over The Vatican City. But in 1917, Benedict XV was a king without a kingdom. At the same time, the Russian Revolution of 1917 resulted in the separation of church and state, leaving the Russian Orthodox Church without official state backing for the first time in its history. So here we had two estranged orphans reaching out to each other in the midst of a world war. Initially it was understood as a desperate move to unite in pursuit of strength and survival. It soon became clear that something far more formidable had frightened them. To make a long story short, the source of their fear was traced back to the Marian apparitions in Fatima that same year." Michael's deep voice seemed to underscore this last sentence with the echoes of a distant clap of thunder. "Later, with the wars come and gone and technology ever evolving, the agency's cryptologic activities morphed and grew until the NSA was formally established by Truman in 1952. Until then, it had not existed, officially. Surveillance of the Vatican never ceased, rather heightened until the agency decoded John Paul II's messages. The astounding finding of the Marian Line warranted the creation of yet another specialized subunit, the MA, to monitor Marian Activities."

He narrowed on the twins who stood rooted to the floor. "Both of you have been on the agency radar since you were seven."

Lily's eyes reflected her deep disenchantment. "Our encounter in Afghanistan was orchestrated."

Michael offered his signature smile, but it failed to appease her. "No. I was there on a mission unrelated to you. I don't usually work in MA. However, once we had met, it was brought to my attention you were on the agency's roster, and logically our friendship was encouraged. Lily, I hope you believe me when I say that it was a task I undertook happily. I truly cherish our friendship."

She responded with a half-hearted smile. It was apparent to Michael it would take some time to regain her full trust.

He proceeded. "When the agency got wind of your research, scrutiny was heightened, and I became an obvious asset for the case, not only because of our friendship, but also because of my Muslim background. You made it easy when you asked for my help. Gabriel was enlisted for his expertise in Judaism. It was clear from the beginning that Fatima was not solely a Christian affair."

"Who were those men at San Miguel's yesterday?" asked Sofia.

"We don't know. For all the years the agency has been tracking the Vatican, we are no closer to identifying who or what is the shadow force pulling the strings. It's there, though. We've codenamed it Red Dragon."

"I've noticed you have been feeding us information," she added.

"Please understand we are on the same side. You both have an uncanny ability to dig up information from the lines that our well-equipped, professional decipherers have barely been able to scratch. We were hoping that by supplying what little we already knew, together we could advance forward faster. Red Dragon is restless. Their moves on you yesterday are extremely rare. It is clear they are getting nervous. Bear in mind that the success of groups like these is to stay anonymous, to go unnoticed. They don't take risks unless absolutely necessary. Yesterday they exposed themselves three times."

"What?" panicked their mother. "Three times?"

"No, mom. In the cathedral we were only questioned, and we didn't even know we were being questioned. That's how harmless it was," clarified Lily.

Michael quickly tried to appease her, too. "I've arranged for reinforcements. You are safe. There is nothing to worry about."

It didn't work.

"Really?" protested Sakwa. "Bode just walked in with four armed men! If he could, so can that red snake or whatever it is!"

"We have you and your home monitored. We were aware Bode was coming. Once Kyv alerted him, we had to let Bode do his part. He is a law-enforcement professional, and it would have been of further inconvenience to our case to contain him recklessly. We are ready to design a reassuring explanation that will satisfy him, if you are willing to collaborate."

Kyv shook his head adamantly. "You haven't offered me anything yet. You could have easily made up everything you just said."

Michael stared at him for an instant. He then consulted with Gabriel who nodded his agreement to whatever their silent exchange meant.

Michael spoke to the air. "Raphael," he called, "have the reservation's chairman call Muwac."

Kyv, Sakwa, and the twins turned and twisted their heads looking in every direction wondering who Michael was talking to. Finally, they set their bewildered eyes back on him.

"You bugged our house?" asked Sakwa. "Is that what you meant by monitored? When did you do it?"

"With today's technology, cumbersome in-house devices are no longer necessary. Now, I beg your patience. This will only take a moment," he said.

"Raphael? Really?" remarked Sofia. "What's with the archangel names?"

Gabriel chuckled. "That was my idea. MA agents are nicknamed Mary's Angels, so I thought of code names in line with it."

No one seemed in the mood to appreciate his sense of humor.

"Anyway, we try to have some fun at the office sometimes," he concluded.

Kyv was focused. "What happens if we don't wish to collaborate?"

"We can't force you, but the sooner we resolve this riddle, the greater the chance that your daughters walk away unscathed."

Lily felt a shiver. She approached her sister and reached for her hand.

Their father's phone vibrated. He glanced at the screen. It was Bode. He was asking permission to come in.

"Yes, Bode," yelled Kyv at the door. "Please come in."

It opened. Bode's brows had thickened and connected in the middle. He spared an instant to give Michael a defiant look. Then he spoke to Kyv and Sakwa.

"I just received a call from the reservation chairman. He asked me as a personal favor to leave quietly and, if possible, to *kindly* erase my memory."

Kyv tightened his jaw in reaction to the display of power Michael had just exhibited. He cleared his throat. "I'm sorry about all this, Bode. It looks like everything is fine. As you know, Sofia collaborates with a specialized magazine as an analyst. Lily called her to look into a delicate matter she had stumbled on. She was right to suspect, but unfortunately, it meant that they inadvertently walked into a highly sensitive case that National Security was already working on. Michael and Gabriel are here to ensure the girls don't jeopardize it any further. They almost exposed it yesterday."

Bode snorted displeased as he assessed 'the girls'. Lily and Sofia nodded with a remarkable semblance of being at absolute ease."

"I've been promised the exclusive if I stay quiet until they resolve it," said Sofia.

Lily simply nodded.

He grunted and turned to Sakwa.

"It's true, they are fine," she reassured him, "We all are."

Bode took a deep breath. Since he too had been guaranteed there was no danger, and that he'd be briefed back in the office, he finally lowered his guard.

"I'll be going then."

"I owe you a beer," appreciated Kyv.

"And a couple of front seats to the game."

"Don't push it!"

Everyone faked a laugh as Bode resisted leaving. He remained stuck to the spot, his eyes wandering over everyone not knowing where to rest.

Kyv walked over to him, patted him softly on the shoulder, and guided him to the door. "Don't worry, I'll tell you all about it when I buy you that drink."

Shaking his head, Bode accepted his friend's assurances and left.

Once alone, Michael congratulated the family. "Thank you, you improvise well."

"Will the girls really be safe?" asked Sakwa.

"Red Dragon appears to be interested in what Lily implied she knew. It struck a vital chord. Nothing has rattled them so hard since the apparitions. Be assured you will be supervised until this is over. The best thing we can do now is find the laminate before they do. Once it is in our hands, we'll ensure they know we have it, and you'll become irrelevant."

"We have to hand it over to you?" asked Lily. Defeat was spelled across her face.

"I'm trying to keep you safe, Lily. In my hands, the focus is off you. If, additionally, it happened to fall in my hands without either one of you seeing it, well, your wellbeing would be guaranteed."

For Kyv, the message was crystal clear. He punched the door. "That's it! Sakwa, we're giving them the golden plate!"

Sakwa shot a look of shock at her husband.

"They can have the darn thing; all of it!"

She seemed paralyzed, unable to react, until she did.

"Kyv, no!" she begged. "What are you doing? You can't give it to them!"

"Enough! They can have it. I want them the hell out of here."

"It belongs to our people. We were chosen to guard it." Sakwa gestured in the direction of Sofia and Lily. "It was their fate to bring it to light."

"I'm sick and tired of hearing about that. To hell with it if it's going to get them killed."

"Don't you understand? It's for a greater purpose, for the greater good." Sakwa's face was one of pure anguish. She pulled on his arm. "Don't, it's wrong. You can't. Please."

He released himself. "You are the one that doesn't understand. It's over, Sakwa."

Sofia and Lily exchanged bewildered looks.

Their father then fixed his fiery eyes on Michael. "I know where that damned laminate is. I want it out of here and you two with it!"

Sakwa hid her face in her hands. "What have you done?"

Kyv pointed a threatening finger at Michael. "I swear: if something were still to happen to one of my girls, there will be nowhere for you to hide. My people will hunt you down." He held his stare for a few seconds, and then slowly turned. "Grab your jackets."

CHAPTER 39

The night was chilly. The clear sky and low moon shed enough light so that, once eyes had adjusted, the trail down the back hill was visible. Nonetheless, Kyv had grabbed a couple of flashlights and a portable rope ladder on the way out. They were going to need them where they were going.

The party moved along without saying a word. Some because they were concentrating on not tripping, others because they needed a moment of silence, but all knowing the destination: The well.

Kyv was the first to arrive. He reached for a set of keys hanging from his belt. One fit the lock.

Sofia felt a cold sweat. As her father opened the lid, the mouth of the well morphed into the void of her nightmares. She steeled herself and asked: "I'm confused. You kept the gold laminate in the well?"

"Honey, this was never a well. We called it so for convenience. When you fell in it you suffered a concussion. You never became aware it was the entrance to a mine."

He looked at Michael and Gabriel. "Mines like these can be found all over Utah. I inherited this land. My father refused to limit himself to a reservation. It was a question of time that someone in my family found it, and I was the lucky one. It was a gold mine abandoned a long time ago and vandalized long before my father bought the land. But it was also something else; not sure what. There are inscriptions on the walls. When I first saw them, I consulted some books and even brought down a retired university professor to see them. He claimed they were forged by whoever vandalized the cave because they were a poor attempt at reproducing an ancient European script. I let it go until I heard of an archaeologist working in Mesa Verde who had the absurd idea that ancient people from the Mediterranean had visited the area over a couple thousand years ago. It's how I met Sakwa."

Sakwa was too upset to acknowledge anything he was saying. She turned her face away.

He continued. "I tracked her down, showed her a photograph of the inscriptions and she agreed to come and take a look. She found them disappointing at first. Most had been defaced, and what little remained did indeed look like a poor forgery."

Sakwa couldn't help herself and stepped in to explain it her way. "Tartessos' inscriptions were not discovered until very recently. That's why experts at the time discarded the inscriptions as a hoax," she reminded them. "When your father contacted me," she said addressing her daughters, "I noticed that some of them looked like the ones on the back of our rosary medallion. I agreed to dig around the mine to see what else I could find. For a while I found nothing. Normally, I would have given up, but since I married the owner, and we built our home up the hill from the mine, it became a hobby to head down in my spare time. There are several tunnels, but only the great room has inscriptions. Bored of it, one day I moved on to check out one of the side tunnels. It had an unusual trapezoid shape. I chose to study the wall that seemed most out of place for its odd inclination and noticed that under the centuries-old grime, it had been plastered." She sighed with a painful long side look at her husband. "I did not have the tools to remove the plaster properly but was able to peal just enough off to find a delicate, fine sheet of gold laminate under it."

"Are you serious?" exclaimed Lily, "Are you saying it is still there stuck to the wall?"

Sakwa nodded.

"Why didn't you call your colleagues for help?" asked Sofia. "That is an extraordinary find!"

"Honey, I was so excited when I found it that I ran to call your father, leaving the opening to the mine unattended. That was the day you fell in. Considering our family legend, and that a mysterious voice led Lily to save your life, I took it as a sign. We closed the lid, put a lock on it, and never dared to go in again."

"Oh, come on! I just hit my head, hardly an omen to keep you away from the discovery of a lifetime."

"You had a clot, Sofia. If Lily had not found you when she did, who knows how long you would have been down there. We had just had breakfast. I would not have looked for you for a while. When Lily alerted me, I was engrossed in making plans on putting a team together and requesting equipment. You would have most certainly died."

Michael interrupted. "If you never saw the plate, what makes you think it is the one that contains Solomon's code?'

Sakwa's cheeks flared. "It's a laminate, it's made of gold, it's in a cave with Tartessos inscriptions, and Divine Lines that talk of relics and secret names lead straight to it. Let's call it a wild guess." She was pissed.

"And now it's yours," added Kyv just as aggravated. He handed over the key.

Michael took it.

"That's not all," said Sakwa, her voice broken. "I also suspect that behind the wall there once was a chamber. The laminate is located to one side that still stands. The rest was destroyed when that side of the room caved in. There is a lot of rubble. Knowing what I know now, my educated guess is that the laminate's purpose was to function as a panel announcing the sanctity of the space behind it, maybe a holy of holies of sorts. If that is the case, it is very possible there may also be other relics under the rubble."

Sofia threw her hands to her head. "That's just great!"

Lily was on the verge of crying. "I can't believe Solomon relics were sitting here all this time, and you did nothing to uncover them!"

"Now you two listen to me. The possibility of this cave being related to Solomon is something we figured out today." Sakwa took a deep breath. She was suffering with this as much as anyone. She didn't need to be reminded of what she was giving away. "Regardless, your father is right. No relic is worth your life. Maybe it was meant to be this way. Maybe our Blessed Mother led you here with Federal security agents on purpose. Who better to safely bring it all to light?"

"It's cold out here," urged Kyv. "I want this over with. Let's go down. I'll show you around and then my family and I will take a long vacation. I trust that when we get back it will look like no one was ever here."

"What?" Lily bounced her eyes back and forth between her father and Michael a couple of times. "I'm not going anywhere. I want to see it when they dig it out."

Michael was firm. "No, you must leave. Red Dragon will be informed we have it and no one else saw it. As I said, it's in your best interest that you become irrelevant."

"That's it?" She pointed back at the house. "We figured the lines out. You can't expect us to just walk away. You can't do this to us. We were meant to find it. I trusted you."

He stood quiet. He had to let her realize on her own there was no other option.

Sofia understood and intervened to sooth her sister with a gentle hug. "Lily, everything happens for a reason. We looked for a message and found it. Our job here is done. You must accept it."

Michael addressed the whole family. "We'll have a team come out. I'm sure Raphael is already working on it. Gabriel and I will escort you on your *vacation*. When all is recovered, he and I will head back to Maryland, and you'll be safe to come back home."

"We don't need an escort," defied Sofia. "We'll go home to the Hopi Reservation. We know how to take care of ourselves up on the mesas."

"What if what is down there is not what we think?" asked Lily, praying it wasn't.

Michael drew a soft grin. "Your mother is right. It has to be."

"What will the agency do with it?"

"That, I don't know."

"Do you trust them?" asked Sofia.

Michael froze his stare briefly on hers. "I deposit my trust on few."

CHAPTER 40

Another long night followed by another long drive; only this one was excruciatingly quiet. During the seven hours it took the Auru-Soto family to reach Old Oraibi in Arizona, not a word of what had happened was muttered within the vehicle; partly because their father had demanded it so, partly because the tension was too thick to talk through, anyway. They had spent the night resting the best they could under Michael's guard until he gave them the green light. Now they were in Hopi territory winding up along a wall of colorful sandstone on their way to the Third Mesa. Beyond the rocky fall on the open side of the road laid a privileged view of far-reaching dessert lands spotted with stunning rock formations beautifully placed as if an exquisite Zen Garden colored red. And off in the far distance the approach of a tourist vehicle was detected by its trailing cloud of road dust. Such a command of their surroundings made them feel safe as it had made their people for hundreds of years.

It had not always been easy for the Hopi. Like everyone else on the planet, they had contended with external hostile forces encroaching on their existence as with their own internal schisms. However, considering how bad others had it through history, their life on the mesas, permeated with their peaceful nature, was appreciated overall as relatively benign. The Hopi made the Arizona mesas their home in the early 12th century after fleeing a series of droughts that brought social instability and devastation to the Ancient Pueblo civilization that once flourished around Mesa Verde. Since then, they had survived colonial aggression, land usurpation, and cultural assaults. Today, the hardships of the past were confined to an unpleasant memory, and efforts were focused on safeguarding their proud identity and traditions.

The sky was blue, the air dry, and since it was a weekday, the town was relatively quiet from visitors. Kyv chose to leave the car parked in the tourist lot at a safe distance from the old Soto family home, which wasn't really all that old. Not all Hopi were resistant to the American cultural influence, at least not when it came to modern conveniences such as better materials to build one's home. Unfortunately, not all current commodities were feasible. Oraibi, for instance, had no running water. Since it was their oldest settlement, it was punctured with sacred underground kivas. Digging to install pipes was out of the question. Though the residents of Oraibi had proven to be among the most loyal to their ancient ways, they weren't the staunchest about it. The Traditionalists had chosen to completely resist outside cultural influence. They founded their own village, Hotevilla, in the early 1900's on the other side of the mesa intent on honoring their old covenant with the Great Spirit. Others had preferred opening up and founded Kykotsmovi. The split had been bloodless but remained deep.

The Soto family found themselves dislodged in the middle. The women of the family had committed to a covenant of their own; yet they understood the need to stay in pace with the evolving world around them if they were to honor their commitment with Providence. In becoming the first member in her family to graduate from college, Sakwa had proven to serve the mission well.

And it wasn't over yet...

She opened the door to their home. There was no key or need for it. They entered solemnly, dropped their things, looked around and, as soon as it was determined that all looked in order, Lily unloaded on her parents as if she held a machinegun full of reproaches.

"How could you?" she said confronting her father. "You gave away God's secret name. Mary wanted us to find it. It was Her message to the world. Don't you realize that choosing us was no coincidence?" She smacked her chest. "We are the Hopitu, the 'Peaceful Ones', Guardians of Balance and Harmony. It was our fate to reveal her message of peace! I would have gladly risked my life for it. You had no right to make that decision for me."

Lily caught her breath to allow her father to respond, knowing that nothing he could say would relieve the profound sense of defeat that tore her inside. He made the attempt, but just as quickly, she changed her mind. Why bother letting him answer. She was too angry to listen.

Her sullen eyes shot to her mother. "Why did you let him? You of all people knew of our destiny. How could you leave the plaque down there like that? I don't care if you were aware it was Solomon's code or not. You should have grasped it was important. You knew Sofia and I were meant to find our way to something. You should have put it in a safe place!"

Rather than waning, Lily's despair seemed to escalate.

"Honey—," started her mother, but was stopped sharp with a dry gesture of Lily's hand.

She wasn't done.

What about her sister? If only she had not called on Michael and Gabriel. Maybe if Sofia had not alerted her father, the laminate would now be in their hands. Who knew what would happen to it now? Had they missed their last chance to save the world? She wanted to cry, but she'd tell her sister off first.

Lily pointed her ire at Sofia ... and froze. Her parents and sister were lined up before her with glittering eyes and displaying suspicious grins. If the realization had not smacked her in the face in that instant, she would have done it herself.

It had all been a charade.

Rather than remaining poised and serene in deference to the habit she rarely wore, Lily had allowed the horror of failing Mary to blur her perception of what was really going on. She closed her eyes and took a slow deliberate breath to collect herself.

Her family watched feeling a pinch of guilt for having put her through this, but in the end, the joy of success allowed for some amusement.

Playfully, Lily went ahead and smacked herself anyway as her family laughed. She shook her head relieved. "I should have known you were up to something when mom hid her face in her hands. Mom weeping helplessly rather than standing her ground and fighting back almost surprised me more than dad giving away a precious Native American object he'd sooner die protecting himself."

"I'm just happy your mother caught my drift," joked her father. "Trust me, I was sweating." Kyv and Sakwa weaved arms around each other's back in a proud embrace.

Lily took a few steps back and forth while she shook her hands to release the adrenaline hangover. "I need to know," she asked, "is there a gold plate in the mine? Actually, is there a mine at all?"

"No and yes," answered her mother. "The abandoned mine is there and once was exploited as a gold mine. The eroded and vandalized inscriptions are also true. And it is true that I did find a corner of a fine gold laminate plastered to a wall, but it was a piece that had remained behind when the rest was extracted, most likely in a hurry. Your dad obviously knew this, so when he announced we were to give them the laminate, *all of it*, I grasped his strategy."

"Thank-you-God," said Lily performing the sign of the cross, "It's not down there. I thought I was going to have a heart attack."

Sakwa's gaze saddened slightly. "Unfortunately, it once was. We did indeed give up an invaluable archaeological site that could shed light on its final whereabouts and much more."

"Like other relics? Could there be some under the rubble?"

"I doubt it, but it is not completely out of the question. It is apparent the cave was emptied before it was vacated. Still, there are signs it was done in a hurry; perhaps because of the partial collapse itself. They may have deemed the mine unsafe and rushed to save what they could. I don't know." She shrugged. "Who knows what they may find with the right resources. I never had the chance. My sentiment that Sofia's fall was a sign to keep it concealed was honest."

"What do we do with Michael when he realizes there is nothing there?"

Sofia responded. "Mom and dad gave Michael what he needed to let us go. You were right, Lily. Michael has his heart in the right place. He was being candid about being on our side."

Lily furrowed her eyebrows. "Still, I don't understand. We didn't give him anything."

"We gave him enough," explained her mother. "That cave is the real deal. As I said, with the right equipment and people it is very possible they can dig something up. Maybe even discover where everything was taken. But that requires time."

"Meanwhile," continued her father, "Michael leaks that the US government has captured the cave, and Red Dragon loses interest in you since whatever secrets it hides are no longer in your hands, nor did you ever see them. I listened between his words and distinctly heard Michael asking us for something, however small, to set you free."

"I can't believe I missed all that." Lily felt silly.

Sakwa approached her and rubbed her arm. "Honey, your soul is too good for devious subterfuges."

Her daughter drew a slow, wry grin. "But not completely clueless. I understand we have bought time to keep looking, right?" she asked her mother.

"Right," responded Sakwa with a conniving wink.

"Without Red Dragon on our heels to thwart our mission?" she confirmed with her father.

"Exactly," he answered.

Lily finally settled her slit gaze on her sister. "And you know where, don't you?"

As Sofia further broadened her already ample smile, her parents showed their surprise. This, they did not know.

"What? You do?" asked her mother.

"What did *we* miss?" asked her father.

"Simple," started Lily, "you've missed the smart aleck smirk she's had stuck across her face for the last five minutes."

Her parents' inquisitive look converged on Sofia.

"Let's go for a walk," she announced.

CHAPTER 41

Temperatures were rising fast. The family had changed into cooler wear and suitable shoes for the trek. They loaded up on water and headed out along the only road access to Oraibi. From there, before reaching the main road, they turned right onto one of the dirt paths that cut the corner to their destination. Sofia led the way.

Sakwa sped up to position herself to her daughter's left. "I can't wait any longer. It is obvious we are headed to Prophecy Rock, but can you tell us why?"

Sofia slowed the pace to let her sister and father catch up on her right.

"The chariot," she started bluntly, "have you noticed how it has been omnipresent along the lines?" She listed a couple of examples. "It was a status symbol associated with power and glory as we saw with the Tartessian warrior steles and yesterday we learned it was the quintessential esoteric symbol thanks to Ezekiel."

Lily added. "And our Hopi Life Plan, as carved on Prophecy Rock, is a chariot as well."

"That's right. However, what business do we have worshiping a chariot as a symbol of anything?" Sofia glanced at her mother. "Yes, I realize you made the case that we may well be related to these Iberian people, and therefore our chariot might be some kind of legacy from them. However, since chariots were never used here due to the lack of horses, this implies we held on to a strange image with ironclad commitment for over three thousand years. Why? And how is it even possible?"

Sakwa considered the dilemma. "Its status symbolism is lost on us. Its value is spiritual; it always has been. Within its lines we see the Great Spirit guiding us to follow the *Straight Path of Peace*."

"And for that reason," explained Sofia, "logic dictates that the answer is in Ezekiel's vision."

"You lost me," confessed her mother.

"What she is trying to say," intervened Lily, "is that our memory is good, but not that good. Instead of remembering a three-thousand-year-old Tartessian chariot, our Life Plan is more likely to reproduce the image of a more recent and tangible source, the golden plate that reached us in the 8th century. Yesterday, we realized that the golden plate not only carried God's name on it, but also His manifestation. Gabriel explained that this aspect of God, Shakinah, is described by the prophet Ezekiel who saw God riding a chariot precisely. Since this imagery matches our Hopi Life Plan, it would indicate that we brought the plate with us to Oraibi. And that's why we were able to reproduce a chariot despite never having seen one."

Sofia smiled satisfied, but she also enjoyed the guilty pleasure of knowing that she was still several steps ahead of her sister.

Her father on the other hand needed things to slow down a bit. "Let's back up a moment," he requested. "I admit I'm not familiar with Ezekiel or his visions, but I'm quite curtain the Bible does not mention a goddess on a chariot in reference to God."

Lily, the Catholic historian and unconditional feminist, happily explained. "Let's go one step at a time. Ezekiel was a Jewish rabbi during the time of the Babylonian destruction of Solomon's Temple and ended up in exile in Babylon with the rest of the rabbis. While there, he started having visions, becoming a notable prophet, and since it was during this exile when the rabbis put the Old Testament together, his seven visions were incorporated as one of its major prophetic books. In it, he decries, among other things, the destruction of Jerusalem as punishment for worshiping foreign idols. As a true patriarch, he chiefly focuses all the blame on a woman, Asherah, a Canaanite goddess who was heavily followed in Judea. So, you are right, Ezekiel would never have admitted to seeing a woman driving the chariot. However, he never said he saw a man either. That is a generalized misconception due to the incorrect translation of the Hebrew text. If you recall, Gabriel explained that God's male aspect is unknowable, His image unthinkable. This aspect is what we know as Yahweh, but, again, it cannot be *seen*. That's what Asherah was for. She was the *Face of the Lord*. So, what does Ezekiel do to describe the Divine Presence without referring to its feminine aspect? He composed a tongue twister. In Hebrew, he says he saw *'the appearance of the likeness of the glory of Yahweh.'* Later, to simplify matters, Jewish sages came up with the term Shekinah, derived from 'to dwell', to designate the Divine Presence, and surreptitiously made the term feminine to honor God's dual essence."

"Understood," said her father. "Now explain why you are so certain that what Ezekiel saw was what was engraved on the table."

"Well, I wouldn't say we are certain, but there are enough hints to it. You see, scholars who study him suspect that his visions reproduce—symbolically—what he knew of the Temple. Remember, he was a rabbi who worked in the First Temple until it was destroyed. Consequently, there must have been an image of the 'glory' on a chariot somewhere in it. We know from the Bible that Solomon worshiped Asherah in the Temple, but then, to make things really interesting, I also happen to know that there is also mention of a golden chariot. According to Chronicles, King David left detailed instructions to his son Solomon on how to build the Temple and its contents. Specifically, when describing the golden items, King David says: '*and gold for the pattern of the chariot.*'"

This caught Sofia by surprise. "Seriously? Well, there you go. We should have started by consulting the Bible."

Lily chuckled. "I never thought I'd hear you say that."

"It's the heat, it's getting to me." And wishing to move things alone, Sofia concluded, "In sum, if there was an image of Asherah and her chariot in the Temple, the most logical place would have been engraved on the Table of the Divine Presence if only because its name gives it away."

Lily had something else to add. "Let's not forget the coincidence that the Table ended up in Spain in a temple with an identical floorplan to the one described also by Ezekiel; the same country where Kabballah later dedicates a whole school of thought to Ezekiel's vision of God's chariot. Clearly, there was a chariot on the Table, and it spawned a power tradition there."

"Fine, but why so much transcendental importance placed on the vision of one man," asked Kyv.

"Leaving aside that Kabballah places a lot of transcendental importance on anything and everything related to God, it just so happens that Ezekiel is the only person in the Bible to actually *see* God. Remember that, technically, God isn't supposed to be *seeable*. Not even Moses had that privilege. Therefore, the fact that it's an esteemed prophet who *sees* God and what he *sees* is particularly strange, made the vision a bottomless pit for esoteric interpretation."

"What was strange about it?"

"Well, Ezekiel describes seeing a human likeness that is half glowing metal, and half fire, seated in a flying throne of sorts, and drawn by four cherubim or angelic creatures. These in turn are described as having four faces each: those of a man, a lion, an ox and an eagle. And to make it even stranger, the chariot's wheels fly detached alongside the cherubim with rims full of eyes."

"That is strange and nothing like the Hopi chariot," observed Kyv.

"True," agreed Sofia, "but as Lily said, his visions were symbolic of what he saw in the Temple. I suspect our chariot is a more accurate but simplified sketch of what was on the plate."

"Do you think it might be a location marker?" asked Lily, hopeful. "Could it be hidden there, under Prophesy Rock?"

Sofia came to a stop. They had reached the main road where it turned south. She took the moment to address her sister. "I don't know if it is physically hidden there or not, but honestly, I don't think we need it. Our Life Plan, however simple, is prodigious. When I show you what I mean, you'll see it is all the evidence we need."

Sakwa had been silently listening, while making more connections in her head. All the years of privately studying the mythical Tartessians and their outlandish equivalences with the Puebloan people were coming to fruition. "I'm not sure what prodigy you're referring to," started her mother, "but if it is evidence that you want, you can be certain the Goddess Asherah and her chariot were engraved on the plate and that it was exactly what Ezekiel saw."

Her daughters showed deep curiosity.

Sakwa turned to Lily. "Your comment about the tradition spawned in Spain around the chariot got me thinking. In Ezekiel's vision the wheels were detached from the flying throne and had a rim of eyes, right?"

"Yes. Why?"

"Remember the picture of the female Iberian bust I showed you yesterday? You know, the one where the woman wears her hair up in elaborate buns like our traditional whorls."

"I believe you called her The Lady of Elche."

"Correct, that one," confirmed her mother. "If you recall, her buns looked like wheels. But to make my point further, in 1987, another similar bust was found, the Lady of Guardamar, not far from the first, only in her case, her buns are actual wheels. And what is also interesting is that she was found together with statues of lions, bulls and eagles or griffins, like the four faces of the cherubim in Ezekiel's vision. Statues of ladies like these are being dug up all over the south of Spain. One of them, The Lady of Baza, was even found whole body seated on a winged throne. And they all closely date to the time following the destruction of Solomon's Temple."

Sofia gleaned immediately what her mother was implying. "These ladies carry all the elements of Ezekiel's chariot ... They embody the Divine Chariot. No wonder Ezekiel's vision was so strange. He struggled to describe it as personified by a Lady-Chariot."

Kyv was getting more confused by the minute. "But he saw God as half shinning metal and half fire."

Lily and her mother exchanged smiles. Both knew the reason. Lily for her knowledge of the Bible and Sakwa for hers of Tartessos.

Sakwa gestured Lily to go ahead. "Dad, shinning metal and fire confirms that he indeed saw a Lady-Chariot and knew it was headed to Tartessos. You see, Ezekiel's exact words when describing the wheels were that *they shone like the Tarshish Stone*, and Tarshish was the Biblical name for Tartessos. This stone is referenced several times in the Bible as a type of precious gem that looked like a gleaming metal or fire. But since it remains a mystery, it's generally translated as beryl or amber."

Sofia chuckled. "I've got the feeling the nice prophet wasn't receiving visions. What he was receiving were reports from the exiled Asher's who escaped to Spain with the Table. That's why he was able to describe the 'New Temple' so accurately."

Sakwa shook her head. She was amazed at how all the pieces were coming together so neatly. "The cubic seal I showed you, the one found at the Tartessian sanctuary, it was telling us all along. It contains all the elements of Ezekiel's vision as well. One side has Asherah and her chariot, while the rampant goats confirm it. Then the other large side depicts a man and three animals, which equate to the four-faced cherubim exactly, and ..." She lapsed into silence. The fourth side contained two cherubim facing each other, their wings extended to the center ... the unequivocal symbol of the Ark of the Covenant ... *Could it be?* Had the Ark been taken to the sanctuary as well?

Meanwhile, Kyv was not too happy standing under the sun. It wasn't doing him any good. "Ladies, do you mind if we continue this chat under the shade of the Rock?"

They were around the corner and, indeed, the high temperatures were sucking the moisture out of the air. They were literally frying. Sofia reached for her bottle and took several sips. Everyone imitated her as if the act was contagious. She checked for cars and initiated the approach to Prophesy Rock. The closer they got, the wider her signature smart aleck smile. She had to hand it to her family. Without seeing the golden plate, they had deciphered God's secret name and identified Her beautiful face.

But she alone would have the privilege of revealing the greatest miracle of all ...

CHAPTER 42

Sofia checked discreetly on her dad. His limp worried her. She now wondered if they should have driven instead suspecting her proud father was withholding the true gravity of his knee ailment. But other than repeatedly rubbing it, he seemed to be holding up under the heat better than her. Sofia took a sip of water and turned her attention back to rolling out the red carpet for her grand revelation. The lead up had to be done right. She wanted to ensure her family appreciated the miracle in all its glory.

"Everyone, listen up," she said. "I'm taking you to Prophesy Rock because there is something I want to show you, however, in order for you to fully appreciate it, I need to organize all the random tidbits we've learned about the golden laminate into a meaningful and chronological summary. So please bear with me as I recount its journey from Jerusalem to Oraibi."

Her family accepted with a nod.

Sofia's chest swelled in anticipation of her own surprise. "Here's what I think happened. Our enigmatic leader Solomon, whose name fittingly means 'Peace', was tasked with building a temple for God's Divine Presence in Jerusalem, the 'City of Peace'. Within it, he diligently secured its most precious relic, the Ark of the Covenant, and refurnished Moses' lamp and bread table with the finest gold to fashion the Menorah and the Table of the Divine Presence. But the latter was no ordinary table; it was a sacred slate upon which to engrave and preserve the essence of God's name and face in the traditional manner of the region." The symbolism of this part made her smile because shortly it would prove to be far more meaningful than her family could imagine.

She continued with a touch of theatrics in honor of her sister. "Alas, dark days would befall the kingdom leading some religious reformers to do what is ingrained in the human heart in times of fear, they blamed the 'others'; in this case, those who worshiped other gods, chiefly Asherah. The patriarchs clamored for a distinct identity defined by the single male aspect of God they felt unique to them, unaware of the curse that the ensuing imbalance of inequality and disunity would bring. The City of Peace would fall in disarray and its Temple destroyed until such time Balance and Harmony were restored."

"Right," interrupted her mother, "but the relics were saved in time, and though we're not entirely sure what happened to the Ark or the Menorah, we think the Table was taken to Tartessos, considered the safe haven in those days ..." Something gave her pause.

Oh no, thought Sofia, her drum roll was in jeopardy.

Sakwa continued. "Did I mention that the sanctuary was destroyed and buried by its own occupants a couple of centuries later, in the 4th century B.C.?"

"Really," said Kyv, "they destroyed their own sanctuary? Why would they do that?"

"It's not quite clear, but there is evidence it was done in a ritualistic manner. I bring it up because following the condemnation of Asherah there was a wave of idol destruction. But there was one in Tartessos as well that affected the Lady-Chariots. Few have been dug up unharmed. The Lady of Elche got lucky. She was found buried in a niche as if hidden there to protect her, while the Lady of Guardamar did not fare as well. She was found hammered to pieces and burnt as they usually did with the Asherah pillars, poles, and statuettes. I'm going to speculate that Lady-Chariots proliferated in Tartessos because the Table's sanctuary was there, but when the idol destruction promoted by the patriarchs reached their corner of the world, the guardians of the Table moved to bury their temple to prevent its sacrilege, and perhaps even eliminate any trace of it being there or where it was taken."

"Of course, I remember now," celebrated Lily. "Asherah was often represented by a pillar or a pole. That's why in the Bible, when cracking down on the worship of idols, they repeatedly call for the cutting down of the Asherah pole or the smashing of her pillar." She shook her head as she turned to Sofia. "How about that? "Now we know why Mary appeared with a pillar during her first apparition in Zaragoza. It makes sense. The Spanish Line was designed with a strong emphasis on the feminine. It starts with Mary's Rosary in Prouille, followed by Asherah's Pillar in Zaragoza, Zohar's Shekinah in Guadalajara, the Ancient Mother Goddess as the Black

Madonna in Guadalupe, Tanit personifying Creation in Medellin, and finally the table with the *Face of the Lord* in Merida."

Sofia heard this as an out of body experience. A straight line, formed through the centuries, collected all the versions of *God's Feminine Aspect*. The Spanish Line had pulled off a feat that rivaled the portent she was about to reveal about Mary's Line. Two lines, each more prodigious than the other. Surely there was a reasonable explanation, but for the moment, it was giving her skeptic mind the goosebumps.

The drum roll interruption had been worth it conceded Sofia, but they were steps away from the Rock. It was time to recover control over her narrative. "Fine, so the sanctuary is destroyed and nine hundred years later the Table is spotted by the Moors in Merida. As for where it was kept hidden until then, we don't know."

"Maybe we do," suggested her mother.

One of Sofia's eyes started to twitch.

Oblivious, her mother offered a suggestion. "It was likely taken to Medellin. The town was an important Tartessian center until the Romans took over and made Merida the capital of the region. We know Asherah, reimagined as Tanit, was big there thanks to the medallion."

"Fine, so via Medellin, and with the coming of the Romans, the Table is ultimately placed in a temple in Merida. I read that the cathedral was built upon a prior temple. Who knows, maybe they named it Basilica of Saint Jerusalem in honor of the relic safeguarded there."

Lily agreed. "And later they consecrated it to Mary as Cathedral of Saint Mary of Jerusalem when it became a Divine Marian Marker."

Sofia surrendered, accepting in good spirits she was not the sole owner of this remarkable story, and continued. "I'm going to guess they sketched copies of the chariot's pattern for the cathedral's archives. That's why, despite the bishops running off with the laminate, a copy was later found by the Grand Master of the Knights of St. James during the renovation."

"You mean they found a map, not the chariot pattern," clarified Lily.

Sofia angled a grin. "I mean both. You'll see as soon as we get there," she teased, and hurried to conclude the summary. "The bishops of Merida, probably knowledgeable of the Tartessian Atlantic crossings, made their way to our Four Corners region, mingled with our ancestors, and eventually settled in our backyard. And with the plate entrusted to us, we became the Hopitu, Guardians of Balance and Harmony. Then, in the 12th century, following a severe drought and the encroachment of other tribes that came pushing down from the north, we moved south and established in Oraibi. At this point we don't know what happened to the gold laminate. We do know, however, that we engraved a simplified copy of it on Prophecy Rock and conserved its significance coded in the oral reciting of the Hopi Life Plan."

"Right, but meanwhile, back in Merida," added Lily, "a dozen years before Columbus set sail, the Grand Master discovers the copy of a map in the cathedral with the route followed by the bishops."

"Map and chariot," clarified Sofia.

"Why do you insist on both?"

"Bear with me, it was both. However, I'm certain the chariot pattern was lost on the Grand Master. It was the map that he most likely found interesting."

"Okay," accepted Lily with an arched eyebrow, "Cardenas finds a copy of the map *and* the chariot but disregards the chariot while finding the map intriguing. Since America was not rediscovered yet, he was not aware of its value. By the time Columbus reports his findings, Cardenas is old and ill, dying soon after ..." A thought crossed her mind. "I wonder if he informed Queen Isabella about the map and that's why she knew to support Columbus' crazy venture ... hmm ... Anyway, it's not until the time of his great grandson that North America's geography is well delineated and the value of the map gleaned, launching the gold rush that continues to this day, keeping dad busy."

The family reached Prophecy Rock from behind. They skirted around it to see its flat surface. Upon it, the sacred Hopi Life Plan was etched into the sandstone, looking so innocent despite its profound significance.

They appraised it with renewed respect.

"Incredible," said Kyv. "Right there before everyone's eyes all this time."

Sofia crouched at the foot of the boulder and placed the water bottle on the ground. She then removed her backpack and reached into it to retrieve the world map they had worked on for the past forty-eight hours. It showed some serious wear. Gingerly, she spread it open on the sandy ground. Her family positioned themselves before it, curious about what she was up to.

Sofia stood back up. She assessed the map first and then raised her eyes to the Life Plan.

Slowly, she took a deep breath. This was a transcendental moment, and she awarded herself a few seconds to enjoy it.

Feeling ready, she searched for her sister. Lily was right there beside her. Sofia reached out for her hand and pulled her even closer. Then she quoted the message Lily had surmised earlier:

"God's secret name is 'Peace'
For his wisdom was to create Balance and Harmony where there was chaos.
Such power is now ours
As attested by the sacred writing engraved on the table."

Directing her index finger to the rock engraving, she repeated the last phrase:

As attested by the sacred writing engraved on the table.

The light bulb in Lily's head burst with light. Her eyes opened wide. "Engraved on the table ... table in Spanish is *mesa* ... our mesa ... as in 'engraved on the Hopi mesa'. Holy Wow!"

Yes, thought Sofia, *Holy Wow!* Her sister better hang onto something. She wasn't done.

Sofia spoke solemnly. "The patriarchs, as they strived to worship a single aspect of God, denied his face, and the sages, believing they were protecting his name by keeping it secret, forgot His essence. Jesus came to remind us of both, hoping to lift the curse of Hell and give us Heaven. Mary, seeing that after Her son's death the new churches perpetuated the same mistake, devised a special path." She pointed down at the map and then directed her finger up to the rock carving. "You see it?" she asked her sister.

"Sure ..." replied Lily somewhat hesitant. "Mary traced a line that ultimately guided us to our Life Plan where her message is contained symbolically. We see the Great Spirit, as if a Hodegetria, gesturing with her hand toward the *Straight Path of Peace*, that is, She is showing us the way to her Son: Balance and Harmony among all people and nature."

Sofia smiled. She could tell Lily would have preferred to have found the original golden laminate. Nonetheless, she was graciously settling for what she had, which was plenty.

But, no, she had not seen it.

"Tell me," started Sofia softly, "when you look at Mary's Line as it makes its way across Europe, the Atlantic, and Venezuela to Medellin in Colombia, and then turns north through Mexico, Texas, and New Mexico to end in Utah, what do you see?"

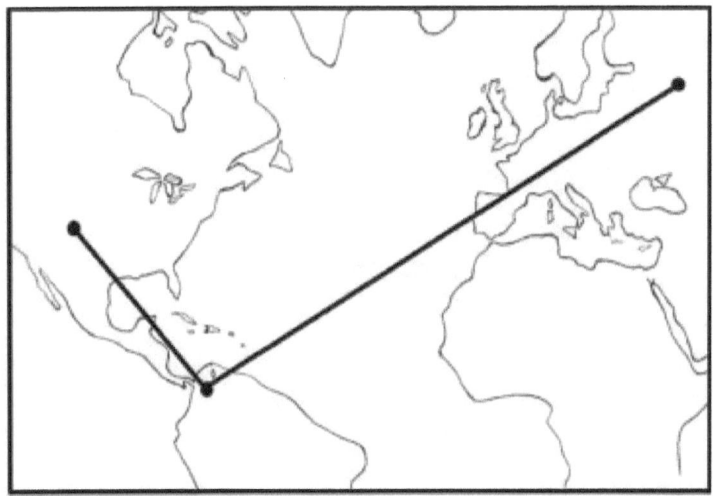

Lily lowered her eyes to study the route on the map. She winced. "I see a large check mark." She was doubtful that was what her sister meant.

Sofia surprised her. "Good, that is exactly what it is. Now look at the chariot. Ignore the crooked line and focus solely on what we interpret as the *Path of Peace*." Sofia squeezed her sister's hand lightly. "Remember that the Hodegetria's first miracle was to make two blind men *see*. Therefore, I'll ask you again, what do you *see*?"

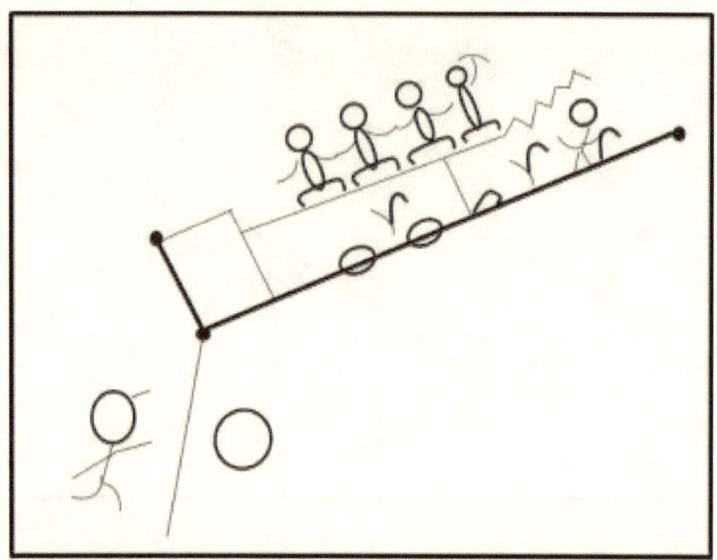

"Well ..." Lily studied the petroglyph, "what's left is the straight path that the Great Spirit wants us to—" Lily lost her breath.

Sakwa's eyes welled as Kyv wrapped his arm around her shoulders in an emotional embrace. It was now clear to all what was to be seen.

They stood speechless and awestruck.

Finally, Lily uttered the answer. "I see a check mark." She fell to her knees and weaved her fingers together.

Sofia joined her parents in the hug.

Unbeknownst to them, or maybe not, the Hopi had miraculously conserved through the centuries *Mary's Way* concealed within the strokes of a chariot together with its extraordinary symbolic meaning; the same *Straight Path* that the Queen of Heaven had replicated on a planetary scale with Divine Markers to guide to its own rediscovery. The chariot had proven to be both the message and the way.

Still, there was more ...

Sofia turned her head to look over her right shoulder. There, behind them, was another boulder with a strange petroglyph. This one few ever talked about, maybe on purpose, since it seemed to only attract the attention of UFO enthusiasts who saw a spaceship in it. To be fair, it wasn't surprising it inspired odd interpretations for it was nothing like other Hopi rock art. It depicted a strange box of sorts with legs and two domes on top that could be understood as two wings coming together to protect what was kept within. On each side, the likes of two holders protruded, similar to those through which in ancient times poles were inserted to help carry heavy arks. To top it off, it seemed to disclose what it held inside: two of something ... tablets perhaps?

Sofia smiled. The quest had taught her to *see* things in new magical ways, and what she saw in this unassuming rendition was the Hopi's simplified sketch of yet another fabulous relic ...

In the distance, standing upon a rock promontory, Michael and Gabriel observed quietly.

"She knows," noticed Gabriel.

Michael nodded, pleased. He always trusted the twins would succeed.

For Gabriel, however, a reasonable concern remained. "Do you think they can do it? It is still up hill from here to rally the world for a global peace project."

"As a friend once said, I believe and know that they can and *will*," settled Michael with a broad smile.

The Beginning...

Dear reader, Gabriel is right, the hill is steep, and the sisters will be confronted with great challenges to complete their mission. But so is Michael in depositing his trust in them. I invite you to join Sofia and Lily, in a new adventure, as they discover that the Divine Lines hold more magical surprises, leading to yet another astonishing message instrumental in advancing the world toward Peace and Justice ...

THE QUIXOTE PACT

A year has passed, Sofia and Lily have published a well-received essay outlining the marvels of *Mary's Way*, which has generated high expectations for their upcoming book, and they have dutifully made sold-out rounds promoting Mary's Message. But it's all for naught. The sisters are discouraged; the harsh reality is that their efforts have had questionable real-world impact.

Meanwhile, Sofia is invited to attend an unrelated presentation by a mysterious professor, Antonio del Mar. Little to nothing is known about Del Mar, yet he has managed to attract the pinnacle of Washington DC's press corps, claiming to know of a private covenant between George Washington and the Spanish King Charles III that could upend what we know of the American Revolution and its aftermath. In sum, the subject has nothing to do with Sofia or her work, but she agrees to attend as a favor to Dan, her boss.

The morning takes a shocking turn when, during his speech, the handsome professor narrowly escapes an attempt on his life and whispers three cryptic words to Sofia before disappearing.

While baffled as to why he'd entrust the enigmatic clue to her and unsettled by its trailing dangers, Sofia can't pass on this exclusive opportunity to track down the obscure pact, suspecting in hindsight it might be connected to their mission due to a couple of hints the professor threw her way during his exposition.

So, joining forces, once again, with her sister Lily, and despite the acute feeling Del Mar has an agenda of his own, Sofia and Lily embark on another remarkable quest, following clues hidden in American icons and Founders' writings that unveil an unexpected connection to the two Divine Lines.

In a timely fashion, **The Quixote Pact** reveals another staggering miracle, and necessary complement to the first one, that may, just may, do the trick to rally the world.

Other Books by the Author

TRAPPED IN A DREAM

Faith and Chris have never met but have the unusual ability to meet in each other's dreams. It was fun growing up and quite enticing in their teens, but lately they struggle with it too uncomfortably aware it is far from normal.

One afternoon, Faith, a harmless schoolteacher dedicated to her community, is unsuspectingly attacked and left bedridden in an odd state of sleep, while alert in her dreams. And, as fate would have it, Dr. Christian Luxford (Chris), a neurologist who specializes in sleeping disorders, is called in. Naturally perplexed, Chris recognizes Faith, and soon enough realizes that her condition is tied to their enigmatic connection, which, incidentally, has intensified since the assault. Faith can now telepathically communicate with Chris during his waking hours, her only link to the outside world.

When a powerful philanthropist with a disturbing reputation suddenly offers to take charge of Faith's delicate care, Chris must race to unravel the secret behind their telepathy, while distraught by her rapidly declining state and slipping custody.

Yet, as painful truths from the past come to light and the battle over her guardianship turns bloody, don't discount Faith. She may be trapped in her own body, but she is not as defenseless as one would reasonably think.

ESSENCE

At the end of *Trapped in a Dream*, Faith and Chris barely survive the cover-up of an illegal experiment that gave them telepathic abilities.

Now, in *Essence*, as they come to terms with their new reality, and while on vacation in Barcelona, Spain, Faith inadvertently connects with another experimental subject and witnesses her commit a crime.

Unable to go to the authorities, Faith and Chris must team up with an old friend of his parents, Professor Xavier Vall, who is uniquely qualified for undisclosed reasons to keep them safe as they set out to find the sinister woman unaware she is the product of a far more advanced science and determined to stop at nothing to protect a formidable secret.